*More . . .*

"Impossible to put down . . . Susan Donovan is an absolute riot. You're reading a paragraph that is so sexually charged you can literally feel the air snapping with electricity and the next second, one of the characters has a thought that is so absurd . . . that you are laughing out loud. Susan Donovan has a very unique, off-the-wall style that should keep her around for many books to come. Do NOT pass this one up."

*—Romance Junkie Review*

"Susan Donovan has created a vastly entertaining romance in her latest book *Take a Chance on Me*. The book has an ideal cast of characters . . . a very amusing, pleasurable read . . . all the right ingredients are there, and Ms. Donovan has charmingly dished up an absolutely fast, fun, and sexy read!"

*—Road to Romance*

"Contemporary romances don't get much better than *Take a Chance on Me* . . . such wonderful characters! You want sexual tension? This book drips with it. How about a love scene that is everything that a love scene should be? There's humor, a touch of angst, and delightful dialogue . . . *Take a Chance on Me* is going to end up very, very high on my list of best romances for 2003."

*—All About Romance*

### KNOCK ME OFF MY FEET

"Spicy debut . . . [A] surprise ending and lots of playfully erotic love scenes will keep readers entertained."

*—Publishers Weekly*

"Donovan's blend of romance and mystery is thrilling."

*—Booklist*

"*Knock Me Off My Feet* will knock you off your feet . . . Ms. Donovan crafts an excellent mixture to intrigue you and delight you. You'll sigh as you experience the growing love between Autumn and Quinn and giggle over their dialogue. And you'll be surprised as the story unfolds. I highly recommend this wonderfully entertaining story."

*—Old Book Barn Gazette*

St. Martin's Paperbacks Titles by
Susan Donovan

# Public Displays of Affection

## Susan Donovan

St. Martin's Paperbacks

This is a work of fiction. All of the characters, organizations, and events portrayed in this novel are either products of the author's imagination or are used fictitiously.

PUBLIC DISPLAYS OF AFFECTION

Copyright © 2004 by Susan Donovan.

Cover photograph of lipstick by Ben Perini.

For information address St. Martin's Press, 175 Fifth Avenue, New York, NY 10010.

ISBN: 978-0-312-36646-9

Printed in the United States of America

St. Martin's Paperbacks edition / June 2004

St. Martin's Paperbacks are published by St. Martin's Press, 175 Fifth Avenue, New York, NY 10010.

10   9   8   7

This book is dedicated to the men in my life.

# ACKNOWLEDGMENTS

The author would like to acknowledge the following people for their assistance.

Susan Burkey, thank you for telling me about your life as a young widow with children. I couldn't have created the character of Charlotte Tasker without your help.

Supervisory Special Agent Will R. Glaspy and the staff of the Drug Enforcement Administration Office of Public Affairs, thanks for being so generous and patient in answering my stupid questions, then, soon after, my stupid follow-up questions. I hope this book answers once and for all the hotly debated question of which branch of federal law enforcement employs the best lovers.

Kim Lancaster, thanks for answering questions about real estate sales, and Celeste Bradley and Marilyn K. Swisher, thank you for reading early drafts of the manuscript.

To my editor, Monique Patterson, thanks for being patient with this one, and to my agent, Pamela Hopkins, thanks for cheering me on.

And finally, to the Reed-Shuster kids a big thank-you for being who you are—Sir Joke-A-Lot, Sir Go-With-the-Flow-A-Lot, Lady Brave-A-Lot, and Sir Loves-Animals-A-Lot. I adore you all, and I trust you will someday forgive me for shamelessly stealing pieces of your real personalities to create the fictional Hank, Justin, and Matt.

# Thirteen Years Ago

The air was thick and sugary with honeysuckle, and Charlotte breathed deep, pulling the sweetness into her lungs until she could taste the possibilities.

Of course she would say yes. In less than an hour, probably right there at Gate B-16 of National Airport, she was going to look into the eyes of the most wonderful man she'd ever known and say yes—yes, yes, yes! For once she was glad that Kurt's roommates couldn't keep a secret. She wondered if the diamond would be emerald cut or a classic round solitaire and whether it would have a platinum or gold setting.

The wind lashed into the convertible, whipping a few strands of hair across her cheek and sending others straight up like tongues of strawberry blonde flame. She looked into the rearview mirror and smiled. She was wild. Carefree. A bad, bad girl.

The thought was so ridiculous that she laughed.

A slap of hair covered Charlotte's eyes, and she eased up on the gas to be on the safe side. She had plenty of time. She should just relax and enjoy the baby blue sky, the heavy green tunnel of leaves along the George Washington Parkway, and all that rich, sweet honeysuckle.

She sighed, thankful for the magic of this borrowed sports car. How odd that just the absence of a roof could make her feel so free. It was as if she'd been given permission to touch the whole big world along with the wind—and it made her feel strong, uninhibited, and, okay, she was going to admit it—she felt *sexy*!

She felt ready.

Charlotfe's foot thumped and her thigh bounced as The Clash poured from the car's overtaxed CD player. She raised her voice to sing along—and why not? Why not sing loud enough to scare the birds? Why not feel the air caress the bare skin of her arms? Why not live in the moment? Wasn't that what life was—just a finite number of moments strung together?

And how could anyone know how many moments they got in this life? How precious was the number?

She checked the rearview mirror again.

That man was still there.

Charlotte first noticed the guy in the black Jeep and even blacker Ray•Bans before she left the Beltway. When he followed her onto the GW, she'd told herself that there was nothing to worry about—it *was* the most beautiful route into the city on a day like this and he was entitled to enjoy his open-air ride, too.

So what if he just flashed that *Top Gun* smile again? So what if he just wiggled his fingers in another flirty wave? So what if one quick look at him made her belly catch fire?

She was a big girl. She could handle him.

Then he puckered his lips and blew her a kiss and Charlotte's pulse spiked. She jerked her eyes back to the road in front of her. She thought of Kurt Tasker, coming home to her in less than two hours. She focused on her future, on everything noble she had planned for her life, everything she had saved herself for.

With a trembling hand, Charlotte reached for the little notepad on the passenger seat. Maybe seeing Kurt's flight number once more would anchor her, keep her safe.

But a gust of wind ripped the notepad from her grasp and sent it flying out the open roof.

Charlotte watched in horror as the man in the Jeep rose and snagged it from midair.

He shot her a blazing white smile.

And motioned for her to pull off at the scenic overlook.

# Chapter One

Charlotte Tasker squinted into the afternoon sun, watching the Buckeye Moving & Storage truck lumber down the cul-de-sac. She turned toward her best friend.

"I guess if the world didn't suck, we'd all fall off, right?"

Bonnie Preston touched her shoulder in sympathy, and Charlotte managed a smile.

No, it wasn't exactly the end of the world when the neighbors next door got transferred. But one look at her son confirmed that the timing couldn't have been worse.

Matthew held the Techno-Spy binoculars up to his eyes, following the moving van as it disappeared in the distance. His narrow shoulders shook. Charlotte heard him sniffle.

"Why did they have to move?" he asked in a small voice.

"Mr. Connor got a new job in Columbus, honey. We talked about this."

"But *why* did they have to go?" The boy let the binoculars dangle from the cord around his neck and glared at his mother, his face contorted with the effort not to cry. "We're never going to see them again, are we?"

"Maybe we can visit someday."

"We won't. *Ever.*"

Charlotte watched her ten-year-old stalk off across the yard and her heart ached for him. Another loss, another change, was the last thing their little family needed, and they all knew it.

As Matt slammed the front door with finality, a pudgy, sticky hand wheedled its way into her palm.

"So who's gonna toss with me now, Mom?" Hank looked up at Charlotte with a pair of deep blue, forlorn eyes, set in a chubby, freckled face.

Before she could answer, Bonnie's husband swooped down and lifted the little girl into the air. "I'll toss with you, Henrietta, but you gotta go easy on your fastball. I'm getting to be an old man."

Ned Preston threw Hank over his wide shoulder and marched away.

"Call me Henrietta again and I'll knock your block off!" she yelled through her giggles.

Ned looked back at Bonnie and Charlotte and grinned. "Hey, ladies, whaddya say I throw some veggie burgers on the grill, whip us up some killer fruit smoothies, and we meet next door in a few minutes? We got any wheat germ, babe?"

Bonnie chuckled and shook her head. "Not since about 1974."

"I'll improvise," Ned said with a wink.

The women stood quietly in the driveway for a long moment, Charlotte feeling Bonnie close to her side. She reached out for her friend's hand, found it, and pressed it tight. "He's a good man, Bonnie, even if he can't stop abusing me for my food choices."

She laughed at that. "He certainly is. And I guess after thirty-five years I'd better start thinking of this as a permanent arrangement."

Charlotte's smile faded at what Bonnie said next.

"I'm sorry Matt's taking the Connors' move so hard."

"He takes everything hard since Kurt died."

"I know."

"He's not bouncing back the way Hank has."

"He needs more time, Charlotte. He's older than Hank. And it's only been—"

"Eighteen months, eleven days, and twenty-two hours."

The women's eyes locked. Bonnie squeezed Charlotte's hand even harder and tried to smile.

Then in tandem, the women turned their gaze to the split-level stone and siding house at 1232 Hayden Circle. With the plastic climbing toys and the BMX bikes removed from the lawn, Charlotte thought the house next door looked downright glamorous—and a little lonely.

She glanced at the red SOLD sticker slapped across the real estate sign, proof that LoriSue Bettmyer had successfully closed another deal.

"Any more dirt on who bought the house?" Bonnie gave Charlotte a sidelong glance. "Because I've got to say that LoriSue's been weirder than usual about this. Maybe a decade of bleach buildup has finally leached into her brain."

"That would explain *so* much."

As the two giggled like girls, Charlotte scanned the house and its sloped, painstakingly landscaped front yard. "Actually, nothing," she eventually answered. "It's strange. All the Connors said is somebody from First National signed the closing documents and the bank is listed as owner. They have no idea who is going to live here—and it's freaking me out. What if some psycho moves in?"

"Then Ned will have somebody to play with!" Bonnie slid her arm around Charlotte's shoulders and guided her back toward the house.

They walked up the drive, past a neat row of yellow tulips in full bloom, past the little clumps of lilies of the valley along the front walkway, and to the front door of Charlotte's tidy two-story Colonial.

Charlotte put her hand on the brass doorknob, then paused. She slowly turned her head. "Tell me I'm being paranoid, Bon. Tell me the new neighbors will be a nice family with two-point-five children and a gerbil."

"Hmm. Not sure about the gerbil, but I bet you'll love them, whoever they turn out to be."

Bonnie pushed open the door and ushered Charlotte inside.

"Besides. You've got to remember that Ned and I were a bit worried the day you newlyweds pulled up in your beat-up Chevette. And look at us now. I can't imagine my life without you and the children."

Charlotte looked closely at her friend, noticing the crinkles at her eyes, the damp sparkle at her lashes, and knew with certainty that she wouldn't have survived the last year without Bonnie and Ned Preston.

*"Ohio?"*

Joe Bellacera's mouth fell open in shock. Then he lanced Roger Hagerman with one of his trademark menacing stares.

But Roger already knew this was not going to be an easy sell.

"Minton, Ohio, Joe." He shuffled some papers on his desktop. "Population of just over twenty thousand souls. An hour or so from Cincinnati. Near the scenic and historic Ohio River. Good schools. Decent, patriotic folk."

"You might as well put a bullet in my brain now and skip the middleman."

Roger winced. "Only living people can testify in a court of law, as you know."

He watched Joe turn up the intimidation level of his stare, and though Roger tried to smile casually at him, he couldn't quite manage it. No wonder Joe Bellacera had a reputation for getting exactly what he wanted—whether it was convincing an informant to talk or a getting a woman he'd just met to eat out of his hand. It was his eyes. They could be pitch-black and threatening one minute and cheerful and sweet the next.

And though he'd known Joe since he was a kid straight out of Special Forces, the guy's intensity still managed to make Roger more than a little nervous.

Roger breathed a sigh of relief when Joe began to let his big body relax into the chair, his glare mellowing to a frown.

"So let's hear it, boss." Joe ran a hand through what was left of the heavy black hair that had been past his shoulders only days ago. "Who am I? What's my story?"

Roger reached for the dossier, flipped open the cover embossed with the Drug Enforcement Administration shield, and read aloud.

" 'You're Joseph William Mills.' "

Joe let out a sharp laugh. "Jesus tap-dancing Christ! *Mills?* Could you possibly have been a little less Wonder Bread?" He shook his head. "Go on."

Roger stifled a chuckle, agreeing that the name hardly fit Joe's infamous Latin-lover looks. "We're going Middle America here, Joe."

"I'm all over it."

Roger laughed out loud at that. "You're a mystery writer trying to get published. You live off your investments. You work at home. Keep to yourself. Divorced. No kids. Moved from the city to start over. A private kind of person."

Joe mumbled something probably crude and probably in Spanish, Italian, or Greek or some combination thereof. Roger raised an eyebrow.

"Go on," Joe said, crossing one long leg over a knee. "This is good. I can't wait to hear the rest."

Roger scanned the file. "Hayden Heights subdivision. Soccer moms and corporate dads. We've done background checks on everyone and the place is squeaky clean. The house is a nice, modern split-level with four bedrooms, two and a half baths, a patio, and a pool. And it's all compliments of the U.S. Marshals Service." Roger winked. "They owed me one."

"Plush. Give the marshal my regards. But why the hell do I need four bedrooms?"

"Well, for one thing, you'll be meeting with the supervisory agent in Cincinnati, a guy named Rich Baum. He could really use your expertise while you're in town."

"Yeah, but we'll be meeting in his office, not my bedroom. What am I supposed to do with a place that big?"

"You can run around the house and dance to show tunes for all I care—just keep a low profile until the trial."

"That could be a while."

"We're well aware of that. We're just trying to make this as pleasant as possible for you."

"I still say shoot me."

"Not an option. The whole case against Guzman is built on your testimony about the year you and Steve spent inside."

"I know."

"Guzman has a million-dollar reward out for your head, Bellacera."

"I know."

"So if you don't disappear, you're a dead man. And years of hard work and countless taxpayer dollars are down the crapper. Not to mention you'll never get justice for Steve and his family. So you go. It's your job to go."

Joe said nothing for a long moment, and Roger watched

the shadow of grief and rage pass through the agent's face. He hoped the downtime would allow Joe to come to terms with the murder of his partner, Steve Simmons, and his wife and son—as much as that was possible. Joe looked him straight in the eye and whispered, "When?"

"Three days. Stay in the safe house until then. Movers will come for your stuff day after tomorrow. Here." Roger handed him a manila envelope. "The usual—driver's license, Social Security card, retail credit report, passport, birth certificate, baptismal certificate, Visa, medical records, your airline ticket, and there's even a Clermont County Library card."

Joe peeked inside the flap, then grimaced. "Guess I'll have plenty of time to read."

"Good luck to you, Mr. Mills." Roger stood up to shake his hand, and he felt a big smile spread across his face. "And for God's sake, Joe—do us all a favor and stay away from the soccer moms."

"We have two minutes and sixteen seconds! Move it!"

Charlotte tossed her laptop case into the front passenger seat and revved up the minivan's engine, tapping her fingers against the steering wheel with one hand while clutching the Palm Pilot stylus in the other. She poked at the tiny keyboard.

Eight a.m.: Do the Gossards' regular grocery shopping and deliver their meal plan for the week.

Nine-thirty: Pick up the Raffertys' dry cleaning, drop off their little dust mop of a dog at the groomer's, then meet their pool restoration man at ten-fifteen. She could work on their weekly meal plan while she waited for him to finish his estimate.

She checked her watch and leaned out the car door. "Matthew! Hank! Let's get a move on!"

Back to her Palm Pilot.

Noon: A lunch meeting with the Jacobsens, potential new clients. The husband was an executive at Procter & Gamble and the wife was a tax attorney. They had two kids and zero time to manage their home life—ooh, how she loved people like that! They were the ideal clients for Multi-Tasker, Inc.

The van bounced as the children threw themselves into the backseats. Without looking up, Charlotte reeled off the usual checklist.

"Seat belts?"

"Yep!"

She heard the click of metal. "Lunches?"

"Yep!"

"Backpacks?"

"Yep!"

"Matt, do you have your volcano?"

"Uh-oh."

Charlotte's head snapped up and she looked at her watch. "You've got forty-five seconds, big guy. Do you need me to help you carry it?"

"No. I got it."

Watching Matt run into the house, she recalled how they'd stayed up until eleven finishing the earth sciences project and pictured all that hard work crashing to the macadam. Charlotte set aside her Palm Pilot and ran after her son.

Matt bit his lip in concentration as he took tiny steps out of the garage. She reached him just before the creation slipped from its cardboard base.

Matt smiled up at her. "Thanks, Mama."

Charlotte kissed his cropped head, stiff with way too much hair gel, and smiled. "You're welcome, honey."

They were now precisely two minutes behind schedule.

"After school we've got playtime from three to four and homework from four fifteen to five." Charlotte turned the van into the William Howard Taft Elementary drop-off lane. "Then you've both got Little League from six to eight. We're having falafel for dinner."

"Awful falafel," Matt mumbled from the backseat.

"I'd rather have monkey chowder," Hank said.

Charlotte reveled in the sound of her kids giggling. It didn't happen enough these days. "And, Hank, your coach called to say they've decided to move you up to the majors this year."

"All *right*," the girl breathed.

"The *majors*?" Matt's voice was high and squeaky. "But that's not fair! She's only eight! I didn't get in the majors until this year! That's totally messed up!"

"Dork butt," Hank whispered.

"Freak," Matt hissed back.

"That's enough." Charlotte was now third in line behind two other minivans. "Get your stuff together. Matt, do you need a hand?"

"Duh-uh! I'm not a total *Dorkus maximus,* Mother. I can carry one stupid little volcano!"

Seconds later, Charlotte slapped herself on the forehead. She'd just witnessed the painstakingly sculpted mountain of flour paste slide off the cardboard into a shapeless blob on the sidewalk. She bolted out of the van and knelt next to Matt, stroking his back as the car horns blared.

"I'm so sorry, Mama." Matt's entire face was clenched tight and his already ruddy cheeks were on fire with embarrassment.

"It's okay, Matt. Let's just scoop this up and—"

"I've got it, babe."

Jimmy Bettmyer nearly flattened Matt in his effort to get his hands on the ruined project. Then he stood, towering over them in his expensive real estate agent suit, grinning down in triumph. "Tough break, little buddy." Jimmy then scanned the crowd of teachers, parents, and kids that had assembled at the accident scene, making sure everyone noticed his gallantry.

"Everything's under control," he said to the crowd, offering Charlotte his free hand.

She rolled her eyes and helped Matt to his feet. "Go on in, honey. I'll call your teacher to explain."

Matt slinked off, his head hanging, his gaze riveted to his shoes. Charlotte felt the fury rise when some of the kids snickered as he walked past. She wanted to take them all by the shoulders and scream, "Hasn't he been through enough?"

Instead she felt Jimmy Bettmyer's breath on her neck and turned to find him dangerously close. The instant his hip made contact with her side she leaped back and headed for the van. He followed her.

"Maybe I could come over and help Matt rebuild this tonight. He could probably use a little male engineering know-how."

Charlotte reached for the door handle as she scanned the crowd for Hank's bright red curls and shocking pink backpack. She was relieved to see her daughter chatting happily with a group of girls as she moved through the school's double doors.

Jimmy leaned into the van window. "Besides, we all know Matt's not the only member of the Tasker family who could use a little male companionship."

Charlotte turned to face him. Jimmy Bettmyer had been trying to get in her pants from the first day they'd moved to Hayden Heights, when his wife, LoriSue, had been six months pregnant with Justin. All these years later, he was still trying to get in her pants. In fact, Charlotte was sure the only reason Jimmy escorted Justin through the school doors every morning was to advertise his availability to the drop-off moms. The man was a predator.

And, apparently, a real slow learner.

"Jimmy, why don't you bless your own family with your male know-how and leave me the hell alone?"

When the driver behind her laid on the horn, Charlotte put her van in gear and pulled away from the curb. Jimmy jogged alongside, still holding the ruined school project.

"LoriSue and I are separated and you know it," he panted. "I'm only living with her because I refuse to give her possession of the house. It's the principle of the thing."

Charlotte said nothing but pushed the automatic window button and smiled as the pane of glass went up between them. Unfortunately, Jimmy stuck his arm in the window and had this to add: "You may be a vegetarian, but I bet a hot little number like you can't go too long without a nice piece of meat!"

That was it. She hit the brakes and got out of her van.

She raised her chin and looked up at him—a thirty-something former jock with thinning blond hair and a very unattractive smirk. "I'm not interested in you, Jimmy."

Charlotte was quite pleased that her voice sounded calm yet assertive—clearly the voice of a woman who had her act together. "In fact, I just plain don't like you. You basically ignore your kid. You cheat on your wife. You have no manners. And as far as your 'piece of meat' goes . . ."

Charlotte let her gaze drop below Jimmy's belt, then shook her head. "Meat makes me nauseous. Now back off or I'm calling LoriSue to tell her all about this little encounter."

Jimmy's eyes narrowed and he gave her a nasty smile. "You know, Charlotte, someday you're going to beg for it."

She got back in the van. As she drove away, she heard

him shout after her, "What the hell am I supposed to do
with this volcano?"

The carpooler behind Charlotte told him precisely
what he could do with it, and Charlotte laughed all the
way to the Kroger parking lot.

That night, she checked on Matt first. Her son lay on his
side curled up in a ball, the long, thin index finger of his left
hand hanging limply from his mouth. She reached out and
gently pulled it away from his lips, aware that it was probably too late to avoid braces, but at least she could go
through the motions.

She watched Matt root around in sleep for the familiar
comfort of his finger—the way he'd done all his life.

Charlotte remembered the ultrasound. She'd been just
over five months pregnant when the indistinct gray and
white image showed the tiny male human living inside
her. He had a tiny head and tiny feet and a tiny penis—
and his left index finger stuck in his mouth. She and Kurt
had been fascinated by this first glimpse of the life they'd
made—the first peek at their family.

She stroked the boy's short brown hair, looked at the
outline of his face in the night-light, and let the tears flow.
Charlotte only cried when the kids were asleep. And usually only when the effort it took to stay cheerful in their
presence had exhausted her to the core. Today had been
one of those days.

Like yesterday and the day before that.

She patted Hoover's head on her way out and smiled
at the big dog. He used to sleep in the hallway at the top
of the steps, but on the night Kurt died he began sleeping in Matt's room. It was like he knew the boy needed a
protector.

She checked on Hank next. Her daughter lay openmouthed on her back in the narrow twin bed, her arms

and legs flung out like she'd stopped in the middle of making a snow angel. The lightweight blanket lay in a heap on the floor.

Charlotte wiped tears from her face and smiled down at Hank. The child had obviously inherited the flaming red hair from Charlotte's side of the family, but everything else about Hank was her daddy. She was round and solid, with a friendly, open face, wide eyes, and a charming smile. People gravitated toward her, just like they'd done with Kurt. She was even named after his mother.

It always amazed Charlotte how children of the same parents could be so inherently different from each other.

Charlotte worried about Matt. She knew Hank would be all right. And she prayed every day that the kids didn't sense the discrepancy.

Charlotte went to her bedroom, closed and locked the door, and arranged the pillows just the way she liked—stacked five high behind her back. Kurt used to tease her, saying that in a bed with six pillows you'd think a man could have at least two, but no . . .

Some nights she simply missed Kurt. She missed his comforting warmth, familiar smell, and the steady in-and-out of his breath in sleep. Tonight, she missed sex. She missed it with such a sharp emptiness that it made her legs and arms ache. So she put the sixth pillow on her lap, unlocked her nightstand, and got out the cloth-covered poetry journal. She opened it to the first blank page and began to write.

She needed this tonight. She needed to release the pressure building inside her, feel the hot, sharp rush and resulting peace, just to survive until morning.

She'd felt so alone today, especially when she sat at the Raffertys' kitchen table, preparing their low-fat, high-fiber, plant-based, protein-centered meal plan. Her eyes kept returning to the well-formed backside of the pool restorer, his broad shoulders, his neck ropy with muscle and tendon. She stared at him as he measured and prodded and climbed down the pool ladder into the dry depths.

Of course he'd caught her staring out the picture window. How embarrassing! But he'd smiled—a little too brightly—and she'd quickly gone back to printing out the recipe for Chinese green bean and tempeh salad.

Charlotte uncapped the ink pen now and closed her eyes, letting the slap of guilt sting her the way it always did. She fought it off, reminding herself that this little hobby of hers hurt no one, telling herself that despite everything she'd ever been taught, it could hardly be considered a sin.

She was a sexual creature by nature. A grown woman. A widow with vulnerable kids. So what other choice did she have?

In fact, if the truth be told, what choice had she ever had?

The hurt rolled through her chest and she closed her eyes. Yes, she'd loved Kurt. He'd been a loyal husband, a fun-loving companion, an honorable man, and a wonderful father.

But the sex. Yes, well . . . the sex.

About six years into their marriage, Charlotte read an article in a women's magazine that said if your partner didn't satisfy you, it was your own damn fault. You needed to speak up. Spell things out. Draw diagrams on a chalkboard like John Madden football plays if you had to—but it was up to you to teach the man what he needed to know.

But she'd wondered—didn't the author realize that some men were too shy to talk about sex? That sometimes in a marriage it was the *woman* who was more sexual than the man? That sometimes a woman's secrets could keep her from pushing too hard, asking for too much?

Fine. So maybe it was all her fault that sex with Kurt wasn't cataclysmic. But that didn't change the fact that when she'd focused on her husband, looked into his eyes, stayed present with him in the moment of passion— *pfft*—nothing. Zilch.

She opened her eyes. She put the pen to the paper and let the truth out: that the only thing that had ever worked was the memory of that day so long ago, and of that man.

Always her fantasy man.

Charlotte began to compose her latest erotic poem. It made her smile that Jimmy Bettmyer, of all people, had given her the idea for the title. And as the words flowed from the pen, Charlotte felt the warmth spread in her veins, because the memory of the man from her past never failed to make her unbelievably, wildly, wantonly . . . *hot*.

She smelled the honeysuckle, recalling how the little blossoms had ground into her damp skin as they rolled together in the undergrowth, the juice mixing with their mingled sweat to create the most arousing scent she'd ever known.

As always, she tasted the blood, because she'd kissed him so violently that she'd sliced open her bottom lip.

Charlotte let her tongue fiddle with the invisible scar as she wrote:

*Meat*

*Three helpings*
*I couldn't get enough*
*It's not polite to devour and run*
*But I had a plane to meet*

*Meat*
*That first time remains*
*In my blood*
*And I'd lie if I said*
*Anything since has been as thick*
*Or juicy*
*And filling*
*As you were*

*Hungry*
*Always so empty-hungry-open-ready*
*Waiting*
*For your meat*

Charlotte put away the poetry journal. She removed her convenient handheld lover from its soft cotton storage sleeve. Then she made that mysterious battery-powered journey through memory and fantasy until she arrived at the only kind of release she'd known since that perfect afternoon thirteen years ago, in the arms of the man with the greedy hands, the insistent mouth, the endless dark eyes that swallowed her soul.

The man of her fantasies.

The man with no name.

# Chapter Two

"My name is Joseph W. Mills and I'm here to pick up my keys."

The bleached blonde he'd been told was LoriSue Bettmyer rose from her desk and produced a saleswoman smile. Then she smoothed out the nonexistent wrinkles of her tight blouse, in case he'd missed her customized upper body at first glance.

As if anyone could.

"Oh!" She brought a red-nailed hand to her boobs and breathed deeply. "Oh, my! You're our mystery man!"

He smiled politely. "I understand you have the keys to Twelve thirty-two Hayden Circle."

"Well, of course, but . . . let me introduce myself." She rounded the corner of her desk, brushed a swinging hip against her in-box, and now stood too close to him, close enough that he got a blast of severe perfume and could see right down into the dark roots of her hair.

She held out her hand. "LoriSue Bettmyer. That's my married name. But I'm not married. I mean, well, we're separated." She shrugged and giggled. "I'll be going back to my maiden name professionally. Very soon now. Probably within the month."

"Great." He gave her hand a perfunctory shake. "I'm kind of in a hurry, so if you don't mind—"

She smoothed her blouse again.

Joe looked at his watch.

"Oh! Please. Just follow me."

Then LoriSue Bettmyer strutted her stuff in front of Joe with such resolve that he feared she'd dislocate her pelvis. They went down the hall and out into the reception area of Sell-More Real Estate, where half a dozen women waited for him with open mouths and wide eyes. A pudgy grandmother type spilled her coffee.

"Everyone, this is Joseph Mills. He's the client who bought the Connor house."

They all nodded and stared at him as LoriSue bent over a file cabinet and rooted through envelopes, wiggling as she worked. Joe thought the woman should just get a tattoo on her rump that read: "I'm LoriSue and this is my ass." It would save time.

"So, are you getting settled in?" the youngest of the women asked. She blinked rapidly.

"Just got to town. I need my keys before I can settle in."

"Oh! Right." She laughed nervously.

Then a rather mousy woman in a brown sweater asked, "Are your wife and children excited to be moving to Minton?"

*Thrilled out of their little nonexistent heads.* "I'm divorced. No kids."

The grandmother let out an involuntary squeak, continuing to mop up her coffee with a soggy paper towel. Joe glanced with longing toward the door and Main Street beyond.

"Voilà!" LoriSue moved triumphantly in his direction, holding the garage door opener in one set of lacquered fingers and the keys from the other. "The movers came yesterday, so you should be all set, Mr. Mills. And if there's anything else you might need—" She breathed in. "Anything at all—" She breathed out, handing him the items. "Please let me know."

"Thanks. I'm on a tight schedule, so I'll be off. Goodbye, ladies."

He got out of there as fast as possible, thinking that maybe he'd be safe in Minton, Ohio, because if Miguel Guzman's men ever came around sniffing they'd be eaten alive—picked to the bare white bones by a pack of starving females—before they could find him.

"His schedule's not the only thing that's tight."

LoriSue pressed her face up against the window while the rest of the Sell-More staff gathered behind her to make a few observations of their own.

"Did you *hear* that? Divorced. No kids. My legs are kinda shaky."

"He had that earring, though. Do you think he's straight?"

"Lord, yes. I could smell it."

"How old do you think he is?"

"Thirty-five, thirty-six max."

"I don't know—his eyes look much older."

"Maybe, but he has the bod of a twenty-year-old."

"And the booty of a Greek god."

LoriSue pushed away from the window and ran back to her office to retrieve her purse, pager, and cell phone. "I'll be out for the rest of the afternoon!" Her hand hit the front door handle. "I've got to catch up with a friend!"

"Quick, Justin. Hand me the Techno-Spy camera."

Justin Bettmyer reached down into the right pocket of his paratrooper shorts and scooted on his belly in the pine needles until he was stretched out next to Hoover the dog. "Did you get the plate number?"

"Negative," Matt whispered over Hoover's large brown head. "Bad angle."

"Was that a Mustang?"

"Affirmative." Matt took a few shots before the garage door closed. He then handed the camera back to Justin, propped his elbows on the ground, and returned the binoculars to his eyes. "The windows were too dark to see in, but it's definitely not the Connors coming back for something they forgot. My guess is we got ourselves a solo male suspect."

"What's our next step?"

Matt turned to Justin Bettmyer and smiled. "In a few days we check out the mailbox and the garbage. And we wait him out. Nobody can stay inside a house forever."

A voice carried across the yard and through the pine trees, causing Matt to wince.

*"Ma-aaatt!"*

"Jeez Louise, my mom's got lousy timing."

*"Ma-aaatt! Just-iiin! Do you want a snack?"*

"Any idea what it is today, dude?" Justin's eyes narrowed.

"Whole-wheat fig bars. They taste like dog turds rolled in sand if you ask me."

Justin's eyes widened. "Hey. Your mom's made those before and I think I kinda liked 'em. What to drink?"

Matt pushed up to a stand and shrugged, tucking the binoculars inside his utility belt, next to his plastic bowie knife, squirt gun, bent coat hanger, and notepad. "You know how weird my mom's been with food lately—probably your choice of soy milk or green tea."

The boys walked companionably out of the pines, the dog trotting between them. Justin looked down at his younger friend. "You ever have Kool-Aid, dude?"

"Three times—at your house. The red kind."

"Right."

"I had Mountain Dew there once, too."

"Yeah."

"Mom'd freak if she knew."

"Yeah."

"I ate a whole bag of Doritos at Steve Jacobucci's birthday party last week."

"No kidding?"

"And a box of Nerds at Tasha Wainwright's skating party."

"Cool."

"Must be nice to eat whatever you want, whenever you want," Matt said.

Justin shrugged. "It's okay, I guess."

The boys came to a halt in the driveway. Matt saw his mom and Bonnie waiting for them on the back patio, a tray of snacks sitting on the table. Hank was already munching away.

"Your mom's pretty cool," Justin said.

"She's okay."

"She's always home when you are. She hangs out with you and stuff."

"Guess so."

"Must be nice," Justin said.

Charlotte took one look at the way her son was outfitted and sighed. She'd gone over this with him before, but it was like talking to a pile of bricks.

"Have you been spying again, Matt?"

His head popped up from his snack and his eyes got big. "Just playing around, Mom."

"But you haven't been invading people's privacy again, right?"

Her son blinked. She groaned and looked over at Bonnie.

Since Kurt died, Charlotte had searched desperately

for something fun and educational to keep Matt busy, keep him excited and positive. Matt had idolized his father and loved him fiercely. When he died, he took the center out of the boy's universe, and nothing seemed to interest him. He skipped baseball last season. His grades plummeted. And then, suddenly, Matt developed a passion for all things related to espionage, and he set about collecting Mega-Wheat cereal box tops and saving his allowance until he could afford to send away for his beloved spy kit—binoculars, camera, decoder ring, notebook.

Charlotte had been grateful for the distraction until the day she dropped off several rolls of film to be developed and got a load of photo after photo of the residents of Hayden Heights going about their daily routines—getting into their cars, going to their mailboxes, taking out their trash, eating in their kitchens, kissing in their bedrooms.

"Matt?"

"What?" He stopped chewing.

"Have you been taking pictures again?"

"Just trees and stuff."

"Uh-huh."

"I learned my lesson, Mom." Matt looked at Bonnie and swallowed hard. "Ned told me I could go to jail."

Bonnie gasped. "He *didn't*!"

"Yep. Juvenile detention for trespassing," Matt said.

"And he oughta know," Justin said between bites. "He's the police chief."

"He's retired, honey," Bonnie corrected him.

"But he still knows all about jail and how people get fried like bacon in the electric chair, right?"

Charlotte leaned toward her son. "I don't want to have to take away your spy kit, Matthew."

"I hear you."

"Excellent fig bars, Mrs. Tasker."

Justin Bettmyer smiled at Charlotte, and though she was aware he was playing the decoy for Matt, she couldn't help but be charmed. The sandy-haired, brown-eyed kid was a sweetheart—no matter who his parents were.

"You sticking around for dinner tonight, Justin?" she asked.

He took a swig of tea. "What are you having?"

"Vegetable lasagna."

"Awesome."

Joe dropped the duffel bag on the white Mexican tile and let his eyes adjust to the cool dimness of the space. It was all very pale and sleek, and the powers that be had done a pretty good job picking out stuff to go in it, he supposed—not that he had any particular interest in interior design.

He walked through the kitchen, running a finger along the cold white surface of the kitchen counter. He flipped the switch to the family room ceiling fan, then bent down to check out the gas fireplace. The idea that he'd be here long enough to watch spring and summer pass into fireplace season made him sigh.

Living room—fine. Dining room—whatever. Like he'd be doing a lot of entertaining. He went up the stairs and looked out over the open foyer—God! If he had kids he'd be scared they'd crash through the railing and plummet to their deaths. Who designed houses like this? He grabbed the polished oak railing and shook it to make sure it was secure.

He poked his head into an open door—his bedroom. Good enough. What concerned him most was his office—he'd told the movers that he wanted the biggest bedroom for his office space, and he was relieved to see they'd followed through.

Joe stood in the doorway of what was probably re-

ferred to as the "master suite" in LoriSue Bettmyer's
world. It had a vaulted ceiling, dual ceiling fans, four
huge windows, two walk-in closets, and a fancy attached
bathroom with a Jacuzzi tub. He could live with that.

The movers had set up his desk against the inside wall.
He'd have to change that. He wanted it by the windows.
He'd be spending a lot of time at the computer, and maybe
an occasional dose of fresh air and sunshine would lessen
the feeling of imprisonment.

He bent down to double-check that all his computer
equipment and files had been delivered. He counted
thirty-two boxes. Everything was here.

Joe ran a hand through his hair and scratched his chin.
His two-week goatee was just starting to feel smooth under
his fingertips, finally past the itchy phase. He hadn't had
facial hair since his Mexico City days, and it was going to
take some getting used to. And the hair on his head—he'd
had a good eight inches hacked off the day after Steve and
his family were killed. He remembered watching the hair
fall to the barbershop floor in dark hunks, visual proof
that another undercover assignment had ended. He stared
at the dark curls, waiting for the sensation of relief to hit
him the way it usually did. That sensation never came.

He sauntered over to the wall of windows and tested
the action in the miniblinds. He saw drapery hardware
still attached to the window frame and decided he'd get
real thick, real private drapes as soon as possible. He'd
better start a shopping list.

His eye was drawn to the big Palladian window in the
master bath, right over the tub. As he walked toward it
and took off his boots, he figured whoever built this house
must have had a penchant for flashing the neighborhood.
When he stepped into the sunken tub to pull down the
blinds, he saw them.

Three kids and two women sat at a wrought-iron patio

table under an umbrella. They were talking and eating, maybe an after-school snack. He checked his watch—it was four o'clock, so that would be about right.

He got a good look at the older woman—the grandmother probably. One of the kids was a redheaded, chubby girl no more than seven or eight. She looked like a pistol. There were two older boys. The mom had her back to him, but he could see nice reddish hair up in a ponytail. She had slim shoulders and she was laughing with the kids.

Joe found himself easing down onto the edge of the tub, in slow motion, his hand frozen on the miniblind pull. He leaned forward, breathing hard. His skin had started to tingle. His blood had begun to hum. And he was hit with the oddest combination of sensations: dread, regret, lust, utter disbelief. The scent of honeysuckle cut through his nostrils and into his brain.

Just then, the mom stood up from the table, bent over to pick up a tray of cups and plates, and he got a good look at her petite, shapely body. Her little round ass. Her dainty waist.

She turned and headed to the back patio door, calling over her shoulder. He saw that graceful throat. That sweet face. That shiny hair.

He slapped down the blinds, nearly tumbling over the edge of the tub in his hurry to get on the phone to Roger.

"Get me the hell out of here," Joe said as soon as his boss answered. "I don't care if it's North-fuckin'-Dakota. You gotta get me out of here."

Charlotte could not recall the last time LoriSue Bettmyer had been in her house. Probably the day of the funeral, but she couldn't be sure. The whole town had invaded her home that day, yet she'd been so numb she didn't recall a minute of it.

But here was LoriSue now, leaning up against Charlotte's kitchen counter in her tight little blue business-woman suit, chatting with her and Bonnie like this was an everyday thing, munching on a carrot stick as friendly as could be. Charlotte had to concentrate doubly hard in order not to lop off a finger while she chopped zucchini, her eyes occasionally moving to Bonnie's face for confirmation of this strange occurrence.

"So we'd love to have you and the kids over for dinner one night, Charlotte. You know, to repay you for having Justin over here every once in a while."

Bonnie's eyes darted to Charlotte's, and she knew immediately what her friend longed to say: *"Every weeknight is more than once in a while."*

Charlotte smiled to herself, knowing that the kid hadn't earned the nickname Justin-Time-for-Dinner for nothing.

"He's always welcome," Charlotte said. And she meant it. There was no point in being cruel to a little boy just because his parents were jerks. "You know, LoriSue, he really misses you and Jimmy. He says you've been working a lot."

"Oh! It's been *crazed,* let me tell you! The market is megahot right now with the rock-bottom interest rates, and we're getting new listings left and right. The office is swamped."

Charlotte grabbed another zucchini and hacked off the end, wondering why some people even bothered to have children if they didn't spend time with them.

"We're lucky that Justin has always been such an independent little boy."

"Uh-huh," Bonnie said from her seat at the table. "So, LoriSue, any idea who's moving into the Connor place? We've been wondering when—"

"A man," LoriSue said, pushing away from the counter. She reached around Charlotte for a zucchini slice and nibbled, not saying more, obviously thrilled that the women now relied on her for information.

Charlotte stopped slicing, wiped her hands on her jeans, and looked at LoriSue. "Okay. I'll bite. A man alone? One guy in that big house?"

LoriSue sucked in her cheeks and pursed her lips, producing a look that announced she had hot news to share.

"Ladies, I spoke to the movers the other day. He's a mystery writer. Isn't that a trip? He came into the office for his keys just a little while ago, and I've got to tell you, he looks like a Chippendales dancer. Not an exaggeration. Absolute male-stripper material."

Bonnie snorted.

Charlotte's mouth fell open. "Are you *serious*?"

"Swear to God." LoriSue held up the zucchini slice, then took another nibble. "Drives a black Mustang. Divorced. No kids. Dark hair just past his ears. A little goatee. Earring. I'm telling you, he is one juicy piece of man."

Bonnie snorted again.

Charlotte went back to cutting vegetables.

"His name is Joseph Mills. I don't know if people call him Joe. He didn't say. He didn't say much of anything, really. Not the friendliest guy in the world, not that it matters." LoriSue giggled. "I'll tell you what—this has been so much fun! We should hang out together more often, just us girls."

Suddenly it all made perfect sense to Charlotte. LoriSue was in her kitchen because of its geographic proximity to the Chippendales' bachelor pad.

"Would you like to stay for dinner, LoriSue? We'll be eating about six, and then it's off to baseball and Boy Scouts."

"Oh! No—but thanks. Got to get back to the office. Do you think you could give Justin a lift to the scout meeting?"

"Of course," Charlotte said. Like tonight should be any different.

When LoriSue was safely on her way and the lasagna was in the oven, Charlotte crossed her arms over her chest and frowned in Bonnie's direction. "Do you think she's right about the guy next door?"

"No way," Bonnie replied, slowly shaking her head. "LoriSue's on the prowl, honey, and when a woman's on the prowl, she can convince herself that the FedEx guy is a man in uniform. I know. I've been there."

Charlotte laughed and set the oven timer. "You're a riot, Bon."

"I speak only the truth. I once was sure that Ned was the spitting image of Robert Redford."

Charlotte spun around, her eyes quite wide. "Whoa. When was *that*?"

"When I was on the prowl. You see what I'm saying?"

He probably shouldn't drink beer in the middle of the day, because that's when he would start to feel a little sorry for himself. That's when he'd start to think of Charlotte Tasker.

He'd wanted that woman for years. And he was certain that if things had been different—if his situation and hers had been different—they could have been happy together.

Jimmy Bettmyer sat at a table at the Creekside Inn and savored his Budweiser, thinking about the conversation they'd had yesterday in the school parking lot. Charlotte was a fighter, that was for sure, but he figured all the stubborn resistance would make the eventual surrender that much sweeter.

And she was going to give it up sooner or later. He knew it. A babe like her couldn't survive without a man. He could see it in her eyes.

Jimmy looked around the bar and counted four women

he'd slept with. Then he counted the total number of women in the place and realized he'd nailed about a fourth of the females present. Not a bad handicap.

Jimmy had no intention of getting drunk this afternoon. He had a showing at 6:00 and a closing at 7:30. He decided to head home, and left a buck on the table. He chuckled to himself at the use of the word *home,* because for the last five months home had been the basement rec room of the custom-designed $400,000 New French château he refused to vacate to the bitch who would eventually be his ex-wife.

Jimmy stood up and stretched, briefly wondering if chasing women would be nearly as much fun once he was divorced. He wondered if being married was half the thrill. He'd find out soon enough, he supposed.

# Chapter Three

Roger was perplexed, but Joe wasn't about to paint a detailed picture for him.

"We met a long time ago. That's all."

"When, exactly?"

"Thirteen years ago."

"Where? Quantico?"

"Not really."

"DEA-related? Was she an informant or something?"

Joe couldn't stifle the laugh that erupted from his chest.

"Joe, for God's sake, does she know your name? Does she know what you do for a living? Help me out here!"

"We never exchanged names."

"Then what's the problem?"

"I can't stay here."

"You've already told me that."

"Just get me out—out of the Cincinnati area entirely."

"You want another temporary assignment? You want another field office? But I promised Rich Baum you'd help him out with—"

"Just make it happen, Roger. Please. I need you to do this for me."

"What exactly happened with this woman?"

Joe couldn't answer.

"Oh, hell, Joe. Not that." Roger sighed. "Look, I'll do what I can, but it's going to take a couple weeks to find another place—and it won't be near as nice. You know I don't have any more country estates up my sleeve."

"A hotel is fine."

"A goddamn hotel is not fine! You are a marked man!"

"But—"

"Unless you believe yourself to be in imminent danger of discovery, you will stay put until I can get something arranged. Do you hear me?"

Joe said nothing. He was on a landline telephone that prevented him from wandering back to the bathroom and peeking out the window, so he just stared at the closed blind, his breathing shallow, thinking of her.

"You still there, Bellacera?"

"Can you send that family's background file to me? Give me an hour to get on the network—my computer stuff is still in boxes. They live in the house immediately to the"—Joe craned his neck to judge the angle of the sun—"immediately to the southwest of this address on Hayden Circle. I don't have a street number. Yellow two-story. Kids, probably."

Roger sighed again. "Yeah. Sure."

"Thanks."

"One thing before I go." Roger's voice was strained. "The nastiest Mexican drug cartel I've seen in twenty years in law enforcement killed your partner and has a million-dollar reward out for your head. I just want to make sure you understand those little details."

Joe closed his eyes.

"Just hang tight until I tell you otherwise."

As Joe disconnected, he told himself he'd be hanging all right—hanging upside down from the doorjamb by a string tied around his nuts at this rate.

How could this have happened? There she was, right next door! After all the years he'd searched for her, she was an arm's length away and he couldn't go to her! He couldn't talk to her! He couldn't get to know her!

Joe methodically sliced open the boxes one-by-one with his pocketknife, aware that the violent slashing motions might be on the verge of overkill. But it felt good. And as soon as the computer was up and running, he'd find where the movers had stashed his punching bags. Then he'd fight himself into a state of oblivion.

Ah, *hell*. She was so obviously married. Those were her kids. She was probably content in her little life here in Bum-Fuck with her lucky son-of-a-bitch husband, whoever he might be.

She probably didn't even remember him.

Joe was sweating by the time he'd reached the last box and caught his reflection in the floor-length closet mirror. He stopped, straightened, and jogged to the glass, where he bared his teeth.

The left front tooth was as straight and white as its companion, but anyone who looked close enough could see it had a story to tell. It was his story, and hers, and dammit, every time he saw that tooth he thought of her, which meant he thought of her at least twice a day. Over thirteen years that was, what—nearly ten thousand times? And that didn't even count all those times she'd invaded his dreams, when she'd come to him sticky with honeysuckle juice, her skin hot to the touch, so much fire in such an innocent-looking little package.

When she drove away that day, he'd forced himself not to turn around and memorize her license plate number. And it was surely the single biggest mistake he'd made in a life full of them. What had he been thinking? He hadn't been thinking at all, of course. He'd been young and stupid and so damn sure that there would be an endless supply of incredible women in the world that he just let her drive away.

Joe let his mouth relax and stared intently at the man in the mirror. He was older and smarter now. He'd seen more than his share of injustice and violence, and it showed in the lines around his eyes, the taut pull of skin over his cheekbones. And lately, he swore he could sometimes see the Carmine Bellacera of his childhood staring back at him—except that his dad never went in for the reclusive writer look; it was GI Joe all the way to the grave.

Joe smiled sadly. He would turn thirty-eight next month holed up someplace alone, where no one knew his real name.

He went back to the boxes, knowing that he'd have to be completely insane to approach that woman before Roger could get him out of here.

He needed to stay alive, stay focused on the trial, and on his duty to Steve and his family. He couldn't afford this distraction.

But *damn*.

She'd grown from pretty girl to beautiful woman, and he hadn't been there to see it.

And knowing that made him feel more alone than he'd ever felt in his life.

It was only nine, so if she were good, she'd use this time to do her Tae Bo tape. No, wait—Charlotte had recently read a magazine article that said it was self-defeating to label yourself "good" or "bad" when the focus should be on the behavior itself. The article said that people make just two kinds of choices in life: harmful ones and helpful ones.

So after she checked on the kids, she headed downstairs and made the choice to find the box of Triscuits and the can of squirt cheese. Then made the choice to sit at the kitchen table and chow down.

"You only live once," she said to no one, popping another salty, crunchy, squishy, artificially flavored tidbit in her mouth, thinking the whole time of the Chippendales dancer next door.

After a few more savory concoctions, Charlotte stuck the cracker box under her arm and tucked the squirt cheese in her shorts pocket and wandered out to the back patio. Though the days were growing longer, it was fully dark by now, and the neighborhood was quiet. She took a seat at the patio table and propped her feet on an empty chair.

Right after Kurt died, more than a few well-meaning people had asked if she planned to sell the house. The answer was no, not if she could help it.

She topped another cracker, a little shocked at how loud the aerosol sounded out here in the quiet.

She loved her home—the acre of yard that provided privacy and plenty of play room for the kids and Hoover, the mature shade trees, the roomy floor plan. She loved that her children felt like they belonged here. She loved that they felt close to Kurt.

What she didn't love was the mortgage—$1,500 a month, every single month, even after refinancing.

She munched down hard on the Triscuit, wiping a few errant crumbs off her scout leader shirt.

She'd told herself countless times that it could have been worse—Kurt could have died with no insurance instead of a modest amount. He could have died leaving a mountain of debt instead of a few conservative investments. It's just that no man thinks he's going to drop dead at age thirty-four. And no woman thinks she's going to walk into the family room to rouse her napping husband for dinner only to find him cold.

The bottom line was they weren't prepared for the wage earner in their family to die. And Charlotte refused to go out and get a full-time nursing job with the kids this young. They needed her attention. They needed her time. They needed *her*—because she was all they had.

Multi-Tasker, Inc., was something she could do while the kids were in school. It was something she could juggle in the summer and something she could set aside if one of them was sick. With the life insurance and social security, it made them just enough money to squeak by.

She squirted out a big, sloppy pile of Day-Glo cheddar on a cracker and shoved the whole thing in her mouth.

She immediately stopped chewing and her ears pricked.

*Thud-a-ba, thud-a-ba, thud-a-ba, thud-a-ba . . .*

It sounded like muffled gunfire. She choked down the cracker and sat up straight, her ears straining to identify its source.

*Thud-a-ba, thud-a-ba, thud-a-ba, thud-a-ba . . .* Then she heard a loud *"Uhmph!"*

Charlotte shot to her feet and stared up toward the children's bedroom windows. It wasn't coming from there.

*Thud-a-ba, thud-a-ba, thud-a-ba, thud-a-ba . . .*

Bonnie and Ned's house was quiet. And it wasn't coming from the Noonans' over the back fence because they were still in Florida and their security system could wake the dead.

*Thud-a-ba, thud-a-ba, thud-a-ba, thud-a-ba . . .*

Her head whipped around—it had to be the Chippendales guy!

Charlotte gathered her snacks and tiptoed around to the driveway, where she stood half-hunched in the darkness, listening.

*"Uhmph! Uh! Mmmm, mmmm, uhmph!"*

"Good Lord," Charlotte whispered to herself. Still hunched over, the Triscuits tucked close under her elbow, she glanced furtively up and down the street, making sure there were no cars or dog walkers coming. She then slipped past the pine trees to the edge of her property and sidled up to the privacy fence around the Connors' in-ground pool and patio.

The sound was definitely coming from behind the fence, but it wasn't the pool pump. It wasn't mechanical.

Charlotte pressed her face up to the fence boards, and though she tried several angles—twisted around until her neck hurt—she couldn't quite find a way to align her eyeball with the small vertical slits. She sure couldn't peek over the fence—it was nine feet tall! So all she saw was a sliver of light and indistinct movement.

*Thud-a-ba, thud-a-ba, thud-a-ba, thud-a-ba* . . . *"Uhmph!"*

Someone was being murdered! That had to be it. She suppressed her gasp and skittered away from the fence, racing full speed to her own patio, running inside the back door. Hoover lay in wait, hair on end, ready to pounce— and his whole big body shuddered with relief that it was only her.

She slipped him a Triscuit. "Good boy, Hoov."

Charlotte bolted the lock on the family room double doors. She did the same to the laundry room door leading to the garage, and the front door.

Then she took the stairs two at a time and, for lack of any other source of reassurance, she spoke to Hoover.

"We may have a situation on our hands," she said.

The dog blinked and yawned, exposing a set of huge white canine teeth. He waited briefly for some kind of command, then burped and went into Matt's room, where he collapsed in a heap.

"You call yourself a watchdog," she muttered.

Then she saw them.

The spy binoculars sat precariously on the edge of

Matt's small desk, the lenses reflecting the hall light. She grabbed them, slinked down the hallway to her bedroom, and locked her door.

Now if this wasn't the lowest point in her life, she didn't know what was. She was going to spy on her new neighbor! And after the lecture she'd given Matt that very afternoon!

But that sound—it could be anything, right? And those animal noises! If it wasn't murder, maybe he was injured. What if her new neighbor was having some kind of spasm or epileptic fit and swallowing his tongue?

She turned off all the lights in her room. She stood at the window facing the drive and tried to figure out how to focus the binoculars. She certainly wouldn't be discovering any new solar systems with these cheap plastic things, but she hoped they could at least put her mind to rest about the tongue swallowing.

She aimed out the window, and in the light from the Connors' patio she guided the binoculars through the tree branches, located the fence, and tilted down until she could see the pool area.

A punching bag. The guy was pounding on a punching bag. That realization took about a nanosecond to register in her brain before the real important information came to the forefront: LoriSue, God bless her slutty little soul, had been absolutely correct. He was male-stripper material, and he'd been thoughtful enough to strip to a pair of athletic shorts on his very first night in the neighborhood.

Charlotte prevented herself from crumpling to the carpet by leaning against the window frame. The binoculars clicked against the glass.

This was so wrong. So illegal. So bad. And so incredibly *gratifying*!

She chuckled to herself and found a comfortable stance, immediately deciding that LoriSue's term "juicy piece of man" didn't go far enough in describing the image now framed in the binocular lenses. In fact, Charlotte didn't think there was a term for a man like him.

And he just kept punching, his back toward her, the little bag blurring and spinning from the impact of his boxing gloves. His longish hair was wet with perspiration and black against the nape of his neck. His cut shoulders, back, and arms rippled, glistening with sweat, an image made all the more surreal by the haze of moths drawn to the patio light.

"Moths to a flame," Charlotte said out loud.

She stared, stupefied, watching his feet dance and his thighs and calves bunch up and release, his tight backside bounce and jut, his lungs pump air in and out of his body.

And just then, a thick, slow-moving fog of déjà vu began to roll through her. It was like she'd once had a dream about this or that her subconscious was whispering to her that this man reminded her of someone she once knew— or wait; maybe she'd once seen a movie where some pathetic, lonely widow stared at her attractive neighbor with her son's cereal box binoculars!

She groaned and was about to put an end to the whole sorry business when the man stopped. He pulled his hands out of the gloves, tossed them on the pool deck, then shook his sweaty hair. He reached around, grabbed a water bottle, and playfully tossed it up over his head.

That's the moment he turned toward her, snagging the plastic bottle in midair. She saw his face.

Charlotte's legs didn't hold.

Bonnie remembered the last time Charlotte told her to come over and bring a spiral cut ham. It was the night Kurt died. But he'd died at five-thirty on a Tuesday, so the HoneyBaked Ham store at the mall was still open. It was almost ten tonight. And the closest thing she and Ned had to ham was a half-pound of smoked turkey breast from the Kroger deli case.

She poked her head in the family room double doors and was greeted by a snarling Hoover.

"Hey, Hoov." Bonnie tore off a piece of turkey breast and the dog trotted happily away.

It took a moment before she located Charlotte. She was sitting cross-legged on the family room rug, wearing her blue and yellow scout leader uniform, her face pale and her gray eyes far too bright.

"Did you bring it?" Charlotte swiveled her head and Bonnie watched most of her hair slip out of her ponytail.

Bonnie held up the Baggie and tried to smile. "Turkey, sweetheart. It's all we had. Do you want to tell me what's going on?"

Bonnie put the Baggie on the table, next to the Triscuits and squirt cheese, and figured it had been a rough evening at the Tasker house. Ever since Kurt died, Charlotte had gone overboard with the health food thing, grabbing onto something she could control in a world that had proven itself unpredictable. Bonnie didn't blame her. But she also knew that ham and squirt cheese were Charlotte's drugs of choice and if she had a craving for both, she'd hit rock bottom. This was going to be a long night.

"Want to join me at the grown-up table?"

Charlotte laughed a little, which relieved Bonnie—because she looked like a zombie.

"How long have I known you, Bon?"

"Hmm." Bonnie draped an arm over the kitchen chair. "Twelve years, I guess."

"And we've never really talked about sex, have we?" Charlotte reached behind her and pulled out the ponytail holder, letting her straight reddish-gold hair fall to her shoulders. She glared at Bonnie in challenge.

"Uh, no. Not much."

"Do you know why?"

Bonnie let her eyes dart around the room. She was waiting for the punch line. "Noooo. Why?"

"Because I've got a whopper of a secret."

Bonnie jumped to her feet. "How about I make us some tea?"

"I'll have scotch, neat."

She stopped in midstride. "You don't drink."

"I do tonight, sister." Charlotte pushed herself up from the floor and passed Bonnie on her way to the dining room sideboard. She came back with a bottle of Glenlivet and two shot glasses. "And so do you, if you know what's good for you. Come on."

Bonnie followed her into the rarely used living room, thinking, *Charlotte's going to tell me she's a lesbian and she wants to do it in the formal living room.*

"Don't worry. I'm not a lesbian." Charlotte plopped down on the sofa cushions, then poured. "I hope this booze is still good. Somebody brought it to the house after the funeral. Here."

Bonnie wasn't sure what toast would be appropriate for the occasion, so she said, "Bottoms up?" then slammed it back.

Charlotte did the same and began thumping her chest, gasping. "That stuff's poison," she choked out. "I'm going to have to pace myself."

Bonnie studied Charlotte as she sank back into the sofa and closed her eyes. She loved this young woman like a daughter. She loved Charlotte's children, and she'd loved Kurt. And over the years the two women had shared everything—childhood traumas, political beliefs, parenting philosophies, thoughts on organized religion, God, death, and the afterlife.

But Charlotte was right. They'd never really talked about sex.

Bonnie learned early on that it was not a topic Charlotte felt comfortable discussing, and she'd assumed it had to do with the difference in their ages. For Charlotte it would have been like talking about sex with her mother. Besides, how many stories had Charlotte told about growing up the daughter of strict Baptists? Bonnie just figured the subject was taboo.

But here was Charlotte tonight, drinking scotch in her scout leader uniform, asking for ham, and apparently getting ready to let it all hang out, as she and Ned used to say.

"Is this about Kurt, honey?" Bonnie asked as gently as possible. "Did you find out he had an affair?"

Charlotte let her head rock back and forth against the couch, not bothering to open her eyes. "No. Extremely unlikely."

"Did you have one?"

Charlotte let loose with a bitter laugh and sat up straight, now fully alert.

"Not technically."

"I'm not sure I follow."

Charlotte poured them each another shot and got herself comfortable. She sipped. "What I'm going to tell you has to stay between just the two of us. I've never told anyone—" She impatiently swiped away a tear. "But if I don't talk to somebody, I'm just going to explode!"

Bonnie grabbed Charlotte's hand. "I won't breathe a word to another soul and I'll help any way I can." She cupped Charlotte's frightened face. "Honey, whatever it is, it's going to be all right."

Charlotte nodded.

"And you know you can tell me anything."

Charlotte struggled with a deep breath and set her shoulders straight. "It's the man next door, Bon. The Chippendales guy—Joseph Mills."

Bonnie reared back, staring at her friend, her mouth ajar. "You mean you did the nasty with the new neighbor already—in your scout leader uniform?"

"What? God, no!" Charlotte shot up from the couch and began to pace in front of the fireplace, pulling on hunks of her hair, eyelids squeezed tight.

"Then . . . ?"

"I *know* him!" Charlotte's eyes popped open, and they were terror-stricken. "I know this Joseph Mills person!"

"Oh. Well, that's nice—"

"Nice?" Charlotte's mouth fell open, then snapped shut. "I had head-banging, mind-blowing, totally anonymous sex with that man thirteen years ago! And I'm talking *minutes* before Kurt proposed to me! Do you hear what I'm saying, Bonnie? He popped my cherry while Kurt was waiting to pop the question!"

"Oh. Oh, dear," Bonnie managed.

"And Kurt thought I was a virgin when we got married. It was really important to him. But I *lied,* Bonnie! I had sex with this guy in the weeds! Three times! And he was . . . oh, my *God* . . . nothing has ever been right since!"

Charlotte swayed, her arms hanging at her sides, the scotch spilling onto the carpet. She looked like she might faint. She began to sob.

Bonnie jumped up and grabbed her by the upper arms. "Charlotte. Look at me. Tell me right now—did he hurt you? My God, honey—did he attack you? Is that what you're trying to tell me?"

Charlotte shook her head and the tears slipped down her cheeks. She looked away briefly, then steeled herself. "Actually, Bon," she whispered, a look of pleading in her eyes, "I think *I* may have attacked *him.*"

# Chapter Four

Her name was Charlotte.

Charlotte Mary Nelson Tasker was a thirty-five-year-old registered nurse who ran an errand service. She had two kids. She was a widow.

Joe blinked, skimming the computer file one last time, rereading the obituary for the man who'd been her husband. Kurt Lewis Tasker was a local boy, an All-State lineman who became a popular sports columnist for the *Cincinnati Enquirer,* apparently known for his straight talk and good humor. He left work early one Thursday with what he thought was a touch of the flu. He dropped dead a few hours later from a congenital heart defect no one knew he had.

The obit photo showed a robust, friendly-looking guy with wide shoulders and questionable taste in ties. The color picture showed him at work on the sidelines at a Bengals game, curly brown hair, a lopsided grin, and pale, laughing eyes. He looked like a good guy. Joe read again how he was mourned by fellow journalists, coaches, players, and readers.

Joe felt a sad smile creep across his face, recalling the little girl he'd seen at the patio table—Henrietta was her name—realizing that she looked just like this man except for the flaming red hair. The other Tasker kid was named Matthew according to the file, and if memory served him correctly, which it always did, the boy looked more like his mom.

Joe rubbed his eyes with the heels of his palms. He must have read this stuff ten times since Roger sent it to him—everything he'd ever wanted to know about what had happened to his mystery woman, all in one convenient little 400 kilobyte file.

Her name was Charlotte—*Charlotte!*—and she would have been just twenty-two that day. All this time he'd thought of her as a Kim or a Jenny or a Terri, but she was a Charlotte. It sounded kind of old-fashioned and stuffy in his opinion, and it made him chuckle to put *that* name with *those* memories.

It was Charlotte who pressed her sweet little hips into him when he pinned her against the car. Charlotte who happily opened her mouth to his kiss. Charlotte who rolled with him in the weeds, tore at his clothes, and whispered, "Hurry, oh please hurry!" when he fumbled with the first condom wrapper.

It was Charlotte who gave herself to him over and over, shuddering on top of his body, tight as a clenched fist around him.

It was Charlotte who said, "I don't have a name and neither do you, all right?"

It was Charlotte who kissed him good-bye with such hunger that she broke his tooth.

Joe shut down the computer and turned off the light. He wandered into the smaller bedroom and dropped his clothes to the floor, then slipped under the cool, clean sheets in the nude.

He lay there a long time—minutes, hours, he didn't have a clue—staring at the indistinct patterns in the ceiling of this strange room, sensing her next door, swearing to God that he smelled honeysuckle through the barely open window, and knowing that if he didn't get out of this house and this town, he'd lose his mind.

*Charlotte.*

He'd found her.

Joe clenched and loosened his fists as they lay at his sides, wondering for maybe the thousandth time in his life whether he'd taken her virginity that day. It had always bugged him. Not because she'd been hesitant or unsure of herself or afraid, but because she'd been so incredibly snug. And at one point, after making her come with his hand, he'd seen bright red blood streaked down the length of his fingers.

But here's what had forever baffled him—what would a virgin be doing acting like a wild thang? Why would a spectacularly beautiful woman who'd held out to the age of twenty-two suddenly decide to give it up to a stranger on the side of the road? It made no sense, and he'd never been able to figure it out.

Joe rubbed his entire face and sighed. If, in fact, he'd been her first, it was something he needed to know. Because that would mean she'd given him the most precious gift imaginable. And his mama had taught him to always say thank you.

Besides, if he was Charlotte's first, that would mean she would always remember him—right? It would make him special to her, if solely for that one reason . . . right? So if he walked over to that cute yellow house and knocked on the door with the wreath on it, she'd answer, smile at him, and know exactly who he was.

Wouldn't she?

The only person he'd ever told about Charlotte had been Steve Simmons, his partner and the best friend he'd ever had. Joe grinned in the dark, remembering how

Steve had helped him in his attempts to find her, the mystery girl in the 1992 Mariner Blue Mazda Miata with Maryland tags.

One hundred and two. That's how many people they called, wrote, or visited looking for her. Nobody fit her description and no one said they had loaned their car to a young redhead that day.

Joe chuckled softly to himself, recalling the night an exasperated Steve observed, "Damn, Bellacera. I have never seen *you* do the chasing before."

And wasn't that the truth?

But, with Steve's help, chase he did, with nothing to show for it. She was out there somewhere, though. He knew she'd been driving one of the 102 cars. He hadn't imagined her. She'd been real. She'd been hot and sweet and funny, and right before Christmas he'd been sitting in the dentist's chair about to let Dr. Lavin of the Quantico Dental Clinic put a cap on that tooth.

But he just couldn't go through with it.

Joe had gotten used to the little chip at the juncture of his two incisors. He'd become attached to the only proof that she'd ever been his. And if he fixed it, it would feel final, like he'd given up on ever finding her.

Joe laughed again to himself in the dark, then heard the sound of his laughter die away. He flipped over onto his stomach and turned a cheek into the pillow.

Life had swept him away that winter. He and Steve got their first assignments with the Administration. They went to El Paso together, four years of gritty border cases. Then there was Houston and Mexico City and it became clear that he'd picked the kind of work that would forever leave him drained and needing his space. The women he'd managed to hook up with all had the same complaint—his job left no room for a relationship. And they were damn right.

No wonder DEA agents had a divorce rate of about 75 percent.

Somehow, Steve had managed it better. Maybe he was just a more laid-back guy, or maybe Reba was such a wonderful woman that it made it worth the effort. But Steve found a way to balance a wife and kid with his job, a way to mix his work with a real life.

For a while, anyway. Until his work got them all killed.

Joe flipped over again, sending the sheet flying off his body. He felt hot. Enraged. He felt that familiar black hole in his gut, and knew he'd never find a way to fill it.

It had been the assignment of a lifetime. Their job was to infiltrate Guzman's Albuquerque cell and get enough evidence to take down the entire organization. The cartel was suspected of smuggling huge quantities of cocaine, marijuana, and methamphetamines into the country and distributing it all over the western United States. He and Steve soon learned the group had expanded its reach by subcontracting to deliver Colombian heroin as well.

It took them ten months to worm their way into the good graces of Guzman's men, making several small buys of cocaine and heroin. Their money was clean. Their word was good. They earned the dealers' trust. And the team did a meticulous job of documenting every encounter, every meeting, every word exchanged. The result was that even if they never caught Guzman himself in the act, the U.S. attorneys had enough evidence to nail the elusive drug lord.

Joe had never met Guzman during his two-year assignment in Mexico City but knew all about him. He was in his early fifties, a man who'd been born in the fetid slums of Ciudad Juárez on the U.S. border and had worked his way up in the ranks of organized crime.

He earned a reputation for killing anyone who looked

at him funny. He had a large and loyal following of men who knew that if they made one misstep, their families would die. It's how any tyrant won respect—with fear. Absolute fear.

Joe laced his fingers together behind his head and let the memory of Steve's murder flood his brain.

They'd been hanging with Guzman's men that evening, putting the finishing touches on the deal that was supposed to go down the next morning. Guzman was already in town to supervise the transaction—fifty kilos of cocaine for $5 million. In hours, they'd catch him orchestrating the sale, on videotape.

Joe and Steve left in separate cars about 2:00 a.m. and met up at the Denny's on Alameda Boulevard, like they sometimes did. They had no idea that just moments before some two-bit informant they'd dealt with in another case had blown their cover. They had no idea they'd been followed, that Guzman's men sat outside like the patient predators they were. Steve reached the door first. It was sheer dumb luck that Joe was two steps behind, still paying the bill.

The henchmen got to Reba and Daniel before agents could. They'd been executed in their sleep. It was Guzman's way of making his point quite clear: Special Agent Joe Bellacera—and anyone close to him—would never be safe.

Guzman was snagged by agents later that night at an airstrip forty miles out on the mesa. It wasn't the Hollywood ending, but agents impounded the cocaine intended for distribution, arrested twenty-seven Mexican nationals, and took the big man into custody.

It was no comfort to Joe that Guzman now sat in maximum security at the federal prison in Beaumont, Texas. Because he still had his followers. And he'd promised a million dollars to whoever brought him Joe's head.

A million dollars was highly motivating.

That's why Joe had to hide. Why he had to live in Ohio. And if all that weren't enough, he was faced with the ultimate irony: He'd finally found his mystery woman and couldn't go to her.

Joe took a deep breath and smelled the honeysuckle again. The mind could play tricks on a man, he was well aware, but another sniff assured him this was no illusion. He made a mental note to find wherever that tangle of weed existed on this property and hack it to pieces.

Burn it if he had to.

Because he saw Reba and little Daniel Simmons in his mind and knew he could never go to Charlotte Tasker, tell her he'd searched for her, that he'd never forgotten her, that he'd missed her every damn day for thirteen years. He couldn't risk getting close to anyone.

Not ever again.


Not fifteen minutes had passed since Bonnie went home, and the poems were coming fast and furious. Maybe because of the Glenlivet but more likely because *he* was here. *He* was real.

Charlotte could feel a crackle in the air around her. She felt like a live wire, her skin raw, her mouth dry. And all she could think of was his face, now thirteen years older and framed in a villain's goatee and longer hair. But it was the same face. It was *his* face. There was no doubt.

At first, when she'd hauled herself off the floor and retrieved the binoculars, she told herself no—it couldn't be him. It was just a man who looked like him. A man who happened to move like he'd moved and smile like he'd smiled. Besides, the man she'd known so briefly was clean-shaven and wore a crew cut. The Chippendales guy's face was harsher. Much more intense, even when he smiled. So, no. It wasn't him.

But there was no mistaking those piercing black eyes, that sensuous, wide mouth, those big but graceful hands. The man's entire body seemed to glide through space, like a sleek jaguar, just like her fantasy man.

She couldn't stop writing.

*Glide*

*Tongue on tongue*
*Slide on me*

*Teeth to flesh*
*Consume me*

*Move inside*
*Fill the void*

*Feel the glide*
*Deliver me*

Charlotte closed her eyes tight and allowed herself the luxury of the ultimate fantasy. Here's what would happen: She'd walk over and knock on his door. He would smile and wrap her up in his arms and he'd say, why, of course he remembered her! And yes, he happened to be single yet adored children, and he was sane, employed, and free of all communicable diseases! And of course he'd love to pick up where they left off thirteen years ago and fuck her brains out on a regular basis!

Would Tuesday work for her?

She sighed. Even if all that were true, what exactly would she tell Hank and Matt? That Mommy had a special new friend? The thought made her queasy.

She chewed on the end of the pen, then stopped, her mouth falling open in shock. This was the end! This moment marked the official death of her sexual fantasy life. For thirteen years she'd built a personal ritual around a mystery man, a man who lived only in her memory and imagination, and now the real man had to move next door—in the flesh—and ruin it!

God! Couldn't a woman even masturbate in peace?

She flipped back through her journal, finding a poem she'd worked on a few months ago. The more she read, the more pissed off she became.

*All I've Got*

*I'll pretend it's you*
*Will you humor me?*
*And for a while*
*I will be free*

*Sweat heat*
*Fiery friction*
*I will burn*
*In my latex addiction*

*I'll burn and scream and writhe*
*So hot!*
*I'll pretend it's you*
*Though I know it's not.*

*But it's all I've got.*

Charlotte choked back a fresh batch of tears, took another swill from the water bottle by the bedside, and wiped her mouth. She needed to stay hydrated. She'd be sure to eat plenty of potassium tomorrow and take her vitamin B supplements. She'd do a three-mile loop at the park once she got the kids off to school. One thing she knew for sure—healthy food and fresh air had always helped to make anything survivable.

She'd get through this as well.

Charlotte closed the journal in her lap and folded her hands. Bonnie had been a good listener earlier that night and had kept her commentary to a minimum—just what Charlotte needed. The last thing she could have dealt with was her best friend expressing shock or disappointment or passing judgment.

Bonnie had simply nodded a lot. Held her hand. Let her talk. And as the words had spilled from Charlotte's lips, she felt somehow separate from the story she told her friend, as if it had happened to another woman.

She supposed it had.

After all, who is the same woman at thirty-five as she was at twenty-two? No one she'd ever met, that was for sure. On that day thirteen years ago, she'd been young and optimistic, ready to graduate, ready to get engaged, ready to start her life. She'd felt like she was ready to step out into the bright perfect world of her future.

But somehow, right there in that convertible on the GW Parkway, it hit her like a cinder block to the forehead—Kurt Tasker would be the first and only man she'd ever have sex with. Sex—that dark territory she'd tiptoed around and shut her eyes against in order to stay a good girl—would be experienced with Kurt and only Kurt. He would define it for her. He would be her travel companion. Her tour guide. The only places she'd ever go would be the places he took her. Just him. One man.

Forever.

Even back then, had she known in her heart that it would be a no-frills excursion? Yes, if she answered honestly, she had. But at the time that had seemed a small sacrifice to make. After all, Kurt Tasker was good for her, just what she needed in so many other ways. And a woman couldn't have everything, right?

Charlotte recalled the conversation they'd had before he flew out to his interview at the *Enquirer*. Once again, it was Charlotte who brought up the subject of sex, only to be guided back to moral ground by Kurt. It was best to wait until they were married, he'd reminded her. It was the right thing to do. It would be worth the wait. They would enter into their covenant of marriage in God's favor.

Of course he'd been right, and she'd felt that familiar sense of guilt wash over her. What was wrong with her? Why did it tantalize her so much? Why wasn't she as patient as Kurt? As in control of her desires?

Then something happened that should have set off the warning bells. They'd been sitting at the gate, waiting for boarding to begin. Kurt had been reading the *Sporting News,* his fingers absently stroking the top of her left hand. She watched his big thumb trace the vein under her pale skin, let her eyes travel up his thick forearm to his biceps under the sleeve of his pinstripe Oxford shirt, then to his eyes the same pale shade of blue, moving from side to side as he read.

She couldn't help it. She loved the way he looked. She'd touched him everywhere, she'd had her hands on his bare flesh, and that one time things got "out of hand," as Kurt referred to it, she'd even had him in her mouth.

He was beautiful. He made her feel hot and soft and female. She wanted to have sex with him. She wanted him inside her. She wanted to surrender to the mysterious pull of sexual desire. And yet she admired him so for his restraint, his strong sense of what was right and wrong. He was such a good man.

That's when she'd said, "Kurt?"

He'd looked up at her and blinked. "Hmm?"

She'd cleared her throat. "How important is sex in a relationship, do you think?"

His eyes went wide. "Charlotte—"

"I'm not pushing. I'm just curious. Listen, if a relationship between a man and woman were like a whole pie—"

"What kind of pie are we talking about? Apple? Boston cream?"

She'd laughed. He could always make her laugh. "I'm serious."

He'd bent down and kissed her cheek. "I'm listening. We're talking about a married man and woman, is that right?"

She grinned. "Sure. A married couple. And the whole of their relationship is a Boston cream pie."

"Sounds good so far." He raised an eyebrow.

"Okay." Charlotte took a deep breath for courage. "Just how important is sex to them? How many pieces of the pie would have to be made up of good sex for them to be happy?"

Kurt frowned and folded the *Sporting News* in his lap. "Are you talking about our pies, Charlotte?"

Her heart beat fast. She licked her lips in nervousness. "Yes. My pie. Your pie. Let's say each has eight pieces. How many pieces of *your* pie would have to be dedicated to sex?"

"Okay." She'd watched Kurt's eyes travel over to the glass wall overlooking the taxiway. He turned to her. "Probably one slice."

Charlotte remembered that her mouth had opened and a sharp bolt of fear shot up her spine. Because, though she could never say it out loud, she'd just pictured five slices of sex. Okay, six—six big, sweet, creamy, melt-in-your-mouth pieces of sex.

But she'd smiled at Kurt and said, "That sounds about right." Then he'd boarded his flight to Cincinnati.

It had been the first time she'd ever lied to him.

Charlotte jumped from her bed and tucked the journal into her nightstand, locking the drawer, placing the key under the base of the reading lamp like she always did, thinking about what had happened three days later, when she went back to the airport to pick up Kurt. The day she met Joe.

Charlotte walked toward her bedroom windows. She could see the tiniest slice of pink on the horizon. Another day was coming. Another day when she'd be mommy and business owner and widow. Another day that she would feel the undertow of loneliness and need, so strong lately she feared it would eat her alive.

She dragged her fingertips along the cool pane of glass, remembering the miracle of letting go in Joe's arms, how perfect it felt to release all the wildness and curiosity hiding inside her. She'd allowed a stranger to see how much passion lived in her, how hot she really was, and she'd felt real for the first time in her life. Free. Alive.

Was it wrong to want that again?

She stared at the Connor house—*his* house now—glowing in the pale daylight and heard a little voice inside her head whisper, *Maybe just once more?*

# Chapter Five

The sun tried its best to cut through the blustery air, but Charlotte's fingers still felt stiff and cold as she hunched over, trying to unravel the tangled pieces of string.

"Here, let me block the wind," Bonnie said, hovering over her.

"Mommy, hurry!" Hank called. "It's almost the time I was born!"

"Hang on. I've got it. There!" Charlotte straightened and held out three purple balloons to Hank, making sure her daughter held them securely.

Charlotte then gave the three yellow ones to Matt, the blue one to Bonnie, and kept the red one for herself.

She imagined that they made an odd picture out there on the knoll in the middle of the Minton Recreation Park, colorful balloons flapping in the wind. But it was Hank's birthday, and this was where she wanted to launch her messages to Kurt, and the Tasker family custom was that you got whatever you wanted—within reason—on your birthday.

Hank raised her face to her mother and grinned, her blue eyes sparkling. "Tell me again exactly what he said when I was born, Mama."

Charlotte was prepared for this part of the ritual, but being prepared didn't make it any easier.

"You came out screaming bloody murder," she answered, just the way she knew Hank wanted to hear it.

"A brat from the start," Matt mumbled.

"And your daddy took you from the doctor, tucked you close, and told you shake it off and get back in the game."

Hank's face blossomed. "Then what happened next?"

"You got very, very quiet. Then you punched Daddy in the nose with your fist."

Everyone laughed but Matt.

"Can we just do this now, please?" he said, rolling his eyes while the laughter continued.

"What time is it, Mama?" Hank jumped up and down in anticipation.

"It's eight after eleven, the exact time you were born. You ready, girly?"

"Yep!" Hank turned her face to the sky, the wind slapping her bright orange hair out behind her. "I love you infinity much, Daddy!" she yelled, releasing the first balloon.

They all watched it sail up, up, until it drifted over the trees.

She turned to Charlotte and frowned. "But I don't remember which note is in which balloon!"

Charlotte smiled at her daughter, recalling how the kids had written three notes each addressed to "Daddy in Heaven," and brought them to the party store. The nice lady had inserted the folded-up paper into their balloons before filling them with helium.

"It doesn't really matter, honey. Daddy doesn't mind what order they're in."

Hank nodded seriously, then wiped her nose with the back of her hand. "I'm pretty sure that was the one where I told him I got in the majors this year."

"Stop the presses," Matt said.

"Dweeb," Hank responded.

"Okay, gang." Charlotte put her hand on Matt's shoulder and squeezed. "Let's let Hank have her turn. Go ahead, birthday girl."

Hank raised her right hand and opened her stubby fingers, and the second balloon was off. "That was the one where I told him I missed him infinity much," she said with a nod of certainty.

Hank released the third purple balloon. "And that one said not to forget my ballet recital at two o'clock on June seventh."

Hank turned matter-of-factly toward her brother and offered him a gap-toothed grin. "Your turn, Matt."

Charlotte had to choke back her sob. One of the hardest lessons she'd learned in the last eighteen months was that the kids had their own way of grieving and it wasn't necessarily her way. It seemed these concrete, simple things let them express their loss the way talking never could.

Neither of them had ever wanted to talk much about their dad's death. Charlotte recalled each long hour she'd ever spent in the worn blue wing chair of Reverend Williams's office in the First Baptist Church of Minton, talking about Kurt. About her fears and hopes and emptiness. It had helped.

But the day the reverend came to the house to chat with the kids, they both ran away, crying.

Matt stepped forward then, causing Charlotte's hand to fall from his shoulder. He let the first yellow balloon fly without comment, waited for it to climb, then released the other two in the same silence.

He shoved his hands in his pockets and stood still for a moment, finally turning his head toward his mother. He nodded and said, "Your turn, ladies."

Charlotte was struck by how grown-up he seemed in that moment.

Bonnie stepped up and let her blue balloon take wing. She smiled and said, "Look out for all of us, Kurt."

Then it was Charlotte's turn. Knowing she was under the watchful gaze of her friend and children, she took a steadying breath and raised her hand. A sudden gust of wind snatched the balloon from her grasp, sending it flying before she was ready.

That struck her as somehow appropriate.

"I miss you," was all she could think to say.

When Charlotte turned around, Matt and Hank were already laughing and running toward the playground equipment and their friends.

"Have you tried the Internet?"

Charlotte nearly spit out her coffee.

Bonnie laughed a little and continued, leaning back on the park bench. "You know, I've read that Internet dating is the hottest way to meet people these days, and frankly, it sounds like the best thing to happen to male–female relations since the Pill."

Charlotte felt her eyes widen. It seemed that since she'd decided to confide in Bonnie about her once-in-a-lifetime fling, all her friend wanted to do was talk about men and sex.

She'd obviously opened up a big can of worms.

"Think about it." Bonnie took a sip from her thermos cup as she watched the kids on the monkey bars. "The Internet lets you meet people anonymously and be totally upfront before appearance has any impact on anything! How freeing! It's got to be better than bars."

Charlotte raised an eyebrow. "I don't go to bars, Bon."

"My point exactly."

"I don't need a man right now," she lied.

Bonnie tilted her head and studied Charlotte carefully, and the scrutiny made her uncomfortable.

"What?"

"Maybe you feel that way now, but someday you're going to be ready for a man to come into your life again."

"Maybe."

"Mama! Can we go to the duck pond?"

Charlotte squinted in the sun, seeing a gaggle of kids running toward the old ice-skating pond on the other side of the park. Matt and Hank stayed behind, waiting for her okay. She smiled.

"Go for it!" she said.

"Is it the kids, honey? Is that what's holding you back from dating again?"

Charlotte bunched her lips together and wondered exactly how to answer her friend. Her children's welfare had been her primary concern, of course, and she just couldn't picture the awkward moment when she had to introduce Hank and Matt to a *boyfriend*. She didn't want to do anything that would confuse them or threaten their fragile sense of safety. And okay—she had a few issues herself.

"I'm just not ready" was all she could manage to say.

"All right."

"I'm doing fine on my own."

"If you say so."

As she watched Bonnie's eyes scan her face, full of affection and challenge, Charlotte felt the knot loosen in her chest. Bonnie Preston had lived a lot longer than she had. She'd stayed married to the same man for thirty-five years, raised two boys to adulthood, and was now a grandmother. She was a hard woman to fool.

"Okay, Bon. I do fine most of the time. But it's been kind of rough lately. There. I said it."

Bonnie's hand patted her knee. "Are you ever going to say anything to him?"

"Him who?"

Bonnie tilted back her head and laughed. "I'm referring to Mr. Male Stripper, honey. Juicy Joe Mills. The man you've not been able to stop thinking about for thirteen years." She grinned. "You know. Your new neighbor."

Charlotte blew out a breath and pulled her fleece jacket close to her chest. Springtime in southern Ohio could be as unpredictable as life itself—bright and balmy one day, biting and gray the next.

"Crazy weather," Charlotte said, attempting to change the subject.

Bonnie shook her head, smiling. "What's the worst that could happen?"

Now *that* made Charlotte laugh. There were just so many bad outcomes from which to choose, and she'd already imagined them all in detail.

"Well, let's see. . . ." She put down her coffee mug and began counting on the fingers of her left hand. "One, he doesn't remember me and I'm completely humiliated, standing there saying things like, 'Oh, come on now! Me? Naked? In the weeds? June 1991?' "

"I see what you mean."

"Or two, he *does* remember me and then tries to avoid me the whole time he lives here because he's always considered what happened between us a huge mistake."

Bonnie frowned. "Honey, I'm not sure any man on the planet would consider what happened between you two a mistake. I think hours of hot, anonymous sex is something men generally approve of."

Charlotte kept right on going. "Or three, and this is the worst, Bonnie, let me tell you. He knows exactly who I am and expects me to do a repeat performance. You know, meet him three times a week for a roll in the pine needles."

Bonnie waggled her eyebrows.

"You know I'm not like that."

"I know, honey."

"I'm not a slut."

"No one ever said you were, Charlotte."

"But maybe I could go over and talk to him."

"You could."

"I could get a feel for the situation." That didn't come out right and Charlotte scowled when Bonnie laughed. "Oh, forget it. What excuse would I possibly have to go over there?"

"Borrow a cup of sugar."

"We don't eat refined sugar."

"A cup of flaxseed, then?"

"I think it's best to just pretend he doesn't live there. So far, it's been a real easy thing to do because the man hasn't set foot outside the house in three days, except to go on his deck."

"Oh, really?"

"No mail delivery. No garbage set out for pickup. His lights are on late every night. And I don't know when the hell he goes grocery shopping, unless it's at three in the morning."

Bonnie stared.

"So it'll be easy to ignore him. As far as I know, the man doesn't exist. Maybe it's all still my imagination, that I'm still making up everything about Joe Mills and his incredible—"

Charlotte stopped herself, realizing that Bonnie was still laughing.

"Go on," Bonnie managed. "His incredible what?"

Charlotte felt her face go scarlet. "Anyway, I did try the Internet once, Bonnie."

"Really? So how did it go?"

Charlotte watched Hank and Matt sprint back from the

pond to the swing set, Hank edging out her brother with a
final push, then laughing loudly in triumph. The girl
never let her brother win, and Charlotte had never asked
her to. She hoped that was the right approach.

"Charlotte?"

*Oh, hell. She'd just avoided one pothole by stepping
into another.*

"I've never signed up for a dating service or anything,
but one night, I went into a chat room." She picked up her
coffee cup, happy for the warmth that spread to her
hands. "It was about six months after Kurt died. I was
feeling sorry for myself. It was a disaster."

Bonnie's eyebrows popped up in a question. "Do tell."

"First of all, they're all psychos or people just as desperate as I am. Pretty slim pickings."

"I see."

"I started chatting with a man who seemed perfectly
normal for the first fifteen minutes. Nice, even. But
then—" Bonnie seemed to be hanging on her every word,
and as embarrassed as she was, Charlotte supposed there
was no harm in sharing this with her best friend—she'd
shared everything else. "He said he wanted to . . . uh . . ."
This was harder than she expected.

"Ahhh. Cybersex." Bonnie nodded. "Did you do it?"

"What? Are you nuts?" Charlotte's voice was so loud
she saw the kids look her way. She waved and smiled at
them and they went back to playing. "He told me to go
gather a bunch of supplies and come back to the computer."

"Supplies?" Bonnie's laughter sailed on the wind.

"Office supplies, mostly." Charlotte dared to look at
her friend's amused face.

"Oh, dear," Bonnie said.

"Paper clips, rubber bands, clothespins, Scotch tape,
and an empty beer bottle."

"And this would be for—?"

"You think I stuck around to find out?" Charlotte took a sip of her coffee, which was rapidly losing its heat.

"And that was your big Internet experience?"

"That was it."

"Huh." Bonnie frowned, looking out at the rolling hills of the park. Then she sighed. "Look, Charlotte. Just go over there, knock on the man's door, and introduce yourself. Feign ignorance. Pretend you don't recognize him. See what happens."

Now that was an approach she hadn't considered. "You think I could pull that off? It sounds like something that would require advanced acting skills."

Bonnie thought for a moment, then put her arm around Charlotte's shoulder. "Well, I can always watch the kids if you want to hit the bars."

Joe knew that spending most of the day spying on Charlotte Tasker and her family was the last thing in the world he should be doing, but he couldn't stop himself. He was damn bored. He was dying of curiosity. Hell—he was just plain dying.

He'd spent the morning packing up his belongings, and everything was back in cardboard boxes except for a couple changes of clothes and the punching bags and computer, his main sources of amusement. He'd called Roger at home last night, only to be told to be patient again, that they were looking for somewhere else safe to move him. Patience, however, had never been Joe's strong suit. He was ready to leave. Now. Ready to get out of this town, this neighborhood. Ready to say good-bye to Charlotte Tasker before he broke down and said hello.

The woman was busy; that much he could say for her. Even on a Saturday, she seemed to be in perpetual motion. She was out pulling weeds by seven that morning, wearing what he noticed was a rather appealing pair of old jeans with holes in the knees. With just the right light, he could see a peek of adorable pink flesh under the shredded denim.

Then, about two hours later, her big oaf of a dog—who looked like some canine genetic experiment gone wrong— wandered out of the yard. Joe watched with a mixture of amusement and pity as she and her kids walked up and down the sidewalk yelling for the dog, eventually getting in the minivan and cruising the streets, calling out what sounded like, "Hoover!"

Bizarre name for a dog, if you asked him.

As luck would have it, Hoover suddenly appeared right on the sidewalk in front of Joe's own house, and he couldn't help but laugh watching how Charlotte lured the beast to the minivan.

She held a mostly melted vanilla ice-cream cone out the open door, continually cooing the phrase, "Creamy Whip, Hoover! Creamy Whip!"

The dog trotted merrily to the van, hopped inside, and devoured the cone before the kids could even get the side door shut.

The Taskers weren't home more than ten minutes before they all piled into the car again—this time with Charlotte's neighbor Bonnie Preston, the pleasant-looking older woman he'd seen with Charlotte that first day. According to the files Roger had sent him, Bonnie was a retired high school art teacher married to the town's former police chief, a guy named Ned Preston. The files said Preston was a former marine MP with two tours in Nam to his credit. Joe had yet to lay eyes on the fellow.

While the Taskers were out, Joe did about an hour and a half on the bags, made himself a roast beef on rye, watched something on Nickelodeon called *SpongeBob SquarePants*—which turned out to be damned funny, actually—then took a nap. He couldn't remember the last time he'd taken a nap. Maybe he'd never taken a nap. Maybe this marked the beginning of the end for him, a sign that it was only a matter of time before he could be found asleep in the Lay-Z-Boy like his dad, a thin line of spittle escaping out of the corner of his mouth, the evening newspaper ruffling in the wake of his snores.

Thank God the Taskers returned home about two, looking windblown and chilly. At least resuming his stakeout would get his mind off whether he was morphing into his father. Just because he might retire from case-work didn't mean his life was over. Hell, he wasn't even forty!

Joe brought his desk chair to the upstairs window and used his government-issue, top-of-the-line Bushnell binoculars to watch Charlotte and the kids pull more weeds. The boy did wheelbarrow duty, hauling loads to a pile behind the shed right on the property line, which gave Joe got his first close look at the kid. He was thin and serious, with intelligent gray eyes. He had straight brown hair cut close to his head, except for a little tuft that stood straight up over his forehead, like he'd just stuck his finger in a light socket. Seemed the kid never met a tube of hair gel he didn't like.

A little later, Joe moved to the downstairs living room window to watch Charlotte toss baseballs with the kids and marveled at the arm that little girl had—she could smoke 'em! Then Matt pitched to his sister, and she'd smacked the stitching off the ball, sending it flying out into the street.

The highlight of the day came late in the afternoon, when a man came to the Taskers' front door. He was a balding blond guy with a bit of a paunch and a loud, everyone-look-at-me voice. Charlotte didn't invite him in. She didn't hide the fact that she wasn't thrilled with his visit. She stayed stiff, her arms crossed in front of her, shaking her head. Joe watched the man continue to smile at her to no avail.

It was then that Joe had to fight the instinct to march over there and toss the guy into the street. He laughed at himself—exactly when had he signed up to be Charlotte Tasker's bodyguard?

He couldn't leave this town soon enough.

But he watched Charlotte send the guy packing without anyone's help. Good for her. She had good instincts. It was plain to see that doofus didn't deserve her.

But now it was nearly dark, and Joe knew it was time to put away the binoculars and head home. He'd done enough surveillance for one day. Besides, he'd managed to slip under the radar of the dog sleeping on a rug just inside the double doors and figured he shouldn't press his luck.

Joe made one last sweep. From his vantage point behind the Taskers' pine trees he had a good view into what was probably the family room, which opened into a big kitchen. Plaid furniture was arranged around a fireplace and entertainment center and the room looked lived in—kids' backpacks hanging on the doorknobs, art projects taped up on the cabinets, dog toys and sneakers on the rug.

Charlotte moved into range. Then the kids. Then the little family of three was sitting at the round oak kitchen table. They made a cozy picture, illuminated by the hanging lamp as they bowed their heads and said grace.

He watched them eat some kind of rice casserole and a fruit salad. He could see them laughing but caught only the barest hint of their voices from inside the house. He longed to hear every word, but that would require either a dinner invitation or a wiretap. Equally ridiculous ideas.

Joe lowered the binoculars and stretched. Oh, well. He

was as good as gone, and he'd be content with taking this mental picture with him: Charlotte in those battered jeans, her silky pale red hair pulled back in a ponytail, laughing as she ate dinner with her kids, perfectly capable and perfectly happy without him.

# Chapter Six

Charlotte had been in a love-hate relationship with Billy Banks for about four months now.

Sure, she loved the way he made her feel: sleek and empowered and primed to kick some serious ass if the need should ever arise. And for a woman alone, that was a handy skill to have.

But she hated the kickboxing tycoon for the way he made her abdominal muscles scream in agony, her thighs burn, and her lungs heave in her chest.

"Get ripped!" he yelled at her from the TV screen, his dark, chiseled body shining with sweat.

"Go rip yourself," Charlotte muttered, trying to follow the complicated routine of kicks and punches.

"Roundhouse, step, step, right jab, roundhouse!"

She was hitting her zone. Entering that place where the endorphins beat down the pain. Her body was humming. Her mind was focused. But then he had to go and change everything.

"Speedbag!"

Charlotte imitated her video classmates, adjusting her weight evenly, knees slightly bent. She began to spin her fists in tight circles in front of her face in an imaginary attack of a punching bag, and as the seconds ticked by, her arms ached, ached, until they turned to pillars of lead.

"Change direction!"

She could just barely hear the phone ringing over Billy's drill sergeant commands and the pounding of her own heart. She jogged to the kitchen cordless phone, keeping her fists flying high in front of her eyes until the last possible second.

She grabbed the phone with a sweaty hand. "Hell . . . oh!"

"Ah. Tae Bo time."

She could hear the amusement in Ned's voice and it made her smile. "Sure is. Hold a sec. Let me catch . . . my . . . breath."

"Listen, I hate to bother you so late—"

She glanced up at the kitchen clock to see it was 9:30.

"—but Hoover's out in the cul-de-sac again. I saw him in the Noonans' yard a few minutes ago and then all the way over at the Rickmans'."

"Oh, hell." Charlotte leaned forward at the waist and drew in air slowly and deeply, shaking her head. Obviously, the seven-hundred-dollar electric dog fence had been a colossal waste of money. The jolt didn't even seem to register with Hoover. And the Rickmans and their trigger-happy calls to the home owners' association were the reason she had to buy the fence in the first place.

"You know, I swore I turned the juice to maximum on that thing the other day," Ned said.

"You did, but it doesn't . . . seem to make . . . a difference."

"Well, honey, you're going to have to get him. I went out with some bologna, but he didn't fall for it."

"Okay, Ned. Thanks."

"And I'm not giving that dog one of my perfectly good Nutty Buddies. That'd be a sin."

Charlotte laughed, pulling a paper towel off the dispenser and dabbing at her dripping face. Everyone in Hayden Heights knew that Hoover could usually be bribed with an ice-cream cone.

"No problem, Ned. I'm on my way."

"Want me to come over and sit with the kids?"

"No, thanks." Charlotte used her left toe to open the trash can lid, tossed the soggy paper towel inside, and pulled on the freezer handle in one continuous movement. She tucked the phone under her chin and pulled out the half gallon of all natural French vanilla, reached into the drawer for the ice-cream scoop, and kicked open the swinging pantry door with her knee, scanning the shelves for the box of cake cones.

She flipped open the ice-cream lid while reaching for the cones.

"It'll just take me a second. The kids are in bed."

"Okay, Charlotte. You all doing okay over there?"

She smiled, feeling safe and well-cared for. She couldn't have asked for a better friend and neighbor.

"We're all doing great. And thanks again for letting me know about Hoov."

It took her exactly forty-seven paces at a quick jog to reach Hoover. He was peeing on the meticulously planted circle of purple and yellow pansies around the Rickmans' carriage light.

"Hoov, come here, boy!"

The dog glanced nonchalantly in her direction and continued to water the Rickmans' flowers. Then, without warning, he took off at a run right past her, ears flying back in streetlight.

"Hey! I've got a Creamy Whip! Get back here!"

Yes, the spring night was chilly but obviously not as cold as the freezer, because Charlotte looked down to see the ice cream melting all over her hand.

She had no choice but to run after him.

Holding the cone like the Olympic Torch, Charlotte took long strides down the sidewalk. At least she was dressed properly for a nighttime run, in her black bike shorts and coordinating black and purple jog bra. At least she'd complete her workout.

"Hoover!" she called out in a voice loud enough for the stupid dog to hear but soft enough not to startle the neighbors.

"He's down at the Connors' place!"

"Oh!" She came to a halt, barely making out the figure of Mrs. Watson at the end of her driveway, putting out her matching set of Rubbermaid garbage cans. "Thanks!"

Charlotte continued on, growing more and more annoyed at the stupid dog, wondering if the kids were okay, hating to be out of the house for even a few minutes.

"Hoover, you dumb thing!" she whispered, now walking in front of the Connors'. She stopped and looked up. The stone and wood house rose up from the slope of lawn, its tall, slanted windows glowing with light from inside.

My God—*he* was in there.

At that instant, she realized that she hadn't thought of Joe Mills for at least twenty minutes—which may have been a record for the last couple days. But she sure was thinking of him now—wondering what he wore as he walked around inside that house. Wondering which bedroom he slept in. Wondering on what section of kitchen countertop he'd decided to put his coffeepot.

She saw a shadow pass in front of a window—and gasped.

The ice cream was running down to her elbow now.

She wondered if that man had even the slightest, tiniest, most minuscule memory of that day on the GW Parkway.

Her knees felt wobbly.

"Hoover! Please, please, please!" She tried to be as quiet as possible. "Come get your damned Creamy Whip!"

She saw a movement in the boxwoods along the front of the house and sighed with relief. She crept up the grass, holding the now lopsided ice-cream cone out in front of her body.

"Hoov?"

More rustling. She saw the streetlights reflected in a pair of beady dog eyes peering out from the shrubs. Then she felt the first sprinkles and cursed the fact that it had started raining, only to realize that the Connors' much-envied automatic sprinkler system had just come on.

"Oh, great." She was about to call Hoover every nasty curse word she knew when she was suddenly off the ground. Her brain seized in panic and confusion as she saw the grass turn to a blur beneath her useless feet, the ice-cream cone falling from her grip. She was being carried. Someone was running with her. . . .

She hit the ground with a thud and that's when she remembered to scream.

"Oh, hell," the voice said, just as she was being flipped onto her back. A big hand came down over her mouth. She looked up to see—this couldn't be right—a *gun*? Pointing in her face? But it was gone so fast she thought she'd imagined it. And then all she saw was . . . *it was him*!

Her scream made no sound, even as her throat burned with the force of it.

"Please stay calm," he said, and she looked up into those black eyes and experienced a sharp plunge into the surreal. His body was fully on top of hers. His hard weight pushed her into the unyielding ground. The water misted over them in a steady spray. He wasn't wearing a shirt—and she could feel how hot his skin was against her bare midriff. She could feel the wiry hair all over his upper body.

Charlotte blinked against the water—against the memories rushing into her—and screamed even harder.

"I apologize for this," he said.

*Apologize?*

She screamed again, this time trying in vain to open her mouth enough to bite his hand.

"I saw somebody in the yard."

She attempted to squirm her way out from under him, but her arms and legs were tightly pinned to the grass. She could hardly breathe. He was squishing her.

In a burst of optimism, she looked around his big body toward the front yard, hoping Hoover would find it in himself to take a chunk out of this idiot's ass and save her. Instead, she witnessed Hoover lick his chops for the remaining ice cream, then trot merrily away down the sidewalk.

"HMMMPPPPHHH!" she screamed. "GMMMMM-PHHHHMMMMM!"

"I am going to let you up now," the voice said. The voice was deep and rich and made something in her brain snap. Because it was *his* voice. She remembered that voice with every fiber in her being.

"I am going to let you up now, Charlotte."

*He knew her name! He'd just said her name!*

"Please calm down and listen to me."

Where was the scent of honeysuckle coming from? She was lightheaded with it. It permeated the air. It was on her skin and inside her nose and throwing a heavy blanket of confusion over her mind. The feel of his wet, rock-hard body against hers was intoxicating. She felt drunk with the realization that finally—after thirteen endless years of wishing and praying and hoping and imagining—this man's body was once again touching hers.

"HMMMMPPPHHH!" she screamed, arching up beneath him, closing her eyes as she used every Billy Banks–honed muscle she possessed to resist him.

It was the worst possible thing she could have done.

Because now she knew he was aroused.

She was being assaulted by a madman with a hard-on and a gun, which was probably not a good combination.

Charlotte's eyes flew open. Nerve endings began to short-circuit from her scalp to her toes.

Then he smiled down at her sheepishly.

"Hello, Charlotte," he whispered, brushing a clump of wet hair from her cheek. "It's really great to see you again."

She was slippery, firm, and thoroughly female crushed beneath him, but never in thirteen years of fantasies had he imagined it quite like this.

And the worst part of it was that Charlotte would not stop screaming.

"I will not hurt you. I am your neighbor. My name is Joe Mills and I promise I will not hurt you. I'm going to release you. This has all been a big mistake. Just please stop screaming."

He raised himself on one hand, his other still cupped over her mouth, his body still in contact with hers from the waist down.

Her eyes were wide with terror and it broke his heart.

"Charlotte?"

She nodded.

"If you scream, the neighbors will think I'm hurting you. I don't want any trouble. I just . . ."

Her brow creased in a frown.

"I'm a little paranoid about burglars. I'm very sorry about the gun—my mistake. Please don't be frightened. I'm going to let you up if you promise me you won't scream again."

Her eyebrows arched high on her forehead and she nodded enthusiastically.

He took his hand off her mouth and rose above her, pulling her to her feet. She screamed.

In an instant he'd flipped her around, one arm tight around her waist and the other hand slapped once again over her mouth.

She was kicking him in the shins with her running shoes.

She was a wildcat.

But he already knew that, didn't he?

He couldn't help but laugh, and that apparently pissed her off even more, because the kicks grew more ferocious.

*God.*

The truth was that if he'd been the subject of some strange test, blindfolded, led into a room filled with twenty women, and told to touch each one and then identify Charlotte—a woman he hadn't laid a finger on in thirteen years, a woman he'd known for less than two hours—he could have done it. No problem.

He knew her. His hands remembered her. His skin remembered her skin. His bone and muscle remembered hers. And the smell of honeysuckle was everywhere, so intense he couldn't think straight, couldn't separate fantasy from reality.

He picked her up at the waist and began to walk across the lawn toward the pine trees. It was a long and painful trip, and he knew his legs were going to be black-and-blue from knee to ankle.

"You know, dumplin', it would be easier for both of us if you just stopped yelling."

She somehow maneuvered a pointy elbow into his gut, and it hurt like hell. Her feet were still thrashing.

"Really, Charlotte. I don't want any trouble."

But he was well aware it was too late to avoid it, because

trouble was right there in his arms, wet and hot and slippery and curvy and pressed against him in all the right places. And though he'd promised himself he'd get out of Minton without seeing her, touching her, smelling her, he'd just failed big-time.

Eventually, they made it through the pine trees and to her driveway, yet she kept squirming and writhing against the front of his boxers. It was more than he could stand. It wasn't fair. And he just couldn't help himself.

Joe lowered his mouth to the nape of her neck, planting one soft, openmouthed kiss on her slick skin. The contact of her hot flesh on his lips was shocking. He pulled away and gasped.

The thrashing stopped. She went rigid in his arms.

He loosened his grip, allowing her to slide down the front of his body and place her feet on the asphalt. He felt every wet inch of her on the way.

The arm that had been around her waist had slipped up to her chest, and—thank you, Lord—he'd somehow been allowed to spread one hand over a wet, spandex-covered breast while the other hand remained over her mouth.

She was silent and unmoving. The darkness gathered around them, and Joe took a second to scan the street. No one was out. Her dog was nowhere to be seen. It was just the two of them in her driveway, under the basketball hoop, in the faint light coming from her upstairs windows.

He felt her shiver in his arms.

"You're wet and cold and you need to go inside."

She nodded, and the slight movement sent a burst of scent into his nostrils. She smelled exactly like she had thirteen years ago. She felt the same. He'd finally found her.

And he'd likely never speak to her again, because he was leaving. And the sooner the better—for everyone.

The nipple under his palm was hard as a .40 caliber

bullet, and he couldn't resist finding out what the other one was up to, so he dragged his hand across her little sports bra to find out. He felt her heart pound and her breath catch. Damn—her other nipple was just as tight and hard.

Her hand suddenly covered his own. It was soft and warm and pressed his palm with urgency against her breast, and it was the most amazing thing he'd ever experienced, and the last thing in the world he wanted.

With that single touch she'd told him everything. Yes, she remembered him. Yes, she wanted him, too.

"Oh, damn, Charlotte."

She whimpered in agreement, as if she somehow understood everything she couldn't know, why this was such an impossibly bad idea. Then Joe felt a hot droplet fall onto his fingers. Tears. Then he felt the subtle pressure of her butt. She was pushing back against him, fitting her hips against the front of his body, where she still fit perfectly.

He let his hand fall from her mouth and he spun her around to face him.

Those eyes looked back at him full of shock, confusion, and need. And he decided he'd go ahead and do it—just once—the one thing he'd longed to do since 19-fucking-91. . . .

He kissed her. And the instant their lips touched, the kiss rocketed out of control. Everything went fierce and hot and deep and Charlotte was all over him and every single detail Joe thought he'd imagined was right there under his mouth as real as real could be—this perfect mix of sweet and sexual, this wild little redhead, this woman of his dreams.

He had to end the kiss. It was a mistake. Too much, too fast, too intense. But as Joe pulled away, her lips sought his. Her nails dug into his forearms as he tried to separate.

"Charlotte. No. Wait."

She looked as dazed as he felt. But he had to tell her this one thing while he had the chance. He was leaving, maybe as soon as tomorrow, but she needed to know he'd never forgotten her.

He grabbed her by her slippery, shapely shoulders and watched her struggle to focus on his face.

"I've thought about you every day for thirteen years," he said.

Her eyes flashed. She took a deep breath. Then she smiled at him with that pretty mouth and his knees wobbled.

"Can I tell you what I've thought about for thirteen years, Joe?"

*Oh, man. . . .* He nodded, because he couldn't speak.

"I've thought about this—"

Her hot little hand landed on the front of his boxers. She cupped him through the soaking wet cotton, then stroked, moving her palm up the underside of his now record-book bulge.

Joe froze. His head buzzed from the staggering amount of pleasure in that touch. A storm blew through his heart. Never in his life had he been this surprised, or this torn. This couldn't happen. This was sheer stupidity.

This felt so damn right.

He managed to grasp her wrist, pull her hand away, and smile politely.

"I can't," he said.

"Oh God," she said.

Then Charlotte let out a moan of anguish and twisted away, running toward her house, leaving him in the driveway in wet boxers, aroused, perplexed, and sorely tempted to chase after her.

Some things never changed.

# Chapter Seven

"Have you talked to him yet? He's been next door for a whole week!"

Charlotte shuddered, taking a quick peek at Bonnie before she tried to answer LoriSue's question. Not even Bonnie knew what an idiot she'd made of herself with the man in question. No one knew but Joe himself.

"We haven't spoken. Not really," Charlotte managed.

LoriSue took a sip of her coffee and raised her eyes to the house beyond the pine trees. "My God. If he were my neighbor, I'd have already brought him a little welcome-to-the-neighborhood gift . . . if you get my drift."

"We get your drift," Bonnie said.

"Well, I can tell the man just *puts it down* in bed."

Charlotte's heart skipped at least two full beats.

"I only meant—" LoriSue laughed and waved her hand in the air, as if to shoo away the bluntness of her words. "Look. I've always had this theory that some men are put on this earth simply to make women happy. I know one when I see one. Joe Mills is one of them."

Charlotte stared at her brown leather sandals, feeling sweat dribble down her spine. How could she have been so stupid? How could she have thrown herself at him like that? She *groped* the man! Just reached right out and assaulted his person! He could file charges against her for a stunt like that! Oh God, if she ever saw Joe Mills again in her life, she'd probably die of shame.

"And Big Jimmy isn't one of the anointed?"

LoriSue laughed at Bonnie's inquiry. "Oh, I used to think Jimmy was a real babe." She tapped her long red acrylic nails on the side of her coffee cup. "Unfortunately, he's always thought so, too, and didn't want to deprive any woman in the greater Minton area of his charms."

"So what's the status of the divorce?" Bonnie was apparently on a roll with the nosy questions today, and LoriSue launched into a twenty-minute update on the couple's dueling attorneys, postponed court dates, and the apartment Jimmy had set up for himself in the basement.

"He's got a little fridge and his remote and his recliner, and being the bottom-dweller that he is, I think he could live there for the rest of his life. Not that I'll let him."

"But what do you say to each other in passing?" Bonnie shook her head. "I mean, isn't it weird to see him standing there in the kitchen, pouring his morning coffee?"

"No weirder than the past sixteen years of marriage."

Charlotte was startled by LoriSue's next comment.

"I just don't understand how you've done it, Bonnie."

Bonnie laughed. "Done what?"

"Stayed happily married." LoriSue sighed, letting her gaze travel across the yard to where the kids were playing. "I honestly don't know how anybody does it."

The women sat at the outdoor table without speaking for a moment, the cacophony of Matthew's, Hank's, and Justin's voices filling in the silence.

Bonnie leaned back in her chair and cleared her throat. Charlotte could see the gears turning in her friend's head.

"It's never been very complicated for us, LoriSue."
Bonnie's voice was soft. "We just made the decision to
love each other, no matter what. Raising the boys. Moves.
Hard times. We just kept loving each other."

Charlotte looked over to see LoriSue's chin quivering
and reached out to touch her hand.

"Well, there you go," LoriSue said brightly, offering
them a big smile. "That's the difference between the
Bettmyers and the Prestons, right there!" LoriSue slid her
hand out from under Charlotte's. "Jimmy and I decided to
give up on each other a long, long time ago. It didn't
seem worth the effort anymore."

"Any more bananas left, Mrs. Tasker?"

Justin appeared behind his mother, and Charlotte was
struck by the similarities in their features—all except the
eyes. Behind the eye shadow and mascara, LoriSue's
were tired and wary. Justin's were wide and bright. Were
LoriSue's ever like her son's?

"In the fruit bowl, sweetie. Help yourself."

"Thanks."

As Justin walked toward the house, LoriSue reached
down at her feet for a large red-leather organizer bag. Before Charlotte realized what was happening, she'd pulled
out her checkbook and begun scribbling.

"Take this." She held out a check, and Charlotte stared
at a sum of "*five hundred dollars*" written out in elaborate
script. Her mouth fell open.

"What in the world is this for?"

LoriSue laughed bitterly. "I probably owe you thou-
sands for food and child care over the last couple years."

"You don't owe me anything."

"Oh, yes, I do."

LoriSue abruptly stood up. She fluffed her hair and
smoothed out the skirt of her fire-engine red spring suit.
"I know I haven't been the world's best mother in the last

couple years. I've let my problems with Jimmy and the business kind of distract me. If it weren't for you, Charlotte . . ." LoriSue let her words trail off, then shook her head.

Charlotte and Bonnie said nothing.

Justin came out with a banana in his hand, already munching away.

"Honey, come here a second." LoriSue crooked a red-nailed finger in the air.

Justin walked up to his mother. "Yeah?"

"Do you remember to say thank you to Mrs. Tasker for the things she does for you?"

Justin's eyes nearly popped out of his head and he stopped chewing. "Am I in trouble for something?"

Everyone shouted "No!" at the same instant.

His shoulders relaxed and he swallowed his mouthful of banana. "Whoa. Good."

The women laughed, and Charlotte watched with amazement as LoriSue put a hand on her son's blond head. She couldn't remember the last time she'd seen the woman touch her own child.

Then LoriSue kissed Justin's forehead. "We're lucky to have the Taskers as our friends."

Justin nodded.

"Scouts tonight?" LoriSue asked.

Justin looked at Charlotte, then at Bonnie and back to his mother, blinking. "Uh. Yep."

"Your uniform should be clean. Want to have dinner with me before you head out?"

"You gonna cook?" Justin sounded a bit scared.

LoriSue laughed loudly and gave him a quick hug. "Heck no. I thought we'd go to Chico's for Mexican."

A huge smile spread over his face. "That's my favorite, Mom!"

"I know."

"Cool."

When Justin ran back into the yard, Charlotte stood up. "I can't take this, of course." She held the check out to LoriSue.

"Why not?"

"Because I don't do things for Justin for money. He's a great kid. I like him. He's always welcome here."

For a second, Charlotte was sure LoriSue was going to cry—her nose wrinkled up and her eyes watered. But instead she sniffed, raised her chin, and hoisted her bag to her shoulder.

"I just wanted to say thank you."

"I appreciate the thought, but that's not the way to do it." Charlotte placed the check in LoriSue's hand, then watched her rip it in half with a flourish and stuff the scraps in the front pocket of her bag.

"All right. Then how about I take everyone to Chico's tonight? The kids, you, and Bonnie—even Ned if he's around."

Bonnie and Charlotte grinned at each other.

"You've got yourself a date," Bonnie said.

"What's going on with Charlotte?"

Bonnie raised her head from Ned's chest and smiled at his question. He may have been retired from police work, but he'd forever have a cop's instincts. She'd seen how closely he'd studied Charlotte at dinner, sitting across from her at the big table at Chico's.

"She's just tired. She's got a few new clients."

"The woman needs a good New York Strip and a side of onion rings."

Bonnie giggled and kissed the curly graying hairs of her husband's chest.

"Did you see what she ate tonight? I'm telling you, human beings are not designed to live on brown rice and fish flakes. Those kids are going to get rickets—just you watch."

Bonnie shook her head. "And maybe they won't have to take pills to lower their cholesterol, either."

"Ouch! That hurt."

She felt Ned's chest rise and fall with gentle laughter as he put his strong arms around her and pulled her tight. "You gotta admit this old geezer's still got it, though."

"You've still got it," she said dutifully.

"And you still want it."

"I still want it."

"You want it again?"

Bonnie laughed and kissed the crinkled skin of his neck. She'd been kissing that same neck for a long, long time.

"You offering?"

"Damn right I am. All I need is a good night's sleep and two cups of coffee and I'll be raring to go again—just like magic."

They both laughed and Bonnie threw her leg over Ned's.

"Actually, there is something going on with Charlotte, honey. It's the new neighbor. She's a little threatened by him, I think."

Ned sat up without warning, causing Bonnie to nearly tumble from the bed. He pulled her up next to him.

"The guy in the black Mustang?"

"Huh? I don't know anything about a Mustang."

"Yeah, well . . . the kids gave me the whole scoop on him."

"The kids?" Then it dawned on her. "Have Matt and Justin been spying on him?"

Ned laughed. "I never reveal the identity of a confidential informant. You know that, dear."

She grinned. "A black Mustang, huh? Wow. That would make a pretty picture."

"Don't think he's gonna be sticking around long, either. The boys say he's already packing up to leave."

"But he just got here."

"Maybe Minton doesn't suit him."

*Or maybe he figured out who Charlotte is.*

"That's too bad."

Ned laughed at that. "Oh, yeah? Did you have plans for him?"

"Not me. No way." Bonnie kissed his bald head. "I've got all the man I can handle right here."

Charlotte didn't even bother with the Triscuits that night. She pushed open the swinging pantry door with her knee, reached for the squirt cheese, and aimed the spout directly into her open mouth.

She leaned up against the kitchen counter and gloried in the way the salty, creamy, sharp pleasure melted on her tongue. She swallowed with a moan of contentment.

It occurred to her that if any of her clients saw her, they'd fire her. The registered nurse who advocated a diet based on legumes, complex carbohydrates, and eight servings of fruits and vegetables a day was bingeing on a snack food made in a laboratory of artificial ingredients she could barely pronounce.

What a hypocrite.

She needed sex.

She needed Joe.

She wanted Joe.

She'd already blown it with Joe.

But maybe she wasn't to blame. Maybe just the touch of him again—his hands and mouth on her—was too much for her to handle. Could it be she'd had a psychotic break, right there in the driveway?

Charlotte liked that theory and celebrated with one last squirt of cheese. Now she was thoroughly disgusted with

herself. She put the can of cheese on the pantry shelf and
shuffled to the family room couch, where she flopped
down and covered her eyes with her crossed arms.

Maybe she wasn't attractive anymore. Maybe men like
Joe weren't interested in nearly middle-aged mommies
with laugh lines and stretch marks. The injustice of that
made her sigh—how come Joe had only become more of
a hottie in the last thirteen years, while she'd turned into a
sex-crazed, wrinkled hag?

Nature sucked.

But maybe it was just that she was sweaty that night
and she didn't smell quite as sweet as he remembered and
her hair was plastered to her head from the sprinkler.
Maybe she'd be more appealing to him if she dabbed herself with her best perfume, wore her shortest skirt—the
black one that hit midthigh—and stockings. Maybe if she
went over and asked to borrow a cup of . . .

*Shit.*

What was the point? She'd messed up. She couldn't
appear on his doorstep in a skirt now. It would be too obvious, not to mention downright pitiable.

Charlotte closed her eyes and tried to relax. But she
was slammed by her own memory instead, treated to a
play-by-play of what had happened thirteen years ago,
what had gotten her into this mess in the first place.

"*. . . some men are put on this earth simply to make
women happy. . . .*"

The images rushed into her head in high-definition
clarity, in bright color, and in painfully exact detail.

Her legs had been shaking as she took the exit off the
parkway that day. She watched in the rearview mirror as
the man drove right up on the bumper of the Miata, his
smile getting bigger and brighter.

She felt like a fish on a hook, aware that she was a fish
who was asking for it, opening her little fish mouth and

pulling out her own little fish cheek so the hook could find purchase in her flesh.

Charlotte had known she was taking a huge risk, but right at that moment, it didn't matter.

It was a small parking lot with about twenty spaces marked by diagonal white lines. A wooden National Park Service shelter displayed a map under Plexiglas. She saw two other cars but no other people—they must have been out walking. And the man had pulled right up next to her. When she got the courage to look over at him, he'd taken off his sunglasses.

She felt the hook pierce her, but it didn't just sink into the flesh of her cheek—she was also hooked deep down in her gut, and it was a fatal wound.

His eyes were dark, shining, and full of the promise of pleasure. She wasn't completely ignorant. No, she'd never actually *done* it, but she knew seduction when she saw it, and the way he smiled at her with that chiseled mouth was primal and dangerous and full of entitlement.

She couldn't swallow. She couldn't move.

He opened the door of the black Jeep, and she watched his long legs swing out before he hopped down with the grace of an athlete. He was the most amazingly male creature she'd ever seen. He hooked his sunglasses into the belt loop of his worn jeans, and her eyes followed his movement, giving her an excuse to look at his long, lean lower half.

She couldn't breathe. She made some sort of squeak and she heard him laugh in appreciation. Then he was standing at the side of her car.

"Hello there." His voice was deep and dangerous. His voice was the sound of sin. And then she watched as the devil himself put his hand on her door latch.

"I think I've got something you want."

Oh God, she couldn't look into his eyes. If she looked

at him, it would be all over for her. She'd plummet into the abyss.

But all she could think was: *One slice . . . one slice . . . for the rest of my life . . . one puny, stingy, dried-up slice of sex . . .*

"Do you want it, baby?"

She felt the hook pulling her, turning her head, and the car door was opening, and she placed her hand in his and he pulled her to her feet and she tried, she tried so hard not to raise her eyes to his, but suddenly he shut the door behind her and backed her up against it.

"Everything you need is right here in my front pocket."

His body was hot and hard and she kept her gaze downcast in order to avoid those dark eyes. Unfortunately, she'd somehow picked the junction of his pelvis and her stomach on which to fix her stare.

She knew there was no way she was going to get out of this in one piece.

"All you have to do is reach in and pull it out."

She wished he'd stop talking. His words were too hot and too sexual and she was getting a little dizzy.

He probably did this to women all the time.

He was obviously the kind of man who chewed up females and spit them out. The kind of man she'd always avoided. The exact opposite of Kurt Tasker, who was going to be her husband.

*One measly slice . . .*

She raised her chin, looked way up, and swore she heard a loud *click* as her eyes connected with his.

"It's yours if you want it."

He was probably a few years older than her, but not many. His skin was a smooth, rich olive. She wondered if he had Hispanic ancestry. He might be in the military—his hair was buzzed that short, and he held himself like he meant business. She watched his smooth lips spread into a wide smile, revealing a set of straight white teeth.

Or maybe he was a male model.

Then he pushed a little harder against her, and it was suddenly clear that this was not a game and this was not a fantasy and that she may have just done something that would turn her into a newspaper headline.

"I know kung fu," she lied.

"Lucky him," he replied.

"Don't hurt me."

The man laughed at that, bringing his hands to the sides of her face. He gently caressed her cheek with one set of hot, rough fingers. "I'm one of the good guys." Then he softly touched her hair. "Besides. You're just about the sweetest little piece I've ever laid eyes on."

That did it. She was horribly offended. And really, really turned on. Her brain was boiling and her body was catching fire, because Kurt had never said anything that impolite to her. He told her she was beautiful and he called her sweetie and told her he loved and respected her, but nothing like this.

"Ask me for it, dumplin'."

The words were forming in her mind. Her mouth was opening. Her lungs were providing the air. . . .

"Give it to me," she said.

One of his eyebrows shot up. "You talking about your little notebook, or something else?"

She liked this teasing. Kurt didn't tease her. Apparently, teasing excited her. A lot.

She pressed her hips against him.

"Something else," she whispered. His hands had taken a slow, hot slide down her neck, along the slope of her bare shoulders, down her arms, and he'd just laced his fingers into hers. His hands were huge.

"Tell me more."

Oh God. This was it. It was finally going to happen to her. She was finally going to know.

"I want to have sexual relations with you."

The man laughed, and her heart sank. That had probably sounded like something a virgin about to get her nursing degree would say. Because that's exactly what she was. She turned her face away in embarrassment.

"You are a wild little thing, aren't you?"

That made her turn back around, and she was in such shock from those words that all she could do was nod her head in silence.

The man scanned the parking lot, released one of her hands, and pulled her toward the trees near the overlook. She followed, stepping over brambles in her sandals, trying not to think too much, trying to be brave, feeling the thud of her heart in her throat.

He stopped under a big tree already in full leaf. He turned to her and tugged on her hands as he lowered himself to the ground. He sat, leaning his back against the tree trunk, and smiled up at her.

She was confused. What did he want her to do?

"Straddle me."

She sat on him, her legs spread over his, and she looked down at her bare thighs against his jeans and for the first time worried about what she was wearing. A peach-colored tank top and a pair of camp shorts—certainly nothing revealing. She wondered if they'd take their clothes off or stay mostly dressed.

"I want to see every inch of that beautiful little body of yours," the man said, running the fingers of one hand down her tummy, then hooking them inside the waistband of her shorts.

She nearly swooned.

Kurt had put his fingers in her several times. It had never been enough. Nowhere near enough.

"What's your name, baby?"

That question sliced through the brain fog and caused her to gasp. Panic cut through her. She tried to get up, but he put his hands on her hips and held her in place.

"Look, it's okay if you don't—"

"I don't have a name and neither do you, all right?" she snapped.

He smiled at that and stroked her hair. The mix of pleasure and uncertainty was unbearable.

"Fair enough."

Then he reached around and cupped her head in his hand and pulled her to him. His mouth was on hers before she could prepare herself, and the sensation was nothing less than apocalyptic.

Kurt didn't kiss her like this. The man's mouth was soft but persistent, and his lips opened over hers, and he sucked at her lips and tongue, and she found herself doing the same to him, and he just kept asking for more, and she gave it to him.

He bit her gently. She felt his fingers undoing the clasp of her bra under her shirt, then moving to the zipper of her shorts. He was so smooth. Clearly, he'd had lots of practice. In a way, she was glad—glad because if she was going to have one shot at wild sex, it was good that it was with a man who might actually know what he was doing.

Then it occurred to her that she was by the side of a road, where anyone could come across them. She pulled her lips from his and looked around nervously. "What if someone sees us?"

He nodded and surveyed the area. "I'm not usually one for public displays of affection myself, but I think we're pretty well hidden."

Then he put the flat of his palms on her belly and slid them up under her loose bra. She gasped—his hands felt so hot! Then it occurred to her that she didn't have a condom—of course she didn't have a condom! She'd never had a condom in her life! She froze beneath his touch.

His hands stilled. "Are you okay?"

"No. No, I'm not!" She knew she sounded borderline hysterical but couldn't help herself. "I don't have a condom! I can't do this without one!"

"Ahh." He smiled at her, then dragged his hands from her breasts down her back, insinuating them into the back of her shorts, cupping her bottom. "I have some," he whispered.

Charlotte felt herself relax into his grip, get lost in the pull of the man's smile. Then he rose and whispered in her ear, "But you're so small. I don't want to hurt you."

She trembled. He kissed her again. She allowed herself to touch him—his hard shoulders and upper arms, his neck, his chest—and the physical sensations began to blur until they were going at each other like they intended to consume each other, a rush of mouths and hands and breathing until he ripped off her clothes and she ripped off his and they made a little bed in the weeds and she was dying of impatience as he tore open the condom wrapper with his teeth.

Not a moment too soon, he was once again leaning against the tree and she was once again straddling him, but this time she was rolling a condom down his unbelievably beautiful penis and she was suddenly grateful for the required public health education courses she'd had to suffer through.

He pulled her up by the waist and positioned her over him. She tried not to shake. She tried not to have any regrets. And before she knew it, he was pushing inside her, and she tried her best to hide the shock she felt and breathed through the burning pain, inch by inch, until it transformed into molten pleasure.

And as she rocked on him and ground against him, she watched his greedy mouth move all over her pale breasts. She felt him kiss and suck her neck and face and lips. And she smiled up at the sky through the leaves, through her tears, breathed in the honeysuckle that seemed to be everywhere, and knew she'd made the right decision.

It was everything she'd hoped for. This man and his mouth and hands and cock were just what she craved.

She looked down into the bottomless dark eyes of this stranger and he smiled at her with joy. Then he urged her on, using words that appeared in no nursing text she'd ever read.

"God, your little pussy is so damn tight," he moaned. "Come all over me. Let go, you sexy thing. I want to feel you bust it."

That's when she had her first orgasm in the presence of another human being. And boy, was it ever better than going solo.

She had many more before it was done. He had three. And they stopped only when they ran out of condoms and she was late to meet the plane.

They left their nest in the weeds and she stood by the Miata again, the man pressed up against her, just where they'd started. Strangely enough, she didn't feel awkward. They both knew what this had been about. She would never be sitting by a telephone that didn't ring. They would never pass each other in a hallway and have to look away.

"Good-bye," she said.

She saw him frown, start to say something, then just offer her another of his perfect smiles. As an afterthought, he reached in his front jeans pocket and pulled out the little notebook.

She laughed as she took it from him. Then she threw her arms around his neck and practically jumped him, kissing him so hard she thought she heard something crack. Then she hopped back into the car and pulled out of the parking space so fast she burned rubber, never looking back, tasting the blood on her lip.

That little trip down memory lane had exhausted her. Charlotte dragged herself off the couch and out of the past and headed up to bed, where she'd likely dream it all over again.

# Chapter Eight

"I really don't want to hear this, Roger."

Joe's supervisor sighed into the phone. "Two weeks. The Cincinnati office is expecting your help. I'm expecting you to stay alive. So you'll give us two weeks."

"I'm getting a hotel, then. On the other side of town."

"The hell you are!"

Joe had known his boss long enough to suspect he was at the end of his patience. Roger's next comments confirmed it.

"Listen. You will remain right there, where we know you're safe, for two fucking weeks, that's fourteen fucking days, and you can do damn near anything for fourteen days, so just suck it up and do it, Bellacera."

Roger hung up, and Joe stared at the phone in his hand.

How was he supposed to live next door to Honeysuckle Mama for two weeks? Especially after what happened the other night? After he'd made the brilliant decision to hold a gun to her head and then kiss her? And how could he stay here after she'd practically begged him to take her right there in the driveway?

He was strong, but not strong enough for this.

Joe put the phone in the cradle and scanned the bedroom

that served as his office, and the boxes stacked against the wall. Two weeks. How could he occupy himself for two weeks? Yes, he was committed to brainstorming with Cincinnati Field Office Supervisor Rich Baum and his agents about a sudden influx of Mexican-made crystal meth into the suburbs. He'd talk on the phone with the assistant U.S. attorney handling the Guzman case. He'd get in two good boxing workouts a day. He'd take naps. He'd keep an eye on Charlotte.

He'd like to keep a few other body parts on her, too—like his lips and his hands. It took every ounce of restraint he had the other night not to give that woman everything she wanted and then some. He couldn't stop thinking about the intensity of that kiss. The instant his lips made contact with hers, he'd been flung back in time. In his mind, he was right back under that tree, under her spell, underneath her sweet body.

Joe sat down at his desk and stared at the computer.

He would never forget the drive that afternoon back to Quantico, where he got his ass chewed for being late for class. He smelled her on his hands the rest of the day. He wondered if she smelled him. He wondered who was on that Northwest flight she was meeting at National Airport but now suspected it was Kurt Tasker.

Had she ever told her husband what happened that day? He doubted it. The file said they'd gotten married about six months later, and he guessed Charlotte kept her mouth shut and her eye on the altar.

So what did that make *him*? A last-minute fling? Just one more wild boink for the road?

But she'd been so tight. And he remembered how shocked he'd been to look down and see his fingers stippled with bright red blood. He should probably march right over there now, pound on her door, and demand to know if he'd taken her virginity that day.

He had every right—

*Crash!*

The unmistakable sound of shattering glass was followed by a soft thud. The silent alarm system triggered and the flash of a red strobe light filled the room.

He grabbed his semiautomatic Glock from the desk drawer and ran down the hall, crouching his way down the steps, low and tight and fast, his mind on fire with all the possible threats that awaited him.

Could they really have found him this fast? How many men had Guzman sent? Every nerve ending in his body jolted with the knowledge that it was about four in the afternoon—and Charlotte's kids were home from school.

The worst possible scenario.

He pressed his back against the foyer wall, steadied himself, then spun around the doorjamb to the living room, knees bent, weapon thrust straight in front of his body—only to be greeted by the sight of a baseball at his feet. Shards of window glass were scattered over the couch and coffee table.

Joe felt his body sag in relief. He took in a deep breath and let it out. He tucked the gun in the back waistband of his jeans and pulled down the loose hem of his T-shirt to cover it.

The adrenaline began to recede, leaving in its wake a wicked headache that struck the instant he bent down for the baseball. Joe examined the ball in his hand, realizing the alarm didn't trigger before he heard the glass break because the ball tripped the motion sensors around the perimeter of the house an instant before it hit the window.

Joe grinned. A broken window was a big pain in the ass, to be sure, but a whole lot better than finding several highly motivated, heavily armed Mexican drug dealers standing in his living room.

He'd take anything over that.

He was heading toward the back of the house, where he figured he'd trot out to the pool area and throw the ball back over the pine trees and all would be forgiven. But before he could take three steps, the doorbell rang.

At least he assumed it was the doorbell, since he'd never actually heard it before.

There was only one possibility. . . .

The instant he opened the door, he was struck by the widely varied expressions of the three people who stood before him.

The girl named Henrietta looked up at him with the most devilish blue eyes he'd ever seen. She was certainly a colorful child—flaming red hair, lots of brown freckles on pale skin, and a checkerboard smile of missing or in-process teeth.

Her brother stared up at Joe with a look he'd never seen on a kid's face—not that he'd been around kids much. But it was the kind of look Steve used to get when he had something up his sleeve. Matt Tasker gave him a slow once-over, then peered inside his house and raised a single eyebrow in surprise.

Joe took a step outside and closed the door behind him.

And right there, not a foot away, with her hands on her children's shoulders, was Honeysuckle Mama herself. Her face was as red as her hair. Her big gray eyes stared at him with embarrassment. She was clearly horrified to be standing on his stoop.

About as horrified as he was to have her.

Then he noticed she was dressed in those jeans he liked, worn and thin and clinging to every one of her petite curves, and a nice little white button-down shirt.

"My daughter . . . she—" Joe watched Charlotte struggle with the words and gloried in the sound of her voice. He wanted her to keep talking. About anything.

"Hi," the girl said.

"We came to apologize for—"

"I smashed your window, and my mom just said, 'Oh, shit,' and she never, *ever* cusses." Hank smiled proudly. "Can I go inside your house and look for the ball? Can I use your bathroom? The Connors used to let me use their bathroom whenever I wanted."

"She's out of control," Matt offered as explanation, rolling his eyes.

"My dad said I'm a power hitter," Hank added.

Joe was struck by the absurdity of the scene. There was so much that he wanted to do. Run inside and hide was at the top of the list, followed closely by grabbing Charlotte around that nice little waist of hers and getting his mouth back on those pretty pink lips—

"I will pay for the repairs of course," Honeysuckle Mama was saying. "Garson's Glass on Main Street repairs windows. Have Mr. Garson send me the bill."

The object of his fantasy was slowly pulling her children back, as if to protect them.

He held out his hand to return the ball, and Charlotte gasped. What? Did she think he was going to shoot them, for God's sake? But he *had* pulled a gun on the woman only two nights ago, hadn't he? And he was armed at the present moment as well.

He uncurled his fingers and held the baseball in his open palm, smiling down at the power hitter.

"Nice swing for a girl, Henrietta."

She grinned and grabbed the ball with a chubby, dirty hand. "Thanks, Mr. Mills. But call me that again and I'll have to bop you one."

Joe stepped back in surprise, laughing, and looked to Charlotte for guidance. Then he realized that Mommy must have mentioned his name to the kids. So she'd been talking about him. This was an interesting development.

"Hank. She prefers to be called Hank." Charlotte backed away further, avoiding his eyes.

God, how he wanted to tilt up that perfect little chin of Charlotte's and explain everything to her. Tell her how he'd looked for her. How he'd kicked himself for letting her go that day. How he much he wanted her—how much he'd always wanted her. And why he had to leave and never speak to her again.

"Why are there red lights flashing in your house?"

Matt's question startled Joe. How long had he been staring at Charlotte?

"You got some sort of fancy alarm system or something? Are you a spy?"

Charlotte pulled Matt by the elbow. "My apologies for the window and the invasion of your privacy. It will not happen again."

Joe watched her practically drag the kids down the diagonal stone walkway that led to the sidewalk. He was sad to see them go but relieved they were leaving. He also had to admit he enjoyed the view of Charlotte in retreat, the sway in her walk, even in a pair of sneakers. She had the nicest little compact butt.

Hank turned around and waved at him. "Wanna toss with us sometime?" she called.

Joe couldn't stop the smile now spreading across his face.

Charlotte scooped up Hank and hustled her along, not bothering to look his way. Matt did, however, and shot him a deadly scowl he wouldn't soon forget.

About an hour later, Joe had the glass cleaned up, the window measured and taped off in plastic, and a replacement ordered from Garson's when the alarm went off again.

"Some safe house," he muttered.

That's when he saw the real estate agent, LoriSue Bettmyer, standing at his front door wearing a tight neon orange suit and holding what he thought for sure was a big straw basket full of . . . of . . . food and crap. What the hell?

He'd made this mistake once before and wasn't making it again. He was supposed to be a reclusive mystery writer, right? Well, the recluse part was about to start.

She kept ringing the bell. But he didn't answer.


"How many fingers am I holding up, Mama?"

Charlotte glanced in the rearview mirror as she turned the van onto Hayden Circle. "I can't see right now, Hank. I'm driving."

"I'll give you a hint," Matt said. "She's holding up her whole hand."

Charlotte grinned to herself. "Okay, guys. Five fingers."

"WRONG!" they both yelled from the back, and Matt quickly added, "The answer is four fingers! The thumb doesn't have a middle joint, so it can't be called a finger!"

Charlotte laughed. "You got me there."

"So, how come Mr. Mills can't toss ball with me?" It was the third time that evening that Hank had mentioned him.

"I just don't want you going over there. He . . . uh . . . may be a little unstable is all."

"What's 'unstable'?" she asked.

"I don't want you bothering him."

"But I think he's nice." Hank's voice was suddenly garbled.

"Yeah, but what were all those red lights flashing in his house? What was up with *that*?" Matt asked.

"I have no idea."

"I thought they were cool," Hank mumbled.

Charlotte turned her head to see her daughter chewing on a Cow Tail candy.

"Where'd you get that, Hank?"

"She always gets them," Matt said.

"Nuh-*uh*," Hank said.

"Yeah-*huh*," Matt replied. "She gets them whenever Justin's dad works the concession stand. He gives them to her for free."

"So? He gave you a box of Hot Tamales tonight. I saw him!"

"Did not."

"Did so."

"Did not!" Matt yelled.

"Tattler," Hank snapped.

"Porker," Matt said.

Charlotte just hated it when the kids chose to work out the challenges of interpersonal relations on each other after 8:00 p.m., when everyone's tempers were short. And she hated to hear her own words come out in the universal boring, whiny, singsong of mothers everywhere, but what choice did she have?

"That is enough. Both of you."

Hank started sniffling, and Charlotte reached around behind the front passenger seat and held out her hand. "Give it to me, please." A sticky, half-eaten chocolate chew landed in her palm. "Now apologize to your sister, Matt."

Matt sighed loudly, temporarily drowning out the sound of sniffles. "Sorry I called you a porker," he said.

"Am I fat?" Hank asked in a soft voice.

Charlotte pulled into the drive, feeling tired to her bones. She got out of the car and tossed the candy into the trash can just inside the garage. Then she took Hank's hand.

"You're not fat, sweetie." Charlotte reached down and wiped the tears from Hank's face, leaving two pink clean streaks across her cheeks. "Let's get you in the tub, young lady. Matt, you can take a shower in my bathroom."

"People say I'm fat, Mama."

Charlotte gripped her daughter's hand tighter as they walked up the stairs to the porch. "People come in all shapes and sizes, Hank, and what you are is healthy and beautiful and athletic and I would ignore what other people say. Just focus on liking yourself and treating others the way you would like to be treated and it will all work out, sweetie."

They were in the kids' bathroom now and Charlotte tested the water pouring from the spout, then pushed the bathtub stopper into place. She turned around to see Hank standing before her nude except for her bright yellow ball cap, her round, firm, wide little girl body flushed from exercise and fresh air. Charlotte sat on the edge of the tub, held out her arms, and Hank fell against her.

"Daddy said I was perfect and graceful and the best ballerina in the world."

Charlotte pulled off the baseball cap and breathed deep from Hank's sweaty head and the crook of her neck. "I know he did."

"But some of the girls say I'm too big to be a ballerina."

She stroked her daughter's hair as the bathroom filled with warm steam. Charlotte wondered if her words would ever have the same impact as Kurt's had and wished once more that he was still with them.

"You love to dance, sweetie, and that's all that matters. I think you are a wonderful ballerina, too."

Hank sniffed. "I wish Daddy could see me dance in my recital."

"He'll see you."

"I want him to see me play in the majors, too."

"He sees you, baby."

Hank stood straight and looked into Charlotte's face. She was grinning once more, seemingly recovered from her brief moment of insecurity.

"I look like Daddy, don't I?"

Charlotte smiled gently at her daughter, seeing the need for confirmation in her eyes. "You sure do, Hank. And you've got his spirit, too—his kind heart and his way with people. You should be very proud of that."

Hank nodded. "So when you look at me, it'll help you to not forget Daddy, right?"

Charlotte pulled back, the air emptying from her lungs in surprise, and she shook her head. "Honey, I will never forget Daddy. What in the *world* made you say that?"

Hank chewed on her lip and briefly looked away from her mother. Then in a soft voice she said, "Don't be mad, Mama. I just wanted to make sure you won't forget him, even when you start to love Mr. Mills."

He was just finishing another report for the U.S. attorney when Joe noticed that his cut had bled through the plastic bandage again. That sliver of window glass must have sliced him deeper than he realized. He saved the file he was working on and walked to the bathroom medicine cabinet, pressing a new strip onto the left index finger.

That familiar twinge of nausea hit him, and he told himself that it was only a tiny drop of blood and it was his own blood, not Steve's. But then he caught sight of his face in the mirror and knew he wasn't going to be able to fight it tonight.

He flopped down on the bed and closed his eyes, knowing that there was no way to change the ending to the scene that was about to replay in his mind. Steve Simmons would always end up lying with his left cheek slapped down in a puddle of blood in the Denny's parking lot, his car keys in his hands, his eyes wide with the shock of his own death. And Joe was always going to be on his belly on the asphalt beside him, gun drawn an instant too late, still breathing despite the spray of bullets, watching the four-door silver Lexus speed away.

The coroner's report later indicated that Steve died within minutes of his wife and son, a sign that Guzman had dispatched two separate crews to two locations that night. And Joe had wondered if maybe that wasn't a blessing, because Reba and Daniel never had to hear that Steve was dead and Steve never had to know that his job had gotten his family murdered.

Joe had been glad that there was no one at home waiting for him that night. Because they'd be dead now, too.

He turned on his side, figuring he was in for another restless night. How was a man supposed to sleep? It had been two months since that night. Since then, he'd heard plenty of reassurances that it hadn't been his fault, from the DEA-appointed shrink, from Roger, from his coworkers. An informant had ratted out him and Steve under torture. There was nothing that could have been done. Risk was part of the job and Steve knew it. They all knew it.

Joe shot up off the bed and paced in the darkness. He had choices to make. Maybe all this free time in the middle of nowhere was just what he needed—time to think.

He could retire. Or go on to something else. God knew what, but something else.

Roger had suggested he move into a first-line supervisor position. The higher-ups had dangled a few choice posts in his face: San Diego. San Francisco. Seattle. And Roger had pointed out the obvious so many times that it made Joe's head spin: he'd put in twelve years with the Administration and had a GS 13 ranking. He had wide-ranging field experience as a case agent. He'd seen most of what the immoral, violent world of drug dealing had to offer and it was his duty to share that knowledge with other agents. A supervisory job was the next logical step.

Logical? Sure. Appealing? Not so sure.

Joe spread his palm flat against the bedroom wall,

leaned forward, and hung his head. He took a few deep breaths, feeling a strange stillness descend upon him, starting at his shoulders, spreading down to his legs, then settling in the soles of his feet, firmly planted in the plush carpet of this strange house.

It seemed he'd slowed down so much in the last week that he was now standing still, and the problem with standing still is that you become an easy mark for your own emotions. And right at that moment, he felt like a sitting duck for everything he'd not allowed himself to feel, from not only the past two months but his entire life.

No wonder he never used his vacation time.

Joe let his neck relax further, and there was so much sensation rushing into his head that he felt it would burst. And the tears felt so foreign, because he really didn't know he could cry. The last time he did, he was fourteen years old, at Nick's funeral, and they were tears of rage.

His big brother—his idol—had OD'd on cocaine at a college frat party. His parents never rebounded from the pointless loss. And Joe vowed to spend his life making up for it.

He let his head hang, thankful for the dark, the stillness. It made it easier for him to label what was bubbling to the surface.

He was almost thirty-eight and felt every single day of it. He loved his job but knew it had sucked him dry. He felt alone. Empty. And if he looked really close, he'd have to admit that for a while now he'd known that a one-bedroom apartment and a string of short-lived relationships was no longer cutting it. For a while now, he'd wanted what Steve had—a place that anchored him, people who needed him, a woman who loved him.

Joe didn't miss the irony—he was coming clean to himself about what he really wanted in life just when he couldn't do a damn thing about it! He was supposed to be invisible, not going around looking for connections, for home—for a woman.

Joe moaned. He wanted Charlotte. He wanted her so damn bad he could taste her, and he always had.

Could it be that he'd fallen in love with her that day so long ago? It seemed ridiculous, but what else could explain the fact that every woman who'd entered his life since had always been subjected to comparison to her?

Was it simply the fact that she was the ultimate challenge? After all, she'd been the hottest woman he'd ever touched, a woman who refused to tell him her name and then burned rubber in her effort to leave him standing alone in a parking lot.

And then, thirteen years later, in her driveway.

Joe smiled, and the twitch of his mouth caused a lone tear to detour down the side of his neck. He swatted at it impatiently.

He'd always believed there was a reason for the way things happened in life, even though he may not know that reason for many years, if ever. He believed the big picture was sometimes just too big for mortals to see.

So there had to be a real good reason why he'd landed in some tiny town in Ohio only to find Charlotte. He couldn't help but wonder if somebody up there was giving him a second chance.

Joe stood up and stretched. He padded downstairs to the kitchen in bare feet and rooted through the drawers until he found what he was looking for—six stubby white utility candles. He grabbed a plate from the cabinet and a box of kitchen matches and went out to the back patio.

He arranged the candles on the plate and lit them, watching their bright flames cut through the darkness. Then he said a silent prayer for his brother, his parents, and Steve, Reba, and Daniel—and threw in one for himself.

# Chapter Nine

"I think he practices Santorini."

"What the heck is Santorini?" Bonnie reached into the concession stand cooler for a Gatorade. "That'll be one-fifty, sweetheart." She took the money from a T-ball player who could barely see over the order window. "Have a good game."

"I think I saw that movie—*The Great Santorini*!" Ned hollered from his post at the large stainless-steel grill. "I love Robert Duvall. Order up!"

He slid a paper plate across the counter to Bonnie, who picked up the cheeseburger and fries and carried it to the window. Then she laughed, turning suddenly toward both of them. "*Now* I get it! Charlotte, do you mean Santeria, the voodoo thing?"

Charlotte nodded with enthusiasm, counting out change for a five. "Yes! That's it!"

"And, honey," Bonnie added to Ned. "It's *The Great Santini*. Santorini is a Greek Island."

"I knew that." Ned flipped a burger.

Charlotte finished counting out change and tilted her head toward Bonnie and whispered, "All I know is I saw him light a bunch of candles out on his pool deck last night, then mumble some sort of spell or something."

"A spell?"

"Can I have some Big League Chew, Mrs. Tasker?" a small voice asked.

Charlotte peered out the window, saw another potential convert, and said cheerfully, "I made some delicious whole wheat fig bars and there's no charge. Would you like one of those instead?"

The little girl shook her head with certainty. "No way."

"Just a second then." With a sigh, Charlotte reached into the bubble-gum bin and handed the bag through the window, taking the child's money while resuming her conversation with Bonnie.

"Yes, a spell. He lowered his head over six little white candles and his lips were moving. It was scary. Between that and the gun, I'm thinking I should call the police."

Ned's head popped up. "What gun?"

"Uh—" Charlotte really didn't want to make a big deal out of this, but she supposed it wasn't a bad idea to let Ned know. "The night Hoover got loose I followed him into the Connors' yard. He pulled a gun on me—told me he was a little paranoid about burglars."

Ned's eyebrow shot up and he stared at her. He didn't look pleased.

"He put it away when he realized it was me."

Ned nodded soberly and flipped the line of burgers on the grill.

Bonnie rolled her eyes heavenward. "I think Mr. Mills is going to get a visit from Sheriff Ned's Welcome Wagon."

"You bet your sweet patoot he is," Ned mumbled.

Bonnie smiled at Charlotte. "So tell us, Charlotte. How is it you know so much about what your neighbor is doing at night behind a nine-foot privacy fence? You're not spying on him or anything, are you?"

"You can go to women's prison for that," Ned offered helpfully.

Charlotte felt herself blush. The truth was she'd had trouble sleeping and was spying on Joe with Matt's binoculars again, not that she'd ever come right out and admit it. She was scrambling to come up with some excuse when a customer appeared at the window. Charlotte spun around, happy for the distraction—for about one second.

"Hello there, Miss Vegetarian," said Jimmy Bettmyer. He stuck his faded blond head through the window to greet Ned and Bonnie, who returned his hello.

"What can I get you, Jimmy?" Charlotte waited, order pad and pencil in hand, as Jimmy carefully considered the menu overhead—as if he didn't know it by heart. The Minton Little League concession stand featured the same five grease-soaked fast-food choices season after season.

"I think I'll try a number two with a Sprite," Jimmy said loudly, then added under his breath, "and a big bite out of you, babe."

She ignored him, ripping the order off the pad and sticking it in the little metal clip over Ned's grill. "Chili dog, large fry," Charlotte said, all business. She turned her back on Jimmy to fill his drink order.

With dismay, she noticed that Bonnie had become occupied with a group of players at the other window and wouldn't be able to act as a deterrent to Jimmy's antics. She was on her own.

"Order up!" Ned announced, and Charlotte retrieved the food and shoved everything toward Jimmy without making eye contact. He grabbed her hand before she could pull away.

"Meet me tonight," he whispered.

"Get your hand off me," she said.

"Ten. The Creekside. Just a friendly drink."

Charlotte extricated her hand from his grip and glared at him. "Not in this lifetime."

"I'm not giving up on you."

Charlotte's eyes flew wide as LoriSue appeared behind her husband, her blond brows knit in a frown. There was nothing she could do to prevent it from happening. . . .

"Ten at the Creekside. See you there, babe."

Then Jimmy turned, knocking the plate of food into his wife's enhanced chest.

"You are such a complete weasel, Jimmy." LoriSue's eyes lanced Charlotte through the clear plastic of the window. "And you—nice. Real nice." Then she turned and stomped off.

As Charlotte raced out the back door of the concession stand to catch her, Ned shouted, "Stay clear of those fingernails!"

Charlotte was panting by the time she reached LoriSue, already unlocking her BMW with the *chirp, chirp!* of her automatic door opener. "Please wait! Just a second!"

LoriSue looked over her shoulder, her face pulled tight with anger.

"Look, I swear there is nothing going on with—"

"Oh Lord, I know that," she snapped. "And I'm sorry for implying there was." She shook her head. "It's all him. He does it all the time. I know it's not you."

Charlotte slowly approached, touching LoriSue's arm. "I'm not going to meet him."

She gave a stiff nod. "I know."

"I never have and I never will."

LoriSue laughed. "Well, I guess that makes you a boat-load smarter than me, doesn't it?"

"I'm sorry, LoriSue."

She sighed heavily, picking chili off the front of her white silk wrap blouse. "Me, too." Then she straightened her shoulders. "You know, I've been thinking. He can just have the damn house. I mean, I can find another one for God's sake—it's my job!"

Charlotte smiled.

"I can't live like this anymore. The asshole can have it—it's just bricks and wood. I need to get on with my life."

Charlotte patted her arm. "Sounds like a good plan."

LoriSue suddenly brightened. "In fact, I think I've already started getting on with my life."

Charlotte was happy for her, happy to see her doing something positive, taking charge. "That's great! What have you done?"

LoriSue locked her gaze with Charlotte's and shook out her ultrablond tresses. "Made up my mind to go after Joe Mills, of course."

The next afternoon, Charlotte sat at the kitchen table in the sunlight and scraped away at what was left of the half gallon of French vanilla. Under Hoover's watchful eye, she slipped a spoonful of the cold, sweet comfort between her lips and wondered how she could possibly compete with LoriSue, the tight-skirt queen of Minton, Ohio.

But if LoriSue was going after Joe, there was no way she could just sit back and watch it happen.

Right?

She needed one more Joe-related encounter, that's all. And she refused to let LoriSue Bettmyer stand in her way.

Charlotte took inventory of what she was up against. She had bare, short nails, and LoriSue had sexy long red ones. She hardly ever wore anything but jeans or shorts, and LoriSue dressed like Fuck-Me Barbie. She kept her racy thoughts locked away in her nightstand, and LoriSue just went out into the world and said what was on her mind and strutted her stuff like a liberated, modern woman.

Charlotte downed another spoonful, trying to ignore how Hoover's eyes tracked every hand-to-mouth movement. He sat at her knee, licking his chops and drooling, and Charlotte couldn't help but wonder if that's how she'd appeared to Joe Mills the other night in the driveway. For the first time ever, Charlotte truly empathized with her dog.

"Aren't we a pair, Hoov?" She set the carton down on the kitchen floor and let the dog lick away the dregs. She stared out the window and wondered what excuse she could possibly have to go over there and talk to Joe again, only this time sporting a pretty dress and dry hair?

She let her mind and gaze wander until she suddenly saw what was right in front of her—the window. She'd go over and inquire about the broken window! She wouldn't even have to make up a reason to see him! And she'd wear something simple but lovely and she'd shave her legs and put on some mascara and she'd call this a do-over.

She had exactly three hours before she had to go pick up the kids, plenty of time to shower and dress and get over there with a couple hours to spare. She already knew what the two of them could do with two hours.

Charlotte used the blow-dryer and a round brush to put bounce in her hair. She dabbed on a bit of blush and a flattering pale pink lipstick. She selected a slinky spaghetti strap sundress in a buttery yellow that she'd worn to a banquet with Kurt a couple years before. She found the matching sandals in their original shoe box at the back of the closet. She didn't have time to polish her toes, but if all went as planned, Joe wouldn't be studying her feet.

She took a flirty turn in the mirror and liked what she saw. And she told herself that win or lose, at least she was giving it her best shot.

Charlotte walked downstairs, holding her head high,

and exited from the front door. She could hardly believe that she soon might be tasting the one thing she'd been starving for all these years. And by God, she deserved it. She deserved one more taste. She was a good woman who followed all the rules. She deserved one more taste of Joe Mills.

She headed down the driveway, aware of the sexy click of her heels as she went.

In fact, maybe that's all she needed—just one more taste. Maybe that would be enough to get him out of her system forever. Then the two of them could go on as neighbors. Normal, friendly neighbors.

She practiced rolling her hips as she walked.

God, how she wanted her slice of Joe. She couldn't wait to sink her teeth into that big serving of melt-in-your-mouth man—

Charlotte stopped dead in her tracks. LoriSue was leaving Joe's house, calmly making her way down the stone sidewalk.

"My God. I don't think I've ever seen you in a dress." LoriSue looked Charlotte up and down. "Where are you headed?"

Charlotte's mind went numb.

"Charlotte?"

"Just back from a new client interview." Charlotte realized her answer was a bit rushed and loud, but it was the closest to normal she could do. Then she added, "And you?"

LoriSue smiled and rubbed a hand on her throat. "Just bringing Joe another one of those welcome-to-the-neighborhood gifts I mentioned."

Charlotte stopped breathing.

LoriSue sighed dreamily. "So where you headed now?"

"Hoover escaped again."

LoriSue laughed. "I don't know why people have

dogs. Well, good luck. Talk to you later." She got into her BMW and pulled away.

Charlotte went home to change her clothes. She couldn't get out of that ridiculous outfit fast enough.

"I have to breathe or I'll turn blue and die," Justin pointed out.

"Then breathe in silence, like a ninja."

Justin closed his eyes and focused on the movement of air into his nose and out through his mouth. "How was that?" he asked.

"I can still hear you breathing."

Justin frowned and looked at the dog in the pine needles between them. Hoover was now scratching and licking his hindquarters, his license tags tinkling, making enough noise to blow their cover.

"Well, at least I don't lick myself," Justin said.

The boys snickered for a few moments, then Matt flinched and held up his palm. "Shhh. Here he comes again! Give me the camera!"

Justin traded the Techno-Spy camera for the binoculars as they both watched the subject step out onto his porch, look left and right, grab the basket, then shut the door.

"That's the fourth delivery this week," Justin said.

"Do you think they're top-secret communiqués?" Matt asked.

"Looked more like pretzels to me."

"So who keeps leaving those things?"

"Dunno." Justin frowned. "But they seem to come while we're in school. So it can't be a kid, right?"

Matt raised an eyebrow at that comment. "Excellent point."

"Unless they're playing hooky."

"True."

"So it could be a kid *or* a grown-up," Justin offered.

"Right, and since that's the only two kinds of people in the *universe*, I think we need to narrow it down some."

"Yeah."

Hoover popped up from his nest in the pine needles, yawned, stretched, then trotted back toward the house.

"Got any more Skittles, dude?"

Justin rooted around in his left pants pocket and pulled out a crumpled pack and handed it over. "Don't eat all the red ones. They've got special powers."

"Get real," Matt said, popping a handful of round candies into his mouth, along with a few stray pine needles that he had to pick off his lips.

"Really. If you eat enough, you can see right through girls' shirts."

Matt stopped chewing. "Says who?"

"My dad," Justin said, smiling.

Matt's eyes got big. "Wow. You think if I ate enough they'd work on Lisa Bertucci?"

Justin giggled. "I knew you had a crush on her."

"Do not. I hate girls."

"Liar."

"Besides, she was there the morning I dropped my volcano on the sidewalk." Matt sighed. "She thinks I'm a nimwad."

Justin shrugged. "What do girls know?" He patted his friend's shoulder. "Besides. I bet she doesn't have anything worth lookin' at anyway."

"Maybe, but she sure smells good."

A faint sound caused both the boys to freeze, then slowly turn their heads. Matt swallowed a mouthful of Skittles and picked up the camera. Justin grabbed the binoculars.

"Dude," Justin whispered as Matt clicked away. "Is he gonna kill us or what?"

The boys watched Mr. Mills take deliberate strides across the grass, machete in hand, heading right for them.

"Like a ninja," Matt hissed, sending a pleading look toward Justin.

They watched as Mr. Mills suddenly veered off toward a clump of bushes between the utility shed and his privacy fence. He began slashing away.

"What the heck's he doing?" Justin asked.

"Yard work?" Matt said hopefully.

"He looks royally pissed. Besides, that bush is in your yard!" Justin swallowed hard. "We'd better report this to Ned."

The boys glanced at each other, scooted back on their bellies in the pine needles, then made a run for it.

Joe sensed the man's presence long before he heard the polite cough, and looked up to see him straddling the property line between Charlotte's yard and his own.

He was a stocky guy, on the short side, balding, with a smile that didn't quite fit the serious look in his eyes. He was holding out his hand.

"Ned Preston, two houses down," he said.

Joe transferred the machete to his left hand and wiped the sweat off his brow with his forearm. He reached out, and Ned's hand gripped his tight—a little too tight for a friendly get-to-know-you visit.

Joe managed a polite smile.

"Joe. Joe Mills."

Still clenching his hand, Ned Preston nodded toward the machete. "Word is you got a got a real nice collection of weapons over here."

Joe pulled his hand away. Charlotte had obviously told him about the gun—he really was going to have to learn to be less antsy—and now he had to placate Dirty Harry here.

"I have a handgun. I've had some unfortunate experiences in the past."

Ned nodded slowly. "Come from a bad neighborhood, do you?"

"The city. You know."

"What city might that be?"

Joe shifted his weight and tossed the machete onto the ground. He put his hands on his hips and studied Ned Preston. Smart guy. Maybe a little too smart.

"Here and there. Out west. Washington, D.C., for a bit."

Ned let out a long and low whistle. "Good ole Minton must be a bit slower than you're used to, huh?"

"I needed a change of scenery. I'm a writer."

Ned bobbed his head in approval. "Anything me or the wife might have read?"

"Sorry. I write mysteries, but I'm not published yet. That's why I needed the change. You know—motivation."

Ned nodded toward the honeysuckle. "I'd say you were plenty motivated to hack the living shit out of that bush. But I think you may have missed a spot."

Joe couldn't help it—he found himself chuckling and shaking his head. "Don't much like the smell. Gives me a headache."

"Really now?"

"Really."

"That's Charlotte Tasker's property you just destroyed."

"It is?"

Ned bent at the waist and pointed to the tangle of stalks coming up from the ground. "The bush is planted in her yard. Some of it hangs over into your yard, and yes, technically you could have trimmed that section. But you had no right to annihilate the whole plant."

Joe let loose with a heavy sigh. He wasn't cut out for

suburbia, obviously. "I wasn't thinking. I'll reimburse Mrs. Tasker for it."

"So what kind is it?"

"Honeysuckle. The smell was about to drive me nuts and—"

"I meant the gun."

Joe frowned. "Pardon?"

"The handgun you own." Ned Preston had straightened to his full height and was no longer bothering with the smile. "The one you stuck in Charlotte's face when she happened to wander into your yard looking for her dog."

Joe didn't blink. "The kind of handgun that comes with a license."

"Mind if I see that license?"

"As a matter of fact, I do mind."

Ned hoisted up his jeans and puffed out his chest. Joe nearly laughed out loud, but something in the man's expression put that idea to rest. What Joe saw was protectiveness—genuine concern that he might pose a danger to Charlotte.

He liked that.

He liked Ned.

"You know, Ned," he said, "I'm extremely sorry that I pulled the gun on Mrs. Tasker. I feel awful about it, and I did offer my sincere apologies."

"So you're not sticking around?"

"Say what?" Joe's pulse quickened.

"Just heard you're already packing up. The kids said something about it."

"What kids?"

"Matt and the Bettmyer boy. They said you were packing up already, so I figured maybe you decided Minton wasn't a good fit after all."

When had the kids seen him packing? *How* had they

seen him packing? And was this old bumpkin *threatening* him? It sure as hell felt that way.

"I haven't made up my mind about staying," Joe said calmly and politely. "But in the meantime, never fear, Ned. I have no intention of bothering Mrs. Tasker. I'm busy writing and I just want my privacy. That's all."

"A man's entitled to a little privacy," Ned said.

"Indeed."

"Speaking of which, I'll let you get back to your—" Ned glanced at the decapitated branches strewn all over the ground. He made a big production of sniffing the perfumed air. "Pruning."

Joe laughed and held out his hand. This time, Ned didn't try to cut off the blood flow to his fingers. "Thanks for stopping by, Ned."

"No problem, Joe."

"I'm telling you, If Joe Isuzu over there is a mystery writer, then I'm the president of General-freakin'-Motors."

Bonnie stood at the kitchen counter, tossing the dinner salad. "You can be so skeptical sometimes, Ned. Give the guy a chance."

"The man's a cop, honey."

She looked up, startled, staring at the potted oregano on her kitchen windowsill. Eventually, she turned her head toward her husband. "What did you just say?"

"And former military would be my guess, but without a doubt a cop."

She dropped the salad tongs. "You sure?"

Ned chuckled. "Of course I'm sure. Just don't know what kind of cop he is or if he's an ex-cop and why the hell he's hanging out in Hayden Heights. I smell something cookin', and it ain't your fifteen-bean soup."

Bonnie busied herself with setting the table, her mind

tumbling with this information. She trusted her husband's instincts—always had—so if Ned said Joe Mills was a cop, he was probably a cop.

But then that meant Joe Mills had lied to everyone. She set out two napkins and two sets of silverware. That meant he wasn't the man he proclaimed to be. That meant he might not be the safest person to be living next to Charlotte and the kids.

Yes, Bonnie had promised Charlotte she would never breathe a word of what had happened thirteen years ago, but if Ned was right, what was the responsible thing to do?

"So, honey . . ." She brought two steaming bowls of soup to the table and passed the plate of corn bread to Ned. She watched him slather the triangle with cholesterol-free spread. "Do you think Joe Mills might be hiding something? Like the real reason he's here?"

Ned took a huge bite and shrugged. "Hell if I know."

Bonnie brought the soupspoon to her mouth and took a sip. She was aiming for a casual tone of voice but didn't know if she could hide her anxiety from the man who knew her so well. "I just wonder, honey . . ."

Ned was dipping his corn bread into his soup. "About what?"

"Well, that maybe Joe Mills's real reason for being here is to be near Charlotte."

Ned stopped dipping and looked across the table at his wife. "Go on."

"Well, I think they might have met each other a long time ago." Bonnie waved her spoon through the air. "I think I remember Charlotte saying something or other about that." She took another sip of soup, cringing when she heard the seriousness of Ned's voice.

"Let's have it, Bon."

"Oh, I can't!" Bonnie jumped up from her seat, the ladder-back chair scraping along on the floor. She pulled her arms around herself, her back to Ned. "It's just that now I'm worried that it isn't a coincidence."

"When did she meet him?"

"Thirteen years ago, right before she graduated from nursing school in Maryland." Bonnie turned back to Ned. "Right before Kurt proposed to her."

Ned frowned but still ate. "I'm listening."

"They didn't exchange names."

Ned looked up at Bonnie with a quizzical expression. "You mean they passed each other in a 7-Eleven or something?"

"Well, no. Not exactly."

"Did they have some kind of fling or something?"

"I can't really say."

Ned laughed, corn-bread crumbs dribbling into his soup. "This sounds hot."

"Ned, it's Charlotte's private business. I'm just worried about her—why that man is really here."

Ned put down his spoon. "So how hot was it?"

Bonnie bit her lip. "Side-of-the-road hot."

"What?" Ned stopped chewing and blinked. "Are we talking about Charlotte Tasker, the good girl we know and love?"

"The same."

"And she's sure it was him?"

Bonnie nodded soberly. "Oh, my. She's sure."

# Chapter Ten

Charlotte checked her watch. She had fifty-two minutes until she had to pick up the kids at school, and with a quick survey of the yard she calculated she could finish mowing and still have time to use the power trimmer along the driveway.

It was truly hot today—the first hot day of spring—and the sun felt deliciously good on her skin. She checked her chest to make sure she wasn't getting red, hoping the SPF 20 would do the trick, and could almost hear the freckles popping to life between her boobs. She adjusted the cups of her swimsuit top for modesty's sake.

Charlotte bumped along, rock music blaring from her earphones, and she grinned with pleasure. She didn't mind mowing the lawn. Kurt had always done it, so she'd only recently discovered how relaxing it was. It was like meditating, only with engine noise. And what a sense of accomplishment a freshly mown lawn provided! All those straight green rows! It was infinitely more satisfying than housework. With housework, no matter how many hours you put in, the kids could erase any evidence of your labor in minutes. But lawns stayed mown up to a whole week! Not even two kids and a dog could unmow a lawn.

Charlotte breathed deep, loving the smell of cut grass, the feel of the sweat beading on her forehead under the brim of her ball cap. As she rounded the side of the utility shed, she cocked her head in surprise. Now that was odd—what in the world had happened to her honeysuckle bush?

Charlotte turned off the riding mower, pulled off her headset, and charged over toward the flowering vines. It looked like it had been run over. Mutilated.

She stomped into the Connors' yard and bent down for a closer examination. At least half of it had been chopped to the stalks!

"Sorry about the bush."

Charlotte jumped. She spun around, saw Joe, and immediately checked to see if he was armed. No gun today. Then she checked to see if LoriSue was with him. She wasn't. Then she let her eyes move to his face. And she stared at him in awe.

The man standing there in the sunshine, his hands at his sides, his bare toes wriggling in the grass, was indeed the man she'd known all those years ago. But he was no longer young. His eyes were deeper. They had mellowed. They were maybe just a little sad.

Joe smiled, and she tried to place what was different about that smile. Maybe it was the addition of the little goatee, which provided a neat frame around that wide, provocative mouth of his. She liked it. In fact, Charlotte could still feel how the short whiskers had brushed against her lips when he kissed her. The longer hair that curled at the nape of his neck and behind his ears—that suited him, too. It gave him that just-rolled-out-of-the-sack look.

Talk about overkill.

This man seemed so out of place just inches away from her, right there in broad daylight. She was used to seeing him only in the dark recesses of her imagination, at night, through a fog of desire.

"You've got a nice singing voice, Charlotte."

"Huh?"

"Just now. When you were mowing."

"You could hear me sing over the mower? I had no idea I was that loud."

Joe's mouth quirked into a half smile. "Well, I couldn't tell if it was Ozzy Osborne or the Osmonds, but I heard you all right."

Charlotte became painfully aware of her own clothing choice for the afternoon: denim cutoffs, grass-stained sneakers, a pink bikini top, and Hank's yellow Minton Little League hat. She didn't know what to do with her hands, so she grabbed onto a decapitated honeysuckle twig.

"You did this to my bush?"

He winced. "Sorry about that."

"But I love honeysuckle! Why did you do that?"

Joe took a step closer to her. "Do you have a minute?"

"For what?" She watched him run a hand through his hair like he was mustering his courage. It seemed that thirteen years ago he'd been a hell of a lot more sure of himself than he was today.

"Talk. I think maybe I need to explain something to you."

"Explain what? LoriSue's little welcome-to-the-neighborhood visits?"

He tilted his head and stared at her. "You know about those?"

Charlotte was getting steamed. "Sure do, Joe. I saw her leaving your place yesterday. Hope you're getting everything you want."

Joe chuckled and shrugged. "It's generous of her, I suppose, but I can't use half of what she's giving me."

Charlotte let out a loud hoot, amused at what an insensitive jerk her fantasy boy had turned out to be. It didn't seem to bother him one bit that he'd pushed her away and then turned right around and done the deed with LoriSue! What had happened between them thirteen years ago meant nothing to him, obviously. It was a godsend that LoriSue got to him first, because the guy was bad news.

Not to mention that he was a liar—Charlotte knew too well that Joe Mills could handle anything a woman might give him.

Joe shrugged. "I mean, a man can only take so much chutney."

"Is that what they're calling it nowadays?" Charlotte tried to walk away, but Joe grabbed her forearm. Despite everything, his touch made her breath catch.

"Charlotte?" He turned her and looked into her face as if he was truly concerned for her feelings. "LoriSue is leaving gift baskets on my front stoop. We *are* talking about the same thing, correct?"

*"Gift baskets?"* Charlotte couldn't stop her mouth from falling open.

"Muffin mixes and fancy vinegars and crap I don't even know what to do with." A crooked smile spread across his face. "That's all she's been giving me."

Charlotte covered her eyes with her gardening gloves and wanted to die right there. She heard Joe laughing softly and she joined in.

She peeked at him. "Sorry."

"No problem." He released his hand from her arm. "Thanks for looking out for my best interests, though."

"We take care of each other in Hayden Heights."

Joe nodded, and Charlotte watched his expression turn wistful. "Look. About the other night—"

"There's no need to explain. I'm sorry I behaved like that. I'm usually not such a—"

"Don't be sorry for anything, Charlotte. Is there somewhere we can sit down?"

"I'm fine here. And the kids are coming home soon."

"Ahh, right." Joe cleared his throat. "Well." He seemed nervous, and his gaze wandered onto her freckled chest and dragged its way down her belly. Charlotte tried to suck in her gut without him noticing.

Joe redirected his gaze to her face. "I have one thing to tell you and two questions to ask, and then I won't bother you again."

The way he looked at her, with such earnestness, made her think of her own little boy. She didn't understand how she made that connection, but her heart softened to Joe and whatever it was he wanted to say. She must be the biggest sucker on the planet.

"Go on."

"You need to know that I tried to find you after that day, Charlotte. I looked a long time."

She could not move.

"And the first question I have is—" Joe shook his head and laughed, his black eyes sparkling. "Damn, girl! Put me out of my misery and tell me whose Miata you were you driving that day, would you?"

She wasn't prepared for that question and found herself laughing nervously. *He'd looked for her?* She felt like the ground was rolling under her feet, like she might lose her balance. "The car belonged to the girlfriend of one of my boyfriend's roommates."

Joe smiled and shook his head. "And I bet she had no idea her man lent it to you."

Charlotte shrugged. "Maybe not. He gave it to me to drive because it was a special occasion. I was on my way to—" She stopped, unable to complete the sentence that would have included the words *Kurt* and *propose*. It seemed like blasphemy, under the circumstances.

He took another step toward her, so close that she could smell him—heat and soap and Joe.

"I looked for about six months, Charlotte—tracked down every blue Mazda Miata in the state of Maryland. Then I got transferred with my job. I always hoped I'd see you again."

This was more than she'd bargained for, and Charlotte turned on her heels and headed back to the mower. She needed to end this conversation. She needed to hop back on the Cub Cadet and put the headphones back over her ears and forget she'd ever heard the words he'd just spoken. It was too much. Far too much for her to handle.

But his hand touched her shoulder.

"Do you know you kissed me so hard that day that you broke my tooth?"

*"What?"* She spun around and examined the smile that greeted her. So *that's* what was different! He had a little snip off the inside of his left front tooth! She'd remembered his smile as blazing perfection, but now it was flawed, rakish, sexy as all get-out.

She absently ran her tongue along her bottom lip, then said, "No shit?"

Joe tapped a finger on his front incisor. "You owe me. And remember, you don't cuss."

"Damn—I really did that to you? I'm so sorry! I . . . uhm—" She couldn't stop licking her own bottom lip, horrified to know that the crack she'd heard had been one of his teeth! She'd been so out of control that day. What had she been thinking?

"I have just one more question."

She raised her eyes and scanned his entire face, nearly falling backward as she looked up at him from under the brim of the ball cap. He was so dark and beautiful that it overwhelmed her. He was too close. He was too real. He'd looked for her.

"The day we met—"

His pupils were bottomless, compelling. She once thought of him as the devil, the devil with a fishing pole, if she remembered correctly. So who was he now, and what did he mean when he said he'd never bother her again?

She felt Joe's gaze as it explored her face, and watched as his smile turned to an expression of tenderness. Worry, even. It was as if he suddenly expected her to shatter into pieces or blow away in the wind.

She flinched at the feel of his fingertips brushing the side of her cheek.

"I need to know, Charlotte. Please tell me the truth."

Oh God. She knew exactly what he was asking. His thumb brushed her bottom lip, tracing the invisible scar, paralyzing her.

"Did you give me your virginity that day?"

Charlotte spun away from his eyes, his touch, his words, and was about to hoist herself into the seat of the riding mower when his arms encircled her. With gentleness, he pulled her back against him. As he continued to talk, she felt his breath on the side of her damp neck.

"It's important to me. I have a right to know."

Charlotte didn't consider herself a coward. She'd faced so much and held it together for so long that she could surely answer this simple question. And the truth was, he did deserve to know. She wanted him to know, in fact.

So she nodded.

"Thank you, Charlotte." Joe swept his lips across her shoulder, released her, and backed away.

"I'll be leaving soon," he said. "I had no idea you lived here. I never intended to interfere with your life or cause you any pain."

She twirled around again. "You're *what*?"

"I have to leave. I'm sorry."

"You're leaving because I live here? You don't want to live near me?"

"It's not that. It's my work."

"You can't live here and write? Why not?"

"It's not that, exactly—"

So he was rejecting her again. Her chest ached and her head buzzed with anger.

"Why the hell did you cut down my honeysuckle?"

"I didn't know it was yours until your friend Ned set me straight. It'll bounce back. Most things do."

Charlotte took a few steps back, circling around the riding mower, putting several hundred pounds of bright yellow steel between them. She shook her head and laughed. "Okay, Joe. So you just show up next door after thirteen years, tell me you never forgot me, hack down my honeysuckle, and *leave*?"

He moved toward her, leaning both hands on the mower. "It's more complicated than that, Charlotte. I'd give anything to stay here and get to know you, but I can't. It's impossible."

"Right. Great." She hopped into the deep leather seat of the Cub Cadet and was about to turn the key in the ignition when his hand grasped hers.

"I'm glad you remember me, Charlotte. It means a lot to me."

The laughter exploded from her just as the tears began. *If the man only knew* . . . Charlotte stared at her grass-stained sneakers and shook her head, thinking of how the memory of Joe had flooded her poetry, her fantasies, her marriage, her life.

"What's so funny?"

If he was leaving, she might as well speak the truth. Charlotte raised her head, looked him in the eye, and said, "Since that day with you, nothing else has ever been good enough."

She turned the key in the ignition and let the roar of the motor drown out his response.

Joe spent the afternoon pacing the rooms of his too-big house. By evening, he knew he had to get out of there or lose his mind.

All had been revealed in that short conversation with Charlotte—words exchanged while he had to watch a single rivulet of sweat roll down Charlotte's smooth, soft, bare belly and into her shorts. And what Joe now knew made him nervous as hell.

Charlotte remembered him all right. What happened between them so long ago meant as much to her as it did to him. Meeting up again in Minton had left Charlotte just as unhinged as he was, as confused and conflicted. He'd seen it in her eyes that afternoon—desire, need, and grief, the same jumble of emotions roiling around in his own heart.

What a recipe for disaster.

Joe closed the automatic garage door and backed down the sloped drive. It was a gorgeous evening for a ride with the top down, but he didn't want to call that much attention to himself on his first leisurely cruise around town. He needed to bide his time for twelve more days. Maybe he'd check out the local cinema. Or see if there was a driving range nearby—he hadn't picked up his clubs in years. Or maybe he'd just see where the road took him.

He passed through the small downtown along Main Street, amazed that many of these sturdy nineteenth-century brick storefronts managed to stay in business as florists and hardware stores and restaurants. He passed by Garson's Glass and made a mental note to check on the new window tomorrow. He shuddered a bit at the sign for Basketful O' Gifts, noting that it was conveniently located next door to Sell-More Real Estate, and chuckled to himself about Charlotte's jealousy over blueberry muffin mix and scented room spray.

God, he would miss her. He would miss Charlotte the rest of his life.

Joe headed west of town past a few developments nearly identical to Hayden Heights, then past the high school campus, a couple of strip malls, and a handful of gas stations before it returned to countryside.

It was certainly pretty enough around here. The land that made up the north bank of the Ohio River rolled and swayed, the freshly paved road curling like a black velvet ribbon through the gentle hills. Not a bad place to live, as far as he could tell, if you had to live somewhere like this. Probably not a serious drug problem, but he knew well enough that the ugliness of the international drug trade didn't spare pretty little towns like Minton, Ohio—or their elementary schools, businesses, or families.

He'd asked himself a thousand times over the years why he chose the life he had. He could have done so many things with his criminal justice degree and his Special Forces background, but he'd picked the DEA. He knew the seed had been planted with Nick's overdose and the realization that his brother was just a tiny piece of a global enterprise of slavery and death. He came to see that the production, distribution, and consumption of drugs was at the heart of much of the world's violent crime, and if you were a cop who wanted to get to the root of what was wrong, the DEA was the place to be.

Joe stopped at a red light at the intersection of two county roads and sat patiently, letting his mind wander. Of course the Administration wasn't perfect. No huge government bureaucracy was, especially one at the whim of shifting politics. But he'd known a lot of good people who worked ungodly hours in awful situations, all in the name of saving people. And he'd always been proud to be one of them.

Joe watched the parade of minivan moms drive by and smiled. He could have chosen to live life like Ned Preston, come to think about it. A big fish in a small pond. The law in these parts. He could have been Minton police chief Joe Bellacera—a man who knew more about stolen bikes than bloodshed.

Joe chuckled, about ready to pull out from the light, when he saw the Minton Little League complex down the road to his left. He blinked. The place was huge! Cars spilled out of the lot and lined up along the roadside bumper-to-bumper. The night lights flicked on, sending a white glow over what looked to be a half-dozen fields. He heard the sound of cheering on the breeze.

Before he even realized what he intended, Joe pulled into an empty spot on the grassy shoulder of the road and walked across two lanes to get to the ballpark. His feet crunched on the gravel parking lot as he read the large blue sign at the entrance: MINTON LITTLE LEAGUE, WHERE DEDICATION, TEAMWORK, AND SPORTSMANSHIP MEET.

He scanned row after row of pickups, SUVs, minivans, and the occasional luxury sedan. Curiously, the first two rows outside the park entrance remained empty. He heard a chorus of "heads-up!" as a foul ball landed smack in the middle of one of the spots.

Good thing the Mustang was across the road.

A little kid with yellow hair ran out to retrieve the foul ball, smiling at him as he hustled back toward the stands.

God knew it was probably not a good idea to wander in here, but he was drawn by the sounds, the lights, the smell of baseball. He'd played in a Little Italy neighborhood league as a kid, in a grungy, weed-riddled lot that made this place look like Camden Yards. The people around here obviously took their baseball seriously.

"Evening," said a fat guy in overalls and a Minton Feed & Seed cap.

"Good evening," Joe replied.

He walked past the first field—the big boys obviously—and he could hear the sharp *crack* when a thrown ball hit the pocket of a glove. Next was a T-ball field, and he watched the batter just barely graze the stationary baseball, causing it to dribble onto the ground. The parents screamed as if the kid had hit a triple.

He released a startled laugh as he looked to his right, directly into the sharp blue eyes of a redheaded third baseman.

The girl put her hands on her hips, then broke out in a big smile. "Mr. Mills!" She waved her glove into the air. "I'm up next! Stay and watch me hit!"

Hank's coach yelled for her to pay attention to the game, and Joe watched her smack the sweet spot in her glove with confidence as she winked at him. It was the last thing he planned on doing, but he found himself wandering along the side of the field to the stands, where he found a spot on the aisle about halfway up.

A few faces frowned, most smiled politely, but Joe knew good and well this group of upstanding citizens was trying to decide if he was just another mystery weekend dad or a child molester.

He nodded politely and kept his eye on the action.

Hank scooped up a grounder at third and shot it to second for the last out of the inning. She ran back to the dugout like a woman with a mission. It dawned on Joe that Charlotte could be close by—and he winced at his own stupidity. He wasn't thinking things through. It was like his brain was on vacation.

The last thing he wanted to do was see her again today, because, more than anything, he wanted to see her again.

Joe did everything but stand up and scan the benches, but a casual look around told him Charlotte wasn't there. He was about to sigh with relief when a pair of sober gray eyes met his from under a maroon ball cap and Matt Tasker stood up and made his way through the crowd to him.

He sat down right next to Joe. "You got a kid that plays?"

Joe observed Hank smacking the top of her batting helmet to adjust the fit, then taking a couple practice swings outside the batter's box. From the way she wielded that bat, he thought maybe she was named after Hank Aaron. "I don't have any kids," he said. "Just driving around and stopped in."

"I saw Hank speak to you through the fence, but we're really not allowed to talk to you. My mom says you're unstable."

Joe looked at Matt in surprise. Man, kids just gave it to you straight, didn't they? It was kind of refreshing. "I'm plenty stable," he said, hoping he didn't sound like he was defending himself.

They both turned when the play-by-play man announced Hank Tasker was at the plate.

"Check this out," Matt said, nodding toward the field, not bothering to hide his pride. "My little sister rocks."

Hank let two low and outside pitches go by. On the third, she relaxed her back shoulder, focused her eyes fiercely on the pitcher, and followed through with a swing so pretty that Joe expected the ball to land on the county highway. It didn't go quite that far, but it sailed over the fence by a healthy margin, and Hank trotted around the bases with a gap-toothed smile on her face.

"It's better when she does that with a couple men on," Matt said while clapping. "Helps her RBI stats."

"Does she do that a lot?" Joe asked.

"At least a couple homers every game. She's one of the best hitters in the majors, better than most of the boys, and she only just turned eight last week."

When the applause died down, Joe felt like he needed to make conversation, because Matt showed no sign of moving from his spot. "How old are you, Matt?"

"I'll be eleven in November."

Joe smiled, remembering how at that age he, too, couldn't wait for the numbers to click by. He glanced at Matt from the corner of his eye, realizing this past year had to have been hell on the kid. Maybe that's why he was so serious all the time.

"My dad used to coach," Matt said, keeping his eye on the game. "He died a year and a half ago. He was a sportswriter—you might have known him. He was famous." Matt swiveled his head and looked Joe right in the eye. "Kurt Tasker."

Joe nodded in approval. "I know of him and I heard that he died. I am very sorry, Matt."

The boy shrugged and fiddled with a loose splinter of a fingernail. "Yeah. Thanks."

"My dad died about five years ago," Joe offered, unable to stop himself. When had he turned into a chatterbox? "My mom died when I was in college."

Matt's eyes flashed briefly, but his gaze didn't linger on Joe's. "That's bad. You got any brothers or sisters?"

"Nope. Had a brother, but he died, too, a few years before my mom."

Matt slowly raised his head. "Wow. That blows."

Joe nodded in agreement, not knowing what else to say to the kid. "Would you like a soda or anything?"

Matt frowned. "You mean a pop?"

Joe smiled. "Yeah. A pop."

It looked like Matt was going to smile, but he stopped himself and shook his head. "I'd love one, Mr. Mills, but my mom's working the concession stand and she'll only give me bottled water. She's kind of a freak about healthy food."

"I see."

"But if *you* go, she won't know it's for me, so that would be cool! So I'll take a large Mountain Dew with no ice and a box of Hot Tamales."

Joe chuckled to himself. Not only had he just been bamboozled into buying junk food for a preadolescent who wasn't supposed to eat it, but now he was going to have to see Charlotte.

Maybe he could use this turn of events to his advantage.

"I'll make a deal with you, Matt. I'll buy you a pop— no candy—in exchange for a little information."

Matt scrunched up his mouth in thought and eventually nodded. "Sounds fair. What do you want to know?"

Joe put a hand on Matt's shoulder and glowered at him, well aware that it might be considered intimidation. "When exactly were you spying on me, kid?"

# Chapter Eleven

Charlotte was feeling particularly sorry for herself tonight. Instead of being in the stands cheering for Hank the way she'd done earlier for Matt, she was stuck filling in for two no-show parent volunteers at the concession stand.

To make matters worse, her coworkers that night were the poster children for passive-aggressive couples everywhere—the Bettmyers.

Twenty minutes into the shift, Charlotte wanted to wring someone's neck. She decided Jimmy Bettmyer's neck would do nicely.

"We need another cheeseburger, if it fits into your busy bachelor's schedule," LoriSue said to Jimmy.

"Comin' right up, Your Bustiness," he replied.

Charlotte decided now was a good time to restock the grill with frozen hamburger patties and excused herself. Once in the back of the concession stand, she leaned up against the large chest freezer and sighed.

It hit her right then—a punch of grief for Kurt. It could still sneak up on her like that, at the oddest moments, with no warning, and before she knew it her stomach was in knots and her eyes stung with tears. She missed him so. He should have been there tonight with her. He would have been the one making everyone laugh. In his presence, the Bettmyers wouldn't bother her. She would take one look at her husband and know just lucky she was.

They'd always been able to talk—about everything but sex, anyway. And spending time with the Bettmyers made it clear just how good her own marriage had been. There was never any of this spiteful snapping at each other. When they argued, they talked it out calmly until it was as right as they could make it. And it might have been a bit boring, but it was good.

She'd give anything to have him back.

Charlotte shook her head and forced herself to stop the tears before they really started, reaching into the chest freezer and grabbing a plastic bag of frozen meat. She was heading toward the front of the snack bar, wiping her eyes, when Joe appeared at the window. She had to blink several times to be sure he wasn't a figment of her apparently relentless imagination.

"Well, hello!" LoriSue nearly screeched with excitement. "It's so nice to see you again, Joe!"

Charlotte absently handed the bag to Jimmy, who dropped the spatula and stared intently at the man who'd so obviously snagged his wife's attention.

"Hello," Joe said to LoriSue. "One Mountain Dew, please. No ice." Joe then cleared his throat nervously and allowed his eyes to land on Charlotte. She felt an immediate jolt deep in her belly.

"Good evening, Charlotte," Joe said.

"Thanks for bringing me the burgers, babe." Jimmy moved close to Charlotte's side. "Now why don't you take your sweet self back there and get me some more wieners?"

*Oh, no.* Charlotte sensed a very strange drama unfolding here, and she knew she was about to have one of the leading roles, whether she wanted it or not.

"Here you are, Joe." LoriSue cantilevered her body into the window so that she could offer Joe her breasts along with the soft drink. "No charge. Enjoy."

Jimmy snaked an arm around Charlotte's waist and brought her along as he approached the window.

"I'm Jim Bettmyer." He stuck his free hand past his wife and offered it to Joe. "You must be Charlotte's new neighbor."

Joe reached around LoriSue's boobs and shook the offered hand. "Yes. Joe Mills. Nice to meet you."

Charlotte twirled away from Jimmy's embrace, deciding that now was, in fact, a good time to get the wieners. Why in the world was Joe here? Had he come to see LoriSue? But he said there was nothing between them. Then had Joe come to see *her*?

Charlotte hopped up on the chest freezer and sat crosslegged a good five minutes, biting her bottom lip, waiting until she was certain Joe was gone. She couldn't face him after what they'd said that afternoon. She'd told him he took her virginity and changed her life, and he'd claimed to have searched for her. But he was leaving anyway, and she knew it had nothing to do with his writing. Joe Mills was leaving because she wasn't the girl he remembered. He wasn't interested in the woman she'd become.

Charlotte climbed down from her perch and returned to the front, only to see Joe still standing at the window.

"There you are, babe." Jimmy held out his hand. "I thought I was going to have to send out a rescue team for you."

She couldn't quite pinpoint what she saw in Joe's face but thought she detected a little bit of irritation and a whole lot of amusement. She noticed that LoriSue was patting his upper arm as she laughed and chatted with him.

"I'm just so glad you enjoyed the muffin mixes," she was saying.

Jimmy looped his arm around Charlotte's shoulders. Joe stared at her. Then Jimmy whispered something in Charlotte's ear, but she couldn't hear because of the roaring of her blood. She untied her apron.

"I'm going to catch the end of Hank's game." Charlotte folded the apron and stuck in it the drawer. "Business has slowed down enough that you two can handle it. Have a good evening, everyone."

In a flash, she was out the back door and breathing again, feeling a surprisingly small amount of guilt for ditching snack bar duties. LoriSue and Jimmy were perfectly capable of selling hot dogs without her. Why did people always assume that she would rush in and fix things? Why did people always assume that they could screw up and she would pick up the slack?

Maybe it was time for her to stop saying yes all the time.

Charlotte found herself nearly running to Hank's field, surprised when she sensed she had company. If it was Jimmy Bettmyer, she didn't think she could be held responsible for her actions.

It was Joe.

He had no problem keeping up with her brisk stride. His legs were so much longer than hers that he seemed to be gliding along at a leisurely pace while she scurried. He smiled down at her.

"Is Jimmy your boyfriend?"

Charlotte hissed. "Oh, please."

"He seems quite smitten with you."

"He's smitten by anything with two X chromosomes." Charlotte sped up, noticing that Joe's full paper cup was sloshing a bit. That pleased her. "Are you sure LoriSue isn't your girlfriend?"

Joe didn't answer right away, and in the silence Charlotte found herself wondering if her original assumption was correct. Then Joe said in a flat voice, "I've decided to ask her to be my bride. I think it was the chutney."

Charlotte turned away so he couldn't see her smile. So Joe Mills still had a sense of humor, did he? The realization made her heart jump. Then she reminded herself that Joe and his sense of humor were leaving town.

"I'm plenty stable, Charlotte. You don't have to worry about your kids around me."

She stopped walking. She looked up at him and frowned, and he frowned right back at her. A little voice in her head told her that this big man ought to terrify her—his eyes looked as cold as black steel; his jaw was set and his shoulders rigid—but for some reason she simply felt challenged by him.

She puffed herself up. "You pulled a gun on me and threw me on the ground. You tell me you always hoped to find me, but you're leaving anyway. In my dictionary, these things pretty much define the word *unstable*."

"I have a permit for that gun and I wish I could stay and I'm sorry. I'm sorry for everything."

"I hate guns. I don't believe they have any place in a residential neighborhood. You scared me to death. And I don't want you to leave. You just got here."

His frown disappeared and his eyes softened. "I agree with you. About everything."

Charlotte huffed and started walking again, Joe at her side. Why was he following her?

"Why do you have a gun, anyway?"

"I'm used to living places where I need to protect myself."

"So where did you live before?"

"I've moved around a lot since D.C.—the Southwest mostly."

"Are you going back there when you leave?"

"Probably not."

Charlotte clomped up the aluminum steps of the bleachers, waving and saying hello to everyone. She took a seat at the top, and Joe sat down at her side. She turned to see him waiting for her next question.

Charlotte wished he'd put her out of her misery and leave *now*. Leave the Little League field, leave town, leave her alone. But he continued to look at her with those intensely dark eyes touched with sadness.

"So have you always been a writer?" The question was the best she could do.

"No. I was just out of the army when we—" Joe paused, glanced around, then shot her a penetrating glance. "The day we met."

She looked away. Having this man sit next to her at her kid's ball game was beyond surreal—it was painfully strange. How was she supposed to engage in small talk with someone she'd envisioned naked and aroused for thirteen straight years?

She didn't even have to look at him to picture every detail of his clothing. She knew perfectly well what he was wearing tonight—nicely fitted khaki hiking shorts, black leather sandals, and a black T-shirt that worked to accentuate his dark hair and eyes. He was wearing that gleaming little gold hoop in his left ear. "So what did you do after the army?"

He cleared his throat. "I worked in the security industry mostly. Didn't start writing until recently."

She turned toward him and looked down at his hands. They were a rich bronze, lean and big, yet they cradled the paper cup gingerly. She wondered why he hadn't even taken a sip of his drink. She remembered what those hands felt like on her breasts.

She shuddered.

"Chilly?"

"Nope. So, LoriSue says you write mysteries."

"I try."

"Are you famous? Should I recognize your name?"

"I wish."

His leg brushed up against hers. The contact of the bristly dark hairs against her smooth skin was excruciating. She jerked her knee away.

His legs were muscular and long and the same smooth, rich hue as the rest of him. Mills had to be an Anglicized version of some name the clerks at Ellis Island couldn't pronounce, because this man was obviously something exotic.

"Did you grow up around here, Joe?"

"Nope. I grew up in Baltimore. Little Italy."

"You're Italian?"

She loved how his lips spread wide, pushing out the black goatee like bat wings, revealing the smile she'd first seen in a rearview mirror so long ago.

That perfect smile had hypnotized her then. The imperfect one made her perspire now.

"My father was Italian and my mother was Greek. A pretty lethal combination. And you?"

Charlotte laughed. She'd been right about the name change. "Nothing anywhere near as interesting, sorry to say. I'm from solid Southern Baptist stock. A little bit of Scottish and English somewhere in the distant past. Boring."

"Not hardly, dumplin'."

She tried not to smile.

"So tell me, Charlotte." Joe's words came out in a deep whisper that she heard loud and clear despite the noise of the crowd. "Why did you do it? And what did you mean when you said that after me, nothing else has ever been good enough?"

It seemed she'd been neglecting her kid, because Hank had apparently just hit a homer and was rounding the bases and everyone was cheering but her own mother!

Charlotte was being corrupted by the presence of Joe Mills. She'd thrown herself at him, dressed up for him, and now she was ignoring her children for him. She needed to get this over with so she could concentrate on her life again.

"I want you, Joe."

Slowly, he turned to her. Both his black eyebrows were hovering way up on his forehead as he stared.

"I need it. Bad." She met his stare straight on. "I need you one more time before you leave. One more time before I die."

There it was. If she hadn't proved it to herself before, it was obvious now. She was a slut. Half of her was relieved, and that part wanted to jump in his lap and kiss him so hard she broke all the rest of his teeth. The other half hoped her words would shock him, make him sputter and hem and haw and get up and leave her sitting there by herself the way she should be, a widow and a responsible mother.

But Joe only laughed, and Charlotte was shocked by the contagious quality of the sound. She remembered that laugh. He'd laughed like that with her so long ago, when he was inside her and his hands were all over her and they were tumbling around on the ground and she was praying and crying and giggling all at the same time because of the shocking intensity of the pleasure. His laughter was the sound of pleasure to her still.

She held her breath. She looked around the bleachers. She tried not to pay attention to how close he was and how good he smelled, because she felt another psychotic break coming on.

"Hey! Thanks for my pop, Mr. Mills!"

Matt squeezed his body between them and plopped

down onto the bench, smiling at Charlotte in triumph as he took a big gulp of the forbidden beverage.

Joe's body vibrated from his scalp to his instep. The woman sitting next to him was Eve herself. And the idea of possessing her one last time before he left was as tempting as it was foolish. Who was he kidding? Did he really think he could get another sample of sweet Charlotte and then turn around and leave?

Hell no.

And he didn't know which was worse—being hunted down by a madman or facing life without this woman.

He listened to Charlotte lecture Matt on the evils of sweetened carbonated drinks while he enjoyed a leisurely look at everything she'd just offered him. God. Charlotte Tasker was all woman.

She was still trim and petite but no longer a girl. She'd filled out, softened, and his fingers itched to touch her. Her hair was still shiny and her face full. There were fine lines at the corners of that delectable little pink mouth and crow's-feet fanning out from those sultry gray eyes, but those were just signs that she'd smiled and laughed a lot over the years. Joe found comfort in that and said a silent thank-you to Kurt Tasker, because he'd clearly been good to her.

Matt elbowed Joe and rolled his eyes as Charlotte finished her scolding. Poor kid. Not only had he endured a tongue-lashing from his mother, but he'd had to admit to Joe that he'd spied on him. It had all been innocent enough—watching him stack boxes and retrieve LoriSue's gift baskets—but after all this he bet Matt would never scam for a soda or turn a pair of binoculars Joe's way again.

Hank's team won the game by a score of 16–4, and the

teams lined up at the plate to repeat the phrase "good game" dozens of times and shake hands. Parents began to stand, stretch, and gather their belongings.

"Did you drive your Mustang to the game, Mr. Mills?"

"Sure did. It's the only car I got, kid."

"Can I ride home with you?"

"That's probably not a good idea." Charlotte was up off the bench in a flash, grabbing Matt's hand and pushing him past Joe into the aisle. "Good-bye, Joe. Have a nice evening. And good luck with your move."

With a shrug from Matt, they were assimilated into the throng and gone. Joe stayed in the bleachers for a while, watching parents hug their children and compliment them on their singles and catches. He watched the families walk to the parking lot.

He sat perfectly still, elbows on knees and hands clasped in front of him. Charlotte's abrupt departure stung quite a bit, he had to admit. But it was obvious that she wanted to keep her kids out of this. She was right, of course, and suddenly Joe couldn't recall why he'd come here in the first place. He had no business here. This was not his life and it never would be. Steve and Reba Simmons had led this life once, and they'd never again be watching Daniel play a Little League game, would they?

Joe felt heavy with exhaustion and pulled himself to his feet, joining the last few stragglers as they made their way to the cars. A man in a Volvo station wagon motioned for him to cross the county road while three kids in ball caps stared at him from the backseat.

As Joe opened the car door, he had to laugh at himself. A month ago, he'd been ready to make the biggest bust of his career. He'd been inches from nailing Miguel Guzman as he personally handed over fifty kilos of cocaine in exchange for $5 million in cash.

Tonight, he was a guy with a price on his head, a guy

so lonely that he hung out at Little League games for kicks. A guy who was going crazy with desire for the one woman fate continued to deny him.

Joe had a feeling that no matter what Roger said, if he didn't leave this town right now—tonight—he'd soon be telling fate to fuck off and die.

# Chapter Twelve

LoriSue leaned up against the cupboards and munched on a raw mushroom. "I have some news. Now don't both you go fainting on me or anything, but I've decided to do some volunteer work for the Little League."

Charlotte glanced up from the marinade she was whisking. "Really? More than just your night at the snack bar?"

"Yep. I've volunteered to redesign their Web site."

"I didn't know you had experience with that, LoriSue," Bonnie said from her seat at the kitchen table.

"I just finished revamping the Sell-More site—and it looks fabulous, if I do say so myself—so I figured the Little League's would be a snap. I'm going to take new photos and everything!"

"Wow. That's nice of you." Charlotte dropped hunks of tofu into the marinade, covered the glass bowl with plastic wrap, and checked the clock. She had one hour and eight minutes to feed the kids and start the evening rush. As she rinsed bok choy, she ticked off the sequence of events in her head. She'd run Hank to ballet class, then take Matt to his game and make a quick stop at Kroger's on the way back to town. Then she'd drop off the groceries at home, throw in a load of laundry, pack tomorrow's lunches, and pick up Hank. They could both watch the end of Matt's game.

She made a mental note to bring a change of clothes for Hank, who refused to wear her ballet leotard at the ballpark. She said it made her look like a Miss Priss.

Charlotte lifted the lid from the simmering brown rice, fluffed it with a fork, and replayed for the thousandth time every word she'd exchanged with Joe yesterday, every shared glance. She was dying here. She'd made it painfully clear what she wanted. All he had to do was come and get it. But she hadn't heard from him today. This was torture.

". . . a damned sexy man, don't you think?"

LoriSue's words jarred Charlotte from her thoughts. She put the lid back on the pot and cheerfully turned toward Bonnie and LoriSue, to find them staring at her expectantly.

"Did I miss something?" Charlotte laughed as she wiped her hands on a kitchen towel.

"I asked if you didn't agree that Joe Mills was sexy."

At the sound of his name, Charlotte felt a flash of heat deep in her abdomen that began to percolate into her limbs. She supposed that answered *that* question. "Sure." She tried to sound nonchalant. "He's handsome enough."

Bonnie coughed politely.

Then LoriSue crossed her arms under her unnaturally perky breasts and made a soft humming sound. "Well, Charlotte, I saw him walk over to the major field with you yesterday and sit down right next to you in the stands. What did you two talk about?"

Charlotte busied herself with getting out the cutting board and swirling canola oil around in the wok. "We chatted about this and that. Nothing in particular. Would you like to stay for dinner, LoriSue?"

"No, thanks. And I'm taking Justin out tonight, so he won't be staying, either, believe it or not. We're going for Italian and then we're looking at a house."

"A house?" Bonnie nearly shouted. "You're moving?"

"Yep. It's an end-unit three-bedroom, two-bath condo over at The Lakes. Fabulous. Skylights. Sunken living room. Hot tub. Landscaping included. Just got listed yesterday—perfect for me and Justin."

"Does Justin know about this?" Bonnie asked.

LoriSue nodded.

"And how is he with it?"

"Fine." She grabbed another mushroom. "Well, a little confused, I suppose, but I've told him I'm going ahead with the divorce. He understands. He's a good kid. He's—"

The deep saw of Hoover's bark made all three women crane their necks out the kitchen window.

"Oh, my God! He's *here*!" LoriSue teetered her way across the kitchen floor in her heels and whipped open the screen door to a startled Joe.

He stood wide-eyed on the back patio, holding what looked like a cardboard box full of weeds.

Charlotte let out a startled laugh and Joe looked past LoriSue's blond head to offer her a shy grin. He held up the box so she could see its contents—honeysuckle vines.

"Pardon me." Joe looked somewhat uncomfortable as the three kids pressed up against his back and the women gathered around him in the doorway. Hoover stopped barking just long enough to sniff the crotch of Joe's jeans.

"He won't smell your butt if you give him something to eat," Hank said.

"Ice-cream cones are his favorite," Matt added.

"Yeah, you could rob this place blind if you gave him an ice-cream cone," Justin said.

"Come here, Hoov." Charlotte grabbed the dog by his

collar and hauled him inside, looking up at Joe in apology. Her heart skipped a beat the instant she saw those eyes—the same eyes that had haunted her soul for as long as she could remember were now literally on her doorstep. Her dream man was one step from being inside her house. He was one step away from forever blending fantasy with reality, and it shook her to the core.

"Sorry about the dog," she mumbled, hoping no one could see that she was rapidly unraveling in Joe's presence.

"Come on in!" LoriSue stepped aside and motioned Joe into the family room with a dramatic sweep of her red-nailed hand. "We were just talking about you!"

"I . . . uh . . ." Joe looked from Charlotte to the box of dirt and vines, then back to Charlotte again. "I just wanted to tell you I was replacing the honeysuckle I damaged. Would you prefer that I plant these by the shed or would you like them somewhere else?"

Charlotte made brief eye contact with Bonnie, and in her friend's face she saw the wise advice to remain calm. It made her damn mad that Joe had this effect on her and that it was obvious to others. She took a deep breath and attempted to sound gracious, which was hard to do while wrestling with ninety pounds of dog.

"That's very kind of you, Joe. Right by the other bush would be great."

With a quick nod, he backed away from the door, and the kids adjusted their positions just enough to allow him to make a quarter turn.

"I'll help you dig," Matt said.

"Can we toss after?" Hank asked.

"Kids!" Charlotte transferred Hoover's control to Bonnie and stood up straight. "Give Mr. Mills some room to breathe, please. We have to eat and get ready for activities, anyway."

The three kids produced openmouthed stares of disbelief.

"But, Mama!" Hank wailed.

"Figures," Matt said.

"What's for supper?" Justin asked.

"You won't like it," Matt assured him, rolling his eyes in disgust. "Stir-fried toe fungus again, with those alien vegetables."

"Tofu makes me barf," Hank said.

Joe glanced up at Charlotte with raised eyebrows and a crooked grin. "Sounds delish. Well, good afternoon, ladies."

Charlotte watched him take the long walk across her yard, cardboard box propped on a slim hip, the kids trailing behind him chattering nonstop, and noted once again how smoothly Joe Mills moved. She recalled the way he'd slipped down from his Jeep so long ago, giving her the first glimpse of his long, strong legs. She remembered seeing him glide and sway at his punching bag his first night in Minton. And she imagined that his footfall would be silent on her bedroom carpet—he could easily sneak up on her. Like a ghost. Or a predatory cat. The first few lines of a poem floated into her head:

*He comes for me in the night*
*To suck the marrow from my bones*
*And the common sense from my head . . .*

"That man is so unbelievably hot." LoriSue peered through the screen as she whispered. "I'm gonna get me some of that if it's the last thing I ever do."

Bonnie let go of Hoover, who flung himself at the doors, doubling his barking efforts. The dog meant well, but Charlotte knew that it was too late to protect her from Joe. The damage had been done.

"I'm going to tell her." Bonnie removed the bifocals from the bridge of her nose and let them dangle on their chain against her cotton nightgown.

"Tell her what?" Ned clicked off the TV remote and the lamp. "That ole Ned Preston thinks her neighbor could be anything from a CIA agent to a retired mall security guard? What's that going to accomplish?"

"I'm just worried about her."

"I know. Any new developments?"

"Well, today he planted honeysuckle to replace what he hacked to pieces."

Ned's laughter boomed through the bedroom. "That weed? It would've grown back on its own. I must have scared the shit out of him." He continued to chuckle as he made himself comfortable under the covers.

"I want you to find out who he is, Ned."

Ned sighed, propping the pillows behind his head. "How am I going to do that? I'm just a retired county police chief. Besides, it could be nothing. Maybe he's just who he says he is. Maybe he's a former cop who started writing books. It happens all the time."

"I don't know about that."

"You been to the bookstore lately, hon? Anybody can write a book. You don't necessarily have to have anything earth-shattering to say or any talent to say it."

"I guess."

"But I could try to get his fingerprints if you want."

Bonnie reached over her husband's body and turned the lamp back on. "You could do that?"

"I could lift his prints off something and run them and see what comes up."

"Are all cops fingerprinted?"

Ned frowned. "Most law enforcement officers will show

up on AFIS—the FBI's fingerprint database. I've heard some feds won't, if they do national security stuff, but most everybody else will. Your average beat cop should be there—not that Joe strikes me as a particularly average kind of guy."

Bonnie put a soft kiss on her husband's cheek and turned over on her side. "I've noticed that, too," she whispered.

Joe bolted from a deep sleep, his bare chest covered in a slick sheen of sweat, his hands shaking.

He couldn't have been out long. His wristwatch showed it was midnight, and only an hour before, he'd been staring at the ceiling, thinking about how he could find a way to get to know Charlotte while keeping her safe at the same time. That meant he'd fallen prey to the nightmare the instant he went into REM sleep, his subconscious answering him with the vision of Charlotte and her children covered in blood, lying right next to Steve in the Denny's parking lot.

He jumped from the bed and nearly ran into his office. At least the feel of his chair beneath him and the familiar tap of the keyboard under his fingers provided some comfort and helped to steady his breathing.

He pulled up the Tasker file, not sure what he was looking for. He'd gone over the details so many times he practically had them memorized. But he found himself reading Kurt's obit once again, drawn to the man he saw in the photo, feeling a link to him, asking him to spill his secrets.

He supposed he wanted Kurt to tell him everything about Charlotte, everything he'd never have a chance to discover for himself. What did she wear to bed? What was her all-time favorite movie? Her favorite music group? How did she take her coffee?

Joe slumped down into the chair and let his head fall

back. He wondered—did Charlotte come for her husband the way she'd come for him? Did she cry because it was so intense? Did she laugh with joy? Did she tremble at Kurt Tasker's touch the way she had at his own?

Most of all, Joe wanted to know this: How did it feel to be the man Charlotte loved?

He straightened again, closed the file, and sat in the pitch-dark, staring absently out the windows that faced Charlotte's house. He never did get those drapes. What was the point? He wasn't staying, didn't know where he was going, and didn't really give a damn.

It felt strange to be so detached from his own future. But in his mind, each day was simply another step closer to Guzman's trial. It remained to be seen how many twists and turns the case would take along the pipeline of the federal court system, but once the trial was over, whenever that might be, he saw nothing but a blank.

It was as if he didn't dare plan anything that far in the future. He just needed to stay alive long enough to testify. That's the only thing that mattered.

Sitting there in that house, in that town, so close to Charlotte, it was tempting to believe he was safe, at least temporarily. But this was a pretend life he was leading, light-years from reality, and he would be a fool to relax. He needed to remember that his biggest danger wasn't the delivery of LoriSue gift baskets. It was Miguel Guzman. It would always be Guzman.

Joe propped his feet on the desk, still looking out the windows, and took a deep breath. The faint scent of honeysuckle hit his nostrils and he grinned to himself, recalling how he'd learned the hard way that garden centers didn't actually *sell* honeysuckle. Instead, he was sent to a farmer's place down the road, where the guy laughed when he asked to buy some, gave him a shovel, and said, "Have at it, son."

At least he'd be leaving Minton with a clear conscience.

Joe thought he saw a figure pass by a second-story window of Charlotte's home and wondered what she was doing up so late. He'd grown accustomed to her daily schedule and knew that she was up at 6:00 in the morning and out the door with the kids by 7:30. She should get more rest.

The figure passed again, and Joe was up out of the office chair and standing next to the window, considering the layout of the Tasker home. That was definitely Charlotte who walked by—he saw a flash of her pale legs. But what room was that? Was she in her bedroom? Or with one of the kids? Joe found himself back at the desk, pulling his binoculars out from the drawer, suddenly determined to figure out where Charlotte was and exactly what she was doing up so late.

He trained the lenses onto the three identical windows. One was covered completely by a white shade. On the other two, the shade was half-drawn, leaving the bottom portion of the window exposed. He dropped to his knees and looked straight into what he could now tell was her bedroom.

Charlotte was propped up on a mound of pillows in a big four-poster bed, wearing what looked like a pair of white silk shorts–pajama bottoms and a little white tank top. She had a book opened in her lap and was writing in it. Her diary maybe. He watched her scrunch up that pretty pink mouth in concentration and absently push a slippery strand of hair behind her ear.

She suddenly stopped writing, laid her head back against the pillows, and closed her eyes—then quickly picked up the pen once more. Her hand raced over the page as her toes tapped in impatience. He was fascinated by the way she glowed in the lamplight—all pinks and peaches and oranges—against white sheets. She looked luminous. She looked beautiful.

She looked so far away.

Joe nearly staggered backward at what happened next. He watched, openmouthed, as Charlotte put the book aside and slowly raised her hands to her breasts. He watched her scootch back against the pillows, let her head fall to the side, and brush her fingers in delicate little circles around her nipples. She gazed out the window into the darkness, her eyes glassy and unfocused.

He'd never seen a woman do this before. Up until tonight, he'd been fairly certain it happened only in porno movies. He'd apparently been wrong.

Joe's hands trembled enough that he had to steady himself against the window frame, anchoring an elbow into the molding. He took a deep breath and adjusted the focus. The image he saw was crisp, painfully erotic, and, his conscience told him, nothing he had any right to witness.

But at that moment, Charlotte arched her back and pushed her T-shirt-covered breasts into her hands. She pinched her own nipples. Then she let one hand slide down her breastbone, into the hollow between her ribs, down her belly, and into the elastic of the silk pajama bottoms.

Joe watched her mouth open in shock from the touch of her own fingers. He watched her arch further, her hips coming up off the bed, her legs falling open to accommodate the rhythm of her hand. Lust poured over him like a flood of hot lava, and Joe felt his own body moving to the sensuous tempo she set, the slight push of his hips in concert with the rock of hers.

His hips. Her hips. Her hand. His hand. It was blurring together in his mind and suddenly it was as if he were with her, right there in her bed with her, her skin and breath hot against him.

In a flurry of movement, Charlotte peeled off the pajama bottoms and flung her tank top to the floor. Joe stared—enraptured—as her lithe body twisted to the side. With one graceful arm she tilted back the base of the lamp and took something from underneath. It was a key, and she was unlocking the drawer to the nightstand, and Joe felt his pulse escalate. He felt clammy and shaky.

He needed to sit down, but there was nowhere to sit that would afford him this view, so he stayed ramrod straight on his knees, not daring to breathe, as the woman of his fantasies removed a flesh-colored vibrator from its storage sleeve and began to pleasure herself.

She first took the tip of the vibrator and ran it over the little raspberry peaks of her breasts. She licked her lips.

Joe licked his.

Then she dragged the vibrator down the center of her body, making a sudden detour around her left hip, across her upper thighs and small mound, then to her right hip. She was teasing herself, prolonging the buildup, pretending she didn't know exactly what she had in mind.

Joe couldn't stand the suspense.

"Do it, Charlotte." The anguish he heard in his own whisper startled him. He sounded desperate.

He was desperate.

Then Charlotte turned a little knob at the base of the vibrator and pointed it directly at a spot Joe remembered well. She'd been so slick and swollen that day—so excited and ready for him. He recalled in detail the feel of his fingers as they danced over the hard little kernel nestled in the split of her body. He remembered in detail how her eyelids drooped, heavy with pleasure, then snapped wide open in surprise.

He laughed out loud at the absurdity! This was ludicrous! She was there and he was here and what a perfectly good waste of two consenting adults! He was going to march right across the drive and give her the real thing. He wanted it. She wanted it. Hell, she'd come right out and *asked* for it!

And it was impossible.

Joe groaned, helpless with longing and indecision, and watched Charlotte slowly, so slowly, spread her legs and insert the tip of the vibrator inside her body. He swallowed hard. He groaned again. And he moved his hips in concert with the cadence of her wrist.

Charlotte obviously knew what worked for her. He watched her bring her free hand back to rub that sweet spot while she continued to plunge in and out, and Joe's heart was racing and his eyes bugged out as Charlotte brought herself to a jerking, rigid climax, her mouth wide open in what he figured was probably a soundless scream that wouldn't wake the kids.

The scream in his own head was primal and neverending, and he felt drained and weak as she pulled the vibrator out and flipped over on her stomach to recover. He watched her stretch luxuriously, then reach up to the bedside table for what he thought might be a drink but . . .

What the hell? It looked like one of those aerosol cans of snack cheese! And she was squirting the bright orange glop directly into her mouth!

Joe laughed again. He laughed at Charlotte for being such a perfect combination of sweet soccer mom and sexual dynamo. He laughed at her for eating that disgusting cheese stuff in secret while she made her kids eat tofu. He looked down at his wet boxers and laughed at himself and the ridiculousness of the whole situation.

Maybe it was time to rethink this. Maybe he'd exaggerated the risk in his head. He was in Minton, Ohio, for God's sake! Miguel Guzman would never find him here! What was he thinking?

Maybe Roger was right. Maybe he needed to stay right

where the Administration had decided he'd be safe. They'd done a risk assessment before they brought him here. They knew what they were doing. Maybe he needed to stay in Minton and disappear into life as Joe Mills, an ordinary man who was entitled to an ordinary life, albeit with an extraordinary woman.

He got another glimpse of Charlotte just as she turned off her light. Right then, he knew the choice had been made in his heart long ago. He'd walked away from this woman once and regretted it with his whole being.

He'd be damned if he'd do it again.

# Chapter Thirteen

"You need to get laid, not get involved."

"Is that right, boss?"

Joe paced along the windows near his desk, the binoculars still trained on the little group assembled in Charlotte's backyard. Watching Ned try to put together that tent under the watchful eyes of Hank, Matt, and Justin was nearly as excruciating as the conversation he was having with Roger.

"You're in no position to cozy up to anyone, Joe—especially somebody like her. Couldn't you find a woman a bit more . . . I don't know . . . disposable?"

*"Disposable?"*

"Yeah," Roger said. "Your neighbor lady is like a hot home-cooked meal when you really ought to be going for drive-thru."

Joe thanked Roger for his observation and promptly told him it was his fault. "I told you to get me out of here. This is why."

"And I told you to stay away from the soccer moms."

"She's the only soccer mom in the world who could have gotten my attention."

"Then take your attention back."

"I can't. I don't want to."

"Are you telling me you've changed your mind? You want to stay in Minton now?"

Joe sighed and closed his eyes and all he saw was Charlotte's face the way it appeared that night at the Little League field, when she looked up at him and said, "I want you, Joe." She'd looked completely vulnerable. Completely beautiful.

And now he was completely smitten.

He had to trust that there was a reason for his being there, even if he didn't see it. He had to trust his instincts—they'd kept him alive so far—and every fiber in his body told him to get to know Charlotte. To at least give it a try.

"I do want to stay. Can we hang on to the house?"

"It's yours for as long as you need it, but, Joe"— Roger's voice had become quite serious—"I'm not saying you don't have a right to some happiness, because God knows you do. Just stay sharp, okay? We've got your back, but you've got to do your part."

It was solid advice, and Joe appreciated it. "Roger that."

Two minutes later, Joe found himself standing on the property line near the shed, eavesdropping. He wasn't exactly hiding, but he wasn't jumping around waving his arms, either.

He watched Bonnie squint at the assembly instructions in her hand. "It says you need to insert Pole A through Sleeve A, honey."

"Oh, yeah?" Ned peered up from his bent position and shook his balding head in disgust. "I'd like to tell the guy who designed this tent exactly where he can insert Pole A, Pole B, and all the other poles."

"Ned, please. The kids."

"Mom will be home in a few minutes," Matt said,

scanning the heap of aluminum poles on the grass. "She's good at stuff like this."

"Excellent idea." Ned stood up and rubbed his lower back. That's when he noticed Joe.

"Hey, everyone." Joe walked toward the group and extended a hand toward Bonnie. "We haven't been officially introduced. I'm Joe Mills." He took her hand in his and watched a reluctant smile enter her pale blue eyes.

"Hello, Joe. I'm Bonnie Preston." She nodded toward Ned. "I understand you two have met."

"Sure have."

Joe studied the collapsed fabric and the scattered poles. "Looks like you got a six-man tent here," he said to Matt. "These can be a real bear to put together. Mind if I take a shot at it?"

Matt's face lit up. "Cool!"

"Ned, you want to give me a hand?"

Within ten minutes, the tent stood erect, its sides pulled taut and even. The kids were experimenting with the zippered screen doorway as Ned and Joe secured the rain fly over the entire structure.

"The new technology threw me," Ned said. "Looks like you've put up a few tents in your time."

"Some." Joe gave him a friendly smile. "Not for a while, though."

Ned nodded. "Army, was it?"

"Yes, sir. You?"

"Marines."

The men smiled at each other. That's when Joe heard the arrival of Charlotte's minivan in the drive. He watched her get out of the driver's side and pause a moment to stare at the group in the yard. Then she opened the trunk and walked toward them, two bags of groceries in her arms and a confused frown on her face.

Joe knew the frown was for him.

"Mama! Mama! Joe fixed the tent!" Hank ran to her and peeked inside the grocery sacks. Then she said in a serious voice, "He looked really stable while he was doing it, too. Infinity stable, Mama."

Charlotte glanced up at Joe and frowned again. Based on how the evening at the ball park had ended, he figured she was about to thank him politely and make it clear she didn't want him around her kids. So he took the bags from her arms.

"I'll get these for you, Charlotte."

"No. Really. I've got them."

She actually tried to pry the bags from his hands—that's how hard she was fighting this. He had to admire her. She had willpower. She had determination. But she had met her match in Joe Bellacera. She just didn't know it yet.

"Let the man carry in your groceries, Charlotte." Ned was picking up little pieces of packaging trash from the ground around the tent. "It won't kill you."

Joe felt a rush of triumph when Charlotte sighed and headed toward the house. He followed right behind, glad that the kids were still fascinated with the tent's screen doors and windows and that the Prestons had decided to keep them company.

"Hosting a campout tonight?"

He saw the back of Charlotte's ponytail bob up and down as she nodded. "Six boys."

"What's the occasion?" he asked, following her across the back patio.

"Just something Matt likes to do every year before school's out."

She reached for the door handle and stopped—Hoover waited on the other side of the double doors, growling, teeth exposed.

"You dumb thing." Charlotte spun on her heels and marched over to Joe. She rooted through the grocery bags until she found the pack of NaturPride organic soy protein hot dogs. Sticks of toe fungus, as Matt would say. It made Joe smile.

Charlotte pulled one gray-tinted fake wiener from the pack and held it up. "Give this to Hoover when you walk in. You'll be friends for life."

She took one of the bags from Joe and led the way inside. He held the hot dog in front of his knees, pleasantly surprised that the dog took it without chomping off his left arm, then let him pass without further ado.

"Strange name for a dog," he said, putting his foot on the carpet runner just inside the double doors. "As in J. Edgar Hoover, I take it?"

Charlotte plunked the bag down on the counter, then reached her arms out for the sack he held. She laughed, and at that instant Joe felt suspended in time. He gazed at her face—her flashing gray eyes, her soft pink lips, her full cheeks. She was so beautiful. He remembered the sight of her arching her back in ecstasy last night and he could barely breathe.

"The FBI guy? No way. He's named after the vacuum cleaner." She pulled items from the bags and began a complicated series of moves that included drawer opening, drawer closing, shelf stacking, and refrigerator placement that unfolded like a choreographed dance. She floated around her kitchen, ponytail flying, hands gesturing, words coming out. He was in awe. He'd never seen a human being move with such grace and efficiency.

"His name was supposed to be Oscar—that's what the kids decided. But the day we got him I spilled a whole box of Cheerios on the floor, and before I could get the broom he'd sucked them all up." She paused a moment and put her hands on her hips, laughing. "I remember we joked that we should go ahead and sell the vacuum, and Kurt said—"

Charlotte stopped in midsentence. She looked at Joe and shook her head, all the happiness already gone from her face. She folded the grocery sacks and stuck them in the pantry with grim competence. The dance was over, apparently.

She must have loved Kurt Tasker something fierce.

"You're a good mom, Charlotte."

She braced her hands on the kitchen sink, her back toward him. Maybe it was for the best. Maybe it would be easier for him to talk to her if they weren't looking at each other.

"I'm so very sorry that your husband died. I've heard wonderful things about him, and I'm sorry for your family's loss."

She said nothing, but he watched her lower her chin toward her chest. She locked her elbows as if to keep from falling.

"Charlotte, I know what it's like to lose someone you love. I'm right next door if you need me."

He watched her shift her weight to one leg and wanted desperately to touch her, drowning in the confusing mess of his own emotions. What did he just offer this woman? And was it something he could even give her? Did that make him a liar? A player? Was this really only about sex?

She stayed silent and kept her back to him. Joe let his eyes travel from her slender shoulders, down her straight back, to that luscious little behind of hers and to those smooth, pale legs that ended in a pair of simple soccer-mom sandals.

Last night, he'd watched this soccer mom catch fire at her own hand. He saw her peach skin incandescent against the stark white sheet. He saw such female magnificence in such a small package that it made him insane, crazy with desire.

Sure it was about sex. But it was also about her. It was about this sweet, funny, good woman who stood just an arm's length away, a woman with so much to give and no man to give it to. They both knew she was supposed to be giving it to him.

At that moment, a plan coalesced in Joe's mind. He would tell her he wanted her. That he planned to stay. He wanted to get to know her kids. Then he'd walk her through this, step-by-step, if he had to. But it was definitely time to get this party started.

"Say something, Charlotte. I can't see you and I can't tell if you're crying or what."

She laughed a little and turned her head so that she was looking over her shoulder. Her eyes were red and her cheeks blotchy, but she looked prettier than ever to him.

"The girl you met that day—that wasn't the real me."

She faced away again and continued.

"I was on my way to pick up Kurt from the airport. I knew he was going to propose to me. I planned to say yes."

Joe watched her pull in a huge breath and steady herself to continue. He took two steps closer to her, in case she collapsed.

"I don't know how to say this except to just blurt it out, so here goes. Yes, you were my first, Joe, and the only other man in my whole life except Kurt. I think I panicked that day." She slipped down onto her elbows and rested her forehead in her hands.

Joe stepped closer.

"I knew that Kurt was very shy about sex, but despite that, I would be faithful to my husband. And I remember driving along and thinking, *This is my last chance to see what I'll be missing.* And whaddya know?" Charlotte shook her head back and forth in her hands and laughed. "Joe Mills appears! Right on my bumper!"

Joe averted his eyes from the sweet little bumper now directly in his line of vision. Charlotte laughed again, raised her head, and stared out the kitchen window.

She sighed. "Kurt and I came from very religious families, and sex was never discussed except in the context of sin, you know, something to resist, rise above, then perform as your wifely duty. Anyway, it was really important to Kurt that I was a virgin, so I let him assume that I continued to be one, even after that day with you."

Charlotte spun around to face him, her eyes widening in surprise at how close he was. "I lied to him, Joe. It was a secret I kept from him our whole marriage. But that wasn't even the worst part."

Joe waited in silence, not sure if it was his turn to talk yet.

"The worst part is I never once regretted what you and I did. I kept thinking that at least I *knew*—I knew what it was like to have incredible sex. I knew what it felt like to be with a man who wasn't shy, didn't hold back." Charlotte paused and looked thoughtfully at Joe. "You showed me what was possible. You made me feel the way I always suspected I could feel."

He waited, and her silence gave him the go-ahead to ask. "And what way is that?"

Charlotte gazed up at him with those luscious gray eyes, then served up a smile that would have incinerated a weaker man.

"For the first and only time in my life, I felt like a sex goddess."

It was time to rock-'n'-roll.

Joe stepped forward. He pressed his body against hers and backed her into the dishwasher. She let out a little gasp. He cupped a hand behind her head and looked down into her upturned face.

"I'm staying."

Her eyes flew wide. "What?"

"You're not getting away this time."

"Joe—"

"Listen up, Charlotte. I've decided to stay. I let you go once. I won't do it again. I want you, so you'd better get used to it."

He could feel her heart pound through her ribs, skin, muscle, and both of their shirts. She was breathing fast, too.

"Get used to what, exactly?" she whispered.

"This."

Joe yanked her head forward and slammed his mouth down on hers. Charlotte was his. She had *always* been his. And if he needed any further proof, it was right there in the way she threw herself into the kiss.

Instantly she was hotter than hell and out of control. Zero to ninety in three seconds, that was the Charlotte he remembered, and God, she made him such a happy man.

She was grabbing his shoulders and clawing at him, pulling him closer. Then she ran the instep of her sandaled foot up and down his leg while she opened her mouth to his hungry attack. Then she dropped a hand to his ass and squeezed.

Joe picked her up and spun her around and plopped her right down on the chopping block so he could thoroughly ravage her. With his mouth hermetically sealed over her own, he pushed his hands inside her T-shirt and ran his palms over the hot, soft flesh of her abdomen, back, and sides. He insinuated himself between her spread legs. Her silky little bra offered little resistance when he reached through the bottom to touch her nipples.

He pinched.

She moaned.

He kissed her harder.

She squeezed his hips with her thighs.

He cupped the weight of her breasts.

She ran her hands down his back and tipped her head to the side to grant him complete access.

Then she said something Joe couldn't quite understand.

"Umm nmmm uh sssssltch" was what it sounded like, though he couldn't be sure, because Charlotte hadn't stopped kissing him. He tried to pull away so she could speak, but she grabbed him by the shoulders and continued to kiss.

"Umm nmmm uh sssltch!" she said again, only louder this time.

Joe managed to pry his lips from hers and push her away. Her eyes were half-closed and her face was flushed and her lips swollen.

"Say again?"

"I am not a slut. I just thought I'd better let you know."

Joe didn't laugh. It took everything in him, but he managed not to laugh. It was a damn good thing, too, because Charlotte was dead serious.

Her body hummed with fear and exhilaration as she accepted the news that Joe Mills—everything dangerous and exciting and wild she'd ever known—was staying!

Doubt hit her hard and fast. What did this man expect? What if she couldn't live up to his expectations?

Sheer panic came next. *Where were the kids?*

She looked past Joe's bemused expression and over one of his perfect broad shoulders to see that everyone was still in the backyard, a safe distance from the house. She must be insane, but immediately she was back to figuring out how she could keep kissing him until the last possible second. But first, she had to be certain he understood.

"That night in the drive, Joe, when I . . . uhm . . . touched you?"

"I think I recall that."

"I don't know what came over me. Or today, for that matter. I've not been myself lately. I told you, I'm not that girl from thirteen years ago. I never was."

"Yes, you told me." He was obviously trying not to smile.

"You don't seem convinced, Joe."

"That's because I'm not, and I don't think you are, either." His smile broke free.

"I'm glad I amuse you."

He stroked her cheek with such a gentle touch that she trembled. "I want to know everything about you. Every little thing."

"There's nothing to know. I'm pretty dull."

"That's just an act, Charlotte. I know better."

"I may not be what you're looking for. That's all I'm saying."

Joe leaned in close to drop sweet little kisses all over her temples and cheeks and chin and throat. She shivered.

"As it happens . . ." He nibbled at her clavicle. ". . . I've been in the market for a sex goddess for about thirteen years now."

"Oh God."

"In fact, you're exactly what I've been looking for." He sucked on the hollow of her throat.

"I am?"

His tongue flicked under her jaw to her left earlobe. "Yep. I've been looking for this one particular hot little redhead in a convertible Miata. She gave me her virginity. Ring any bells?"

"Lots of 'em."

She jolted at the feel of Joe pressing his erection against the vee of her thighs. "So it's okay with you if I stay?"

"Yes."

Joe's black eyes drilled her. "Tell me how much you want me to stay."

She could barely get the breath to say what he wanted to hear. "I need you to stay, Joe. More than anything in the world."

"Now show me."

She couldn't help it. Only Joe did this to her. Only Joe. So she threw her arms around his neck and pressed her lips to his and let it all flow out of her—more than a decade of pent-up need for this man found its way into that one kiss. So much need that it made her dizzy.

Joe didn't seem to mind.

His hands felt so damn good all over her breasts and then he pinched harder, kissed her harder, and pushed aside the fruit bowl, climbed up on the chopping block, and pushed her down on her back.

That's when Hoover started barking.

LoriSue threw open the family room door and tried to shoo away Charlotte's big doofus dog with a three-inch spike heel. She tossed him the after-dinner mint she'd just dug out of the bottom of her purse, which seemed to do the trick.

Ugh. She now had a long trail of drool on her panty hose.

She set Justin's sleeping bag and backpack on the couch and looked around.

"Everybody decent?" She heard a ruckus in the kitchen and turned toward the noise.

*Well, damn.*

Charlotte and Joe had apparently been going at it on the butcher block! And now they were scrambling down and smoothing out their clothes and looking at her with the most guilt-ridden expressions she'd ever seen on two adults.

As Charlotte stepped around Joe, LoriSue watched her pretend nothing awkward had just happened—that Joe really wasn't about to take her to heaven next to a bowl of Bartlett pears.

"Hi, LoriSue. Come on in. Let me get Hoover."

Charlotte lunged for the dog's collar and pulled him into the mudroom off the garage, where he continued to bark. LoriSue wasn't sure if she should tell Charlotte that her bra was a bit discombobulated. She decided not to mention it.

She let her eyes slide from Charlotte back to Joe. "Well, *pardonnez-moi* and all that. I just needed to drop off Justin's stuff for the overnight."

*Damn Charlotte Tasker!* She looked like she'd just hit the Powerball. And all LoriSue wanted to know was how the *hell* did the Good Widow Charlotte snag the likes of Joe Mills? What in the *world* did he see in her?

"Thanks. That's great," Charlotte said.

"Well. Obviously, I had no idea it was so *cozy* in here."

Joe cleared his throat. And didn't he just look too delicious?

"Hi, LoriSue."

She had to laugh. At least she could stop buying those goddamn gift baskets now. She looked at Charlotte and gave her a sweet smile.

"You know, I was going to ask if you needed help with the cookout, but it looks like you've got all the extra hands you need."

"I'd love your help." Charlotte crossed her arms over her chest, apparently just now aware of her little bra problem.

"That's nice of you to offer," Joe added.

LoriSue made her smile as big and bright as she could, considering she wanted to cry. "Have fun, kids." Then she turned and exited the family room, making sure she slammed the door as she left.

. . .

Charlotte slowly returned her gaze to Joe, who leaned up against the dishwasher, his fingers laced on top of his head.

"That was bad. I'm so sorry, Charlotte."

A thousand thoughts raced through her head as she went to the mudroom door and guided the still-barking Hoover outside. Bad? Yes. Stupid? Oh, that was about as stupid as they could get!

She'd lost control with him—again—and now LoriSue knew. It could've easily been the children. She needed to get ahold of herself. Fast.

"We need to set up some rules if you're staying."

"Of course."

"I have no idea how we're going to do this."

"It's okay, Charlotte. We'll work it out together."

She turned away from Joe, suddenly overcome with shyness, and shoved her boobs back into her bra, then adjusted the straps.

When she turned around he was smiling at her with . . . well, *affection.* That was the only way she could describe it.

"LoriSue seemed pretty pissed."

Charlotte decided to busy herself with getting things ready for dinner and walked past Joe to the sink. She started to wash spinach.

"She's going through a rough time right now, Joe. She's in the middle of a divorce and getting ready to move out on her own. She's made no secret of the fact that she's got the major hots for you."

She looked up to see Joe's eyebrows arch high.

"Until you moved in, she rarely came over here."

"No kidding?"

"You're the most exciting thing to happen to us Minton ladies in a long while."

"O . . . kay."

Charlotte laughed a little. "Just don't kick the woman when she's down. That's my only advice."

She put the spinach in a colander. "The rest of the kids will start arriving soon. I need to get everything ready."

"I'll get out of your hair, then." Joe pushed off from the counter and moved toward her. As she watched him advance, she couldn't stop marveling at the fact that he was really in her house. His feet were on her floor. His hand was trailing along her countertop. He was breathing the air she breathed. He was real, and the rooms seemed to shrink in the presence of all that male energy.

It had been a long time since any man other than Ned was in her house. A long, long time.

"Unless you'd like me to help," he added, now standing just inches from her. "I'm not doing anything today."

Charlotte looked up into his face and remembered how the heat of the Miata door had radiated through her hiking shorts and into the flesh of her bottom. She recalled the press of his loins against her belly. She heard the words he used to tease her, tempt her, take her where she longed to go.

*"It's yours if you want it."*

"You're not writing today?"

Joe shrugged. "Not particularly inspired. At least not to write."

There was no mistaking the intensity of what was happening here. There would be no more fooling herself that she could devour just one heavenly piece of juicy Joe Mills and be satisfied. They were looking at all or nothing now, and she knew it.

Charlotte's gaze wandered out the window to her kids, slowly making their way up to the house. She did what any prudent mother would do.

"I won't have any time to spend with you today. I'm going to be busy." She hoped her voice sounded calm and assertive. She hoped her knees were not visibly shaking.

Joe nodded. "You certainly are a busy little beaver."

Charlotte didn't appreciate the double entendre. . . . At least she didn't think she did. But if she didn't, why was she tingling between her legs? Why did she start to laugh?

"What is that supposed to mean?"

"It means—" Joe reached for her hand and brushed his thumb across her lifeline. "You're an extremely busy lady. You do everything in the world for your kids. You run around like a headless chicken every day."

Charlotte felt her spine stiffen and her jaw tighten. Was he criticizing her? "My children are the most important thing in my life."

Joe widened the sweep of his thumb to include the delicate inside of her wrist. Her whole body tingled from the contact. "I really admire that about you."

"You do?"

"I do."

"You really want to help out today?"

"I really do." Joe's smile and expression mellowed. "Please let me, Charlotte."

That's when the kids and Hoover burst through the door and Joe dropped her hand and said, "Looks like it's showtime."

# Chapter Fourteen

LoriSue charged in the front door of her house, knowing exactly where she'd find her husband. And sure enough, there he was, hoisting himself off the family room sofa, a chip bag falling to the carpet.

"Basement time again," he mumbled. "Have a nice day, LoriSue."

"Wait just a second, Jimmy. We need to talk."

On the thirty-second drive from Charlotte's house, she'd made some decisions. Things were going to change for LoriSue Bettmyer, and they were going to change now.

"What is it, O eventually-to-be-ex-wife?" Jimmy shuffled past her to the basement door off the kitchen, clutching his chip bag.

"Would you please tell me what is so damn appealing about Charlotte Tasker?"

Jimmy guffawed. "For God's sake, LoriSue! Not this again!"

"I'm totally serious, Jimmy. Tell me."

He turned toward her and got a panicked look on his face. "I've never been with Charlotte Tasker."

It was LoriSue's turn to laugh. "Only because she

won't have you. But that's not what I asked. I asked you what's so attractive about her."

Jimmy crossed his arms over his chest and leaned back against the basement doorjamb, frowning. "You want to know if I find her attractive?"

She nearly howled this time. "God, Jimmy! I've watched you drool over that woman for over a decade! What I want to know is *why*? What is it about her that draws men like flies to shit?"

"Ah," Jimmy said with a smirk. "This is about Joe Mills, isn't it?"

She stiffened. "What?"

"Come on, LoriSue. I saw the way your eyes lit up when that Rambo wannabe showed up at the snack bar. The way you poured on the charm."

"Stop it, Jimmy."

"I saw the way you reacted when he put the moves on Charlotte and went to sit with her in the stands."

"Oh? And I saw the way you reacted, too, Jimmy." She took a step closer to him. "It must really suck to see Joe just waltz right into town and take what you've wanted nearly a third of your life."

A nasty smile creept across Jimmy's face. "Okay, LoriSue. You wanna know what's so hot about Charlotte Tasker?"

"Yes, I do."

"She's every man's fantasy, that's all." The quiet reverence in her husband's voice didn't escape her. "She looks totally wholesome on the outside, but I can smell it. I can tell that deep down, with the right man, she'd be insatiable. And that's what is so hot about Charlotte Tasker. Any man would tell you the same thing."

LoriSue felt her mouth fall open. "That little mouse?"

"See, there you go, LoriSue. You see a mouse. I see an untapped nympho."

Her head spun. Maybe she'd gone about this backward. Maybe subtlety was the key. She hated to have to ask Jimmy this, but he *did* know her better than anyone. Sixteen years of marriage will do that to two people, for better or worse. "So I come on too strong? Is that what you're saying?"

Jimmy rose from the doorjamb and his eyes got big. "You're asking for my opinion about your sense of style?"

"Yes, I am."

"And you want the truth?"

She scowled at him. "Yes, I do."

"Well, yeah. Maybe you do come on too strong."

She tossed her head and jutted out her chin. "I thought you liked my look."

"I . . . uh . . ."

LoriSue let out a big sigh of impatience. "Jesus, Jimmy. We're getting a divorce—and I've decided to let you have this house, by the way, so I can get on with my life—so just answer my question."

"I get the house?"

"I made an offer on that end-unit condo just listed over at The Lakes. I think they're going to take it and we'll be moving as soon as possible. Now, just do me do me a huge freakin' favor and tell me what you think of my look. I won't get mad."

Jimmy's face burned with suppressed glee. "I really get the house?"

"This place only reminds me of what a disaster our marriage has been. I want a fresh start for myself and for Justin."

"We haven't resolved the custody issue."

"I realize that."

"I want joint custody."

"We'll reach a mutually agreeable arrangement."

"And we haven't figured out how to divide ownership of the agency."

"We will. Just answer my question. Do you, or do you not, like my look?"

"I've never liked your dye job."

*"What?"* The exclamation came out so forcefully that LoriSue hurt her own ears. "You always told me you liked me as a blonde, you son of a bitch."

Jimmy shrugged. "I told you that because you seemed to like yourself as a blonde. I never really did."

"Well, I'll be damned."

"And your suits are about a size too small. It makes you look cheap."

LoriSue widened her stance. Put her hands on her hips. If she'd been wearing a gun holster, this was where she'd pull out her six-shooters.

She gave him a nasty little smile of her own. "You've let yourself go to pot, Jimmy. I fell in love with a fit and athletic man. Now you just sit in your recliner in the basement and eat chips and salsa and watch other men be fit and athletic on TV."

"I don't like your fake fingernails."

"I don't like the way you've tried to make it your personal vision quest to screw every woman in Minton."

"I wouldn't have been looking elsewhere if I'd gotten what I needed at home."

"Ha!" LoriSue leaned in and went nose-to-nose with him. She felt invigorated by this exchange. They were breaking new ground today, getting right to the point, and it felt wonderful. Hell. It felt *empowering*.

"You didn't even *know* what you had at home, you fool. You didn't deserve me."

Jimmy's eyes narrowed to slits. "You're exactly the opposite of Charlotte." He backed into the doorway to put some room between them and shook his head. "See, your outside says 'hot,' but I know better, LoriSue. You're an ice-cold bitch inside, and you always have been."

She didn't want to cry. She never cried. But that hurt. It was so unfair, and so inaccurate. And she felt so sad that her husband of so long knew so little about her.

"Look, LoriSue. We really need to get this divorce over with. I need to live aboveground again. I think I'm getting rickets from lack of sunlight."

Her hand trembled as she wiped her cheek, smearing her black eyeliner. "You'll be hearing from my lawyer, Ricket Boy," she said.

Jimmy apparently understood that was his cue to return to the basement. About halfway down the steps he turned and said, "I did always like the boob job, though."

Joe had no idea that entertaining kids was so exhausting. As if he didn't admire her enough, he held Charlotte in even higher esteem after several hours on the job.

There were a total of seven of them—six fifth-grade boys and Hank, clearly the odd man out. The little girl fascinated him, not just because of her athletic prowess and blunt commentary, but because of how affectionate she was.

More than once that day, Joe felt a small stab in his chest he recognized as sadness for the girl. Hank obviously missed her father. He could tell by the way she followed him around and chattered nonstop, then hung on any response he might have.

It was a little embarrassing and he wasn't sure what he was supposed to do. He didn't want to get her hopes up, but he didn't want to hurt the kid's feelings by being too brusque. He decided he'd be friendly and hope for the best.

The truth was that the world of children was an alien land to Joe. He had no nieces or nephews, and Daniel

Simmons was the only kid he ever really had much contact with, and Daniel had been downright reserved in comparison to the in-your-face Hank and the gleefully cynical Matt.

At the moment, the group was involved in a chaotic game of pickle in the backyard, Charlotte and he manning the makeshift bases, tossing the baseball back and forth as the kids took turns trying not to get tagged out. When kids got caught in a pickle, they would invariably laugh so hard that they'd fall down in the grass, grab their bellies, and roll around as the tears trickled down their faces. Joe figured the hilarity must be contagious, because he'd been laughing right along with them.

He and Charlotte were a good team, and there had been many times when he'd catch her eye and know intuitively what her strategy was, whether the next motion of her arm would be a fake-out. He wished the game would go on forever. It gave him an excuse to have constant eye contact with her, in a way he hoped she found nonthreatening. It gave him an excuse to join her in every smile, every burst of laughter.

It was another way they could communicate without words. Kind of like sex, but not near as much fun.

And Joe found himself wondering if this was what Steve once had. If so, he could see why his partner had been happy—for as long as it lasted, anyway.

"Soup's on, campers!"

The boys ran hard for the back patio, where Ned and Bonnie had been setting two tables for the crowd, but Hank stayed behind. As Charlotte gathered up the old seat cushions that had served as bases, the little girl sidled up to Joe.

She grabbed his right hand and squeezed it hard.

Joe froze. He had no earthly idea what to do. So he just stood still until Hank started tugging and led him up the slope of the lawn.

"I like you, Joe," she said.

"I like you too, champ."

"Infinity much."

"Uh, thanks."

Charlotte arrived at his other side and offered to take the baseball mitt still stuck on his left hand. "I'll go put this stuff away in the shed and meet you in a minute."

Joe relinquished the mitt and walked hand-in-hand with Hank.

"That was my dad's glove," she said.

"I kind of figured that."

"You don't play much ball, do you?"

He laughed. It was true that his arm was a bit rusty. "I managed to throw you out a few times, as I recall."

She offered him that patchwork grin, and he noticed for the first time how strange her newer teeth looked this close up, all corrugated at the edges. He didn't know if that was normal. He suddenly couldn't remember why the hell he thought it was a good idea to hang out with the Taskers.

Then he saw Charlotte glance over her shoulder and smile as she walked to the shed, and it all came back to him. He squeezed Hank's hand in response.

The actual dinner struck Joe as a combination of theater of the absurd and a three-ring circus. The six boys were relegated to a picnic table under a tree while the adults and Hank sat at the wrought-iron patio table.

Joe was amused by the boys' conversation, which centered on bodily functions, how much they hated females, and which boy could perform any number of physical feats better than the others present. It reminded him of a typical staff meeting at the Albuquerque field office.

At their table, Charlotte regaled them with the healh hazards of trans-fatty acids found in commercial baked goods and the bovine growth hormones found in meat and dairy products.

Ned patted his round belly and said, "A little bovine growth hormone never hurt anyone. Look what it's done for me!"

In the half hour it took to eat, Bonnie, Ned, and Charlotte got up and down from their own meals a dozen times to replenish plates and do everything from clean up spilled juice to put baking soda on a bee sting.

Hank never budged from his side. At one point she refilled his iced tea and looked up at him with huge blue eyes full of adoration.

She pulled on his shirtsleeve. "Wanna come to my ballet recital in two weeks? I get to wear a tutu and everything."

Joe felt his eyes widen. "Hey, sure. I'd like that."

"Ever had that hummus stuff?" Hank said it in a whisper, nodding toward the barely touched dip at the center of the table.

"Mighty tasty." Joe scooped a wedge of toasted pita bread into the beige substance and took a big bite. "I think my mom made something like this when I was growing up."

Hank's mouth hung open. "For real?" She reached for a triangle of pita and held it over the bowl, a dubious expression on her face. "You didn't puke or anything?"

Joe laughed. "Not once."

After a moment spent steeling herself, Hank scooped the bread through the air and popped it into her mouth, plain. "I'd have puked, for sure," she mumbled, then once more bared those weird-looking kid teeth in that big smile of hers.

Then she said, "Wanna see my tutu?"

After the campfire tale spun by Ned and Joe, it took Charlotte nearly an hour to get the boys settled down. Everyone agreed it was a real treat to have a professional storyteller like Joe contributing to scary-story time, but Charlotte was relieved that in the end Sasquatch only wanted to eat s'mores and not little boys.

Otherwise, she'd *never* get them to go to sleep.

Ned and Bonnie had just headed home. And Joe was drinking his iced tea on the patio keeping an eye on the tent while Charlotte put Hank to bed.

She tucked the sheet around Hank's body and kissed her sweaty forehead.

"I had fun tonight, Mama."

"Me, too."

"Can Joe come up and tuck me in next?"

She tried not to react too much to that question, though it concerned her. "I'll just tell him you said good night."

"I already said good night to him. Three times. He hugged me. He gives real good hugs."

"That was nice of him."

"I think he was stable tonight, Mama, don't you?"

Charlotte smiled down at her little matchmaker, her heart breaking. She'd seen Hank stare at Joe today, seeking out his attention whenever she could, sitting next to him, holding his hand. And Joe had been kind. But Charlotte knew that she needed to nip this puppy love in the bud. For Hank's sake.

"You know, sweetie, Joe probably won't live in Minton forever. He'll move one day."

Hank shook her head, her curls tumbling on the pillowcase. "Nope, Mama. I think he's gonna stay. He likes it here."

"Hank." Charlotte heard her voice grow stern. "I don't want you to grow attached to Mr. Mills. Do you understand?"

Hank shook her head with conviction. "Joe likes us. He's going to stay forever. Matt agrees with me."

Charlotte frowned—why had she let Joe hang around

tonight? The last thing in the world she wanted was to expose her children to more disappointment.

"We talked about it during the pickle game, Mama. Joe likes us. He likes you—a real lot."

"Sweetie, I need to explain something to you." Charlotte smoothed her daughter's curls from her forehead and leaned close, bracing herself on either side of Hank's shoulders. "Remember that night you said that I was going to start loving Mr. Mills? Please don't let that worry you, all right? I don't have plans to love anybody but you and Matt."

In the faint glow of her night-light, Hank's face broke out into a wide grin and her eyes sparkled mischievously. "Whatever you say, Mama."

"Good night, Hank."

Knowing she'd accomplished nothing, Charlotte kissed Hank's forehead again and walked toward the bedroom door.

"Daddy won't mind," Hank whispered to her back.

Charlotte came to a sudden stop in the hallway, those words reverberating in her heart and skittering down her spine. She glanced heavenward, her gaze cut short by the white ceiling, thinking just how wrong Hank was. She pictured Kurt up in heaven, peering down on her, not exactly judging her—he'd never really judged her—but he'd have that disappointed look on his face. He'd be disappointed in her current state of lust, her surrender to the needs of the flesh.

That look on Kurt's face always made Charlotte feel so uncomfortable in her own skin.

She arrived in the kitchen and her eyes immediately were drawn to the double glass doors in the family room and the vision of Joe seated at the wrought-iron table, his long legs stretched out to rest on an unoccupied chair in front of him, his right hand absently dangling down to rub Hoover's ear. The two of them seemed to stand guard, watching the flashlight beams dance inside the tent across the yard.

It was tempting indeed, tempting to look at Joe's silhouette and think of Kurt and everything her husband had been—guardian, provider, father, lover, friend. Charlotte straightened her shoulders and prepared to go outside, telling herself that Joe could never fill the space Kurt once occupied. Joe was her sexual fantasy man, and fantasy men didn't make good husbands and fathers. Everybody knew that.

But Joe had helped clear the table that evening, hadn't he? He'd been so loving and patient with Hank. He'd formed an easy friendship with Bonnie and Ned. He'd been a good sport with a pack of rowdy boys. And those were all things a girl didn't usually expect from her sexual fantasy man.

Right?

She opened the back doors and Joe looked up and smiled. There was a small lantern on the table, which cast a soft bluish light over his features, making his black eyes that much more mesmerizing. He removed his feet from the chair and sat up quickly, wiping off the cushion, then patting it to indicate he wanted her to sit close.

She wondered what in the world they'd have to talk about. They knew nothing about each other, except for that brief encounter so long ago and the few quick conversations they'd had in the last two weeks. Had it been two weeks? On one hand, she still felt the shock of recognizing him at the punching bag like it was yesterday. On the other, it was difficult to remember a time when he wasn't right next door, when her body wasn't alive with the proximity of him.

She sat down and crossed her legs and folded her hands in her lap. Joe just looked into her eyes, silent, a hint of a smile at the corner of his lips.

Charlotte returned his gaze and pondered the mystery of sexual attraction. Why did one man, like Jimmy Bettmyer, make her skin crawl, while another, Joe Mills, made her libido do the Lambada? Sexual attraction had as many layers as organic whole wheat phyllo dough. What she felt for Joe was based in the physical senses, of course, the resonance of his voice, the breadth of his hand, the male scent at the crook of his neck, the black liquid passion of his eyes. But another part of the attraction was intangible. She felt joy in his presence. She felt sensual and alive. She felt like herself.

She couldn't stop her thoughts—they came racing at her too fast and hard to fight back—and Charlotte found herself comparing Joe to Kurt. It was unfair, like comparing a Ferrari to a Volvo, and she knew it.

With Kurt, she felt safe. He was strong and steady and reliable, and when he touched her, it was with the same reserved strength he used to interact with the rest of the world. When they made love, it was pleasant and sweet and usually over too soon. Most often, it was with Charlotte beneath him—that was the way he preferred it—and despite his position, he always left it up to her to control the pace and timing. Her favorite part was when he would hold her afterward and stroke her hair.

That was when the dark thoughts would rush into her, as she hid her face in his chest. That's when she'd admit to herself that she longed for so much more, something elusive and wonderful that she and Kurt just couldn't seem to produce together. She wanted certain physical sensations, yes. She wanted her legs up over her ears. She wanted to ride a man's body hard. Every once in a while, she wanted to be flipped over onto her belly and taken from behind by a man who was blinded by a need much like rage, a force that would propel her into the dark rushing swirl of sex.

But she also wanted something beyond the physical. She wanted that otherworldly sense of connection she'd had with Joe, the way he'd used his mind and words and emotions to push her past the corporeal into oblivion. She wanted to know she was being loved by a man who'd surrendered to his desire for her, who wouldn't hold back, who couldn't stop himself even if he wanted to.

Once, only once, she'd summoned the courage to come right out and ask Kurt for what she wanted. It shocked him. He pulled away from her, paced the bedroom, and told her he respected her too much to degrade her that way.

"What in the world are you thinking over there?" Joe asked.

Charlotte shook her head. Like the grief, the regret could attack her without warning. Tonight, it was relentless. She felt powerless against it.

She thought of her wedding night. She was completely exhausted. Ironic as it was, after all the years of wanting and waiting, she was not at all interested in having sex on her wedding night. By the time the reception was over and the revelers left their hotel suite, it was two in the morning. Her head throbbed from the champagne and the lack of food—she'd been too excited to eat. Her feet hurt from the narrow heels she'd worn with her wedding dress. Her mouth hurt from hours of smiling. She could barely keep her eyes open.

But Kurt had swept her up off the hotel sofa and carried her lovingly to the big king-size bed, where he murmured to her to not be afraid, that he wouldn't hurt her, that he loved her more than anything in the world.

Charlotte's body shook. She was scared to death that at

this most sacred moment Kurt would discover that someone had been there before him and she'd be found out—
her ruse exposed—and he'd want the marriage annulled.
Tears sprang into her eyes. She opened her mouth to tell
him everything, her lips forming the first words of the
sentence that would spell her doom—"Remember the day
I picked you up at National Airport?"—when her new
husband's mouth came down on hers and he'd kissed her
hard and his hands went to her breasts and she surrendered herself to whatever fate would bring.

Fate brought a pleasing but silent coupling, followed
by Kurt apologizing because he knew it must have hurt
her. He told her he felt her shaking, saw her tears, and
hoped that she could forgive him for being so rough.

*Rough?* she'd asked herself. *That* was rough? And so
began thirteen years of comparing her husband to the
mystery man who'd made her lose her freaking mind in a
firestorm of lust and forceful language, the man now sitting across from her on her back patio, gently stroking
her knee, and staring at her like she was some odd creature on display at a petting zoo.

"Charlotte?"

Then she thought of the evening she found her husband dead. He didn't answer when she told him dinner
was ready, so she walked toward the family room, repeat-
ing his name while she wiped her hands on the green-
checked kitchen towel. Her brain had started to buzz with
alarm before she reached him. Something about the way
he lay on the couch didn't look right. He appeared too
loose. His chest wasn't rising and falling. The instant her
warm fingers made contact with the cold skin of his
cheek, she screamed.

It wasn't until hours later that she remembered her
hideous secret wish. That Kurt would just disappear, so
she could take a lover.

"Charlotte? Are you all right?"

She took a deep breath and straightened in the chair. She tried to smile at Joe. "Do you have any idea how strange it feels to be sitting here with you? You're not supposed to be real. You're my fantasy."

He laughed a little. "I think I know exactly how strange it feels."

"Do you have any idea how weird it was to have you here today for the barbecue?"

"Yes, I do."

"Do you know how often I thought of you over the years?"

"How often, Charlotte?"

"Every single day."

"I can beat that," he said, his white smile flashing in the night. He tapped his front tooth with his index finger. "At least twice a day for me."

She laughed, stopping his hand from continuing the warm circular movement around her knee. "You're never going to let me live that down, are you?"

"Never—especially if it makes you feel so outrageously ashamed that you decide you need to make it up to me."

Charlotte shook her head and smiled. "I already feel guilty enough."

"Maybe it's time you stopped feeling guilty at all."

His hand was back, but this time it was higher, and his palm was stretched hot over the surface of her thigh, where it kneaded gently.

"Joe—"

"I'll go crazy if I don't touch you, Charlotte. I've been looking at you all day, thinking about touching you, wondering when it would be safe to touch you again, knowing exactly how you feel in my hands."

She couldn't do this with a tent full of kids not twenty

yards away. She knew how it was with Joe—five minutes and she'd be on him like white on refined rice. Charlotte decided it would be best to end the evening with a warm "thank you" for all his help and a kiss on the cheek. No lip-to-lip contact. She tried to rise from the chair, but Joe caught her hands and pulled her back down.

"What I've always remembered, so clearly, is how dainty you were. How big my hands felt on your hips and waist, how feminine and soft and sweet you were."

"Oh, please." She tried to get up again, but his strong hands held her in place.

"You had this tiny waist and trim little knees and the sweetest round breasts with the perkiest little pink cherry nipples—"

"Stop right there—"

Joe bent close to her, his face not an inch from hers, her hands still gripped tight in his own.

"And this beautiful small perfect peach between your legs, Charlotte. A ladylike little split fruit covered in peach fuzz—so juicy and hot that I've never been able to forget it."

Charlotte felt numb. No one had ever spoken to her like this before—well, just once, thirteen years ago—and she couldn't help but notice that Joe's words sounded like something right out of one of her poems. She wondered if his voice had been the poetry inside her soul all the while.

The thought startled her.

"Sorry, but I'm not so dainty anymore."

Joe pulled back a bit and smiled.

Charlotte hoped her voice didn't sound shrill. She hoped she didn't sound as hysterical as she felt. She wanted to come across as practical, because someone needed to be practical here and it didn't appear as if it was going to be Joe. "Like I said—"

"You're not that girl anymore."

She huffed. "That's right, Joe. I'm not that girl from the side of the road. What I am is a thirty-five-year-old widow with a mortgage and a job, a woman who's carried two babies inside her, squeezed them out, nursed them with those little cherry nipples you seem to have liked so much, and frankly, all my dainty parts have been put to hard use."

He continued to grin and said nothing. It was definitely time to say good night.

"You are beautiful to me, Charlotte." Joe's words came out in a rough whisper. "From what I can tell, you're still dainty and feminine, and I'll be damned, but you smell exactly the same as you did back then. You feel the same in my arms. Your kiss still tastes the same. And I swear, Charlotte, if I don't get another one of those kisses right this second—"

He raised his hands to cup the sides of her face, then slowly, so slowly, brought his lips down onto hers. Charlotte felt as though all the blood in her body rushed to her mouth, as if not a single red blood cell wanted to miss out on the sensory block party now taking place on her lips and tongue.

He pressed on, pushed open her lips to receive him, and kissed her senseless. He kissed her until she couldn't breathe and couldn't remember her name. He kissed the living hell out of her.

Just the way she liked.

# Chapter Fifteen

"I've been thinking about it and I believe you have to sleep with more than two men in your life before you can be considered a slut, Charlotte."

Joe watched her nod seriously, and he couldn't resist the urge to trace the outline of her jaw. Her chin ended in such a soft little rounded point. He marveled at how smooth her skin was. How pale she seemed beneath his darker hand.

She was kicking him to the curb tonight, but she was doing it sweetly, like she did most everything. There was no doubt about how much she wanted him—he felt it in her kiss, the way her hands gripped him, the feverish look in her eye—but she was right. It wasn't the time or place.

Joe glanced over Charlotte's shoulder toward the tent. Most of the dueling flashlight beams were now off, and only an occasional flicker of light appeared, followed by a brief exchange of whispers. The campers were finally falling asleep.

"You going to be okay with the boys?" He rubbed her upper arms as she stood in front of him in the driveway.

She smiled. "Of course. I'll sleep on the family room couch in case they need anything."

"Want me to stay?"

He saw a flicker of interest in her eyes, followed by a polite shake of her head. "No, thanks. I can handle it."

"Obviously."

He pulled her to his chest and wrapped his arms around her small frame. He sighed in contentment when she returned the hug—a surprisingly tight grip coming from such a small woman.

"You've handled a lot, Charlotte. You are a very strong person."

Her entire body sagged against him. She weighed next to nothing. He wanted to pick her up, cradle her in his arms, kiss her face, and carry her right into his house and up the stairs and to his bed.

In his dreams.

He'd already thought this through. Now that he was staying, it would be too risky to let Charlotte or the kids wander around inside his house. The pool area would probably be okay, but he didn't want anyone getting anywhere near his office. It's not like he had his DEA shield mounted on the wall or his reports to the U.S. attorney scattered all over the floor, but it made him uncomfortable to think of anyone seeing anything that would put them at risk.

"I don't feel very strong sometimes, you know?" Charlotte's voice was muffled by the front of his shirt. He felt her snuggle close, and he pulled her even tighter.

"Nobody can feel strong all the time, sweetheart."

He felt her head bob up and down in agreement. He wanted her to hang on to him like this forever, but she was already extricating herself from his embrace.

"So. How many lovers *does* a woman have to have before she's a slut?"

Joe laughed—not only at her question but also at the earnest look on her face. Charlotte had somehow managed to keep an interesting combination of innocence and passion, even into her midthirties, and it intrigued him. "You really worried that you might be considered a slut?"

She pursed her lips in thought. "At first, yes. I was sure I was going to go straight to hell."

"Seriously?"

"Yes." She broke into a wide smile. "As it turned out, I only went to Ohio."

Joe laughed again, taking her hands in his. He dragged his thumb over the delicate bones in her fingers and her small, smooth nails. He wanted to know every single inch of her, every nook and cranny of her body and her mind and her heart.

"I was sure that everybody could see a change in me, because I *felt* so different. I was afraid Kurt could see it, and my mother, and my roommates. I was completely paranoid." Charlotte quirked up her mouth. "The day before my wedding, my mother gave me this pamphlet called *Duties of the Christian Wife*. I nearly died."

"Any good pointers?"

Charlotte laughed softly. "Not that I remember. But I gave it to Kurt to read."

"Good move. A man can always do with a slightly different perspective than 'Penthouse Forum'."

"Oh, my God!" she blurted out. "Kurt never read anything like 'Penthouse Forum' in his life! He never even . . ."

Joe waited, then realized Charlotte had chosen not to finish her comment. She pulled her hands from his and crossed her arms over her chest, as if to close herself off.

"Kurt never even what?"

"Nothing."

"It was obviously something."

She shook her head. "I really need to get some sleep."

Joe bent close to get a better look at her downturned face. "Can I ask you a question, Charlotte?"

She looked up, suddenly scanning the darkness as if to check that no one was listening. It made Joe smile.

"I guess."

"Did you eventually have a satisfying sex life with your husband?"

"I really need to go to sleep," she said, walking away.

"Hey, wait! What are you doing tomorrow?" Joe hadn't meant to yell loud enough to wake up the boys, but a single flashlight beam sprang to life inside the tent.

Charlotte spun around. "It's Sunday. Nothing much. Why?"

"I want to see you tomorrow. That's why."

She briefly brought a hand to her mouth before she said, "We'll see, Joe." Then she walked into the garage and lowered the automatic door.

LoriSue stopped brushing her hair in midstroke, pausing to check if she felt fully empowered yet. Maybe. She peered close to the vanity table mirror and studied her face. Yes, she was still beautiful, but she wouldn't stay that way for much longer, would she? Ten years, tops, and then what would she have?

LoriSue put the brush down and separated the darkening roots of her hair, trying to jog her memory, trying to recall her face in a brunette frame. She couldn't do it, sighed, and wandered out of the dressing room to her king-size bed. She flopped down on her stomach and kicked her feet in the air like a kid.

Today had been just chock-full of surprises. First there'd been the sight of Joe and Charlotte nearly getting it on by the fruit bowl. Oh, hell—she couldn't exactly indict the woman. Charlotte had been married to the most strait-laced guy on the planet and then left a widow. Of course Joe Mills proved too much to resist. The poor sex-starved thing never had a chance.

And that little soul-baring discussion she'd had with Jimmy that afternoon? *Bring it on,* that's what she had to say about it! The truth will set you free, and all that shit. So here she was, thirty-six years old, getting a shot at freedom, no longer needing to give a rat's ass about what some *man* would prefer. It turned out she'd been wrong all along anyway, so from now on it would be all about what *she* wanted. What *she* preferred.

From now on it was going to be LoriSue, unchained.

She hopped off the bed and stood before the floor-length mirror of her closet door. After that talk with Jimmy, she'd soothed her soul with a search-and-destroy boutique shopping spree. Nothing like three thousand dollars in clothing and accessories to take away the sting. And she couldn't wait to unleash her new look on the world.

What else could she do now that she was free? She could live anywhere she chose, of course. Change her hair. Get her MBA or law degree. Run for Congress. Train for a marathon. Well, maybe that was stretching it . . . but the point was she could do anything at all and never again have to worry about it affecting Jimmy's wandering eye or fragile ego.

So maybe this was her first little sample of empowerment. LoriSue decided it suited her. And first thing tomorrow, she planned to get her ass out there and get herself some more.

Bonnie woke up in the middle of the night, her heart beating wildly in her chest.

She reached over and shook Ned awake.

"Hmmph?"

"Ned. Wake up."

"What? What is it?" He was up in a flash and the lamp was on. He blinked back against the bright light.

"I just realized we can't go visit Raymond and his family next month. We can't leave Charlotte here alone with Joe Mills."

Ned moaned. "You woke me up to tell me *that*?"

"I had a bad dream." That was an understatement. The dream was more than bad. It was horrible—Charlotte was crying and Hank and Matt had vanished and there was blood all over the driveway.

"Don't worry about Joe." Ned clicked off the light and fell back against the pillows.

"What?"

"He's a good guy. I can tell. And I got his prints tonight."

"You did? How?"

"A drinking glass from dinner. I'll take it into the station Monday morning and see what we can find out."

Bonnie felt some relief. Maybe they'd get enough information that she'd feel comfortable going ahead with their planned visit to Arizona. She really wanted to go—she hadn't seen her oldest son and his wife and kids in months.

"You really think he's okay?"

"He's cool. Don't worry, babe." Ned patted Bonnie on her hip, let his hand linger there a moment, and gave her outer thigh a tight squeeze. Then he rolled over.

"How long will it take to get fingerprint results?"

"Couple days. Not more."

"I'm really worried, Ned."

Her husband rolled back toward her, insinuated a warm hand up the front of her nightgown, and gave her a playful caress. "Good thing I know a way to get your mind off your troubles."

Charlotte gave up trying to fall asleep. Part of her knew she should remain awake in case one of the boys needed something.

Another part of her couldn't sleep because of Joe. He was staying, and that changed everything. He was offering her more than one last taste. He was offering her another chance. And now that it looked like she'd get everything she'd always wanted, she wondered if she was ready for it.

And whether she deserved it.

The first issue was the kids, of course. Should she try to keep her family and her love life separate? Was that even possible when the love life lived next door? He said he wanted to see her tomorrow—but that was Sunday, a family day. She couldn't pawn the kids off on Bonnie to frolic with Joe, and she couldn't seem to wrap her brain around the image of Joe heading to the park with them, joining them for popcorn and a matinee, or sitting down with them to a big Sunday breakfast. She didn't even know if he'd be comfortable with those things.

Then Charlotte winced, wondering how many hours it would take before every living soul in Minton knew that the Widow Tasker had taken a lover. She imagined facing everyone, knowing that they knew. The Noonans. The Rickmans. Old Mrs. Watson. Everyone on the Little League Board. Everyone in Troop 492. Everyone at the William Howard Taft Elementary PTA meeting.

The Bettmyers. Bonnie and Ned.

Hank and Matt.

Kurt up in heaven.

"Ohmigod." She flopped over again on the couch, angry that the sun would be coming up in a couple hours, still feeling Joe's arms around her and his mouth on hers, aware that his presence was dragging to the surface everything she'd spent her whole adult life trying to ignore.

She'd brought her poetry journal downstairs earlier,

just in case she felt the urge to write. She was sure feeling it now. She turned on the lamp and picked up her pen.

*Slut*

*When did she appear, the slut in me?*
*At the spark of creation, when I was two cells,*
*The way we all start?*
*Sex from sex?*
*(Though my mother would never admit to this)*

*Does she have a name, this wanton?*
*I'll call her Charlotte—for she is me, one and the same*
*I've just always insisted she have an early curfew*
*Because she can't be trusted*
*And she would like to dress provocatively*
*That slut*

*So the answer may be zero—it took zero encounters*
*To make me all I am*
*Because she was always there*
*Just laying in wait*
*For Joe's touch*
*To set her free*

*The slut in me.*

Charlotte closed the journal. Turned off the light. And wondered how it would feel to go through life comfortable with who she was—everything she was.

Maybe she'd soon find out.

# Chapter Sixteen

LoriSue didn't feel one lick of guilt about asking Jolene to open her beauty salon early on a Sunday morning, because she'd made the woman an offer she couldn't refuse. Jolene had four kids to support and a house LoriSue knew very well cost a good $1,700 a month.

She'd sold it to her.

Jolene appeared slightly stunned when she unlocked the doors to the Hair You Are salon on Main Street. She looked LoriSue up and down. "Are you sure you want to do this?"

"Absolutely certain."

"Well, okay." Jolene shrugged, getting out a plastic cape. "Have a seat. You look real nice today, by the way."

She sure as hell hoped so. This was the first public outing of her new look, the first of nine outfits she'd hauled away from that boutique in Mount Adams that promised that style was an attitude, not an age.

And that morning she was wearing three hundred bucks' worth of attitude—cream yellow linen crop pants and a little matching jacket with retro buttons. The low-heeled slides were ninety. The earrings—simple little things that didn't even dangle, for God's sake—had been sixty-five.

She had no idea it cost so freakin' much to be subtle.

"I like the way you've toned down your makeup, too," Jolene said, quickly adding, "Not that it didn't look good before."

"Let's talk cut." LoriSue whipped out the folded page from a magazine and pointed. "That one."

Jolene's eyes bugged out. "But that's a layered shag! You've got a long page boy! This will take a lot of cutting, probably five inches on top!"

"I realize that," LoriSue snapped. "I'm going for the no-fuss, casual chic look—something classy and low-key. Something totally different."

"No shit," Jolene said under her breath. She put the magazine page on the surface of her styling station and smoothed it out. "I guess I can do something like that."

"Great." LoriSue was feeling more empowered by the minute.

"Now. What about color?" Jolene snapped the cape around LoriSue's neck and combed her fingers through the pale blond locks. "You said you wanted to go a couple shades darker than usual."

LoriSue spun around in the salon chair and looked Jolene right in the eye.

"I said I want to go back to my natural color."

Jolene's mouth fell open. "Uh," she said, looking worried. "I don't think I even know what your natural color *is*, LoriSue."

She probably wasn't exaggerating. Jolene had opened this shop ten years ago, and every four weeks, like clockwork, for a decade, she'd been helping LoriSue disguise the fact that she was born with a head of medium brown hair.

LoriSue sighed. "Then go get those sample hunks of dyed hair you have in the back and we'll figure something out. I want to get this over with. Oh, and don't forget my eyebrows."

"Why are we going to the lake, Mama?" Hank asked.

Matt yawned. "And how come you woke us up so early?"

Charlotte wasn't proud of herself, but after tossing and turning on the couch all night she'd greeted the day with a plan: avoid Joe at all costs.

So she'd called all the parents to pick up their boys by 9:00 a.m., packed the van with lunch and supper picnics, a change of clothes, rafts, beach blankets, towels, books, sunscreen, beach chairs, and drinks and snacks, then told the kids to put on their swimsuits and get in the car. They were going to Pike Lake for the day—the whole day.

"I just realized we haven't been in a while, that's all. I thought it would be a nice treat."

"I guess," Matt said, unconvinced. "But I'm kinda sleepy."

"You can sleep in the sand."

The lake wasn't crowded, possibly because it was still early when they got there and many families didn't arrive until after church. Charlotte hadn't been to church since Kurt died, much to her parents' horror. The last long-distance conversation she'd had with her mother, which was several weeks ago now, had ended when she reminded Charlotte about the eternal fire pit of hell. She'd thanked her mother and hung up.

Charlotte took a deep breath of the mild morning air and smiled. This would be her church today—the soft roll of Ohio earth, the sun, and the happy voices of her kids.

From behind her gray-tinted sunglasses and from her comfortable perch in her beach chair, Charlotte watched

Hank and Matt swim and splash. She wiggled her toes in the light brown sand. This lake would always remind her of Kurt. They had taken the kids here often. She could almost see him now, his burly body bursting through the water, roaring in his best impersonation of a grizzly bear, making the kids scream with delight.

She scanned the horizon of blue-green water and the uneven line of tall sycamores, maples, and oaks that rimmed the lake. There was no Kurt and there never would be again. Life was so much quieter without him.

How could she have ever wished him away?

By six, everyone was pink from the sun, worn-out, and waterlogged. Charlotte opened the cooler to pull out the food she'd packed for supper—rather limp-looking veggie roll-ups, fruit and flaxseed salad, and oatmeal-raisin bars—and sighed. The resigned looks of suffering on Hank's and Matt's faces sealed the deal.

"We're going to Fritz's," she announced, slamming the cooler lid shut. Hank and Matt cheered and gave each other high fives.

They drove down the state highway to Fritz's Snack Shack and Driving Range, where they sat at an outdoor picnic table under the eaves and gorged on greasy fried cod and chicken planks, French fries, coleslaw, and soft drinks, the way they used to do when Kurt was alive. Then they played a round of cutthroat putt-putt.

At the fifteenth hole, the par three loop-to-loop space rocket, Matt curled his arm around Charlotte's waist and said, "Remember how Dad used to nail this one?"

What amazed Charlotte was that her son said it with a smile.

Both Hank and Matt fell asleep on the fifteen-minute drive home, which she felt like doing herself. The combination of lack of sleep the night before, the sun, and the heavy food was making her eyelids droop. She rolled down her window all the way for fresh air, then adjusted the mirror so she could see her children's faces, sated in sleep. They were such beautiful creatures. They were her whole life. She'd been blessed.

As the headlights arced past her in the twilight, she did the math. Hank had just turned eight. In ten years she'd be looking forward to starting her freshman year at college and Matt would be a junior. In ten years Charlotte would be forty-five.

And alone.

They arrived home late, and she had to drag the kids up to their beds, where they fell on top of their covers in their T-shirts and shorts, with sandy feet.

Charlotte took a quick shower, then went downstairs to let Hoover out for a tinkle. When she opened the double doors off the family room, she saw a piece of paper taped to the glass. She read it by the porch light:

*Hope you all had a good day. I really missed you.*
*—Joe.*

The DEA field office was on Third Street in downtown Cincinnati, a city Joe had never seen firsthand and one he'd never really desired to see. It was surprisingly pretty, with hilly streets and restored vintage buildings tucked right next to modern steel and glass. The downtown was nestled against the Ohio River, surrounded by hills.

He spent the morning in meetings with Supervisor Rich Baum and his staff, his thoughts equally divided between Charlotte and the job at hand. The Cincinnati office did indeed have a mounting crystal meth problem and Joe was surprised by the numbers—six major busts in the last four months, three dead dealers, and two fatal overdoses in one area high school that had politicians and parents demanding answers. Joe was happy to help and gave them the benefit of his expertise, and by lunch he seemed to have told them everything he could.

Also by lunch, he'd relived Saturday at least three times in his head. He remembered each of Charlotte's touches. Her kisses. The sound of her laughter. The way she'd peeked around Hank's curls to smile at him across the campfire.

That's when it had hit him. He was nearly thirty-eight and had never been in love. It had never bothered him, up until that moment, seeing Charlotte with a child in her lap. Because that's when he realized that if he'd done things differently that day so long ago, if he'd only gotten the Miata's license plate number, he might have been looking at his own child cradled in her arms.

He hadn't been able to shake the thought since.

Rich Baum stayed behind as the conference room cleared out of agents, and chatted with Joe for a few minutes. Rich seemed nice enough and had a good reputation in the Administration.

"How's Clermont County treating you, Joe?"

Joe leaned back in the swivel chair and shrugged. "The hectic pace is killing me."

Rich laughed loudly. "I heard we could have a hell of a pool party at your digs—mind if a few of us single guys borrow the place one night?"

"Have at it."

Rich chuckled some more and cleared his throat, then fiddled with his pen. "Listen, Joe." He wasn't looking him in the eye. "I was talking with Roger the other day—"

"Uh-oh."

"And he wants me to send a couple agents into your neck of the woods a few times a week, just to put extra eyeballs on the situation."

He didn't like the sound of that. "What's up?"

"I'm sure you're fine, but—" Rich frowned. "Did Roger tell you Jay Mauk was murdered Friday?"

Jay Mauk had worked on the Guzman case with Joe and Steve out of the Albuquerque field office. He'd been a civilian computer engineer. Extremely bright. Jay was only twenty-three years old.

"No."

"Here. I printed this out for you."

Joe took the sheets of paper, incensed that Roger would keep this from him, feeling the black hole grow bigger in his chest as his hands began to shake. Jay Mauk had been a fucking *kid*. And by the looks of the report, the way he'd been murdered was pure Guzman—a drive-by in broad daylight, AK-47s out the car window, in front of a popular steak house. Albuquerque Police found a stolen Chevy a few blocks away and no sign of the suspects.

Joe folded the report and stuck it in his pants pocket.

"I'm right here if you should need anything," Rich said.

Joe left the offices and headed toward the parking garage, stopping at a newsstand on the way for a pack of bubble gum, pulling the brim of his Reds cap down over his sunglasses as he walked.

He felt the familiar nervous hum through his body, the cold fingers on the nape of his neck. And what amazed him most was the realization that he'd been living without this for a few weeks. He'd forgotten how the baseline fear coiled inside him, ate at him, emptied him of everything but a sharp awareness of his surroundings.

It had been nice while it lasted.

On the drive back to Minton, he thought of Jay Mauk and the million-dollar price on his own head. He told himself again that there was no way Guzman would ever link Special Agent Joe Bellacera of the Albuquerque

DEA to the reclusive Joseph Mills of Minton, Ohio.

He told himself that it was still possible to get to know Charlotte and her kids without putting them in danger. It could be done. It had to be done, because he'd already told them he was staying.

Joe was still trying to convince himself of this when he arrived in Minton and saw the Kroger grocery store to his left. Since he'd found nothing in his refrigerator for breakfast that morning, he pulled into the parking lot.

For the time being he was still alive. And a man had to eat to live.


By one in the afternoon Charlotte had done everything listed on her Palm Pilot—picked up three separate dry-cleaning orders, dropped off a chair cushion at the uphol-stery repair shop, taken a cat to the vet, and finished the weekly grocery shopping and meal planning for three families.

She still had to stop at the grocery for her own family and figured she had just enough time to get a few things and get home by two, leaving an hour to do her Tae Bo tape before she had to pick up the kids.

Then the evening rush would begin. On tonight's agenda: ballet class and Matt's game.

Charlotte was in the frozen food aisle when she felt it—someone was watching her. She glanced around, saw no one, and tried to shrug off the uncomfortable buzz that coursed through her. She didn't often feel unsafe in her life—harried and exhausted, yes, but not in any danger. But right then, goose bumps covered her arms, and she didn't think they were from the freezers.

Charlotte rounded the corner and locked wheels with Joe.

He'd obviously been absorbed in thought, his brow deeply furrowed and his eyes lowered. The instant she smashed into him, his face lightened, his eyes widened, and his goatee spread with the force of his broad, chipped, impossibly sexy smile.

"Hey, Charlotte."

How strange—it was like he really didn't expect to see her. But if it hadn't been Joe watching her, then who was?

"Hey, Joe."

But Joe's gaze had never once caused her that feeling of discomfort. When Joe looked at her, she felt hot and soft and sexy—and guilty, of course—but never scared.

Charlotte told herself she'd worry about it later and went on to more important matters, like scrutinizing the contents of Joe's shopping cart. She had to admit it could have been worse—a lot worse. Nothing too heinous that she could see, just fresh fruits and vegetables, a frozen cheese pizza, yogurt, a taco dinner kit, coffee, bagels, cereal, chicken breasts. Not bad for a guy living by himself.

She noticed him checking out her cart and stiffened in embarrassment at the three cans of squirt cheese balanced on top.

"Wild party tonight?"

Charlotte didn't like the teasing in his voice or the way his eyebrows arched, as if he knew something she didn't.

"No," she said. "I mean, yes. For the kids."

"I see."

"Well, I need to get going." She tried to disentangle her wheels from his, but they kept turning into each other. It seemed she couldn't even go *grocery shopping* without this man disturbing her peace of mind.

"I was hoping I'd get to see you yesterday. Did you and the kids have plans after all?" Joe nonchalantly reached down and straightened one of her wheels, then backed away, leaving the carts separated. He was always so cool and collected—he never seemed ruffled.

"No. Yes. We went to a lake we like."

Joe nodded. Then he crossed his arms and leaned forward on the handle of the shopping cart and smiled at her. "Is it possible you're having second thoughts, Charlotte?"

"What?" she huffed, turning her cart so that she could pass by him. She really needed to get home. "Of course I'm not. I just need to do my kickboxing video before the kids get home from school, so I guess I'll catch you later." She smiled at him in a way she hoped conveyed assertive flirtatiousness. "Have a nice afternoon."

"I do a little boxing myself," he said as she passed by.

"I know. I saw. I'll—" It dawned on Charlotte that the only reason she knew he boxed was because she'd spied on him with binoculars. She closed her eyes and prayed he wouldn't catch that little detail.

"How do you know I box?" he asked, now turning his cart and rolling right along next to her toward the checkout. "I never told you I was a boxer."

"Hmm." Charlotte started to load her groceries on the belt, knowing she was a terrible liar and always had been and wasn't going to get out of this unscathed. She tried for something close to the truth. "I heard you punching over there one night. At least I assumed it was a punching bag. It sounded like one."

"Wanna come over and hit the bags with me tonight?"

Her arm stopped its movement, a box of Kashi hung in midair over the checkout belt. Eventually she set it down. "I don't think that's a good idea, Joe."

"Oh. So you *did* have a change of heart."

She grabbed a box of tabbouleh mix and threw it on the belt, laughing softly. "And if I did?"

She watched Joe nod and compress his lips, as if carefully considering her question. He straightened to his full height and looked down at Charlotte with eyes that intrigued her, challenged her, and basically sexed her up. She started to breathe fast.

"Then I'd change it right back, dumplin'."

Oh, how wrong LoriSue had been—Joe Mills wasn't as hot as a Chippendales dancer. He was much, much, much hotter. And the way he was toying with her had the flames shooting higher than ever.

Charlotte hoisted up a mesh bag of organic navel oranges and studied him, noting that the playful gleam in his eyes was being replaced by a scorching stare.

She gulped.

"If you stay . . ." Charlotte set down a package of dry White Northern beans and tried to keep eye contact with him. "What happens if you're like those potato chips, and I can't eat just one?"

Joe's mouth twitched. He rested his elbows on the shopping cart. "That's all right with me."

"What if I have to have some every day?"

"No problem."

"What if I—"

"Do you have your preferred shopper card today, ma'am?"

Charlotte whirled around to the checkout girl and handed her the card with trembling fingers.

*That sure took long enough,* Jimmy thought, watching Charlotte exit through the automatic doors and push her cart into the parking lot. He wondered why the lovebirds had arranged a rendezvous at Kroger's when they lived right next door to each other. Maybe they already needed a little something to liven things up. Maybe they had one of those kinky preferences for doing it in public places.

Jimmy was admiring Charlotte's ass as she unloaded her groceries into the minivan—much like he'd done in the frozen foods section moments before—when his eye caught Joe Mills coming out the door. The guy made him sick. He hated men with earrings. He couldn't see why some women—like Charlotte and the entire office staff at Sell-More, including his own friggin' wife!—would find that appealing.

Charlotte drove off, never even glancing at Joe. Ha! At least she'd waved to *him* that morning in front of school. Jimmy found comfort in that.

He climbed out of his Excursion and headed over to earring man and his shiny little Mustang. Jimmy hated little cars. He'd take a big-ass SUV any day, one that could take a Mustang like it was a speed bump in the church parking lot.

"Well, good morning, Joe!" Jimmy was a good-sized man, so it annoyed him that he had to look up a few inches to meet Joe's eye. He saw a flicker of surprise in Joe's face.

"Hello. Jimmy, right? LoriSue's husband?"

Jimmy thought, *Fuck you,* but just smiled.

"Hey, Justin's a great kid. I got to know him the other day at the campout."

Well. Wasn't that a smooth way of letting him know he'd spent the night in Charlotte's bed? Jimmy sniggered a little and shook his head, knowing an outright challenge when he heard one. Was this just Joe's way of letting him know that LoriSue was next?

"Good to know you're enjoying yourself here in Minton—getting real comfy, it sounds like."

Joe finished placing the last of his grocery bags in the trunk of his gigolo mobile and shot him a look that any man with a background in athletics would recognize as an outright physical challenge.

"It's a nice town."

"Stay away from both of them."

Joe looked so innocent. Jimmy guessed that made him a gigolo *and* an actor. Those poor women never stood a chance.

"Who would that be, Jimmy? Are you talking about Justin?"

"I'm talking about Charlotte and my *wife,* you loser. Mess with them and you're messing with me—Jim Bettmyer. Got it?"

"Excuse me just a moment." Joe pushed his cart down the row of cars and gave it a push into the cart exchange lane. Then he walked back, got out his car keys, and said, "I'm sorry, Jim, but I need to be heading back. I think you might be jumping to some inaccurate conclusions."

"The hell I am." Jimmy took a step closer to Joe and put his index finger in the man's solar plexus. He felt Joe's body flinch—he also felt some real solid abs and he had to give the man credit where it was due, but they weren't here to discuss his workout regimen. They were here to decide who got the women.

"LoriSue is still my wife, so back off. And Charlotte and I have had a relationship for many years, and she is not available. So your little fun ends right here, right now. You feel me?"

He watched Joe's face empty of all expression, and frankly, it spooked him. It was scary to see a man turn into a stone statue right before your eyes. Then, without a word, Joe got in his car and drove off.

Jimmy shook his head. What a total psycho case. Just because somebody lived in a nice house in a nice neighborhood didn't mean shit these days. There were psychos everywhere.

He looked at his watch and cursed—he was late for his Rotary Club meeting.

Bonnie sensed that things were moving fast with Joe. She just didn't know how fast. At the campout, she'd seen the way Charlotte and Joe looked at each other. Oh, they'd been perfectly polite. And it made the attraction between them all the more obvious. It zinged around like an electrical storm. It was pulled as tight as a tension wire between them.

They wanted each other—bad.

And now, as Bonnie watched Charlotte zoom around the kitchen the way she did nearly every afternoon, she looked for telltale signs that it was too late to do anything to stop it.

But Charlotte didn't seem particularly relaxed or dreamy eyed. She wasn't sighing without provocation. She wasn't looking off into space. In fact, Charlotte seemed a tad snippy.

"How's your day been, honey?"

"Same ole shit, Bon." Charlotte blew a strand of hair away from her face. "Shit to do for my clients. Shit to buy at the grocery. Shit to do around the house. You know—shit that's supposed to be upstairs is downstairs. Shit that's supposed to be downstairs is upstairs. Shit that's supposed to be cooked is frozen. Shit that's supposed to be clean is dirty. Same old shit."

Bonnie had never heard Charlotte say the word *shit* in all the time she'd known her—and she'd just said it nine times without taking a breath.

Interesting.

The family room door flew open. "I'm hungry, Mama," Hank said.

"You've already had your snack. Go back outside and play."

"But I'm starving!"

"No, you are clearly not starving, Hank. You can wait for dinner, which will be in about an hour. Now go back outside with Justin and Matt."

"But Justin and Matt are out riding their bikes and I don't have anybody to play with."

Charlotte tossed the carrot peeler into the stainless-steel sink with a loud sigh. "Then go ride with them."

"But they rode into town and we're not allowed to ride into town."

"They did *what*?"

"Uh-oh."

"How many times have I told that kid not to ride into town without telling me first?" Charlotte massaged her forehead. "Just come on inside and read."

"I don't have anything to read."

"You have an entire bookshelf full of books, Hank."

"But—"

"That's it!" Charlotte jogged around the kitchen counter and whipped open the doors. "Out! Now! Get some fresh air! I'll call you when dinner's ready."

She ushered a miserable Hank outside, then slammed the door.

Nope. Charlotte hadn't been laid yet.

Ned had been right, of course. Bonnie wasn't withholding any actual information from Charlotte about Joe, because she had no information to give. Not until tomorrow, at least, when Ned got the results from the fingerprint analysis. Bonnie wanted Ned to be right—she wanted Joe to be a good man, a man worthy of Charlotte.

"So what happened Saturday after we left? Did Joe stay?"

Charlotte stood at the stove, her back to Bonnie. "For a while. We sat outside and talked."

"That's it? Just talked?"

Charlotte spun around, and that's when Bonnie saw the confusion in her young friend's face. It nearly crushed her heart.

"Honey, are you okay?"

"No!"

Charlotte flung her elbows down on the butcher block

and hid her head in her arms. Bonnie rose from her seat at the table and rubbed her shoulders.

"What is it?"

"Can we go into the other room for a minute?"

Charlotte stalked off into the living room without waiting for an answer, and Bonnie was fully aware that the last little chat they'd had in that room was the one when Charlotte first told her about Joe.

What would it be this time?

They got comfortable on the sofa and Bonnie felt Charlotte reach out for her hand.

"I can't hold back any longer." Charlotte looked at Bonnie with wide, damp eyes. "But I'm trying to figure out if there's a way to balance it all, my life as a mom and a provider with . . . a little . . . I don't know—"

"Passion?" Bonnie patted her hand.

"Yeah. That."

"A love affair?"

Charlotte nodded.

"Wild sex?"

A moan escaped Charlotte's lips.

"You know, honey, it's possible to have both a life *and* a sex life."

Charlotte shook her head sadly and whispered, "I wouldn't know, Bon."

That was a bit of a surprise, and Bonnie straightened up on the couch and patted Charlotte's hand some more. "Do you want to talk about it?"

Charlotte nodded, cast her eyes downward, and cleared her throat. "I've never told anyone this, so bear with me, but the thing is that with Kurt, I always felt like I was abnormal, too interested in sex, too, uh—"

"Horny?"

Charlotte's eyes went huge. "I guess."

Kurt had always struck Bonnie as a nice combination

of maleness and sweetness. Granted, she'd never wondered much about the Taskers' sex life, but as she sat there
with Charlotte now, she wracked her brain for a time when
she might have noticed the two were having trouble in
their marriage. She couldn't think of one.

"So you weren't happy sexually?"

"Not at all."

"And you thought it was your fault?"

Charlotte nodded, and Bonnie watched her fight hard
not to cry. She reached out and stroked Charlotte's hair,
feeling the pain radiate from her small body. *The things
we put ourselves through!* "And you felt guilty for what
happened with Joe?"

Charlotte turned away from Bonnie's hand and buried
her face in her palms. Bonnie watched her thin shoulders
shake, knowing there was nothing at all she could do except be a good listener. She waited a few moments and
then said, "Honey. You need to get this out and get on
with your life."

Charlotte's shoulders stopped shaking. She looked up
at Bonnie with a determined nod. "Except for the times I
was trying to get pregnant, Kurt would have been perfectly happy making love about once a month. And when
we did, it was so damn predictable and polite and over so
quickly that I hardly even knew I'd had sex."

She'd asked for the details, Bonnie reminded herself.

"And when I told him what I really wanted—things I'd
had that one time with Joe—he was appalled. Embarrassed. A little worried about me."

"Good Lord, Charlotte."

"So I went through my whole marriage thinking I was
a pervert because I wanted him to smack my butt and talk
dirty to me. Am I a pervert?"

Bonnie felt herself experiencing the hot flashes she
thought she'd left behind five years before. "Uh, no."

"He was just so shy about sex—wouldn't talk to me about it—and one day he caught me . . . he caught me . . ." Charlotte flew off the couch and started pacing. "I've always kept this journal of erotic poetry—things that pop into my head at the oddest times that I just can't keep locked inside. Some of it is very hot."

She looked to Bonnie for a sign she should continue, so Bonnie managed a nod. She tried not to look too astonished as she kept thinking, *Charlotte writes erotic poetry?*

"Well, one day he caught me with my journal and . . . well, I was touching myself. He freaked. He picked up my journal, read a few lines of what I'd written, told me he was afraid for me, and walked out of the bedroom. He wouldn't talk to me about it."

"Oh, Charlotte—"

"After about three days, I left him a note in his brief-case. The note said that I really needed to talk to him about my sexual frustration and how lonely I was for him. I told him I wanted to talk to him about my poetry. I told him I loved him and I wanted desperately to share the sexual part of myself with him."

Bonnie hardly dared ask. "What happened?"

"He never acknowledged the note. He never said a word to me about it."

Bonnie couldn't help it—her mouth fell open. "Oh, my God, honey. Are you sure he got it?"

"I'm sure. He always got the notes I left him in his briefcase."

"And when was this?"

Charlotte shrugged. "About three years ago. Hank was five. I didn't know what to do, Bon. I was scared that I wouldn't be able to love him anymore."

"Oh, sweetie." Bonnie got up from the couch and put her arms around Charlotte, aware for the first time how much pain her dear friend had been in and ashamed that she'd not seen past Charlotte's veneer of competency all these years. "I'm so sorry."

"Me, too," Charlotte said into Bonnie's shoulder.

"Did you try counseling?"

Charlotte shook her head. "He said he refused to talk about something so personal with a stranger."

"Even if it meant losing you?"

Charlotte pulled away from her embrace. "I never gave him that ultimatum. There were times I thought about leaving him, but all I had to do was look at Matt or Hank and that idea lasted about three seconds. But, Bonnie— can I tell you something?"

Charlotte's chin started to quiver and Bonnie felt her own tears coming. "Anything."

"I even fantasized that . . ." Charlotte broke loose with a sob, wrapped her arms around herself, and rocked back and forth on the balls of her feet until she could continue, and it rushed out of her in one long burst: "I fantasized that Kurt would die peacefully in his sleep, and I'd be free, and then he *did* die! Just like I imagined! And I know this isn't rational, but I thought maybe I was being punished for putting so much emphasis on sex. And, Bonnie—God!—this sounds so stupid when I say it out loud, but I have this fear that if I give in to Joe, give in to lust, something else awful is going to happen. I must sound nuts."

Charlotte sobbed again and Bonnie just barely got her onto the couch before she collapsed. She lay curled on her side and cried so hard, for so long, that Bonnie was afraid Hank would hear her.

Bonnie perched on the edge of the sofa, stroked Charlotte's arm, and told her to go ahead and cry—get it all out—and kept an eye on the door to make sure she had the privacy she needed.

When Charlotte's tears slowed, Bonnie rubbed her back and said, "It was not your fault that Kurt died."

Charlotte nodded in silence, her face still hidden in her arms.

"I don't think the universe sets out to punish any of us, sweetie. You're so young, with so much life ahead of you. Please don't be afraid to live it."

# Chapter Seventeen

"Can't you let things slide for one night, Charlotte? Just keep the kids home and not run around like a crazy person? For one night?"

Bonnie's suggestion sounded tempting but impossible. "We're hosting the Loveland Little League tonight. The place is going to be a zoo, and I've got snack bar duty."

"Good Lord, Charlotte."

She laughed. It felt good to laugh after all that crying. She'd cried for over a half hour, and now she was behind schedule. The kids were finishing up their dinners but had yet to change their clothes.

"Hank, honey, go put on your leotard. Justin and Matt, put on your uniforms and grab your gloves."

The kids dispersed—her two running up the stairs and Justin bolting out the back door for his own house a block away.

"Let me do something for you tonight," Bonnie said, loading the dishwasher. "How about I take your concession stand duty?"

"No. That's okay, Bon. Really."

"Then let me take Hank to ballet and pick her up."

Charlotte looked at her friend and smiled. Because of Bonnie, she was starting to feel better about things. She felt lighter inside, more hopeful, and a little less burdened by guilt. Bonnie had been right about so much. It wasn't her fault that Kurt had died. God—whoever he or she was—didn't take Kurt's life to punish her for having a sex drive. The idea was almost laughable, and one day she hoped to be able to laugh at herself for ever thinking that. Right now, she'd focus on trying to find a way to love and honor Kurt's memory but grab hold of her own life—the only life she'd ever get.

"Thank you, Bonnie," she said, taking a deep breath. "That would be great if you could drive Hank tonight."

The phone rang. The news she got caused Charlotte to reach into the pantry and shoot a steady stream of squirt cheese into her mouth. It was either that or cry some more.

"That was the Liebermans." Charlotte took a big swallow. "They just canceled on me for the concession stand. All three of them."

"Give me that," Bonnie said, holding out her hand for the aerosol can and squirting the cheese on her tongue. "God! This stuff is hideous!"

They laughed loud and long, and Bonnie was saying that she and Ned would take two of the Lieberman spots when they noticed a nicely dressed woman at the back door. Charlotte was surprised when the stranger poked her head inside the house like she was an old friend.

"Everybody decent?"

Charlotte studied the woman, looked to Bonnie for confirmation, and the two of them screamed out at the same time, *"Ohmigod! LoriSue?"*

She was getting used to the fuss by now, having spent the last couple days dressed like Hilary Clinton.

It was kind of fun seeing everyone's reaction to her transformation. The girls in the office went ballistic, especially over her hair. Jimmy, the scum bucket, told her she hadn't looked that hot since high school. Justin hugged her and told her she was the prettiest mom in Minton, and she had to admit that that one made her a little teary eyed.

But nothing could compare to the shocked looks on Charlotte's and Bonnie's faces.

"So what do you think, girls?" LoriSue twirled around to give them the full effect of outfit no. 3—a cotton-rayon blend pencil skirt that hit midcalf, topped by a complementary summer-weight twinset, both in a hand-dyed dusky blue. She kicked up her heels to show off her simple but elegant sling-backs. She shook out her hair, which she had to admit felt delicious as it moved freely against the back of her neck, unencumbered by hair spray.

The two women stared in stunned silence. Bonnie was clutching a can of something in her hand, and a little poof of orange goo went shooting out onto the kitchen floor.

"Well?"

Charlotte was the first to speak. "Wow, LoriSue. You are beautiful and sophisticated and stunning—absolutely stunning."

Bonnie nodded in agreement, her mouth ajar. Finally she spoke. "You're Julia Roberts in *Pretty Woman*—toward the end."

LoriSue liked that analogy. It didn't offend her in the least. In fact, she really did feel like Cinderella.

Justin burst in the door at that point wearing his uniform, baseball mitt in hand. It seemed like Charlotte had everything in control, as usual, and was about to take the boys to the ballpark. LoriSue thought maybe it should be her turn tonight.

"I'll drive Matt and Justin," she said, holding up her

digital camera. "I'm taking pictures for the Web site, so I have to be there all evening."

"Isn't she megapretty?" Justin asked, leaning against her side and gazing at her. LoriSue kissed the top of his ball cap.

"Yes, she's megapretty," Charlotte said.

LoriSue locked eyes with her. Charlotte was mega-pretty, too, in her own way, and LoriSue wondered why she'd never really seen that before. Charlotte had always seemed plain to her, kind of washed-out and moving around too much. But tonight, as she stood still in her kitchen in a ratty pair of jeans and a simple V-neck T-shirt, LoriSue noticed a glow in her cheeks and a sparkle in her eyes that she didn't recall seeing before.

And LoriSue couldn't help but think that maybe all women were beautiful—even Bonnie, who was still staring at her—each in her own way.

"I don't suppose you'd like to do concession stand duty?" Bonnie asked. "We're short a grill cook."

*Not in this outfit.* LoriSue held up the camera. "Otherwise occupied tonight, sorry."

Bonnie suddenly grinned real big, looked at Charlotte, and said, "Know of any other warm bodies?"

Charlotte didn't answer. Her eyes were focused on something right behind LoriSue and Justin, something that had transformed Charlotte's face. If there had been a glow about her a minute ago, the woman was now on fire from the inside out. LoriSue knew exactly what she would see when she turned around.

Joe Mills—everyone's favorite warm body.

He'd gone over the situation in his head so many times that his brain hurt and had decided just moments earlier that he really should talk to Charlotte, tell her a little bit about what was going on in his life, enough that she could make an informed decision.

He just couldn't bear the thought of ever doing anything that would hurt her.

As Joe glanced at the house full of people, he realized their little chat would have to wait. Then he sensed that something had changed. And as Hank ran through the kitchen in a little black ballet outfit and raced toward him, Joe felt like he'd walked onstage in the middle of act 2.

Then it registered. It was Charlotte. She was completely different—transformed. She was looking at him with naked greed. Desire. Not a trace of ambiguity anywhere. It was like she'd decided to stake her claim and stake it now.

The force of it knocked the air right out of Joe's lungs—but that could have been the impact of Hank's little body, which had just thudded against him. Her chubby arms were squeezing him around the hips.

He blinked at Charlotte.

Then, with a little smile barely pushing up the corners of her mouth, Joe felt her slide her gray gaze up and down his body like she was painting him with long, steady strokes of a brush. It was a blatantly sexual move. His favorite kind.

Then he realized he didn't know the woman standing just inches away from him at the back door. He was about to introduce himself when he let out a startled laugh. LoriSue should go into undercover work.

He nodded at her in approval. "Nice," he said.

"Thank you," she whispered back.

He watched a hot wave of embarrassment wash over LoriSue, and he couldn't help but feel sorry for her. She was married to Jimmy Bettmyer. Nobody deserved that fate. And Joe hoped to God that this drastic makeover wasn't for him. Yes, she looked about five hundred times more attractive than she did a couple weeks ago, but the look didn't reach out and grab him.

His gaze returned to Charlotte and he smiled at her.

The only woman he wanted—the only woman he'd ever really wanted—was Charlotte.

She shot a full-throttle smile right back at him and he felt his insides melt. He knew right then, as his hands patted Hank's red curls and his eyes couldn't leave Charlotte's face, that he was, in fact, falling in love with her.

"Joe?" Charlotte said. "Can I ask you something?"

Matt burst into the room at that instant and waved his baseball glove in the air. "Hey, Joe!"

"Hey, Matt."

"Hey, Joe," said another voice.

"Hey, Justin."

"Yo, Joe," said Bonnie.

"Yo, Bonnie."

And Joe sensed that whatever Charlotte was about to ask him was going to be big—life changing, even—yet she was brave enough to ask him in front of all these people.

He gave her his full attention. "Yes?"

Charlotte tilted her head and said sweetly, "You any good with a spatula?"

As a matter of fact, he was damn good with a spatula. But he suspected they weren't talking about the same thing.


Charlotte watched Bonnie's Toyota head down the drive with Hank buckled in the backseat, followed by LoriSue's BMW, Matt waving to her out the rear window. And suddenly they were alone, just Charlotte and Joe, in the driveway.

She could feel him, though he wasn't touching her. It was the memory of his touch that she felt, the ghost touch she'd lived with for all these years. But he stood right next to her now. All she had to do was reach for him, and he'd be real.

The thought left her breathless.

"Charlotte, we need to talk."

"No more talking, Joe. I want to kiss you."

She heard Joe make a little strangled squeak. "There's something I should tell you first." He took a step away. "Slow down just a second."

She couldn't help herself—she laughed. She reached out and touched the silky sleeve of his polo shirt, staring at how her fingers played on the hem of the fabric, noticing how pale her hand looked near his rich brown skin. It occurred to her that he really should change clothes before his stint at the grill, because this nice shirt would be ruined. She'd tell him that in a minute. Right now, she wanted to put her lips on him. And they had about ten minutes before they absolutely had to be on their way. The two of them could accomplish a lot in ten minutes.

"You know, Joe . . ." Charlotte raised her eyes to him. She could see him holding back. His jaw was clenched. His lips were tight. She saw the air rushing in and out of his nose—like a bull trying his best not to charge. "Things have been mighty slow for me the last thirteen years."

One of his eyebrows twitched.

"I don't think I want slow anymore."

The other eyebrow twitched.

"In fact, I'm damn sick of slow."

Joe shifted his weight and licked his lips, never taking his black eyes off hers. Those eyes held that familiar look of entitlement, along with a touch of surprise. The look advised her to be damn sure of what she was doing, because there would be no turning back.

She remembered that look. She liked that look.

"Do I have to ask for it, Joe?"

His eyes got big.

"Because I'll beg for it if you want me to."

Joe's lips parted. The man looked stunned.

"Give it to me, Joe," she whispered. She pressed her body up against his and used her tongue to lick up the front of his silky polo shirt, her eyes locked on his.

Joe let out a sigh and a moan and took a step in to her and just kept walking. Charlotte strained her neck to keep focused on his face, now so close, and reached her arms behind her in case he backed her into the side of the house.

Which is exactly what he did. She hit the siding with a thud.

"Ask for it again, Charlotte."

She stood on tiptoe. She reached her arms up over his shoulders and hooked them around his neck. She smiled at him. She grabbed a handful of his hair. And pulled him down close.

"Please," she breathed. "Kiss me, Joe."

She attacked him like he was a Honeybaked Ham. Like he was her first decent meal in more than a decade. Which he was.

Joe's hands were all over her bottom and the back of her thighs. He was kneading her, pushing her on, and on she went, kissing him, eating him, as snippets of her poetry and their recent conversations floated through her mind and propelled her kiss into higher gear—*"meat . . ." "slut . . ." "ladylike little split fruit . . ." "perkiest little pink cherry nipples . . ." "lying in wait . . ."*

Charlotte jumped him—just threw her legs around his waist and gloried in the feel of his hands clamping her butt. Joe pulled her tight against him and ground her against the wall with his pelvis.

Her head hit the siding, and a dull discomfort radiated

down her neck to her shoulders only to be erased by the searing pleasure, pleasure that had no beginning and no end because of this mouth, this tongue, *this man*. All over her.

"Oh God, Joe," she whispered against his kiss. Joe's arms went tight around her. She couldn't get close enough. It was as if she wanted to push herself inside him, obliterate her own being, and become part of him.

"I've wanted you forever," he said, his hands in her hair, his kisses moving across her cheek and down her throat and onto her collarbones. "I've missed you the last couple days, Charlotte. The last thirteen years."

"God, I've missed you so much, Joe."

The kissing stopped and they just held each other. Joe propped his chin on her shoulder and hugged her so hard she thought she heard the crunch of the cartilage between her ribs. It didn't matter. Nothing mattered but that Joe was real and he was in her arms again.

He backed away from the house and began walking, Charlotte's body stuck to the front of his. He crossed the drive toward his yard. Charlotte laughed.

"Where are you taking me?"

He stopped in his tracks. He said nothing, but just hugged her even harder.

"Joe?"

"I was going to take you to my bed, but I realized that probably wouldn't be a wise idea."

"Yeah. We need to be going."

Joe laughed. "Right. Want to ride in my car?"

Charlotte pulled back a little so she could look down into Joe's face. That baseline melancholy she sometimes saw in Joe was back, not quite hidden by his gentle smile. She kissed that smile, brushed her fingers through all his thick black hair, and wondered what made him so sad.

"I'd love to go for a ride in your car. The boys talk about it all the time."

"So I hear. Let's go."

She unhooked her legs and slipped down the front of his body until her feet hit the driveway. Joe took her hand. "Oh, wait! You really should change your shirt," she said.

Joe frowned and glanced down at himself. "You don't like this shirt?"

Charlotte laughed. "I love the shirt. But I don't think you have any idea what you're getting into—the concession stand is a pit of grease."

"Ah. Then come with me and I'll change."

Charlotte hadn't been inside the Connor house since before they began packing, so the bareness of the place shocked her. She stepped inside through the pool patio door to the kitchen, immediately noticing that there was no fruit on the counter. No art on the walls. No candles on the family room mantel. Just a black leather couch, one lamp on one end table, and a dinette set with two chairs. Joe lived simply.

"I'll be right back." He began walking toward the center hallway.

"I'm waiting down here?"

He turned to face her, the sadness back with a vengeance. "Please. If you don't mind."

The hurt was immediate. Apparently, Charlotte was good enough to grope in the drive but not good enough to let upstairs. She shrugged and looked down at her sandals.

Joe walked back to her. "Charlotte?"

At the brush of his fingers on hers, she looked up.

"I am not used to having a woman in my life. I've been alone a very long time."

She nodded and swallowed, overwhelmed by the serious tone of his voice and the pleading in his expression.

Whatever he was about to tell her was difficult for him.

"Okay," she whispered.

"There are things about me that I don't usually share with anyone."

"Your writing."

He smiled a little. "Because of the nature of my work, I've become a very private person."

"So you don't want me in your bedroom."

Joe's eyes closed, and she marveled at how long and lustrous his eyelashes were against his cheek. Joe's children would be beautiful creatures. And the next thought hit her before she could protect herself—*their* children would be beautiful creatures.

"I want you in my bedroom bad, Charlotte."

"We have about thirty seconds until we have to leave. Go change your shirt."

"I'm going to have you."

"Yes, you are, Joe."

He didn't have to say a word. They were driving along the state highway just past Main Street when the scent of honeysuckle whooshed down on them through the open roof of the Mustang. Charlotte's little hand landed on the top of his right thigh, telling him everything he needed to know.

She remembered, just as he did.

She'd cried that day so long ago. He'd never been with a woman who cried during sex, and it baffled him. She assured him she wasn't crying because she was sad or hurt, but only because it felt so good.

That first time, she'd straddled him. He thought it would make her feel more in control and less in danger. He didn't want to scare her or make her run. He only wanted to fuck her. He wanted to fuck her from the instant he saw her zoom by in that little car on the Beltway, red hair flying around that angelic face. It had been a primal urge. He had no choice but to follow her and get her.

He nearly hooted with joy when that notebook flew up and out of her car. If that wasn't a sign, he didn't know what was.

The surface of her skin had been satin smooth and hot from the sun. Her entire little body was covered in that creamy pale satin. She felt ethereal under his hands. Fragile and delicate. But the way she kissed him—goddamn— that was anything but delicate. She was greedy and pushy and kept making these blissful little moaning sounds as her hands ran over his body and her lips attacked his. She might have been petite, but she had a big appetite for sex.

The second time, he took her standing up, much like the kiss they'd just shared in her driveway. In fact—feeling her ass in his hands, her legs clamped around his hips—it was like those thirteen years had never even happened. She tasted the same. She felt the same. And Joe wondered if he'd ever really existed outside her flesh and her heat and the sound of her voice.

He glanced over at Charlotte next to him and watched her hair whip in shiny flames around her face. Today was then or yesterday was now, he didn't know which, but he knew that he was right where he was meant to be—at this woman's side.

"Do you remember the third time we made love?" she asked.

Joe laughed. Apparently, his brain was the projector and his forehead the movie screen and she'd had a front row seat for the show.

"Hell yes, I remember." The third time had been the best. And the most intense thing he'd ever experienced.

Joe took her hand from his thigh and raised it to his

lips. Then he put it right back where it had been, only his hand now cupped hers.

As he looked at the profile of her face in the mellow evening light, he told himself that he would find a way to love this woman and keep her safe. It was possible. Every day he spent in Minton made him feel closer to normal. Every day he spent in her presence made him believe that anything was possible.

"I couldn't help myself that day, Charlotte. I wanted you so much. I just went crazy."

"It was a good crazy, Joe."

"A great crazy."

He'd never gone soft that day with her so long ago. As soon as he came, he was ready again. One look at her—from her smoky gray eyes to the sweet patch of honey red fuzz below her belly—and he'd felt like there would never be adequate release. She was a drug, and he couldn't get high enough.

So he'd eased her down on her back and spread her thighs wide, running a finger along her to be sure she was ready. He found her swollen and tender and so slippery that his finger disappeared inside her with the slightest pressure. When he removed his hand, he'd seen the blood. It wasn't much and he wasn't quite sure what to make of it, but he'd stared at his finger for a long moment before he dared look up at her face.

What he'd seen in her expression blindsided him—naked vulnerability and pure female lust. Tears spilled down the sides of her face and into the hair fanning out beneath her in the honeysuckle. She offered him a shy smile, in spite of the tears, and whispered, "Thank you for this."

He'd been unable to come up with a reply.

Her smile widened.

"Why are you crying?" he'd asked her.

She'd reached up and touched his face, caressing his brow and cheek. "Because you're everything I needed."

And that's when it hit him—this woman wasn't a playful conquest. She was a gift—a rare and beautiful gift.

He'd nearly begged her, "Tell me your name, baby. Please."

She'd pressed a fingertip to his lips. "Shhh."

He'd licked at that finger, then pressed his mouth on hers as he penetrated her. He'd cradled her in his arms, feeling the sheen of tears, sweat, and honeysuckle blossoms that seemed to cover every inch of their skin. She'd cried out into his open mouth, shuddered beneath him, and gripped him so tight he could feel every bone in her body.

That third time, it had been like he'd reached out through the universe and touched joy. That third time, Joe had made love to the woman and she'd made love to him.

Now, with the wind in his face and her at his side, he marveled at how young and stupid he'd been that day. He'd just stood there in the parking lot, so concerned about not showing his real feelings that he'd frozen. The big badass right out of Special Forces couldn't bring himself to ask the woman for her name again—let alone her number, her address, her date of birth, and whether she believed in love at first sight.

Instead, he'd grunted something unintelligible and was wondering how he was going to get out of there with his pride intact when she'd thrown herself at him, kissed him, and broken his tooth.

She'd raced out of that parking lot so damn fast that there'd been no time for an awkward good-bye. No time for any good-bye at all. Joe had just spit out his tooth chip into the loose gravel and forced himself not to look up at the license plate.

As he pulled into the Minton Little League parking lot

and cut the engine, Joe ran his tongue over the chip in his tooth. He turned to see that she was watching him, smiling, her face radiant from the wind and sun, her hair a bit disheveled. He couldn't remember ever seeing anything as lovely in his whole life. Something about Charlotte made him believe in happiness. In miracles.

"You sure you're ready for this?"

Joe didn't know whether she was referring to snack bar duty or love, but one answer would work for both.

"I'm sure."

He held her hand as they walked toward the obnoxiously bright blue concession stand, its white aluminum shutters raised for business. Bonnie and Ned waved at them from inside as a faint aroma of hot grease wafted through the air.

Joe leaned down and whispered in Charlotte's ear, "I won't be able to keep my hands off you in there."

She looked at him sideways. "I was about to say the same thing."

"Gonna be a long night," he said with a sigh.

Charlotte laughed. "You have no idea."

"Four more number fours and two number fives!"

At that instant, Joe realized it was a good thing he'd gone into law enforcement and not fast-food management. His head was spinning.

"You hanging in there, Joe?" Ned looked over at him with an impish grin. "Only got two hours to go."

"Smooth and in the groove, Ned." He slapped four more burgers onto the open buns lined up on the wooden countertop.

Ned laughed. "And it pays just about as well as police work, doesn't it?"

Joe's brain buzzed in alarm, but he kept his eyes on the grill and his breath steady. So Ned knew, or at least suspected. Part of him wanted to believe that Ned was an ally. Part of him remembered Roger's warning not to lose his edge. There wasn't room for a single mistake now, not since he'd made up his mind to bring Charlotte and her kids into his life.

No mistakes. Ever.

"I suppose you'd know, Ned."

"Yeah, well, I hear the pay scale is a little better at the federal level."

Joe said nothing, thankful for the string of orders now being recited in Charlotte's melodious voice.

"I need a number one, three number fours, and a number two without the chili!"

"A number two without the chili is a number three, Charlotte," Ned mumbled.

"One three then," she said impatiently.

How did Ned know? What had Joe said or done to tip him off? Did it mean he had to leave Minton? Would Charlotte ever consent to go with him?

"Your secret is safe with me," Ned whispered over the hiss of the grill.

"And what secret is that?"

"Why don't we go for a beer sometime and talk about it? Is Friday good? Nine o'clock at the Creekside—you know where that is?"

"I've seen it."

"Good, then." Ned slapped his shoulder. "By the way, you're a natural at this. I'm impressed."

Joe took his time flipping the burgers, then turned slowly toward Ned, shooting him a look he'd perfected long ago. Ned's eyes widened and the older man tugged at the collar of his golf shirt.

"Now it's your turn to impress me, Chief Preston."

Ned swallowed and gave him a nod. "Duly noted."

The next two hours passed in a blur of burgers and

buns and frozen bags of French fries and it had just occurred to Joe that he was dying of thirst when there was a little tap on his shoulder. Charlotte stood behind him, holding out a bottle of water.

It was the only touch he'd had from her since they walked in the place. So much for not being able to keep his hands off her—the only thing he'd had in his hands was frozen beef.

"Thank you for working so hard, Joe," she said, opening the bottle and handing it to him. "We get ninety percent of all our operating revenue from this concession stand. Did I tell you that?"

God, she was sweet. And watching those pretty pink lips recite Little League fund-raising facts was making him hard. "You don't say?"

"Yes. So you are now officially a Minton Little League volunteer. Wanna serve on the board?"

"No." He couldn't take his eyes off her lips.

"You got a couple burgers about to combust back here, Joe." Ned didn't even try to hide the laugh in his voice.

"Right."

Joe rescued the orders and Charlotte went back to her post. Moments later, he heard LoriSue's voice at the snack bar window, chatting with the women about the Little League's Web site or something.

"LoriSue is lookin' real good lately," Ned whispered. "I always suspected that woman could suck a golf ball through thirty feet of garden hose."

Joe roared—laughed so loud that everyone turned to look at him. And honest to God, he couldn't remember the last time he'd laughed like that.

Charlotte suddenly raced behind him, on her way to the back room for freezer pops, he overheard. Joe was feeling frisky. He was feeling happy. He handed Ned the spatula and ripped off his apron. "Take over for me for a minute, would you?" He didn't give him time to say no.

When Joe reached the back room, Charlotte was on tiptoe, leaning down into the chest freezer. Her little heart-shaped ass was displayed like a Valentine with his name on it. Joe shut the door softly and took a few silent steps toward her.

"Hey, dumplin'."

She gasped and tried to straighten up, but Joe flattened a hand on her spine. "Stay right there. I like you like this."

He felt Charlotte shiver under his palm. He felt the cold air rush from the well of the freezer around her body. He pressed into her behind and brought both hands to cup her breasts. Her nipples were little rocks in the cold.

"Joe . . ." The word was part plea and part moan.

"I know. I'm not usually one for public displays, either, but you make me crazy."

She looked back over her shoulder and smiled. "I feel how hard you are," she whispered.

He pinched her stiff little nipples, then relaxed his hands to cradle the weight of her breasts in his palms. He pushed her up against the freezer and moved his hips into her. "I want to take you like this. I haven't taken you like this—yet."

Charlotte's smile disappeared. Her expression grew serious and hot, and her lips trembled. "Oh God." She closed her eyes. "I want . . . I want . . ."

"I want it, too."

She shook her head. "I'm not sure you understand, Joe. I'm so . . . well . . . *deprived* that I'm afraid once I start I won't ever get enough."

"The potato chip scenario again."

"I'm afraid so."

"We're going to get along just fine."

"Joe? Do you take a multivitamin with iron every day?"

"I do."

"You're going to need it."

"Are you on the Pill?"

"No."

"Good. I want to have babies with you."

*"Oh my God."*

Joe immediately closed his eyes in horror—his DNA was speaking without his permission. The idea of bringing any more children into this situation should make him sick with fear—it's just that Charlotte made him want so much. She made it seem possible.

"I didn't mean—"

"Hey—we've got a line for the freezer pops out here!" Bonnie's voice was coming closer. Obviously she was giving them ample warning that she was on her way to the back. She was a good woman.

"Damn!" Charlotte straightened up and turned toward the doorway. Joe pressed his pelvis against the cold, reached inside for the pops, and handed them back to Charlotte without turning around. He hoped the commercial-sized freezer would be sufficient cover for his raging erection.

"Here you go!" Charlotte's voice sounded overly enthusiastic as she handed the pops to Bonnie, and Joe let his head hang into the frozen food and laughed. They were like teenagers. It felt so reckless. It felt so damn good.

"All righty, kids," Bonnie said. "You two can take off. Ned and I will close up."

"Thanks, Bonnie."

"Don't forget your children, Charlotte. Matt's game just ended and Hank is running around here somewhere. I've got her ballet bag in my car."

"Right."

"See you, Joe." Bonnie was obviously enjoying herself. "Everything all right down there?"

"Better than ever," Joe answered.

The ride home was magic. The kids reached up into the wind, laughing and shouting as their fingers played in the rush of cool night air. Charlotte leaned back on the headrest and gazed at the stars above. Joe held her hand. And it dawned on her that the Mustang was the first convertible she'd been in since that day thirteen years ago.

The stars raced by, like time did, and it made her dizzy. She thought of holding Matt and Hank for the first time, just seconds after they were born. She thought of the feel of Kurt against her at night. The scent of honeysuckle hit her nostrils, and Charlotte recalled the way Joe had looked deep into her eyes when he took her.

She found herself saying a silent prayer to Kurt. She hoped that God was eavesdropping and that both of them would understand.

*I will always love you, but it's time to let you go.*

"Mama! Look!" Hank and Matt screamed in amazement as a shooting star flashed on the horizon.

Charlotte felt a smile curl her lips.

"Shooting stars are actually small asteroids burning up in the earth's atmosphere," Joe said. "They're not really stars at all."

"Coolio," Matt said.

"Guess how many fingers I'm holding up," Hank said.

Joe laughed. "I have no idea."

"I'll give you a hint," Matt said. "She's holding up all the fingers on her left hand."

"That would be four fingers then" was Joe's answer.

Charlotte turned around in time to see her children

stare at each other in shock, their mouths open, then start to howl with laughter.

Joe pulled into Charlotte's drive instead of his own, which made her smile, and the kids tumbled from the backseat and raced for the door. Charlotte had barely gotten out of the car when Hoover bounded toward them, barking like a hound from hell. His nose immediately went to Joe's crotch.

"Your dog needs obedience classes, Charlotte."

"I took him. He flunked."

Then Joe had his arms around her, and she felt herself melt against him with a sigh. What would life be like if she could end every day in this man's arms? Hoover shoved his big head between their knees.

"It's damn hard to be alone with you," Joe said, chuckling.

"I know. I'm popular." Charlotte pulled away from his embrace. "Anyway, you smell like a giant number five with cheese."

Joe grinned down upon her and planted a sweet kiss full on her lips. "How about I take a shower and come back over?"

This was the part that was going to be the most difficult, but Charlotte knew she had to get it over with. Yes, she was falling for Joe, and yes, she'd decided to give in to her unbearable need for him. And no, she wasn't a damn bit ashamed of herself for doing either.

But she wouldn't do anything that would harm her children.

"Joe? I don't feel comfortable having you in my . . . well, my bedroom. Because of the kids. It's just—"

"I understand."

Sometimes she thought Joe was too good to be true. This was one of those times. He looked down at her with affection even though she'd just put the kibosh on his plans. How could a man be so carried away by passion one moment and so patient the next? What made a man like Joe tick?

She looked forward to spending a long time finding out.

"I'd like to make it really special for us—like when it's not a school night and the kids can sleep over with friends. I'll make you dinner. We won't be rushed. We can—"

"I've waited thirteen years. I can wait a couple more days."

"Mama!" Hank's face was pressed up against Charlotte's bedroom window and she peered down on them. "Matt won't let me take a shower first and it's always my turn to go first on Tuesdays!"

"Creepy little cow-butt tattletale!" Matt's voice rang out from somewhere inside the house.

Charlotte looked up at Joe and sighed. "Good night." She planted a kiss on his cheek, which felt clenched tight beneath her lips. "I guess this mixing fantasy with reality isn't an easy thing to do."

"We'll find a way, Charlotte. Just you watch."

# Chapter Eighteen

"I want a turn, Matt."

Justin applied the brakes and waited for his friend to stop his bike. "It's not fair—you've been getting all the good pictures this week: the one of Lisa Bertucci's mom's slip hanging out of her skirt on Tuesday, and then on Thursday the mean guy outside the library who looked like a mental patient, and then yesterday that dude at the gas station kissing that fat lady. It's my turn."

"Whatever." Matt lifted the spy camera strap off his neck and passed it over to Justin. "Just don't waste any film."

They rode for a while down Main Street, avoiding pedestrians and parking meters and the occasional suggestion that they ride their bikes somewhere other than the sidewalk.

The boys rounded the corner of Queen and Main and were debating whether they had enough money between them to split a blueberry freezee from the Creamy Whip and whether they had enough time to eat it before dinner when Justin skidded to a stop.

"Check out those guys," he said, nodding casually toward two men sitting in a car parked at the curb. "Man-oh-man."

"CIA, do you think?" Matt motioned for Justin to walk his bike into the side door of Garson's Glass, where they could monitor the situation discreetly. Matt pulled out his binoculars to get a good look.

"Too creepy looking for the CIA. I think they're hit men or spies." Justin started snapping pictures.

"I don't know. CIA agents can be pretty creepy looking."

Justin took one last picture and laughed at Matt. "Like you've ever met a CIA agent in real life?"

Matt snatched the camera away. "Like you ever met a hit man or a spy?"

The two boys walked their bikes back up to Main Street, then hopped on and began pedaling.

"I think we should show these pictures to Ned," Justin said.

"And how we gonna do that?" Matt asked. "I can't have my mom develop these pictures—she'd have a spaz attack. You know I'm not supposed to be spying."

"Then give 'em to me. I'll have my dad get 'em developed."

"No," Matt sighed heavily. "This should stay on a need-to-know basis. I'll figure something out."

It was turning out to be one of those weeks that went by in a blur. Charlotte had as many clients as she could juggle, Hank's ballet recital was that weekend and the kid had a rehearsal schedule more suited to the Kirov Ballet than The Minton Dance Factory, and both Matt's and Hank's teams had advanced to the play-offs.

Charlotte was exhausted. She'd hardly seen Joe at all. He'd stopped by for coffee the last two mornings before she took the kids to school, but she hadn't had time to say two words to him. It dawned on her today that Joe actually liked the morning chaos. He was always so chipper at 7:00 a.m.

She lay in her bed with the covers thrown off because it was so warm. The only sounds that infringed upon the night silence were the faraway bark of a dog, the chirp of crickets, and the soft hum of the ceiling fan above her bed.

She stretched, letting her arms and legs fall loose, feeling the caress of the air on her skin. Summer was nearly here. It would be the second summer without Kurt, the second cycle of seasons without her husband. She was well into her second year as a widow.

Charlotte trained her eyes on the slow whir of the fan blades, trying, in the wash of moonlight, to isolate one blade as it spun around in an unbroken rhythm, like the earth around the sun, like the moon around the earth, like the days and weeks and months cycling through her life. The one life she'd ever get.

Was she about to screw it up?

She did a few deep-breathing exercises, then surrendered. She got the key. With more force than she planned, she yanked open the bedside table drawer. She clicked on the lamp.

Charlotte grabbed her notebook and removed the cap from her ink pen and stared at the blank page.

The fear welled up in her the second her hand began to move across the paper, leaving in its path loops and swirls that revealed every uncertainty she felt.

*Dark Stranger*

*Who is this man I've let inside,*
*And how much will he take?*

*His feet walk on my kitchen floor*
*His words seduce my injured heart*
*His hands burn my weakened flesh*

*But I don't know him*
*Though he laughs with my kids*
*And pets my dog*
*And sits on my porch*
*He is a dark stranger*
*With black eyes and a troubled soul*

*He says he wants babies*
*But it's only part of rough play*
*Don't play with me, Joe*
*Don't hide from me*
*Dark stranger*
*Already inside*

*Don't hurt me, Joe*
*Please*
*Don't*
*Hurt me*

The notebook went first—hurled across the bedroom—and she watched the pages flutter like bird wings as it sailed. It hit the wall with a thud, which was immediately followed by Hoover's deep *woof* from across the hall.

That's all she needed—to wake up the kids.

Then she threw the pen, and it, too, hit the wall.

"It's okay, boy." She'd cracked open her bedroom door and peeked into the hallway. "Everything's all right. Go back to sleep."

Hoover gave her a look that indicated he didn't really believe her, then sauntered back into Matt's room.

She couldn't help it. She was weak. Joe was so close. Close enough to touch, taste . . . to love. And she wasn't strong enough to resist him. She'd never been strong enough to resist him.

Charlotte felt herself walking across the hall to Matt's bedroom, where she grabbed the binoculars off his desk, then, like a zombie, returned to her own room, shut the door, and allowed herself to be enticed by the moonlight at the window. She felt like a third-party observer as she watched her own hands raise the plastic spyglasses, felt them settle upon the rise of her cheekbones. With a quick blink, she set her focus on the window beyond the trees.

She gasped, stumbled backward, but kept her eyes open.

A pair of big black binoculars was aimed right back at her.

Well, *hot damn*!

Joe laughed so hard that the image of Charlotte began to jump up and down and side to side in his sights. He noted with pleasure that she took a shocked step back; then he saw that she had to be holding up the cheapest pair of plastic binoculars he'd ever seen in his life. They looked like something a kid would get in a box of Cracker Jacks. They had to be Matt's.

He raised one hand and waved to her. He watched with pleasure as her mouth fell open in what he only hoped was indignation.

Like she had any kind of moral high ground here.

Joe didn't hide the fact that he found the situation amusing, and smiled big in her direction. It crossed his mind that she might not even appreciate this little exchange because she might not be able to see a thing out of those Pacific Rim goody bag stuffers she held up to her eyes.

He mouthed these words to her: *Hello, dumplin'*.

Then it was his turn to drop his jaw.

She'd felt this jolt of awareness just one other time in her life. In that Miata. Alive. Sexual. Free. Absolutely herself.

*Ready.*

Charlotte set the binoculars on the bed, seeing this moment for what it was. It was the end of thirteen years of sexual anguish.

She took a deep breath, realizing that she wasn't even mad at Joe for spying on her. In fact, she loved it. She loved it so much she was trembling.

Charlotte spun around to face the window and reached up to unclasp the barrette that held her hair in place. She shook her head and let the mess fall where it would and licked her lips. It was so strange performing for someone she couldn't see—just an open window. But then she'd never stripped for a man in even the most private of settings.

Her shaking hands rose to touch her breasts, as if she knew instinctively what Joe would want to see. She let her fingers brush around the prod of her nipples under a thin layer of cotton, then let her caress sweep down, down, until she put her hands where she wanted Joe's to be.

Charlotte let her fingers play inside the elastic of her underwear, barely brushing the silk of her damp flesh, and allowed her head to fall back from the pleasure of her own touch. She knew the effect she must be having on Joe, and a sense of power surged through her. She felt like such a bad girl. So lustful. So out of control. So wonderful.

Such a slut.

Charlotte leveled her gaze out the window and moved both hands to her hips, then her waist, grabbing the bottom of her tank top as she went, pulling, pulling, until her face was covered and the rest of her was not. Then she tugged the shirt with a bit of drama, held it out to her side with a straight arm, and let it fall to the floor.

Joe's window must have been open, because at that instant she heard him shout.

Next she raised her hands and fluffed her hair real good, then puckered up in a kiss, running an index finger down the center of her lips, her chin, her throat, her sternum, her belly, her belly button . . .

Her phone rang. She picked it up.

"Not fair," Joe said, breathing hard.

"I can't wait anymore," she said.

"We don't have to."

"You like this?"

"Oh, fuck yes."

"Want me to keep going?"

"Are you serious?"

She hung up and went back to the window, wearing just her panties and hoping to God that the angle of the window prevented Mrs. Watson or anyone else on Hayden Circle from seeing her little show. But if she was honest with herself, she was beyond caring. She was beyond stopping.

Charlotte twirled to expose her back to the window, feeling the air on her spine, the sensitive flesh where her back flared out to create her hips. She raised her arms straight up over her head and clasped hands, then peeked around. She slowly swiveled her butt, smiled big, and lowered her hands to the waistband of her underpants.

Deliberately, teasingly, still looking over her shoulder, she eased them down. She felt like a snake shedding its skin. And knowing that Joe watched her every move made her body do a slow burn. She ignited as the curve of her ass cleared the fabric and she knew that everything she was now belonged to Joe. It always had.

The phone rang again, and Charlotte nearly tripped on the panties twisted around her ankles as she dived for it.

"I'm coming over there—now. Get ready."

"The dog."

"What?"

"Hoover will wake the kids. Bring an ice-cream cone."

"Are you kidding me?"

Charlotte giggled and summoned her sexiest, throatiest voice. "Do you want me, Joe?"

"God yes."

"Do you want me right now, right this instant, naked and hot and shaking for you?"

Silence. Then, "You want sprinkles on that?"

The line went dead.

Joe had been in a number of tight spots over the years, and many of them required him to think on his feet. But this was ridiculous.

He stood in the kitchen in a pair of boxers, harder than he'd ever been in his life, rooting through the cabinets for something—anything—that resembled an ice-cream cone.

It was nearly midnight on a Tuesday. The Creamy Whip stand was closed. And looking down at his full-mast state was all the reminder he needed that a trip to the convenience store was out of the question. He needed to focus. *Focus.*

A quick peek revealed no ice cream in the freezer, but he already knew that. The refrigerator featured beer, olives, yogurt, milk, and apples.

*Yogurt.* He pulled it out.

He ran to the pantry. Crackers. Coffee. A taco kit. Pretzels. Tomato soup.

*Taco shells.* He grabbed the box.

Then with shaking hands and a string of foul words, Joe got the cellophane off the package of tacos and spooned in several globs of vanilla yogurt. He held it up, gave it a quick examination, and figured a dog wouldn't know the difference.

Then he bolted out the patio door, threw open the privacy fence latch, and ran barefoot across the grass, pine needles, and driveway until he arrived, breathless, at Charlotte's back door.

She was waiting for him, wearing a little red silk robe and a huge smile, Hoover at her side.

Charlotte glanced down at the concoction in his hand and laughed. Her laugh sounded so damn good to him that he had to join her. But Hoover growled low and deep and bared his teeth and looked ready to bark his head off, so Joe shoved the yogurt taco next to his snout and they both waited.

After what seemed like an eternity, the dog began to lap at it with delicate little strokes of his tongue and they both sighed in relief. The yogurt was soon gone, and Hoover took one bite out of the taco shell and spit it out, looking at Joe like he'd offended his palate.

"Will he stay quiet?"

Charlotte reached out and touched Joe's bare forearm. "I think so. You did good."

Joe dropped the taco shell and hooked a finger inside the lapel of her robe—her skin was hot and smooth and he felt ready to bust. "Where exactly is this going to happen, Charlotte?"

A shadow crossed her face. "I'm not sure. I can't leave and you really shouldn't come in."

*Oh, this was just great.* Joe looked around and noticed that the campout tent was still up. "Ever done it in a tent?"

"A long time ago."

"Can you grab a sleeping bag and a couple pillows?"

Charlotte nodded, then allowed her gaze to travel down the front of Joe's body. She bit her pretty pink bottom lip. Joe watched her breath come fast and hard.

"Can I help with anything, Charlotte?"

"No." She continued staring at his boxer shorts, then shook her head. "Hold on a second." Charlotte ran toward the mudroom and Joe watched her sweet little ass bounce around under the robe. She came back with two flashlights and handed him one through the door.

"Make sure there aren't any spiders in there, and I'll see you in a minute."

"Hurry."

She gave him a serious nod. "I've haven't been in this big of a hurry in my whole life."

This was not exactly how she'd pictured it. Charlotte wanted candlelight and wine and she wanted to hold his hand and talk to him . . . then take him into her bed, where he'd remind her how it felt to be fully alive.

Instead, she had a couple couch pillows in her left hand, a SpongeBob sleeping bag in her right, a utility flashlight stuck in the sash of her robe, and she was running across the yard, barefoot, in the dark, praying she wouldn't step in dog poop.

She saw a flashlight beam bounce inside the tent and smiled. None of the details mattered, she supposed— because Joe was in there waiting for her. She was going to be his again.

Charlotte poked her head inside the tent flap and saw him sitting cross-legged on the tarp, peering into an open bag of marshmallows. He looked up and smiled at her.

"Care for a fresh hors d'oeuvre?"

"No thanks."

He jumped to his feet and removed everything from her arms, then took her hand and led her inside. She watched his body move in the flashlight beam as he stashed the marshmallows into the corner of the tent, spread out the sleeping bag, arranged the pillows, and eventually lay on his back with his arms tucked under his head, smiling at her like he planned to make her the happiest woman alive.

*Some men are put on this earth simply to make women happy.*

"Oh, my," she breathed.

Where Kurt's body had been big and brawny and male, Joe's was like fine art, and seeing Joe stretched out nearly naked caused the floor of her abdomen to open like a trapdoor, and her heart fell through it. Seeing the long, defined muscles in his arms and legs made her knees go wobbly. Seeing how his black eyes flashed and his white teeth gleamed made her want to cry out.

Here he was—her dark stranger. In the flesh.

"Come lie with me, Charlotte."

"I'm scared."

"It's just me."

"I don't know you."

"You know me better than anyone."

She dropped to her knees, the silk robe covering her thighs. His hand brushed her knee and his fingers insinuated under the hem, parting the silk.

"Why did you get divorced, Joe? What happened?"

Joe's eyes shut, but his hand still explored her skin. "I want to tell you everything, Charlotte. But I'd like to do it later."

Charlotte tilted her head and studied him. She had a feeling that getting to know Joe was going to be like peeling back layers of an onion the size of Ohio.

"I haven't been with a man in over eighteen months, Joe."

He smiled. "I'm damn happy to hear it."

"I'm just not used to this."

"I'm glad."

Charlotte grinned at him. "So you want to be my first again?"

"Hell yes." He slid his hand up the inside of her left thigh, and his touch made her shiver. "I plan to be your first and your last."

She laughed at that. More of his intense sex play, it seemed.

Joe frowned. "I'm completely serious. For thirteen years I hated the thought of any man putting his hands on you. It made me insane. I want to be your man, Charlotte. Don't you know yet that I was supposed to be your man?"

Her laugh died. Her whole body shuddered. "Joe—"

"I only wish I'd found you sooner."

"I wasn't ready to be found, Joe." She smiled sadly at him. "I married Kurt. I had the kids I was supposed to have. I wasn't ready for you to find me."

"Until now," he said.

"Until now," she said.

His other hand reached up to stroke the line of her jaw. She turned into his touch, rubbed into his palm, and closed her eyes at the pleasure in that simple gesture.

"I've been watching you, baby."

His voice was low and rough and Charlotte gazed down to see his expression full of need. She nodded. "Okay—"

"I've watched you work in your garden, eat with your kids. I've seen how much you love them, how much you give them." Joe paused and made sure his eyes were locked on hers. "Tonight wasn't the first night I've watched you with my binoculars. I've seen you masturbate, Charlotte."

A hum of terror moved through her body, starting at her toes and rushing up to her brain until she feared her head would explode. *He'd seen her?*

"I watched you write in your diary the other night. I watched you make yourself come."

"Oh, my God!" She tried to get up. His hand clamped down on her thigh.

"It was the sexiest thing I've ever seen a woman do in my entire life. I love how hot you are, Charlotte."

She barely had the courage to look at him. Kurt had been so disgusted with her that he couldn't even discuss this, and Joe thought she was *hot*?

"What were you writing about, baby? Tell me." His fingers continued their soft slide into the vee of her legs.

"I . . . nothing."

"Tell me."

"Poetry. I write a little poetry." Her heart hammered and her hands began to sweat.

"Really? What kind of poetry?" He stroked the sensitive skin at the juncture of her legs, and his touch felt like magic, like a familiar dream. . . .

"Erotic poetry—" she breathed, arching her neck with the pleasure. "About you and me, mostly."

His fingers spread, separating the puffy lips of her sex. She could feel herself opening to him as her legs fell apart, her arms fell to her sides—hands loose and palms up. Her breath was coming fast and shallow.

"Do you have any memorized?" Joe sat up and leaned close. His hand remained just at the opening of her, toying with her, teasing her until she knew she was wetter than the kitchen faucet.

"Of course I have them memorized. I wrote them—ahh!" His finger scarcely brushed over her erect clitoris and she saw black spots dance in her vision.

"I want to hear one. The hottest one you've ever written. Give it to me." His soft lips were grazing her face, her temples, her hair, the side of her neck . . .

She was having trouble concentrating. "How about something short and to the point?"

He chuckled against the juncture of her neck and shoulders, and his goatee tickled her. Then his fingers slid more purposefully over her clit, and she gasped.

"Go for it," he said.

"It's called 'Nice Pants.'"

"I like it already. Let's hear it." His warm lips and tongue were now trailing down her shoulder to her upper arm, the robe falling away as he went, his fingers still coaxing her, pinching her, flicking at her.

She could barely get the words to form. "'Nice Pants,' by Charlotte Tasker," she whispered. Just then, a finger slid inside her and she bucked from the invasion.

"I'm listening," he said, his voice muffled by the flesh of her breasts.

"It's only two lines. . . ."

Two long fingers slid into her. "Uh-huh."

His lips and teeth tugged on a nipple while she felt what she swore were at least eight fingers all over her between her legs—on her clitoris, inside her pussy, pressing into her bottom.

She rose up so he could get at anything he might want; then she shouted out:

*Nice pants.*
*Take them off!"*

Joe's laughter rumbled into her skin as she came. He was all over her then, wrapped around her, holding her tight as she rode through the rough pleasure. It was intense, complete, and so familiar.

When she regained some sense of where she was, Charlotte noticed Joe struggling to remove his boxers. She gave him a hand, then put both hands on his ass.

"You have real talent, Charlotte."

She giggled. "So do you, Joe."

His mouth crushed hers. She drowned in his kiss, his heat. And as he untied her belt and slid the robe completely from her body, Charlotte felt the years fall away, felt her heart come to life and her body unfurl like a flower. In her mind's eye that's exactly what she witnessed: Charlotte Tasker, business owner, scout leader, widowed mother of two, was a deep red rose captured in time-lapse photography, opening into full bloom in this man's hands—only for this one man.

Joe broke the kiss to cradle her face and look her square in the eye. "You were a virgin that day, but you came so much. You can't help it, can you, Charlotte? You really are a sex goddess. You were made for sex, weren't you?"

She nodded, so full of desire, so ready for whatever he was about to ask of her—and so excited by the way he spoke to her.

It seemed that Joe was as raw with his words as he was thirteen years before—raw power, raw sexuality. She thanked God that the years hadn't changed that.

"I want you to do something for me." Joe broke out into a lopsided grin. "Will you?"

She nodded again.

"I want you to be the little soccer mom slut that you really are."

Charlotte heard her own gasp, felt the lightning bolt of sexual greed strike her down.

"Nobody will know. It'll be our secret. Just be who you really are, for me, tonight, because I have to tell you, Charlotte—I fuckin' love it."

Joe eased her down onto the SpongeBob sleeping bag, covered her with the hard glory of his body, and kissed her ferociously, his lips crushed against hers. Charlotte welcomed Joe into her arms, into the arms of the little slut she was.

# Chapter Nineteen

How could a man feel so grounded and be flying at the same time? Joe couldn't grasp it, but there he was, inside Charlotte at long last, flesh to flesh, his body soaring through space even as his heart hit the ground with an audible thud.

*He was home.*

Charlotte was with him, right there with him, her eyes locked on his as he took her. He felt the force of her welcome, her love, as her legs opened wide beneath him.

The impulse to drive into her was unstoppable. The surge of power that coursed through him was equaled only by tenderness he felt for her. She was his safe haven, his perfect fit, his lover. And he would die before he'd let her go again.

Joe smiled when she shouted out his name. She'd been shouting his name so often and with so much gusto that he feared she'd wake everyone in Hayden Heights. He tried to keep his mouth on hers but couldn't stop himself from occasionally making a detour to bite those tasty cherry nipples.

He also needed to keep his mouth free to talk to her. It didn't take a genius to see that words did the trick for

Charlotte. Every time he said something even remotely racy to her, her eyes flashed and her body clenched him tight.

"Come for me, you beautiful, sweet, sexy little soccer mom slut."

There she went again, his cock the lucky recipient of the wet velvet vise treatment he hoped to God would be his for the taking the rest of his life.

"You can't stop, can you, Charlotte? Tell me you want some more."

He reached down into the slippery juncture of their bodies and found the hard little peak uncovered by her position. He circled his fingertip around it.

"I want more!" She wrapped her legs around his butt and squirmed to meet his thrusts.

"How much more?"

"I want everything! I want you, Joe!"

He slammed his lips on hers, his wide mouth engulfing her from her silky upper lip to her adorable chin. He felt her bring her arms around his body and squeeze. He tasted tears, but he didn't know which of them was crying. And he kissed her hard and breathed her in and got lost in the scent of their union—skin and sweat and summer air and honeysuckle—and knew this was the only real thing he'd ever known. He soared higher and then exploded inside her—giving her everything. He gave her himself. Just as she'd asked.

They hung on to each other in the single flashlight beam. Joe felt his skin fused to hers. He felt her breath against the side of his neck and her heart beating wildly beneath him.

Charlotte trembled, and he rolled until her small body stretched out on top of him. She burrowed her face in the crook of his neck and the tears trickled down his shoulder.

"Tell me what's going on in that brain of yours."

She sniffled. He stroked her hair.

"I was thinking that I'm glad. I'm just *so damn glad* I wasn't making it up all these years!"

Joe laughed, hugging her tight. "Neither of us made it up. It was all real." He pulled a strand of damp hair from the side of her face and kissed her hot cheek. "It still is."

"I needed this, Joe."

"I did, too."

"You have no idea how much I needed it. How long I've needed it."

"Tell me."

Charlotte pushed herself up on her arms and looked down at him. Her face was relaxed, open, and a wistful smile played on her mouth. In the strange light inside the tent, she seemed to glow from the inside.

"I loved Kurt and he loved me. He was a wonderful man and a great father. But this wasn't important to him." She glanced down at their bodies still joined. "Sex wasn't important to my husband."

Joe wasn't sure he'd heard her right. "Want to repeat that?"

Charlotte pushed herself up until she straddled him. He was still inside her, growing soft and malleable, but enjoying the sensation of her heat. The peace.

She nonchalantly pulled her hair back off her face and tied it in a knot on top of her head, a move that put her breasts on display. He was in love with her breasts. He wanted to know what they felt like full of milk when she was pregnant with his child. He wanted to drink hot milk from her and then lie down next to her in the spoon position, holding those full breasts in his hands while he took her from behind.

"Kurt was not a very sexual man."

Joe blinked. He *had* heard right.

"I was frustrated through my whole marriage, Joe. I felt immoral because I wanted it so much more than he did. The only thing that kept me going all those years was fantasies about . . ." Charlotte dropped her gaze and shook her head gently. He reached up and lifted her chin.

"Tell me."

"You. I fantasized about you, Joe. All the damn time."

There was something seriously wrong with the concept that any married woman—especially a beautiful, sexual, loving woman like Charlotte—had to rely on fantasy for satisfaction.

"Was your husband gay?"

Charlotte scrunched up her pretty mouth and shook her head. "You know, I wondered that a couple times, but I really don't think so. It was more his personality. His upbringing. He never wanted to talk about sex. He never wanted to experiment—be adventurous with me. He never saw sex as the gift it really is."

She shrugged, letting her fingers fiddle with Joe's chest hair. It was such a small thing—but so intimate—that his breath caught.

"I think he was ashamed when I asked him for things he couldn't or wouldn't do. He was ashamed of me. And over time, I became ashamed of myself."

Joe was getting hard again. "Details, please." He brought his hands around to cup her sweet behind.

With a tilt of her head and a wicked little grin, Charlotte said, "You aren't anything like Kurt when it comes to sex, are you, Joe?"

"Doesn't appear that way." He pinched her plump little ass. She yelped and squirmed on him. Joe was getting stiffer, quick.

Her voice became a soft whisper. "Once, I got the courage to ask him to spank me."

He was at full attention now. "And he didn't?"

"He said he felt foolish."

Joe smacked her butt—real hard. She squirmed again and let out a contented sigh. So he did it again. He frowned as if in deep thought, then smiled. "Nope—I just double-checked and I don't feel the least bit foolish."

Charlotte's laugh disappeared into a moan when he spanked her again, then again. She gazed down at him with a hot, half-lidded look of lust. Her hair had slipped down out of its knot and fell in straight shiny strands around her face.

This woman clearly needed to be fucked some more.

"And once, I asked him to tie me up," she whispered.

Joe licked his lips, wondering if the SpongeBob sleeping bag had string ties. "Too foolish?"

"No. He said he respected me too much to despoil me or treat me in such a sadistic way."

The guy was definitely gay.

"Well, baby, I'll tell you what." Joe smoothed his palms over her bottom, the flesh hot from spanking. "I would consider it an honor to tie you spread-eagle to the bed and despoil you until you can't see straight—in a completely respectful way, of course."

As they moved in unison with laughter, Charlotte made a smooth segue into raising and lowering her body on his cock. Before Joe could anticipate it, she was riding him with purpose and he was back in serious fucking mode, as if he hadn't just come a few minutes ago.

This woman made him crazy. He had to slow down. He clamped his hands on her thighs to keep her still.

"You can always tell me what you need, Charlotte. If it works for you, it'll automatically work for me."

"Thank you, Joe."

"I love how passionate you are, how sexual you are. You don't have to hold back anymore. Ever."

She pushed his hands away without further comment and moved on him, varying her tempo and pressure and angle to coax the pleasure, drag it to its acute phase. She was a marvel, a redheaded vixen who seemed quite pleased with her official sex goddess status. It was obvious from the gleam in her eye and her self-satisfied smile. With a sigh, she lowered herself down on him, pressing her breasts against his chest.

Joe stroked her hair, delighting in the cool, silky feel of it slipping between his fingers. "Did you ever ask for anything else?"

She let go with a small laugh. "Well, one night, I asked him for one of my favorite fantasies." Charlotte left little kisses along Joe's throat as her lower half undulated over him.

"I can't wait to hear this one." He nibbled at her neck.

Charlotte stopped moving and simply laid her head on his chest. "It wasn't wild, Joe. I just asked him to sleep with me under the stars. Naked. I wanted to make love under the stars. That's all."

Joe had to close his eyes against the sadness that swept through him. He almost didn't want to know the answer to the question he was about to ask—he wasn't sure he could bear to hear it.

"Please tell me your husband did that for you, sweetheart."

"He tried." Charlotte rubbed her cheek against Joe's shoulder. "We got out here in the backyard and he couldn't . . . he was just too worried and embarrassed—"

That was it. Joe saw it happen in his mind—he'd just handed his heart to Charlotte Tasker on a platter. He just silently uttered the words, *Here it is. It's not much, but it's all yours.* And right then, he knew that whatever she might ask of him, it would be his honor to do it. As her man, it would be his job.

A job he desperately wanted.

Joe sat up, tucked Charlotte's legs around his waist, and told her to hang on. He stood, grabbed the sleeping bag, and unzipped the tent door.

"You and me and SpongeBob got some love to make," he said.

Joe tossed the sleeping bag on the grass and stood with Charlotte still attached to his naked body. He could feel her giggling. "Now, tell me exactly what you want, sweet-heart."

She lightly touched his hair, then his cheek, then the smooth, clean lines of his goatee. It amazed her that he was so eager to please. She felt the tears build again but saw no reason to force them down—nothing she'd revealed so far had scared Joe away. Maybe nothing ever would. "What I want—what I *really, really* want—"

"Tell me." He pressed his soft lips to hers. "Tell me everything."

"I want to feel the power of you and me. I want you inside me, part of me. I want to look up and see your face surrounded by a thousand stars. I want to know that it's true—that we were supposed to be together."

"Comin' right up." Joe supported their combined weight on one arm as he lowered her back to the sleeping bag. He pushed inside her, gazing down at the woman beneath him, her pale skin glowing in the night, her eyes as bright as the brightest star in the heavens.

"I'll never leave you again, Charlotte."

"I'm so glad."

"I want to love you."

"I want to love you back."

Charlotte smiled up at him, then felt her eyelids slide shut at the consuming pleasure, feeling Joe going deep, deeper than she'd ever allowed a man to go, deep into her secret heart, her secret passion, her secret self.

She felt the truth and opened her eyes in time to see that Joe felt it, too.

"Let me do that, Joe."

"Nope. No deal, soccer mom."

Charlotte sat at her own kitchen table feeling quite useless. She took another sip of the coffee Joe had poured for her a moment ago, watching him root around in the cabinets for the stove's griddle attachment and then hunt for plates, utensils, and ingredients stored on pantry shelves.

"Organic stone-ground whole wheat pancake mix?" Joe held up the box and frowned as he read the directions. "What's that gonna do for us, exactly?"

"It's a complex carbohydrate. More fiber and vitamins than white flour. Plus there's oat bran in it."

"I feel healthier already. How are we doing on time?"

Charlotte looked up at the kitchen clock. "I've got to get them up in about fifteen minutes. Sometimes Matt will wander down on his own, but Hank is not a morning person."

Joe turned and looked over his shoulder, his little gold earring gleaming in the overhead kitchen lights. "And her mommy?"

Charlotte smiled back, unashamed that she hadn't stopped smiling since Joe had arrived with the yogurt taco more than six hours before. "I think I'm a night person forced to be a morning person. But I'm feeling legitimately perky this morning."

Joe nodded and opened the refrigerator door. "I'm feeling pretty perky myself. You got any real milk in here or just the soy stuff?"

"Just the soy, which is real, too, just devoid of lactose, antibiotics, and growth hormones." *Oh, my,* but Joe looked exceptional bent over in his jeans, scanning her refrigerator shelves. He'd run home a few minutes ago to take a lightning quick shower and put on something other than his boxers, insisting that he make the kids breakfast before school. She watched him straighten and laugh as he examined the soy milk carton.

"I suppose what doesn't kill us only makes us stronger."

"Ain't that the truth," she said, laughing, too.

Charlotte watched the ripple of muscle and tendon in his forearm as he whisked the egg, oil, and milk. She smiled to herself, recalling how that muscle and tendon had felt under her hands. She recalled how glorious he'd looked hovering over her with the night sky behind him, how perfect he'd felt inside her, how she'd allowed herself to fall in love with a veritable stranger.

*Who is this man I've let inside . . . ?*

She took a giant swig of coffee for fortification and said, "Who the hell are you, Joe?"

The question popped out without a bit of adornment—and she heard her words hang in the early morning quiet. He stopped whisking in midstroke, leaving the hum of the refrigerator and the pounding of her own heart the only audible sounds.

"I don't have a simple answer for that." His wrist gave a few last twirls and he set the mixing bowl aside, keeping his back to her. She watched him measure out the pancake mix and level the cup with a sweep of his finger. He was precise. Careful. He was stalling.

"Then give me the complicated version." Charlotte stood and walked to the coffeepot to refill her cup. She tipped the carafe over Joe's empty mug. "Need another shot?"

"Is the pope Catholic?" He began to stir the batter with a wooden spoon, not meeting her eye.

"Are you?"

"No, I'm not the pope."

She sniffed. "I should hope not, after last night. But are you Catholic?"

"Recovered." He continued to stir. "And you're Baptist, right?"

"Recover . . . *ing*."

That got a smile from him, and he crooked his head to let his gaze meet hers. "If the kids are coming down in fifteen minutes, I don't think I have time for any version at all."

Charlotte checked the clock. "Fourteen minutes now. Just do your best."

He chuckled, pouring out four puddles of batter onto the hot griddle.

"You know everything about me, Joe, and I know nothing about you. It's a bit uneven, don't you think?"

"It is."

"So let's hear it."

"All right, Charlotte." Joe sighed. "Both my parents are dead. My older brother died in college of a drug overdose. I got my bachelor's degree in criminal justice from American University and did two years in the U.S. Army Special Forces. I've traveled a lot for my work since. I've never been married—that was just part of my cover story. I've had a couple serious relationships, but the women always left me because I wasn't around enough to make a go of it."

"I'm sorry about your family." Her voice was soft. Then she frowned. "What do you mean by *cover story*?"

Joe took a deep draw of air to clear his head. He tapped the edge of the spatula against the griddle, realizing it sounded like the ticking of a time bomb. His time was surely up—he couldn't hide the details from Charlotte a moment longer. He was in love with her. She had a right to know what she was getting into. The real trick would be telling her enough so that she could make an informed decision but not enough to frighten her away.

"I'm not a writer. I work in federal law enforcement and I can't tell you much more, for your own safety." Joe cringed at the sound of her laugh.

"Oh, really? As in you'd tell me, but then you'd have to kill me?"

He felt his stomach lurch, thinking, *I won't be the one doing the killing.* "Not exactly, Charlotte."

As she watched him flip the four pancakes, it dawned on her that he wasn't joking. Joe's shoulders had stiffened and his mouth was pulled tight in seriousness. Charlotte began to feel a bit dizzy. She didn't like this. Not at all.

He placed the golden-brown pancakes on a platter and started four more.

"I'm waiting, Joe."

He turned to her and leaned a hip against the counter. "Do you trust me?"

She'd been asking herself the same thing, and though it was a simple question, it made her head spin. How could she trust a man she didn't really know? Yet how could she be in love with a man she didn't trust? And how could she tell him she wasn't sure if she trusted him when it was obvious he wouldn't tell her anything unless he had that trust?

"I'm sure trying."

"That's a start."

Charlotte sipped her coffee, studied the grim line of his lips, and thought about the big picture for a minute—the gun, the alarm system, the secrets, the underlying seriousness. It seemed a little far-fetched, like something Matt would conjure up, but she couldn't help herself. "So what are you, Joe? Some kind of secret agent? The Austin Powers of Minton, Ohio?"

His grin lasted a split second. "Not exactly. I work for

the U.S. Department of Justice. And I'm in a bit of a bind. I was sent here to disappear, Charlotte." He locked his eyes on hers. "And that needs to stay between you and me."

Her hand fell to the countertop with a thud, sending a plume of coffee into the air and onto her wrist. "Ow! God! You're kidding me! Hold on a second!" As she let the cool faucet water run over her arm, Charlotte tried to collect herself. Joe was some sort of cop? What kind? Why did he have to disappear?

"It's better if you don't know the details. That's where the trust comes in." Joe had moved close behind her and whispered this in her ear, his hands cupping her hips. "The less you know, the safer everyone will be."

His hands stayed put as she spun around to face him. "What do you mean, *safer*? Who do you mean by *every-one*? Are you in some kind of danger? Are my *kids*?"

Joe kissed her hairline, ran little smooches down her temples, and nibbled on her ears. "I pissed off a few bad guys, is all. And I have to testify against them in court."

"Stop right there." Charlotte pushed him back enough to look at his face. "They're after you? You came to Minton to hide from criminals of some kind?"

"Yes."

"My God, Joe! How bad are these guys?"

"Real bad."

"Will they find you?"

"They won't find me."

"Are you sure?"

"Pretty sure."

"What do you mean, *pretty* sure?"

"Yo." A small voice caused them to jolt away from each other.

Matt stood in the kitchen doorway in his jammies, studying them from under raised eyebrows and an uneven thatch of bed hair. He yawned. "Who won't find you, Joe?" He frowned. "Were you just kissing my mom or something?" Then he glanced at the now smoking griddle. "Can I have cereal instead?"

Matt ate another spoonful of Mega-Wheats and banana, keeping a real close eye on Joe.

The guy had obviously been chewing face with his mother, and there was a tiny place inside his heart that felt sad about that but a bigger place that smiled. Joe was outrageously cool. He knew better than to expect that he'd suddenly jump in and be his new dad, and Matt didn't want that anyway, but if his mom had to kiss somebody, he was glad it was Joe.

"You sure I can't talk you into a pancake or two?"

Matt smiled, remembering that his dad used to make pancakes on Sunday mornings—sometimes even the awesome fluffy, white ones. Matt looked at the stack Joe offered and shook his head. "No offense, but those things taste like hockey pucks even when they're not burnt."

Joe smiled at him. "I hear you, kid." Then he sat down, doused them in maple syrup, and took a few huge bites. "Your mom says they'll Roto-Rooter your insides, though."

Matt laughed, nearly choking on a mouthful of cereal. Joe was funny, too. He was all right. "So you like my mom, or what?"

He watched Joe dab at his mouth with a napkin and take a sip of coffee, the way grown-ups do when they're fishing for the "appropriate" way to say something.

"I like her a lot," Joe said.

Matt nodded, a little embarrassed that his thoughts had suddenly turned to Lisa Bertucci, of all people! But he figured it was because lately he'd wondered what it would feel like to kiss her—her cheek, not her mouth the way

Mom and Joe probably kissed. No way would he ever do something as disgusting as that.

"Is that okay with you, Matt?"

Matt looked up at Joe and wondered if he could bounce a few ideas off him. He wondered if Joe would mind. "That's cool with me. You know, I was kind of wondering. . . ."

Joe raised an eyebrow. "Yeah?"

"How exactly did you let Mom know you liked her? I mean, did you blurt it right out like, you know, 'I like you, Charlotte,' or what?"

Joe thought for a moment. "Basically, yes."

"And girls like to hear that crap?"

Joe cleared his throat. "Absolutely."

"Huh." Matt held up the bowl and slurped down the leftover soy milk.

"Is there a particular girl you're thinking about?"

Matt felt his face get hot. "What? No way. I just . . . well . . ." Matt got up and put his bowl in the sink, thinking maybe he ought to let out the truth. Who else was he going to rely on for advice? His mom? Justin? Ned? *Yikes!* "Actually, there is . . . sort of . . . this girl."

Joe leaned an arm over the back of the kitchen chair and gave his head a quick nod. "That's cool."

"Her name is Lisa. And I feel like such a dweeb when I see her, like my brain's broken or something. Is that normal?"

"It is, Matt. Happens to the best of us."

That was surprising news, and a big relief. "Did it happen to you with Mom?"

Joe laughed a little and took another big bite of hockey puck pancake. "At first, yes. I said and did some real stupid things, because your mom is so special and so pretty that I couldn't think straight."

Matt watched Joe go to the sink and rinse his plate and cup and stick it in the dishwasher.

"I think I'm doing a little better with your mom lately."

"Cool."

"Is Lisa special like that?"

Matt felt his heart slam in his chest. He didn't want to get all gross about it, but maybe Joe would understand. "Sorta. It's the weirdest thing, but when she walks past me, her breeze smells so good I have to close my eyes."

Matt felt Joe's hand come down soft on his shoulder.

"I feel you, man," Joe said.

Matt couldn't help but smile. Joe was even cooler than he thought. Maybe he could help him out with something else, too.

Just then, he heard his mom and Hank upstairs and knew it was now or never. "Hey, Joe?" Matt looked up at him, hoping like heck he'd take pity on him. "Can I ask you a really huge favor?"

# Chapter Twenty

Joe leaned over the lengthy to-do list sitting on the kitchen counter and figured this must be the kind of strategic challenge Charlotte faced every day.

He should probably go to the jeweler first. Since he'd never bought an engagement ring in his life, he had no idea what he was doing and would have to rely on a knowledgeable salesperson. A jeweler's wet dream, no doubt—some love-struck doofus with an open wallet.

If the ring wasn't exactly what Charlotte wanted, they could always return it. It was the thought that counted, right? His heart jumped and he drew in a hiss of breath—God help him if she said no. It was a distinct possibility and he knew it.

After the jeweler, he'd hit the wine shop for champagne. At least he knew what he was doing in that department—maybe a good vintage demi-sec or a nice blanc de noirs?

Next would be Wal-Mart for decorations and then the florist. Then Kroger's. He felt himself grow hard just reviewing the grocery list he'd made: spray cheese, crackers, grapes, chocolate, and strawberries. *Oh, the things he had planned. . . .*

For insurance, he'd enlisted Bonnie to conveniently stop by Charlotte's the moment she came home with the kids from baseball. That way, Charlotte would have no excuse not to accept his invitation for a few munchies and a night swim.

Joe grinned to himself in amazement. Yes, this was spontaneous. Yes, this was completely insane. Yes, it felt utterly right.

But for all his enthusiastic planning, there was something he'd forgotten, he just knew it, and he tapped the felt pen against the pad of paper until he'd created a big black blob that began to seep into the fiber, spread just the way Steve's blood had soaked the pavement of the Denny's parking lot. . . .

He jumped when the phone rang.

"You need to get an answering machine or a cell phone, Bellacera."

"If I wanted to talk, I would have called you."

Roger laughed. "You can run, but you can't hide."

"Why didn't you tell me about Jay Mauk?"

"Shit, Joe." Roger's voice went low and soft. "Did Rich Baum give you the news?"

"Yes. Last week."

"I should have been the one to tell you. I'm sorry. I just didn't have anything concrete to pass on."

Joe let loose with a bitter laugh. "Like Guzman's men aren't the only possibility?"

"The witness statements are a mess. It happened so fast, we've got nothing much to go on."

"He was just a kid."

"It's been hard on all of us."

Joe nodded in silence, knowing that the Albuquerque field office had been dealt more than its share of loss in the last few months. It made him sick. Guzman made him sick with fury.

"Are you doing all right, Joe? How's it going with the girl next door?"

"Ah, well, funny you should ask." Joe cleared his throat, knowing this was probably going to be as big a shock to Roger as it was to himself. "Tonight, I'm going to ask her to marry me."

The line was silent.

"You still there, Roger?"

"Here." Roger paused a moment, then said, "You're pulling my leg, right?"

"No."

"Damn, Bellacera. This is not the best time to be playing house. The woman has kids for Christ's sake, doesn't she?"

"Yep. Two great kids."

"Joe—"

"Just say you're happy for me."

"I'm—" Roger chuckled nervously. "I'm stunned. I mean, this is going to make things infinitely more complicated. What if you have to up and leave?"

"I can't live in fear like that anymore, Roger. I'm tired of it. I want something else for myself."

"Look, I understand, but—"

"I want a real life. Other people manage it and so can I."

"Are you telling me you want out of the DEA? Have you made your decision?"

"No. I'll talk to Charlotte about it. We'll decide together at some point. The trial comes first. Then I'll worry about my job."

"Have you told her everything?"

"I'm telling her a little at a time. I hope it'll go over better in small doses."

"Uh-huh. And when do you plan to tell the woman there's a million-dollar contract on her fiancé's head?"

"Tonight. I'm going to tell her tonight."

"And you expect her to say *yes*? Jesus, Joe! You're going to get your heart stomped!"

Joe let go with a bitter laugh and shook his head. "I gotta at least try, Roger."

"So if by some miracle there is a wedding, do I get an invitation?"

Joe laughed again. "I haven't thought that far ahead."

"Stay sharp, Joe. There's no reason to think Guzman will ever find you, but please just stay focused and think sharp."

"Of course."

"Keep me posted. Oh, and happy birthday, Bellacera."

The DEA hotshot sat across from Ned at one of the Creekside's small outdoor tables, crossing and uncrossing his legs, nursing his beer, and fiddling with the whiskers of his goatee. The man was tense as hell, and Ned hadn't even said anything yet. He figured he'd better just blurt it out, put the guy out of his misery.

"Okay, so I pulled your prints off an iced tea glass the night of the campout, Special Agent Bellacera."

The blank look on Joe's face was pure cop—Ned could see the internal wheels spin as Joe struggled with how he was going to play this, how much he could safely reveal.

Ned couldn't say he blamed the man for being careful. From what he'd learned from his little bit of nosing around, Joe had put his ass on the line more than a few times. Ned figured he'd survived this long only by being real cautious.

It took a moment, but Joe's face eventually softened into a wry smile. Then he shook his head and laughed.

"Sneaky piece of police work, Ned."

"Thank you."

"You ran my prints through AFIS?"

"Yep."

"Nice. You mind telling me why?"

Ned watched as Joe took a huge swig from his beer bottle, which was somehow comforting. Maybe they'd be able to talk, after all. "Three reasons why—Charlotte, Matt, and Hank."

"Ah."

"Had to be sure."

Joe's smile widened. "Thank you for looking out for them since Kurt died. I appreciate that more than I can say."

That was an unexpectedly possessive response, and Ned squirmed a little in his plastic patio chair. In Joe's voice—and in his words—had been an implication Ned couldn't quite pin down. It almost felt like Joe was giving him his pink slip, like he'd be taking over with the Taskers from now on.

"Is that so, Joe?"

The federal agent picked at the label of his beer bottle, staring at his moving fingers for a long time before he raised his gaze to Ned again.

"I met Charlotte thirteen years ago, and I've loved her ever since. I looked for her—you have no idea how I tried to find her."

"No shit?"

"It was pure luck—or fate if you believe in that kind of stuff—that I ended up here."

Ned leaned back in his chair and laced his fingers together over his belly. He had a feeling this was going to be a good one.

"And exactly why *are* you here?"

"I'm hiding. A fairly nasty drug dealer has a million-dollar reward out for my head—which I've kind of grown attached to over the years."

Though fascinated, Ned heard himself let go with

a loud laugh. "Whoa. A million big ones for that ugly mug?"

Joe gave him a short-lived grin, then sighed. "When our cover was blown a couple of months ago, he killed my partner and his wife and little boy. We don't believe the man is joking."

Ned felt his body go numb. *Good God*—this kind of bad shit was a little out of his league and he knew it. He kept his mouth shut and nodded for Joe to continue.

"I'm the U.S. attorney's star witness in the case against this man—his name is Miguel Guzman. My supervisor sent me here so I could stay alive until the trial."

*"Fuck-in'A.* When's that gonna be?"

"God only knows. Maybe a couple years."

Ned shook his head and straightened, leaning across the table so they could whisper. If ever there was a conversation the rest of Minton, Ohio, didn't need to hear, this was it.

"Are you safe here, do you think?"

Joe shrugged. "I think I get safer every day that goes by. The Administration believes the risk is minimal for me here, even though a civilian employee from our field office was murdered just last week."

"Hell! In Albuquerque?"

Joe smiled sadly. "Right again."

"Does Charlotte know any of this?"

Joe's mouth pulled into a tight line and he shrugged. "I told her I work for the Justice Department and that I need to lay low, but not much more. I do plan to tell her everything eventually. But right now, I think it's best for her and the kids if she doesn't know everything I've just told you. That way—"

"Hell, Joe! Don't even say that!"

"Look, nothing's going to happen to anybody. I'm just being extra-careful."

"I don't like this. Does she know your real name?"

"I'm going to tell her tonight—just before I ask her to marry me. I want to spend my life with her."

Ned was up out of his seat, feeling his eyes bug out. "You sure as hell didn't waste much time."

Joe stood up, too, and didn't look happy. "I've wasted thirteen years, Ned, and I plan on making up for every single one of them starting tonight."

It wasn't lost on Ned that Joe could kick his ass and sweep up the deck with his lifeless form. But this development was going to take some getting used to.

"Has she loved you back all these years, do you think?"

Joe's whole face changed at his question—the grimace instantly replaced by the goofiest love-struck grin Ned had ever seen. Damn. No wonder Joe had been so nervous! Tonight was the big night!

"Well? Answer me, son—does Charlotte love you?"

"I'm counting on it."

Then Joe sat down, asked the waitress for a pen, and wrote a bunch of names and numbers on his bar napkin and handed it to Ned.

"My supervisor's name, his office, cell, and pager, plus the local field office supervisor and all his numbers. Just in case."

Ned accepted the napkin with astonishment, hoping to hell that Joe Bellacera knew what he was doing.

Charlotte turned down the invitation to his little get-together, despite Bonnie's words of encouragement, saying it had been a long day. She was right—neither of them had gotten any sleep the night before, as Joe well knew. So to get her over there, he had no choice but to admit it was his birthday.

Now here she was, poking her head inside the gate,

staring in wonder at the fairyland he'd had created just for them.

"Whoa," she breathed. "Oh, boy. Joe—"

Small paper bags filled with votive candles lined the edge of the pool and patio. All the outdoor lights were off except for the underwater pool light, and he'd twined bits of honeysuckle in strands of tiny white Christmas lights, which twinkled in a crisscross pattern overhead. The table was covered in a white linen tablecloth on which he'd displayed all of the evening's treats—except for the spray cheese, which he'd hidden until the time was right.

"Would you like some champagne?"

Charlotte stepped inside and clicked the gate shut behind her. She stood perfectly still, staring.

His heart filled with delight when she began to giggle. "This is *so unbelievably cool,* Joe!"

He took a step toward her, loving the way her little sleeveless yellow sundress rode her curves. It was the first time he'd ever seen her in a dress, and it had been worth waiting for. "I was kind of aiming for hot, Charlotte."

She smiled and held out her hand to him. "You're always hot, Joe Cool."

As her silky little hand slipped inside his, Joe closed his eyes with the realization that she'd soon wear his ring, that he'd be able to feel the hard line of the platinum band and the three stones under the pressure of his palm.

"Is it really your birthday, or did you say that just to lure me to your cave?"

"I'm thirty-eight today, and I'm glad you came to my cave to celebrate with me."

Joe watched Charlotte's neat auburn brows knit together. "How come you didn't tell me this morning? We could have planned a party for you."

"This *is* a party." He pulled her close and let his hands slide up her slender back. The warmth of her skin radiated through the thin fabric of her dress. "A party of two."

"Mmmmm . . ." If Charlotte had planned on saying more, the words melted on contact with the heat of his kiss, and he gloried in the way she sighed and eased her body into his.

"I didn't even get you a present," Charlotte whispered, then nibbled on the soft flesh of his earlobe.

"That's what you think." As they laughed, he pulled her tight, so tight that her feet left the patio. He hugged Charlotte close for a long moment, then eased her back down. "Come have a seat." He guided her to a poolside chair and made sure she was comfortable. "How did the rest of your day go?"

Charlotte let her head relax against the cushion and gave him the widest, most glorious smile he'd ever seen on a woman's face. That woman right there glowing in the candlelight was *his* woman, and that smile was for him and no other man on the planet, and Joe had to admit there was something ass-kickingly wonderful about that.

"My day was busy but good. I had a new client interview. I think this one will be the last I can take on. Isn't that great?"

"It is. What else happened today?"

"Oh, Matt made a great catch tonight, a screaming line drive. Hank had four RBIs."

"You've got terrific kids, Charlotte."

He hardly thought it possible, but her smile just got wider. "Thanks for noticing. How was your day, Joe?"

He had to chuckle. "Good, thanks." He took his seat across from her and popped the champagne cork, then poured two glasses.

After a quick little tap of their glasses, Charlotte said, "Happy birthday, Joe Mills," then eased back into her chair and took a sip. "You know, I've been assuming that Mills is a simplified version of Milani or Mizzelli or something like that. Do you know the history of your name?"

"Ah. Yes, I do." Joe took a deep breath and smiled at her. *Here it comes.* "My last name means 'beautiful evening' in Italian."

The little frown returned to Charlotte's brow and she shook her head. "What name? I'm not following you. Your real family name?"

"Yes. My last name is Bellacera, a takeoff on the words *bella* for beautiful and *sera* for evening, just like the one I hope to have tonight with you."

Charlotte looked perplexed. "How in the world did anybody get Mills out of *that*?"

Joe laughed. "They didn't, sweetheart. What I'm telling you is that Mills is just a name my bosses gave me about a month ago when I moved here—to help me stay below radar. My real name is Joseph Salvatore Bellacera."

He reached over for Charlotte's hand, lying on the table limp with shock, and raised it to his lips. "And it's a pleasure to make the acquaintance of such an extraordinary woman."

Charlotte's eyes grew wide and she pulled her hand away, immediately crossing her arms over her chest.

"I suppose the name's another secret I've got to keep?"

"If you wouldn't mind."

"How many more of those you got, Joe?"

"Just a few more. Here, baby, have a chocolate-dipped strawberry." He leaned forward and pressed the tip of a big, juicy strawberry against her lips. She didn't budge. "Come on, Charlotte; I checked—there are no artificial preservatives in the chocolate."

That made her laugh just enough that he could insinuate the fruit between her luscious lips. She took the whole thing on her tongue, her eyes sparkling in the light as she chewed.

"Yummy," she admitted.

"I got crackers and grapes, too."

"Anything else I should know?"

"I got squirt cheese."

"I'm serious."

"So am I." Joe rose from his chair and moved to Charlotte's feet, where he knelt down on one knee and took both her hands in his.

"Charlotte, I have something very important I'd like to ask you."

During her first proposal of marriage, Charlotte was distracted by shameful thoughts of Joe. While Kurt asked her to be his wife, her entire being wallowed in the essence of Joe—how his touch melted her fears, how the dark power of his voice drew her out of hiding, how his gaze locked onto her soul.

It was the same this time around, only without the shame. All she felt was joy—a full-body rush of joy because what she craved and what was being offered were one and the same.

"Do you think you've always loved me, Charlotte?"

She heard herself let go with a soft laugh. It was a legitimate question—one she'd asked herself repeatedly in the last few days. She knew her answer hinged on the definition of the word itself—a word people used for nearly every relationship there was.

Of course, she loved her children unconditionally. She loved Bonnie and Ned. She loved her parents, despite the years of distance. And the love she'd had for Kurt had been steady, comforting, and very real for a very long time.

But what she felt for Joe was something else entirely—it

was passion, and it felt bottomless, exhilarating, consuming. She'd come to see that Joe was the great passion of her life. But was passion love? And if not, could passion grow into love over time?

She wondered which path she and Joe would take as a couple. Would they go through life as loving companions, like Ned and Bonnie? Or crash through the years like Jimmy and LoriSue, making a mess of most everything along the way?

"Can't you answer me?"

She blinked, unsure how much time had passed, but the wounded look on Joe's face told her she'd hesitated too long. She answered as honestly as she could.

"It's like nothing I've ever felt before. It's big and it's wild and it's a little overwhelming to me, but it's exactly what I need."

His face relaxed, and she watched him lower his head for a moment, as if immensely relieved. His shoulders moved in a slow sigh; then he looked up at her, smiling.

"Scared me there for a minute."

She stroked his glossy black hair, felt his hard skull under her fingers, and thought how lucky she was. She'd had two men love her in this lifetime—two very different men—who'd given her the gift of themselves.

"It really is possible, you know."

She smiled at his comment, letting her fingers trail down onto his cheek, then feather across his exquisite mouth. "What's possible?"

Joe looked past her in thought, giving her an opportunity to study him—so fine, so funny, so giving. He turned his dark eyes on her again, quite serious now. "It's possible to have both with one man—a companion *and* a sexual soul mate. I treasure you, Charlotte, as much as I desire you, and it will always be that way. You don't have to settle for one or the other any longer. And if I have to,

I'll spend the rest of my life convincing you of that."

Her chest clenched and her lips trembled. She didn't want to ruin this moment with tears, but his words had just cut through the last layer of doubt. Joe apparently saw everything—and wanted everything he saw.

She felt the metal ease down onto her left ring finger and she stared in wonder at how beautiful it was. Then she saw that Joe was choked up, too.

"It's exquisite, Joe."

He nodded, biting his lip. "It's technically an anniversary ring. The jeweler said the three diamonds represent past, present, and future and tried to talk me out of it—but I thought it summed up things pretty good for us."

"Oh, Joe—"

"Marry me." He traced a fingertip over the three stones, then raised his eyes to hers. "Be my wife and my lover and give me a place to call home."

Charlotte felt her heart jump into her mouth. "I—"

"Wait. Before you answer, there's one more thing I need to tell you."

Charlotte watched as Joe looked away for a brief moment and swallowed hard. When his gaze met hers again, he seemed very sad.

Cold dread seeped into the pit of her stomach. So this was the big secret he'd been building up to.

"Tell me."

"First, let me say I do think I'm safe here, Charlotte. The Administration has done a thorough risk assessment and they believe I'm out of harm's way."

"But?"

"Those bad guys I mentioned? They want to kill me."

She licked her lips, feeling her pulse spike. "Okay."

"There's a million dollars waiting for whoever can bring back my head."

Her mouth fell open. "What do you mean, your *head*?"

"My head. As in not attached to the rest of me."

Charlotte looked down at the glittering ring on her finger and tried to stuff down the panic but failed. Her hands began to shake and her overwhelmed brain vibrated inside her skull.

"I know it's a lot to ask, and if you want some time to think about it, that's fine. Just please don't say no to me."

"Joe—"

"Please."

"I'm sorry." She started to cry, reeling from how fast the joy had turned to anguish. How horrible it was to think he was in so much danger. How crushing it was to realize it was over with him before it could begin.

Because she could never marry a man being hunted down by killers. She could never put her children at risk like that.

"This is way more than I can handle." She began to pull the ring off her finger, but Joe's hand clamped down hard over hers.

"Don't give it back to me. I love you and it's yours."

"I can't. I—"

Joe was suddenly around her, against her, his arms gripping her tight to his hard chest, his mouth kissing her hair.

"Charlotte, I understand. But please keep the ring. It's yours forever. I'm yours forever. It doesn't mean you've said yes to anything. It only means that if things are ever different, you would consider it."

Charlotte buried her face in his shirt, breathing in the complicated essence of Joe Mills. She corrected herself. His name was *Bellacera*. And not a single thing about this man had ever been ordinary or simple, starting with the way they met.

All she wanted was Joe. Just Joe. That's all she'd ever wanted.

"Stay with me tonight. Let me love you. Wear the ring
and stay with me. Just for tonight."

She threw her arms around his neck with enough des-
peration to send him sprawling on the patio beneath her.


It wasn't Joe's intent to give Charlotte every one of her
sexual fantasies that evening, but he found it difficult to
deny her anything. Especially now that he feared it was
the last night he'd ever have her to himself.

So he'd tied her up, just the way she'd always wanted,
and the two of them couldn't stop giggling. He'd roped
honeysuckle vines around her wrists and throat and waist
and ankles, but they were bonds that shackled her to nothing but his love for her.

"Honeysuckle Mama," he muttered, leaving wet kisses
all over the front of her body, on her collarbone, the swell
of her breasts, down the slope of her soft belly. "That
nickname has so many of my favorite words in it."

"It does?"

He loved how husky Charlotte's whisper had become
after hours of lovemaking on the family room couch, in
the swimming pool, and now on the patio furniture cushions spread on the pool deck. He loved how she instinctively arched into the press of his lips.

"Oh, yeah." He let his tongue slide along the ridge of
her left hipbone, down into the valley between her legs,
and he used his hands to gently spread her open. She was
so swollen and well used that he worried she might be too
sensitive even for the gentle attention of his mouth. There
was only one way to find out.

"The first word I like is *honey* . . ." he said, just before
he flattened his tongue into the hot folds of her body and
lapped her up. He loved how deep her moan was.

"And then there's the word *suckle* . . ." He brought his
lips to her clitoris and nursed on her, noting what she

loved and what was too intense and what made her nuts, and smiled when she shook and went rigid yet again. Joe held her, smiling to himself, wondering just how many times this woman could come in one night.

After a few moments he asked, "Think you could hop up for a second, soccer mom?"

"Do I have to?"

He took her by the hands and eased her to a sitting position, once more admiring how good her little female body looked wrapped up in their binding of choice. She appeared a bit dazed.

"I want to watch you walk."

"Walk? Now? I don't know if I can."

He laughed. "Just over to the table and back. Can you do that for me?"

He loved the teasing smirk she offered him, her hair falling across her face as she stood to do his bidding. Charlotte's playful streak was proving to be a hell of a lot of fun.

He stretched out along the edge of the pool and made a half-circular motion with his finger. "Turn around and walk."

She did so but glanced over her shoulder at him. "And what are you going to do while I'm walking?"

Joe smiled. "Something I should have done thirteen years ago, baby—I'm gonna memorize your license plates."

Her laugh was the background music to her swaying walk, and as she moved, he watched. Her ass was a thing of majesty, small and round and sporting two big handprints visible in the dim light. She stopped when she reached the table and looked over her shoulder again.

"Well?"

"Hmm. Bend down and look under the tablecloth. Bring me what you find."

She did as she was told, which in itself was sexy as hell, and revealed that perfect peach between her thighs.

She turned and walked back toward him, holding the can of spray cheese. She looked down on him and crooked one eyebrow. "Let me guess what's on the menu. A number five with cheese?"

Joe nearly choked laughing.

"Cock con queso?"

He laughed so hard he had to lie down and hold his sides.

Charlotte knelt next to him. The sensation of aerosol cheese clinging to his shaft was close to otherworldly. She topped him off with a festive swirl, and he groaned with pleasure. He decided to hoist himself up on his elbows to watch.

Joe nearly lost it when she straddled his shins and bent toward him. She seemed to enjoy his predicament, licking at him through a devilish smile, her eyes sparkling with the pool lights, her sweet breasts dangling so that her nipples just brushed the surface of his thighs.

He had no idea how much of this he could take—he'd never seen anything so hot in his life.

Then she placed her lips around him and her moan vibrated all the way down into his balls and that was it— one mouthful of squirt cheese was served.

# Chapter Twenty-one

"Would you *please* hold still for one second, Hank?"

Charlotte jammed the safety pin through the elastic strap and poked herself in the finger.

"Ow! Shi—"

"Don't cuss and don't get blood on my tutu, Mama."

"Believe me, I'm trying to avoid both." Charlotte placed the pad of her index finger on her lips and sucked away the bright red droplet. She reached for the hairbrush, then studied the strand of purple silk flowers that was supposed to adorn a bun at the back of her daughter's head. She sighed. "Okay. Let's tackle your hair, kiddo."

"Mom!" Matt's voice boomed up the stairs.

"What?"

"Can Justin come to the recital?"

"Is that all right with you, sweetie?"

"I don't care." Hank shrugged. "He comes everywhere else with us."

"Sure!" Charlotte shouted back, tugging the hairbrush through Hank's tangle of curls. She knew from experience that getting all this hair into one little bun was going to be an engineering feat. "Hand me a few more bobby pins, honey."

"Hey! Don't pull it too tight or my brains will hurt."

Charlotte smiled, then looked up long enough to see the two of them reflected in Hank's dresser mirror. "You're going to do great today."

"Everybody ready?"

The sound of Joe's voice caused Charlotte to freeze. Her heart jumped into her mouth. She heard his footsteps on the stairs and three things occurred to her simultaneously: she was still in her bathrobe, she'd forgotten to un-invite him to the recital today, and she wasn't wearing his ring.

She'd tucked it away in her jewelry box when she got home late last night, after Bonnie nearly fainted at the sight of it and she had to explain that she was merely *thinking* about marrying him. Someday.

"It's Joe!" Hank bolted the instant he appeared in the hallway, and all the hair Charlotte had just twirled into a tight ball burst free. As Hank hurled herself against Joe and he hoisted her up into the air and hugged her, Charlotte noticed a huge run in Hank's ballet tights and knew she didn't have a spare pair.

She chuckled to herself—she'd never been without extra tights on recital day, so it must be that falling in love had her falling down on the job.

"Don't you look gorgeous!" Joe leaned back to inspect Hank's lavender spandex costume, touching the poof of stiff white netting around her hips. He kissed Hank's cheek. "You're gonna knock 'em dead, slugger."

The look on Hank's face was a balm to Charlotte's frayed nerves. Her daughter beamed at Joe, and the way Joe beamed back, it was obvious the affection was mutual.

LoriSue stared at the phone message in shock. Her bid on the end-unit townhome at The Lakes had been rejected—*rejected*—when she'd offered two thousand over the asking price and knew damn well there were no competing bidders.

She smelled something extremely foul. She smelled Jimmy.

With a blunt index finger—she still hadn't gotten used to these bland, stumpy fingernails, but she had to admit they were less hassle—she held down the intercom button.

"Ruth, where the hell is Jimmy?"

"Hold on. I'll check." She heard the office administrator click at the computer keys. "He's got three hours blocked out this morning to show the executive relo over on River Rock. Want me to page him?"

*Three hours for one showing?* "No. Thanks."

LoriSue tapped her stubby fingernails on the desktop. Would Jimmy sabotage her bid simply out of spite? Wasn't he satisfied that she was giving him possession of the house? What in God's name was that man's problem?

She grabbed her purse and cell phone, hit the speed dial for her divorce attorney's home number, and zipped down the hallway and out the door. She was headed for the vacant house on River Rock, where she planned to have it out with Jimmy, once and for all.

LoriSue was so focused on her mission that she nearly flattened two dark-haired men in expensive suits standing on the sidewalk. She ignored it when one of them whistled at her, and the other said something offensive that she didn't fully catch, because it was in a combination of English and a foreign language.

It sounded like Spanish.

"Hope I'm not interrupting anything." Joe's eyes traveled to where Charlotte stood by the bureau, his smile widening. He put Hank down. "How long before we need to leave?"

"Twenty-two minutes," Charlotte said, motioning for

Hank to come back so she could redo her hair. "Hold still for a second, would you, please?"

"Am I dressed all right?" Joe patted his slacks nervously. "I've never been to a ballet recital before."

Charlotte had to laugh. Joe looked more than all right in a pair of gray linen slacks and a black polo shirt—he looked good enough to devour on the spot. She returned to the task at hand, pinning the flowers down over Hank's bun and applying a thick coat of hair spray. Hank coughed dramatically.

"There you go. Perfect."

The phone rang. Charlotte had to sprint by Joe to get to it and she felt his hand pat her robe-encased hip as she passed.

When she hung up a moment later, Joe was leaning a shoulder against the doorjamb of her bedroom, grinning.

"That was Bonnie—they're running late and will meet us at the auditorium."

Joe nodded and looked around the bedroom.

This was so awkward—Joe was in the room she'd shared with Kurt. And she realized that there was so much unresolved between the two of them that she hardly knew where to begin. She loved him. He was too dangerous to be in her house, near her kids, in her life. Her head spun.

"So. This is where it all happens, eh?"

Charlotte laughed. "Where what happens?"

"Where all those poems get created."

"Oh." Charlotte heard Hank clunk down the steps and looked at her alarm clock. "I need to get ready."

Joe straightened. "Sure. How about I do a little light reading while you dress?"

Charlotte pulled the lapels of her bathrobe tight across her chest. "You want to read them?"

"You betcha, dumplin'."

Charlotte tried to act calm, but she was beginning to sweat. "Now?"

"Why not?"

"It's just—"

"It's okay, Charlotte. You don't have to."

He was disappointed, clearly. Hadn't he told her he loved her sexuality, loved how hot she was? He wouldn't have the same reaction Kurt did—it was impossible. So why was she making such a big deal about this?

"All right, Joe."

Charlotte walked to the bedside table, removed the key from under the lamp, and unlocked the drawer. She handed him the book. "Please put it back if you hear one of the kids come upstairs."

Joe accepted the clothbound journal and leaned down to kiss her gently. "I will. And thank you."

LoriSue had always loved this area just outside Minton and had made more than a few profitable sales in the exclusive River Rock neighborhood. That's why it surprised her that this particular corporate relocation hadn't sold after two months on the market. Sell-More had four months left on the contract, and with fall and winter on the way, they really needed to move it.

She pulled into the circular gravel driveway and saw two cars parked outside—Jimmy's phallic insecurity blanket of an SUV and a little beat-up Nissan with Kentucky plates. With a sigh, LoriSue figured her husband was inside giving the grand tour of the inside of his pants and not the roomy walk-in closets.

As she inserted her key into the padlock on the front door, the strangest sense of dread hit her. It started as an eerie skittering over her skin and ended with a thud deep in her chest. She looked behind her—it was a reflex—and saw nothing but the minimally maintained yard, the drive, and an empty road beyond. But she swore she felt someone's eyes on her.

LoriSue shook it off, figuring it was simply the disgust she felt at finally catching Jimmy in the act. She removed the digital camera from her purse and clicked on the power.

Two could play this game.

Joe was amazed. He suddenly felt a little pang of sympathy for Kurt Tasker—because Charlotte's poetry was hotter than hell, so hot that he was feeling a bit uncomfortable himself.

She'd dated each poem, and they started four years ago. He wondered if there were earlier journals anywhere. He wondered if he could read those, too.

He had a few favorites, but the poem titled "Slut" just about did him in. The one where she worried that he would hurt her felt like a knife to his gut.

Joe barely got the drawer closed and locked before Justin and Matt clomped up the stairs and arrived breathless in the bedroom.

Matt looked around furtively, then whispered, "Did you get them?"

"Get what?" He hoped the boys didn't think anything was odd about him being in Charlotte's bedroom, standing in front of her nightstand.

Matt looked toward his mother's closed bathroom door and walked close to Joe. *The pictures,* he mouthed silently.

Hell—he'd forgotten to pick up Matt's pictures! He knew he'd forgotten *something*!

Joe sighed. "They're going to have to wait until after the recital. Look, I'm sorry. I just forgot, Matt."

"Forgot?" Justin's eyes went wide. "Man, we really

wanted Chief Preston to look at those pictures! We found these two spies in town the other day, Joe—two creepy-looking guys hanging around for no reason. We'd never seen them before!"

Joe smiled, remembering being this age, when adventure and danger were the mainstays of his imagination. Then he got a load of Matt's expression and stopped smiling. The kid was devastated.

"You promised me" was all Matt said.

Joe looked at Charlotte's clock. He'd be cutting it close, but failing to follow through on the first promise he'd ever made to Matt was no way to start this relationship. It would be hard enough easing into Matt's life with a clean record.

"Okay. I'll get them."

Both boys exhaled in relief.

"Please tell your mother I'll be back in ten minutes, tops. Okay?"

"Sure, Joe!" Matt's smile took over his whole face. "No problem."

Joe was glad he'd left the film at the drugstore at the intersection of Hayden Circle and the state highway—it took him three minutes to get there. He ran into the store and took his place in line at the photo counter, cursing the other two people ahead of him, repeatedly checking his watch.

Finally, it was his turn. He handed three small tear-off receipts to the teenage clerk and had already pulled money from his wallet when the kid returned with a clipboard.

"We got a problem," he said.

Joe closed his eyes for an instant, then said as calmly as possible, "What kind of problem?"

"Your negatives were part of a group that was damaged when the machine went haywire the other night. You have to sign for the damaged prints." He held out the clipboard and pen.

"Damaged? How?"

The kid opened an envelope and flipped through a stack to reveal a bright yellow streak that cut through the center of each print. "You need to examine your prints and sign this waiver that you accept them in their damaged condition and don't plan any legal action against the store."

"Legal action? Jesus-tap-dancing-Christ! Here—just take my money and give me the pictures, okay? I'm in a hurry."

The kid looked hurt. "There's no charge, sir, and it's store policy and I'll lose my job if—"

"Okay, okay. I'll examine them for crying out loud. Hand 'em over."

Charlotte nearly tripped in her attempt to put on her left sandal and her right earring at the same time, and she stumbled into her bedroom expecting to see Joe but seeing the boys instead.

"Where's Joe?"

Justin and Matt looked at each other; then Matt said, "Not sure, exactly. He mentioned that he had to run an errand and that he'd be back in ten minutes."

*An errand?* She looked at the clock. *Now? But they had to leave now!*

Then it hit her—Joe had read a few of the poems and bolted. Charlotte finished buckling the strap of her sandal and took just a moment to focus on breathing, because it almost felt as if she was going to black out.

Wait. She was being ridiculous—of course she was. Joe hadn't been scared away by her poems. Sure, some were a bit *earthy,* she realized, but Joe liked earthy, didn't he? Joe loved earthy.

*Didn't he?*

"Oh God," she sighed, ushering the boys out of her bedroom. "Go wait for me downstairs. Make sure Hank is ready."

. Charlotte checked under the lamp—yes, the key was back in its place. She unlocked her nightstand drawer— yes, the journal had been returned.

She grabbed her purse, and as she raced down the steps she told herself that it was for the best that she'd scared him away. Then she whispered, *"Please come back, Joe."*

The moment her feet hit the foyer floor, she heard the kids shouting, "Hoover just ran out of the yard!"

LoriSue's digital camera silently took photo after photo of Jimmy—well, Jimmy's flaccid white rump, anyway— flailing away at some girly with a dragon tattooed on her inner thigh.

He'd obviously been using the vacant house as his hose palace and, vintage Jimmy here, had spared no expense in setting the scene for seduction—a bare inflatable mattress lay on the floor, next to a little battery-operated lamp.

No wonder the house hadn't sold. She bet Jimmy, as the listing agent, had been turning away potential buyers in droves so he could keep his little hideaway.

LoriSue cleared her throat, and the next shot she got was a keeper—Jimmy disengaging himself in a panic, his eyes wide in horror. Too bad the Little League Web site had gone live three days earlier, or she could have used this picture on the home page instead of the one of Joe Mills doing concession stand duty.

Oh, well—Joe was far better looking, even in a barbe- cue apron.

"It's not what it looks like, babe."

LoriSue howled with laughter at her husband's com- ment. And as the naked chickie screamed and lunged for her clothing, LoriSue noted the array of condom wrappers flung all over the Berber carpet. At least Jimmy wasn't completely stupid, and for that she was grateful.

"So how did you do it, Jimmy?"

He tried to divide his attention between the girl, now running past LoriSue into the hallway, and his wife but couldn't quite manage it. "Do whaaa?"

"Block my bid on the townhome, you needle dick."

"Hey!" He held out his hands, palms out and fingers spread in surrender. "We can talk about this, LoriSue."

She bent down and grabbed his briefs, khakis, shoes, socks, and dress shirt, wadded them up in a ball, and held them behind her back. She promised herself it would be *the last time* she ever picked up the man's dirty clothes, so help her God.

"So talk. What did you do, advise the sellers to hold out for a higher bid? Bid higher yourself?"

"Uh . . ." Jimmy dropped his head in his hands. "I just didn't want you and Justin to leave."

For a second, LoriSue was speechless. Then she snapped out of it. "Cut the crap."

"I'm serious!" Jimmy struggled to his feet, nearly losing his balance as the air mattress gave under his weight. He righted himself, then cupped a hand over his crotch. "I think we can work this out!"

LoriSue laughed again. "Whatever you did, undo it, Jimmy. I want my bid accepted by nine a.m. Monday or your naughty bits are going on the Minton Little League Web site and I'm going to e-mail everyone I know and tell them to have a look—with a magnifying glass, of course."

"Bitch."

"Good-bye, Jimmy." She turned to leave, clutching his balled-up clothing to her front.

"This is all because of Joe Mills, isn't it?" Jimmy's voice was a high-pitched shriek. "He's doing you, too, isn't he? Did he do you and Charlotte together?"

She whirled around, suddenly seeing her husband for what he was—pathetic, and crazier than a hoot owl. "Joe Mills is in love with Charlotte, you idiot. And as amazing as this now sounds to me, I've never been unfaithful to you once in our entire marriage. Well, gotta run—gotta get these snapshots to my attorney."

LoriSue left, ignoring Jimmy's ranting. On her way out, she noticed that the little Nissan was gone from the drive, which meant her husband would have to drive home naked. That made her laugh.

LoriSue continued to chuckle as she drove along River Rock, seeing a shiny black Lincoln pass the opposite way. Her mind struggled to recall where she'd seen the driver, because he looked vaguely familiar; then she stopped worrying about it because her cell phone rang. Her lawyer was calling back!

Joe flipped through photo after photo of car license plates, garbage cans, mailboxes, front doors, people kissing, people parked in cars and simply walking down the street—each with a bright yellow streak through the center. Fine. He'd inspected them. Joe took the clipboard from the kid and scrawled his name, catching himself when, in his haste, he nearly wrote "Bellacera." Then he headed for the exit.

Charlotte was going to kill him for being so late.

When his hand hit the door, Joe froze. Then, in one long, seamless movement, he raced back to the counter and ripped open all three envelopes, throwing prints into the air until he could find it again.

"Hey, man—what's the issue here?"

Joe sped through the images as fast as humanly possible, only half-noting that a group of people were now circled around him.

There it was—in his hand was a picture of two men he'd known in another life. *"Two spies . . ."* Joe's brain seized. *". . . two creepy-looking guys . . ."* He stared at the date at the corner of the photo—two days ago! They'd been in Minton at least two days!

Joe fought the sensory overload, the black, naked fear and rage that were trying to shut him down, trying to keep him from functioning. And that's when he heard a moan of anguish roar inside his soul, growing louder and louder in his head until he knew he couldn't contain it.

*"No."* The single word escaped in a whisper that no one else could hear.


"Oh for God's sake! What now?"

Charlotte had really, really hoped to have thirty seconds to use an actual mirror to apply her mascara and lipstick, but it looked like her beauty routine was going to take place in the car at a stoplight, as usual.

She raced into the kitchen, where Justin and Matt were flinging ice cream all over the floor in their effort to assemble a cone for Hoover.

"Guys! Look at the mess! I just mopped the floor and we're supposed to have people over after the recital!"

That's when a shrill, high-pitched scream pierced everyone's eardrums. "Mama! I have a big rip in my tights!" Hank came running into the kitchen, her face a mask of despair.

Charlotte looked up from her bent position near the floor, where she was wiping up blobs of French vanilla with a damp paper towel. "We don't have another pair, Hank, and besides, you can't really see it."

"But all the other girls will make fun of me!" Hank began to cry. And as the boys raced out the back door with their cones, Charlotte pulled her daughter close. "It's going to be okay, sweetie, really. You can hardly tell. Now get your dance bag and make sure your ballet slippers are in there and let's get in the car."

"I don't want to dance in ruined tights!"

"Then we'll stop at the drugstore on the way, but we can only get regular tights, because there's no time to go to the ballet store. Please just get in the car."

*Where the hell was Joe?*

"We got him!"

Charlotte turned to see Matt dragging Hoover through the back door by his collar. Justin's dress shirt was now smeared with ice cream. She sighed. They were hopelessly late, and Hank was going to have to endure a lecture from her old crone of a ballet teacher.

"Matt, put Hoover in the mudroom. Justin, run home and get a clean shirt. Be as quick as you can—we'll wait for you."

Hank's sobs had subsided into occasional hiccups as Charlotte used the van's visor mirror to apply a quick layer of Desert Rose to her lips and a coat of Brown-Black to her eyelashes, noting that she didn't feel pretty at all—she felt panicked.

*Didn't Joe say he loved her?*

Matt jumped in the van and slammed the door so hard that it startled Charlotte and she poked herself in the eye with the mascara wand.

"Shit!"

"Mama, my ballet slippers aren't in here."

Charlotte whipped her head around and through smarting eyes saw Hank fling everything out of her dance bag. That's when she knew it with certainty—she was going to lose it. Now.

"Then where the hell—?"

"Here they are!" Hank held up a pair of worn pink slippers and smiled. "Don't worry, Mama. Found 'em!"

Just then, Justin piled in the backseat, sporting a T-shirt

advertising a Florida seafood shack that screamed: *"We're proud to have crabs!"* but at least it was clean.

"Let's roll, Mom," Matt said. After a moment he added, "Earth to Mother?"

Charlotte turned toward her son. He wasn't telling her something—she *knew* it! "Where did he go, Matt? What did Joe say when he left?"

Justin and Matt rolled their eyeballs toward each other while keeping their heads stationary, a very bad sign, Charlotte knew from experience.

"Tell me."

Matt shrugged. "He just said he'd be back in ten minutes. Maybe we should go without him."

"I'm late, Mama." Hank's voice sounded small and pitiful.

"Hold on a second, kids. Just stay in the car—I'll be right back."

Jimmy hoped to hell that the sound he heard was Brenda—or Belinda, he couldn't remember her name—coming back in the house. Maybe she'd agree to go get him a change of clothes.

Since he hadn't thought to bring sheets, there was absolutely nothing in the house he could use to drape over himself, so Jimmy sat down on the air mattress and bent his leg nonchalantly in a pose that he hoped looked sexy to Belinda—or Brenda.

His blood turned to ice the instant he saw them. Two men in black suits blocked the doorway. They stared at him with dark, cold eyes that did not reflect the stiff smiles on their faces. Jimmy felt his mouth open.

"Excuse me," one of them said, his voice thick with a foreign accent. "We saw the sign outside and hope this house is still for sale."

"A friend of ours lives nearby," the other man said.

Jimmy had never shown a house naked before. He was so stunned he didn't know what to say.

"We hope you can help us find a house close to our friend."

Jimmy laughed, suddenly getting the joke. He started to look around for the hidden cameras. He should have guessed LoriSue would do something like this, the evil harpy. She'd pay for her little fun.

"Do you know our friend? He moved to Minton recently."

Jimmy recoiled as the first guy walked toward him, holding out a sheet of paper. This was weird shit. He was naked, for God's sake! He didn't want some pretty boy invading his personal space!

Then he caught a glimpse of the paper—a computer printout of the Little League's Web site. He accepted the single page and stared at it long and hard—right there were Joe Mills and Charlotte, staring at each other like a middle-aged Romeo and Juliet on concession stand duty. It was vomit inducing. But he had to admit that the Sell-More banner ad at the top looked great. LoriSue had done a bang-up job!

Then it dawned on him.

He raised his gaze slowly and smiled. Jimmy Bettmyer was a man of the world. He couldn't be fooled. He knew the game these guys were playing, and he'd help them out. Why not? They were the answer to his prayers!

"So ole Joe owes you some cash, does he, and you tracked him down?" Jimmy handed back the sheet of paper and checked to be sure his privates were still obscured.

The man glanced at his associate, then grinned down at Jimmy. "Yes. Joe owes us big."

Jimmy nodded knowingly. "I'll make a deal with you—you two run along and get me something to wear, and I'll give you his address."

The man's smile got wider, but it wasn't friendly in the least. Jimmy never saw the man move until his arm was painfully wrenched behind his back. Then he was dragged, naked, down the steps and out the front door.

"No deal," the man said to him, shoving him in the backseat of a sedan and nearly sitting on top of him in the process. He got real close to Jimmy's face as the car sped away toward town. "Give us the address. *Now*."

Jimmy pressed the back of his head against the seat, now very afraid. Who *were* these guys?

Then he saw the gun.

*He was going to die.*

"Oh, shit."

"*Sí*, sheeit," the man said, smiling for real this time. "Address, please?"

Jimmy took a breath so he could speak, finding his mouth painfully dry. "Hayden Heights subdivision. Twelve thirty-two Hayden Circle. Two-story contemporary stone and siding. Hey! What the fuck?"

Jimmy didn't know which hurt more—the way his skin shredded when his body slid along River Rock Road or the pain shooting through his left shoulder. Either way, he was now naked, hurt, and bleeding and at least five miles from home. Plus, his fucking car keys had been in the front left pocket of his pants.

He hoped those bean-eating bastards ripped Joe Mills a new asshole.

The first thing Joe did was grab all the photos—who knew what might be important in a few hours? The next thing he did was lean real close to the kid behind the counter.

"The store office. Where is it?"

The kid pointed to the far right corner, his mouth ajar.

Joe had Roger on the line in seconds.

"Guzman found me."

"Fuck!"

"Get Rich Baum's guys here—now. Get Charlotte and the kids out. *Now.* Find out how my cover was blown. I'm ditching my car and moving on foot. I'll call in fifteen minutes to give you my pickup location."

"Got it. Fifteen minutes—no more. Stay alive."

Now that she was inside the house, staring at the kitchen phone, Charlotte didn't have a plan. The truth was, she didn't even know if Joe had an answering machine. Come to think of it, she didn't know which of the four pancake syrups he would pick at IHOP, or his parents' first names, or if he voted in every presidential election.

She didn't know his blood type.

She didn't know what kind of bed he slept in: Queen? King? Water?

She was losing it. Correction: she'd already lost it. Her hands shook and her face was wet from crying and the only reason she was in here was to hide her breakdown from the kids, who at this very moment might be fed up with waiting for her and already walking in the garage door.

She needed to pull it together. Fast.

But she was so confused! Why would Joe reject her? He said he loved everything about her. He said she'd never have to hold back again.

Then he read her poems and left!

Hoover would not stop barking. He hadn't stopped barking for the last several minutes, and it felt like her head was going to implode. She had no patience to deal with him at the moment.

Charlotte used a square of paper towel to wipe her face and blow her nose.

Then a horrible thought occurred to her. What if Joe

really did just run an errand, but something happened to him? What if he was lying in the street? *Decapitated?*

Charlotte froze.

Good God! Now it sounded like Hoover was going berserk in there, letting go with a combination howl and bark she'd never heard before. Next, she swore the dog was throwing his body against the mudroom door.

This morning had been one for the record books.

She picked up the phone. No answer. No machine. No Joe.

# Chapter Twenty-two

Everything her lawyer said made perfect sense—she needed to stay civil for Justin's sake. She needed to keep a level head and think before she spoke. Yes, those photos of Jimmy would come in handy, but Justin's welfare had to be more important to her than revenge.

LoriSue finished stuffing Jimmy's clothing into the plastic grocery sack and paused a moment before she tossed the bag down the basement steps.

Jimmy hadn't been the only screwup in this family and she knew it. She'd messed up with Justin, and now it was time to make amends. She would spend more time with him and less time at work. She would apologize for losing sight of what was really important. She'd ask him for another chance. Then she'd do whatever it took to see that her little boy made it through the divorce with his laid-back happiness intact

The grocery sack hit the basement floor with a loud thud, and LoriSue groaned at what she saw—Jimmy's keys, phone, and wallet had just spilled onto the floor. That meant that Jimmy was at that house with no clothes, no money, no transportation, and no way to call for help.

As she went down the stairs to retrieve the bag, LoriSue

told herself that she was going to be decent for Justin's sake.

So she got back in her car and drove east of town toward River Rock. About two minutes from the listing, she passed a homeless man shuffling down the side of the road in the dappled shade of the trees. She hit the brakes, checked her rearview mirror, and slammed the car into reverse.

"Jimmy? Oh, my God!"

He peered at her with hollowed eyes as she lowered the passenger side window. Inexplicably, he wore a pair of baggy work coveralls smeared with grease, and his hands and face were cut and bleeding. He stood lopsided, cradling an elbow.

"What the hell happened to you? Damn, Jimmy—get in the car and I'll take you to the hospital." She unlocked the door.

"Just take me home," he mumbled, gingerly lowering his body into the seat.

"Are you hurt?"

He blew out air. "What the fuck does it look like?"

"I'm taking you to the hospital. Tell me what happened."

LoriSue saw that his feet were cut and bloody, too—the man looked like he'd been thrown from a moving train.

"Nothing."

"Jimmy—you could be seriously injured. You need to—"

"You need to shut up and drive me home!" He glared at her.

"Fine." She'd drive him home all right—then call his doctor. The doctor could call an ambulance and have him forcibly taken to the hospital if need be.

Jimmy slouched in silence as she drove.

"Tell me what happened."

"I've just had a real shitty day."

"You and me both."

They drove on in silence for a while. Then, out of nowhere, Jimmy said, "I'm sorry for everything, Lori-Sue."

She scrunched up her mouth and took a deep, slow breath through her nose. That statement was a little too little and a little too late, but it was the first time she'd ever heard Jimmy apologize for anything in his life, so she figured she'd better honor the occasion with a response.

"Thank you for apologizing," she said.

"I know I've been a failure as a husband and a pretty crappy dad, too."

She didn't expect him to keep going like that and figured he must be in severe pain. LoriSue glanced across the seat and saw his profile. He looked very old and tired.

"Thank you for saying that."

"You deserve better than me. You always have."

Oh, my. Which of the hundred possible smart-ass responses would she choose? She counted to ten instead, then said, "I wish you happiness, too, Jimmy."

"I'm going to try my best with Justin."

"So am I."

"I've pissed away so much precious time." He looked at her with clear eyes. "Things are going to be different, starting right now, LoriSue."

She nodded. Things felt different already.

Joe left through the drugstore's service entrance, made his way along the back of the strip mall, and boarded a County Commuter bus just pulling up to a stop across the street. He got off at city hall in downtown Minton and used the pay phone in the lobby of the Minton Police Department to call Roger.

"Rich Baum and four agents are on their way to Charlotte's."

"Thank God."

"It's not good, Joe. It took me exactly three minutes to figure out how they found you."

Joe let his forehead fall against the cool metal of the pay phone. "Tell me."

"I did an Internet search on Minton, Ohio, and there you were—on the Little League home page, flipping burgers."

Joe straightened. "Say again?"

"The Minton Little League Web site has a big picture of you and your soccer mom, describing you as dedicated volunteers. I don't know how they were tipped off, but that's how they found you."

Joe's head buzzed. His heart was now in his throat. "Charlotte? She's with me in the photo?"

"And the way you're looking at each other says it all. Any fool could tell you love her."

*Oh God—no.* "Was her name on the site?"

"No."

*Maybe that would buy a little time.*

"Look, Joe. I just tried her number. No answer."

*Please, God, let them be all right.*

Joe checked his watch. "They've probably already left for Hank's ballet recital. It's at the high school auditorium. Reroute the agents there."

"Will do."

*They have to be all right.*

"Wait—call Ned Preston down the street. I told him everything. He may still be at home and he could get to Charlotte and the kids quicker than anybody—tell him to get them out of the school, then call with a pickup location for Rich."

"Done. Do not move, Joe. If you move, I'll kill you myself, and I'm not kidding."

"I'm going back for them."

"Dammit, Joe! Five minutes! I need five minutes to take care of this before you commit fuckin' suicide. It's an order—stay put and call me back in five!"

The line went dead.

Joe looked at his watch and began counting the seconds.

She was in no mood for games, and Charlotte rubbed her forehead with force, hoping the pressure would prevent her head from exploding.

She called the kids once more. Not even a giggle from behind the pine trees. Nothing.

Charlotte took two halting steps toward the van. Both side doors were shoved open. Their stuff was in there—Hank's ballet bag, Matt's Game Boy, and one of Justin's sneakers—but there wasn't a sign of the kids.

She stood utterly still, feet planted on the driveway, hands at her sides, suddenly feeling as if she were the only object on the surface of the earth that wasn't starting to spin. At her core she was calm, but everything around her began to gain speed, spin faster and faster . . .

*Why did Justin take only one shoe? Why had Hoover been barking like that? Where was Joe?*

Then her gaze landed on the three bobby pins scattered on the empty seat, right next to the little band of purple flowers Hank had worn in her hair. Then she saw the strands of red curls.

Charlotte went cold. She felt the urge to vomit.

From somewhere far away she heard a car squeal into the drive, but she could only stare into space as Ned's words reached her.

"Thank God! We need to get you guys out of here!"

Her body was shaking violently by the time Ned gripped her by the upper arms. She stared at him and

Bonnie, not really seeing them, as Ned continued to shout at her.

"Charlotte! Where the hell are your kids?"

She tried to open her mouth to speak, but the words were lodged in her throat.

Ned snatched a piece of paper off the steering wheel. Charlotte heard him start to read it aloud, then stop himself.

"We're too late" is what he said instead.

They didn't even have time to scream.

Somebody had smacked Matt across the face and put a hand over his mouth and he'd watched a man do the same to Hank and Justin. Then they threw them in the backseat of a car. Then the driver hit the gas even before the other guy jumped in and pulled a gun on them. Then the doors locked.

And they'd all just sat there in the backseat, crying, and Matt was thinking, *So this is how you get kidnapped*; then he got a real good look at the men. He caught Justin's eye and they both said it silently in their heads— *we were right*!

Then, while they drove, one of the men told them the weirdest stuff about how some kid played third base on the Garvin Glass Little League team, his sister's stepkid or something. Matt didn't recognize the name and didn't know what this had to do with anything and was too scared to pay real close attention anyway. Plus, his nose was bleeding.

Now the three of them were locked in a walk-in kitchen pantry in some empty house with Justin's dad's face on the sign out front. It was totally dark in there. Every once in a while they heard the guys talking to each other in Spanish in a nearby room, but otherwise it was silent.

"They gonna kill us, Mattie?"

How was he supposed to answer that? He couldn't very well come right out and tell his baby sister that, yes, he was pretty sure they were going to die. But he couldn't lie to her, either. If they were going to at least try to get out of this, they needed to work together.

"I think that's their plan." Matt heard sniffles and immediately regretted his answer. "Don't cry, Hank."

"That's not me. It's Justin."

"I only have one shoe," Justin said in a small voice.

Matt felt sad for his friend. "I know."

"I want my mom," Justin said.

"I want my mama, too," Hank said. "And Joe."

"Yeah," Matt agreed.

After a few seconds, Hank said, "My tutu is itchy and I gotta pee real bad. Where am I supposed to pee?"

"Damn, Joe—they got the Tasker kids."

*"What?"*

"Took 'em right out of the driveway. Neighbor kid, too."

*"Charlotte?"*

"No. She's at the house. Look, there was a ransom note."

*"Tell me."*

"You for the kids. The FBI's hostage negotiators are on the way and—"

Joe hung up the pay phone and ran to the police department reception desk, knowing this was going to be a delicate sell without his badge.

"My name is Special Agent Joseph Bellacera, U.S. Drug Enforcement Administration, and I need a patrol officer immediately. It's an emergency."

Charlotte had regained some of the feeling in her hands, but Bonnie still held the paper bag to her mouth and repeated the instructions to breathe slowly. The last time

Charlotte had hyperventilated like this, she'd been in labor with Hank.

That memory caused her to burst into tears again. She ripped the bag from her face, crumpled it, and tossed it into the bed of marigolds near the garage door, where someone had apparently propped her up.

The driveway was jammed with cars. The FBI was there, and so were a bunch of guys in black ball caps and windbreakers slapped with three huge white letters: *DEA*. And now there was a Minton Police squad car screeching up to the curb and she didn't understand—the note Ned had read to the agents specifically said no police. And the neighborhood was swarming with them!

*Joe.*

She watched him run across the lawn and cut through the sea of men in suits and windbreakers and squat down right in front of her—so close that she could see that his eyelashes were wet. He shook when he squeezed her hands in his.

"I'll get them, Charlotte."

How she *hated* him for endangering her family! She *hated* him for leaving! But he was back, and the relief flooded her, bringing with it a small bud of hope.

She wanted to hit him. She wanted to hold him.

She wanted to tell him all of that, but she was drowning in fear. The fear was stronger than anything else, and it was pulling her down.

Then she felt his kiss on her lips and his breath on the side of her face.

"I swear to you, nothing will happen to your children." His whisper was rough and he clutched her hard to his chest. "I will make sure they come home to you."

Joe pulled away, and as he lanced her with his dark gaze she understood that he was saying good-bye—that he fully expected to trade his life for the lives of her kids, just like the ransom note said.

"I love you, Charlotte."

She nodded then, able to get her mind around one pure thought, one true feeling—that she loved this man with her heart and soul. She always had and always would.

"I wanted all of us to love each other, Joe."

He nodded, tears streaming down his cheeks. "We do, baby. We already do."

That's when the DEA agent who seemed to be in charge walked up behind Joe, put a hand on his shoulder, and spoke in a gentle voice. "We don't have much time."

Joe shared the photos with agents and reread the note, scrawled in black felt tip marker on a piece of ripped notebook paper.

> *Pretty Lady: Have Agent Joe Bellacera here in two hours for exchange. No police or your children will die.*

Every single word in that note filled Joe with anguish. The expression "Pretty Lady" made him sick to his stomach.

"What's the best guess on the timing?"

"I got here just a little after nine," Ned said. "Charlotte said she'd been inside for no more than five minutes, so I'm estimating the abduction occurred about four minutes before nine."

Joe's mind raced—it was already 9:37. Every minute the kids stayed with those animals brought them a minute closer to dying. He couldn't afford to let his thoughts wander to Steve and Reba and Daniel. He couldn't look at Charlotte, sitting cross-legged in the driveway, her face contorted with fear and grief. He couldn't even think that this was all his fault—what good would that do now?

And what good would it do to admit that Roger had been right—that he'd had no business getting involved with Charlotte and her kids?

He and Cincinnati Field Office Supervisor Rich Baum had already had a little private chat: There were only two ways this situation could have a happy ending. One, FBI snipers could take Guzman's men at the exchange before Joe and/or the kids got killed; or two, if they could figure out where the kids had been taken—and get there in time— they might be able to use the element of surprise to get the kids out alive.

The only problem was that no one even knew which way they'd turned on the state highway. The neighbors saw nothing.

Joe was about to discuss sniper placement with the FBI agent in charge when another car pulled into the drive. LoriSue Bettmyer got out of her BMW along with what looked to be a street person. The closer they got, the more the guy looked like Jimmy.

"What in the world is going on?" LoriSue's fists rested on her hips, and Joe watched her eyes fall on Charlotte, then widen in horror. "Where's Justin?"

Rich Baum stepped forward. "Mrs. Bettmyer, it seems that your son—"

*"Where is he?"* LoriSue's voice hit a supersonic screech just before she began to sob. "Oh, my God!"

"What's this about?" Jimmy demanded. "Where's Justin?"

Rich seemed too flustered by LoriSue's hysteria to answer, so Joe told the parents as calmly and quickly as he could, storing for later the obvious fact that Jimmy had just had the snot beaten out of him and was wearing something straight out of someone's home garage. "We believe all three kids were taken as hostages. We are doing everything we can to determine where—"

"Hostages?" they both screamed.

Joe and Rich wasted at least five precious minutes getting the Bettmyers calm enough to listen to all the specifics they could give them. When they were done, Jimmy mumbled something under his breath that sounded a lot like "holy shit" and looked around in a panic. Then he said to Joe, "Can you describe these guys?"

It struck Joe as an odd question, but he asked one of the FBI agents to give Jimmy the photo of Guzman's men.

Jimmy took it in one bloody hand, and Joe watched the edge of the photo tremble. Jimmy looked up, his eyes full of what Joe identified immediately as guilt.

Ned put a hand on Jimmy's shaking arm. "Do you recognize them?"

Several agents heard Ned's question and gathered close. Charlotte and Bonnie pushed into the circle. Lori-Sue raised her head from Rich Baum's jacket and glared at her husband. "Jimmy?"

"I know where they are," he whispered.

Between them, they had four bobby pins, a penknife, three shoelaces, a safety pin, and a half bag of Nerds. It wasn't much, Matt knew, but it was a start.

They'd explored every inch of that dark pantry with their hands and discovered a fire extinguisher bolted to the wall just inside the door. They'd determined that the wooden shelves were removable. They found a metal towel rack on the inside of the pantry door.

They'd also explored the doorknob and door frame, figuring that the men had somehow jammed the door from the outside, because the knob turned freely and there was no bolt or lock that they could find.

So the challenge was how to use the resources and

information they had to get them out of there.

Justin suggested using the pocketknife to unscrew the door hinges, which would have been good, except that they couldn't get to the hinges when the door was shut.

Hank suggested using the shelves to beat down the door, which was stupid, because they'd make such a racket that the men would know what they were up to and be waiting for them even if they managed it. But Matt thanked her anyway, figuring she didn't need to hear that her idea sucked eggs.

He was wondering how they could use the fire extinguisher to their advantage when he heard the men's voices coming closer, getting louder. It sounded like they were arguing.

"Do you think now's a good time to tell them I need to use the bathroom?" Hank asked.

"No!" he and Justin said in unison.

Joe studied the papers in his hand, immensely grateful that LoriSue had snapped out of it long enough to suggest her office fax over a copy of the listing, which included a floor plan, photos, and a detailed description of the property. Within moments, it all arrived via the portable fax machine in her car, and with that one stroke of luck the odds had shifted dramatically.

There had been no time for a search warrant and this wasn't exactly a textbook operation, but they had little choice. He and Rich Baum had instructed the FBI to back off, let them go in alone. The fewer agents at the scene, the less likely anyone would be spotted. And now Joe and Rich were on their stomachs in the tall grass behind a storage shed to the southeast of the house, about to go in.

They'd seen no movement through their binoculars and hadn't heard a sound. Yet they knew they were in there—the car Jimmy and LoriSue had described sat in the circular drive out front. What Joe and Rich were still debating was whether to go in now or jump the men as they left.

Joe's vote was to go for it. He knew all too well the way Guzman's men thought—they'd probably kill the kids before they even left the house. That way, if they didn't nab Joe or died in the attempt, they'd already have made their point.

His only prayer was that it hadn't happened yet.

It appeared a kitchen window had been broken to gain entrance and Jimmy had said the only furnished room in the house was the second bedroom on the right upstairs, but the kids could be anywhere. Joe knew they could be tied up, drugged, injured, or even stuffed in the trunk of the car. The men who took them were capable of anything.

Joe shoved away the gruesome images and handed Rich the key to the front and back padlocks, another gift from LoriSue. "Let's go in here." Joe pointed to the floor plan, tapping his finger on a laundry room entrance off the kitchen.

Rich nodded, and they began to move, low to the ground, taking cover behind every bush or tree they could find along the way, then hugging tight to the house as they crouched beneath the windows, weapons drawn.

Joe covered Rich for the five seconds it took him to ease off the padlock and open the door. Rich slipped inside and Joe followed.

An instant after entering the small laundry room, the men heard voices and moved toward the door that led to the kitchen. The first words of Spanish that registered with Joe turned his blood to ice.

The men were just feet away, in the kitchen, arguing about whether to murder the children. One said the kids were friends with his nephew and should be spared, and the other said he didn't care—the children could identify them, and he planned on being able to enjoy his half-million dollars in peace.

While they argued, Joe cracked open the laundry room door just a fraction, enough that he and Rich could scan the kitchen for any sign of the kids. That's when he noticed a wooden shelf shoved up under the doorknob to what was probably the pantry.

Joe looked at Rich to be certain his partner saw that the children were likely in the pantry, and watched with approval as Rich did just what Joe had already done— calculate at what angle they'd have to shoot to miss the pantry door. Rich nodded to Joe to indicate he understood.

Just then, the argument escalated, and Guzman's men began to hurl loud insults at each other. Joe signaled to Rich that it was time to kick in the door.

Joe took a deep breath, feeling the sharp rush of adrenaline in every muscle fiber of his body, his mind focused on only one thing: getting the kids out alive. On the silent count of three, the two agents slammed the soles of their shoes against the door and sent it flying.

"Freeze! Federal agents!"

Joe saw that one man cradled an assault rifle and was opening the pantry door. The man was momentarily confused at the intrusion but then spun toward Joe with the gun. Joe fired before the other man could, and he fell backward from the force of the single bullet in his forehead.

At the same time, Rich shot the second man in the back of the knee as he tried to run.

Then the screaming began.

Joe raced to the kitchen pantry and flung open the door the rest of the way. There was Matt, frozen in position, standing guard with a fire extinguisher, his face displaying the unflinching scowl of a warrior.

Hank and Justin huddled together on the floor behind Matt's legs, screaming their heads off.

"It's all right now, Matt." Joe touched the boy's white knuckles, clutched tight around the extinguisher's metal handle. "It's okay, Matt. I've got you."

Rich worked quickly to disarm and handcuff the second man, then radioed for an ambulance. Then he pulled the first man's body around the corner out of view of the children.

Joe reached down around Matt and placed a hand on Hank's shoulder. "It's okay, sweetheart. You're safe now."

She wouldn't stop screaming.

There was blood all over the kitchen floor, spreading around his feet, and Joe realized they'd have to carry the kids over it.

"C'mere, Matt. Let's go. We're getting out of here."

Matt would not let go of the fire extinguisher, so Joe just grabbed him and hoisted him up in his left arm.

"Hank! C'mon, slugger—we need to move."

Hank raised her head, her terrified eyes softening when she realized it was Joe. Then she jumped up and climbed his body like it was a piece of playground equipment. Joe held her tight.

Rich helped Justin to his feet and stroked the boy's hair. He told him to grab on.

Joe said, "Don't look, kids. Do you understand? Keep your eyes closed."

"No problem," Matt said, just before he buried his face in Joe's shoulder.

Joe carried Matt and Hank over the blood and out the laundry room door, Rich right behind him, already radioing for pickup. Matt wiggled to be put down the instant they were outside, but Joe thought Hank might be permanently latched onto him.

They stood quietly in the front drive, Matt's hand grip-

ping his, as the line of cars pulled up. Joe's heart was just
beginning to steady and his brain clear, and that's when
he realized that, for some reason, he was wet from his
chest to his knees.

Hank raised her face from the crook of his neck. "I'm
sorry, Joe. I think I peed my pants."

"No problem, slugger." He kissed her cheek and
watched Charlotte bolt from a car door, then stumble
toward them. "I think I'm about to pee my pants, too," he
whispered.

Charlotte skidded in the gravel and threw herself into
them. Her hands went flying over her children, over their
faces and hands and chests, as the tears ran. "Oh, please
be all right. Please—"

"We're okay, Mama." Matt grabbed her arm. "We're
fine."

"They're not hurt, Charlotte." Joe knew she didn't hear
a thing they were saying.

"Joe saved us," Hank said. "He was totally stable, too."
*"Oh, my God!"*

She hurled herself against Joe and Hank, pulling Matt
against her as she went. Joe used his free hand to grab
Charlotte around the shoulders and hold her up. He stood
perfectly still, three people stuck to him, as he observed
the familiar buzz of a crime scene around him. Two am-
bulances wailed in the distance. Rich Baum was motioning that they had to leave.

He'd almost gotten them all killed.

Joe felt the sorrow build from below his knees, which
now felt strangely weak, all the way up to his scalp. He
was overwhelmed with it. Flattened by it. Rich motioned
for him again. He needed to say good-bye to them all.
Right now.

"I'd better go," he whispered into the top of Charlotte's
head. She pulled her face away from him and frowned.

"Where are you going?" all three asked together.

He nodded to Rich to give him a second. "I don't know. I just have to leave. You won't be safe until I'm gone."

"What?" Charlotte's eyes were huge. Hank and Matt said nothing.

Joe decided the hell with it. He was thirty-eight. He'd proved himself as a man and a cop. He'd only loved one woman in his entire life and she was standing right in front of him for the last time. He would miss her with every breath he took for the rest of his days.

So he let himself cry.

"I am so sorry, Charlotte. I never meant to put you or the kids in danger. I only wanted . . . I'm so sorry. . . ." His voice broke and he lowered his head.

"Please don't cry." He felt Hank's little arms squeeze his neck.

"I don't blame you for anything, sweet Joe." Charlotte touched his face with her hand. "It's not your fault."

"Duh! You saved our lives, dude," Matt added.

"You said you were gonna stay!" Joe looked into Hank's face and saw her lower lip tremble. "You promised."

Joe didn't think his heart could break any more than it already had. He was wrong, apparently. "I know I did, champ. I wanted to stay more than I've ever wanted any-thing. But it's not safe for me to be here anymore. I have to go."

"Can we come with you?"

He almost didn't hear Matt's question above the in-creasing chaos.

"Can we, Mama?" Hank was squirming in Joe's arms. "Do you think maybe we could go with him? Can we, Mama? Can we?"

Charlotte looked up and gave him one of her smiles, the kind that warmed his insides and made him feel whole. Then she said, "Yes."

• • •

Charlotte would not let them go. There'd been so much discussed, so many decisions being made, in that ten-minute car trip, but all she could do was hold her children in her arms and keep her eyes focused on Joe.

He wore the black cap and jacket of a DEA agent. The concept was going to take some getting used to. Along with everything else.

"It will not be easy, Charlotte." It was Rich Baum saying it this time, like she hadn't understood it the first five times Joe said it.

"Your life will not be your own for a long while— maybe many years—until the risk is acceptable."

"I understand."

"I want to hear what the kids think," Joe said.

Charlotte had noticed how both Hank and Matt held on to Joe's hands even as they pressed up against her chest. They were knotted together, like a family.

"Hank?" Charlotte kissed the top of her daughter's disheveled hairdo. "You won't be able to play in the Minton Little League again and you'll have to leave Taft Elementary and we'll have to get a different house."

"It's okay," she said through her sniffles. "Can we take Hoover?"

Charlotte looked at Joe. The sad smile he gave her nearly made her cry again. She didn't know all the details yet, but she knew that Joe had done what he'd said he'd do. Just moments before, he'd killed a man to save her children.

"You mean that obnoxious ice cream–inhaling moose of yours?" Joe asked.

Hank smiled a little. "Yep. That one."

"Of course you can," Joe said. "How about you, Matt?"

Her son raised his chin and looked calmly at Charlotte, then Joe. "Do I get any say in where we live?"

Joe and Charlotte exchanged a quick glance.

"You got someplace in mind?" Joe asked.

"Maine—it's my favorite state."

Charlotte let out a surprised laugh. She'd never once heard her son mention Maine. "It is?"

"Yeah. The mountains. The ocean. The snow. I want to live in Maine and learn to ski jump."

Rich Baum cleared his throat. "I'm sure there are some nice houses in Maine."

They pulled up to her driveway, and it hit Charlotte that what they'd just been discussing was no longer theoretical. They had ten minutes to get whatever they couldn't live a couple weeks without, as Rich put it, and then they had to leave.

Hank ran inside in her tutu, and Matt walked slowly up the front sidewalk, letting his hands skim along the bushes and the porch railing, as if saying good-bye.

Once upstairs, the first thing Charlotte did was put on the ring that symbolized past, present, and future. She packed a suitcase with some basic clothing, the family's legal papers, her poetry journals, and a couple photo albums.

Then she threw her vibrator in the trash.

Charlotte got Hank out of her tutu and helped her pack things other than her baseball trophies and a pile of sweaters and mittens, explaining that even if they went to Maine right away it was summer there, too. Then she made sure Matt was making progress. She found him sitting on the edge of his bed.

"Are you okay, Matt?" She sat down next to him.

"I'm thinking of Dad."

Charlotte put an arm around him.

"I won't be living in his house anymore. I'll miss being close to him like that."

"I will, too."

"But you have Joe now."

Charlotte hoped that what she wanted to say to Matt would come out the right way. "We all have Joe now. That doesn't mean that we don't love your father, because we always will, or that we won't miss him, because we miss him very much."

"Yeah. Okay."

"Let's just take it slow. You know that Joe's a good man, Matt."

That's when Matt raised his gaze to Charlotte and nodded seriously. "He's the way coolest man I've ever known—except for Dad."

High praise indeed.

There wasn't enough time to say everything she needed to say to Bonnie, except that she loved her. And Ned hugged her so hard she stopped breathing momentarily, and LoriSue and Justin were crying and LoriSue was promising to take care of everything involved with selling the house, and Hoover was barking, and then they were in a strange car, Joe driving, and Rich Baum was in the car in front of them and two other agents in a car behind them, and Joe told them they were headed to the airport.

About fifteen minutes out of town, once the silence had almost begun to seem normal, Charlotte turned around to check on the kids. They were sound asleep, Hoover between them. Matt had a hand on Hank's shoulder.

Then Charlotte looked over at Joe. He must have sensed her eyes on him, because he turned his head and gave her a sweet smile.

"You ready for this, Charlotte?"

She nodded. "I'm a strong woman, remember? Are you ready?"

Joe grinned. "I am."

She reached for his hand. She'd be lying if she told him she wasn't scared to death, but it really came down to one simple thing.

"Do you love me, Joe?"

His eyes lanced hers, and he nodded. "Infinity much. I always have."

She smiled at that. "I love you infinity much, too."

Joe pulled her hand to his chest, pressing her palm against his heart. "Then the rest is just detail."

# Four Years Later

Charlotte stood up to her ankles in the chilly water, thinking that while her own life had been transformed, this little piece of the world hadn't changed a bit.

The same sycamores, maples, and oaks framed Pike Lake in a heavy green fringe. The familiar squish of the sandy bottom greeted her toes. The squeal of happy kids filled her ears.

They'd come home, and home had welcomed them back with open arms.

The mayor of Minton appeared at Charlotte's left side, Bonnie at her right.

"I have to stop sniveling," LoriSue said. "Mayors aren't supposed to cry."

Bonnie snorted. "Yeah, and until you, mayors weren't supposed to get bikini waxes, either."

LoriSue dug a polished toenail into the sand and slung an arm around Charlotte's waist. Bonnie added hers and the three women were linked.

"You look so beautiful, Charlotte," LoriSue said. "In all the years I've known you, I've never seen you look so beautiful. So happy."

Charlotte smiled at that assessment, pleased that what

she felt inside showed on the outside, that the world could see she was comfortable in her own skin.

"I was thinking the same about you." Charlotte saw LoriSue blush, of all things.

"Thanks."

The women stood without speaking for a moment, observing what looked like half the town gathered for the picnic. Charlotte and Joe and the kids had been shocked when they arrived a half hour earlier, driving underneath a huge WELCOME HOME banner suspended between trees at the park entrance.

"Glad we're not trying to hide anymore," Joe had said dryly.

Charlotte looked at her friends. "It's really good to be back. I've missed all of you more than I can say."

Bonnie squeezed Charlotte and leaned in to whisper, "She looks just like Joe, you know."

The women smiled at two-year-old Tula Bellacera, propped on Matt's shoulders as he splashed his way along the lake edge. The little girl laughed and tugged on her brother's hair, her dark brown eyes sparkling with happiness.

Then Joe burst out of the water with a roar, and even the big kids screamed in surprise.

Charlotte could hardly believe her ears. "Good grief! It's bad enough that Justin is like seven feet tall now, but when did his voice change?"

LoriSue laughed. "A couple months ago—scared the bejesus out of me, let me tell you, because Rich was already at work and suddenly there was this *man* in my kitchen!" She shook her head. "And it was *my* little man."

Charlotte had missed so much, including LoriSue and Rich Baum's wedding, which occurred about a year after the kids were rescued and just a month after her divorce from Jimmy was finalized.

She'd also missed being there for Bonnie during Ned's triple bypass surgery, which happened right in the middle of the trial. Even if the DEA had let her return, she couldn't have. She'd had to stay in Maine with the kids while Joe was testifying in Dallas. Not to mention she was seven months pregnant with Tula at the time.

But she'd prayed for Ned every day. Looking at him now tossing a Frisbee with Hank in the sand, she was relieved to see that he was exactly the same man, just thirty pounds lighter on his feet.

"C'mon, Henrietta—can't you give it any more jazz than that?"

"Careful what you ask for, Ned." Hank put one hand on her hip and flicked her other wrist so that the disk bounced off the water and nearly scalped him.

"Still got it, I see," he said with a laugh.

They'd all stayed in contact through Rich, but the DEA had forbidden any direct communication between Charlotte and her family and friends until they determined it was safe. That had happened just six weeks ago, when Guzman died of cancer two years into his ninety-year federal prison sentence.

"Did you hear what Jimmy is up to these days?" LoriSue's blue eyes twinkled.

"Is he still doing missionary work in Guam?"

LoriSue laughed. "That lasted only a couple months after he let me buy him out of Sell-More. He's in cosmetology school now. He married Jolene down at the Hair You Are and they're opening a day spa in town."

Charlotte's mouth fell open.

"I hear he gives a killer pedicure," Bonnie said.

"I've got to hand it to him," LoriSue said. "He's doing great with Justin, and that's all that matters to me."

"So when's the book coming out?" Bonnie asked. "Ned said something about Joe going on TV—is that true?"

Charlotte nodded, letting her gaze fall on her husband, the professional storyteller. While in Maine, Joe tried his hand at writing a suspense thriller based on his undercover years. He'd often told Charlotte it was his way of exorcising his demons, grieving for Steve and his family, and helping him get his head together about what he wanted to do next.

His therapy session ended up in the middle of a bidding war between New York publishers and was recently picked up for a movie option in Hollywood.

"It's being released in November, and yes, he's been asked to do a bunch of talk shows."

Charlotte felt it then, that familiar zing of appreciation she got every time she made eye contact with her husband, now striding out of the lake and moving toward the women, a wide grin on his face and a pair of soaking wet swim trunks clinging low on his hips.

"Good gracious, it suddenly got hot out here," LoriSue said.

"Somebody put some clothes on that man." Bonnie fanned herself.

"So was I right, or what?" LoriSue shot Charlotte a sideways glance. "Is Joe one of those men put on earth just to make women happy?"

Charlotte watched Joe move toward them, his cropped hair sticking up in wet spikes, his clean-shaven face brown with sun, his lean, hard body streaked with lake water.

The last four years had been a roller-coaster ride, but through it all Joe had amazed her with his love of life, his passion, and his steadfast devotion to her and the kids. He truly was her fantasy man.

"You were wrong, LoriSue." Charlotte held out her hand for Joe. She saw that familiar gleam in his eye and wondered if he'd dare kiss her in public—she sure hoped so.

"Wrong?" Bonnie and LoriSue said in unison, sounding

so disappointed that Charlotte had to laugh.

"Joe's only here to make one woman happy—and that woman would be me."

Charlotte got the words out just before Joe flipped her up into his arms and carried her off into the lake, kissing the living hell out of her in front of God and everyone in Minton, Ohio.